THE LOST STARS: IMPERFECT SWORD

"A fast-paced thrill ride that leaps nimbly from harrowing to heartbreaking to heroic . . . Both new and returning readers will dive right in."　　　　　　　　　—*Publishers Weekly*

"A wonderful, action-packed installment. This is the kind of book that leaves me hungering for another helping of Campbell's space combat!"　　　　　—Fantasy Literature

THE LOST STARS: PERILOUS SHIELD

"I struggled to put [*Perilous Shield*] down and didn't want it to end . . . One thing Jack Campbell really does very well indeed . . . is writing space battles. They are fabulous, and there are enough here to give you a real taste of what it would be like to be up there and shot at."　　　　　—SFcrowsnest

"The universe [Campbell] has created is full of things to marvel at, and his ability to depict both positive and negative aspects of society remains a strong suit in his writing."
　　　　　　　　　　　　　　　　—Fantasy Literature

THE LOST STARS: TARNISHED KNIGHT

"Campbell focuses on the human element: two strong, well-developed characters locked in mutual dependence, fumbling their way toward a different and hopefully brighter future. What emerges is a fascinating and vividly rendered character study, fully and expertly contextualized."
　　　　　　　　　　　　　　—*Kirkus Reviews* (starred review)

"As can be expected in a Jack Campbell novel, the military battle sequences are very well done, with the land-based action adding a new dimension . . . Fans of The Lost Fleet series will . . . enjoy this book."　　　　　　—SFcrowsnest

ACE BOOKS BY JACK CAMPBELL

THE LOST FLEET

The Lost Fleet: Dauntless
The Lost Fleet: Fearless
The Lost Fleet: Courageous
The Lost Fleet: Valiant
The Lost Fleet: Relentless
The Lost Fleet: Victorious
The Lost Fleet: Beyond the Frontier: Dreadnaught
The Lost Fleet: Beyond the Frontier: Invincible
The Lost Fleet: Beyond the Frontier: Guardian
The Lost Fleet: Beyond the Frontier: Steadfast
The Lost Fleet: Beyond the Frontier: Leviathan

THE LOST STARS

The Lost Stars: Tarnished Knight
The Lost Stars: Perilous Shield
The Lost Stars: Imperfect Sword
The Lost Stars: Shattered Spear

WRITTEN AS JOHN G. HEMRY

STARK'S WAR

Stark's War
Stark's Command
Stark's Crusade

PAUL SINCLAIR

A Just Determination
Burden of Proof
Rule of Evidence
Against All Enemies

THE LOST STARS

SHATTERED SPEAR

JACK CAMPBELL

ACE
New York

ACE

Published by Berkley

An imprint of Penguin Random House LLC

375 Hudson Street, New York, New York 10014

Copyright © 2016 by John G. Hemry

Excerpt from *Vanguard* by Jack Campbell copyright © 2017 by John G. Hemry

Penguin Random House supports copyright. Copyright fuels creativity, encourages
diverse voices, promotes free speech, and creates a vibrant culture. Thank you for buying
an authorized edition of this book and for complying with copyright laws by not
reproducing, scanning, or distributing any part of it in any form without permission.
You are supporting writers and allowing Penguin Random House to continue to
publish books for every reader.

ACE is a registered trademark and the A colophon is a trademark of
Penguin Random House LLC.

ISBN: 9780425272282

Ace hardcover edition / May 2016
Ace mass-market edition / April 2017

Printed in the United States of America
1 3 5 7 9 10 8 6 4 2

Cover illustration by Craig White
Cover photographs: clouds © Mr Twister / Shutterstock;
metal plate © Eky Studio / Shutterstock
Cover design by Judith Lagerman
Book design by Laura K. Corless

To Bud Sparhawk,
sailor, gentleman, writer, and explorer of new worlds.

For S., as always.

ACKNOWLEDGMENTS

I remain indebted to my agent, Joshua Bilmes, for his ever-inspired suggestions and assistance, and to my editor, Anne Sowards, for her support and editing. Thanks also to Catherine Asaro, Robert Chase, Carolyn Ives Gilman, J. G. (Huck) Huckenpohler, Simcha Kuritzky, Michael LaViolette, Aly Parsons, Bud Sparhawk, and Constance A. Warner for their suggestions, comments, and recommendations. Thanks also to Charles Petit for his suggestions about space engagements.

THE MIDWAY FLOTILLA

Kommodor Asima Marphissa
(all ships are former Syndicate Worlds mobile forces units)

ONE BATTLESHIP
Midway

ONE BATTLE CRUISER
Pele

FOUR HEAVY CRUISERS
Manticore, *Gryphon*, *Basilisk*, and *Kraken*

SIX LIGHT CRUISERS
Falcon, *Osprey*, *Hawk*, *Harrier*, *Kite*, and *Eagle*

TWELVE HUNTER-KILLERS
Sentry, *Sentinel*, *Scout*, *Defender*, *Guardian*, *Pathfinder*,
Protector, *Patrol*, *Guide*, *Vanguard*, *Picket*, and *Watch*

**Ranks in the Midway flotilla (in descending order),
as established by President Iceni**

Kommodor
Kapitan First Rank
Kapitan Second Rank

Kapitan Third Rank
Kapitan-Leytenant
Leytenant
Leytenant Second Rank
Ships Officer

CHAPTER ONE

FREEDOM or death.

Dignity or slavery.

Give life to something new or die in the collapse of the old.

When empires fall, the outposts of empire do not immediately disappear. Men and women continue to hold the walls they have defended. The cause they once served may no longer exist, but they stay on, holding a line that no longer has meaning.

Some of them find new reasons to fight. At such times, each man and woman must decide whether to hold on to the past, or to fight for the future.

In Midway Star System, President Iceni and General Drakon were building a future different from the oppressive and brutal rule of the Syndicate Worlds. Nearby star systems were choosing whether to align with Midway, risking devastation at the hands of vengeful Syndicate forces, or to cling to loyalty to the Syndicate, which had never worried about repaying loyalty in kind but had maintained stability for generations.

Taroa, Ulindi, Kane, and Kahiki had either joined with Midway or were seeking ties.

Iwa Star System, facing a threat much greater than anyone yet realized, would soon have to deal with the same decision.

"WHO is in command of your ships?" the woman demanded, her image visible to Kapitan Kontos on the bridge of the battle cruiser *Pele*. She wore the suit of a Syndicate CEO, but some of the details of her clothing reflected sub-CEO status. Kontos wondered what had happened to the last CEO. Iwa hadn't revolted against the Syndicate, but there were unmistakable signs that the Syndicate presence at lonely Iwa was as frayed as the cuff of the CEO's suit.

"We have not received appropriate entry reports following your arrival," the woman said in tones not quite arrogant enough for an experienced CEO. "You are to explain your presence at Iwa and subordinate yourself to lawful Syndicate authority without delay. Forthepeople, Vasquez, out," she finished, running together the words of "for the people" in the usual Syndicate manner that reduced a supposed tribute to an empty string of sounds.

Kontos didn't have much experience with the diplomatic side of being a senior officer. Truth to tell, he didn't have much experience at all. Rebellion produced some amazing promotion opportunities. It also produced a lot of opportunities to be killed.

Still, despite his lack of experience, it wasn't hard for Kontos to understand why the authorities at Iwa Star System would be worried when a battle cruiser and a troop transport showed up from Midway. Midway was both a fairly well-off star system and the center of rebellion against the Syndicate in this region of space.

In contrast, Iwa was the sort of star system that was often summarized as "too much of nothing." A lot of asteroids and small barely-planets, a single gas giant that had nothing special about it, and beyond that several larger worlds that were simply giant balls of rock and ice. Only a single planet about nine light minutes from the star was marginally habitable, but too cold for human comfort, and its atmosphere contained too little oxygen while containing too many toxic compounds that would ravage human lungs. The Syndicate had nonetheless planted a colony there, the buildings and streets and factories mostly buried under the surface to allow easier heating. Iwa had once been a fallback position if Midway had fallen to the alien enigmas, with extensive fortifications and bases begun, then abandoned in various stages of completion as the Syndicate first diverted resources for the far-off war with the Alliance, and was later forced to refocus internally on its crumbling empire.

Kontos considered his reply for a few more moments. According to the rules by which the Syndicate worked, those in a position of strength were expected to lord it over individuals with weaker power bases, and those who were weaker were expected to bluff against their peers but to offer submission to the powerful. Every action was judged in terms of how it displayed strength or weakness, respect or insubordination.

The transmission from the Syndicate CEO had been sent just over three hours ago from the main inhabited world at Iwa. Kontos's reply would take another three hours to make its way back, because light only traveled at about eighteen million kilometers per minute, and there was still three light hours' distance between *Pele* and the planet where the Syndicate CEO resided. But by the rigid rules of Syndicate protocol, that CEO would be timing the reply to see how long Kontos took to transmit his answer. A subordinate was expected to reply within seconds. An equal could take a few minutes. A reply that was received in anything longer than six hours and a few minutes would be considered either a deliberate show of strength or a deliberate insult.

So Kapitan Kontos waited, purposely taking his time, while the specialists on the bridge of *Pele* pretended not to watch the clock and hid smiles at the way their Kapitan was disrespecting the Syndicate CEO. Kontos himself had little use for Syndicate CEOs. But the specialists, once all known as "workers" under the Syndicate system, tended to hate the CEOs who had been the highest level of official enforcing their subjugation to the Syndicate. Though "hate" was probably far too mild a word for the workers' feelings.

About ten minutes having elapsed since the receipt of the message, Kontos composed himself, trying to look every bit an officer of his rank and one who cared little for the expectations of a Syndicate CEO, then activated his reply. "This is Kapitan Kontos of the Free and Independent Midway Star System battle cruiser *Pele*. My ship is escorting troop transport HTTU 458, which is carrying ground forces and mobile forces personnel of the Syndicate Worlds who were captured by the forces of Midway at Ulindi Star System. In keeping with our agreement when they surrendered, our prisoners will be released to your custody. Do not bother claiming that you cannot take these people. We know that with the now-empty barracks that once held construction workers, the existing living facilities at Iwa are more than adequate to handle the additional Syndicate soldiers and crew members who are in the troop transport. Those personnel will require further transport to other locations in Syndicate space," he added, knowing how it would enrage the Syndicate CEO to be given a job to do by someone like Kontos.

"Once we have dropped off the Syndicate personnel," Kontos continued, "we will return to Midway. We have no hostile intent toward Iwa and will not launch any attacks while here. Unless we are first attacked, in which case we will reply with all the force of which this battle cruiser is capable. For the people, Kontos, out," he concluded, saying the last phrase with slow emphasis.

CEO Vasquez would not be happy with that reply, but unless she was a complete idiot she would limit her objections to bluster and legalisms. "Have we spotted any signs of possible hidden defenses?" Kontos asked.

"None, Kapitan," *Pele*'s senior operations specialist replied. "The Syndicate records of the work being done here match what we can see, but most of that work is incomplete or clearly abandoned, showing no weaponry, no signs of human presence, and not even traces of power sources."

"Some defensive weaponry had been installed," Kontos said. "I saw those completed work orders in captured files."

"Yes, Kapitan. But those installations are now vacant. From what our sensors are showing, it looks like the Syndicate has been recently again cannibalizing Iwa for weapons, sensors, and anything else that is easily removed."

"It does," Kontos agreed. "Is this right? Communications we are intercepting within the star system indicate that only a single company of Syndicate ground forces remain?"

"Several messages that we intercepted reference that, Kapitan," the comm specialist replied, her voice confident. "There is only an Executive Third Class commanding them."

"An Executive Third Class?" Kontos questioned. "That is the senior Syndicate ground forces commander in Iwa at this time?"

"Yes, Kapitan."

It seemed impossible that even the Syndicate, overextended everywhere, would leave such a junior executive in command of the forces at Iwa. But, then, Iwa had little worth defending. "The Syndicate probably would have abandoned Iwa completely by now if Midway had not revolted," Kontos commented. "As it is, they are doing the minimum necessary to keep it as a potential staging ground for further attacks on us. Try to spot any indications that the Syndicate has shifted resources from here to Moorea. And try to pick up any comm chatter about the situation at Moorea and Palau. Anything about Syndicate activity, or other threats. President Iceni wants to know anything we can discover about the warlord or pirate who rumors say is operating in the region near Moorea Star System."

After that, it was only a matter of waiting as the battle cruiser and the troop transport crawled at point one five light speed toward the inhabited world. Forty-five thousand kilometers per second sounded fast on a planet, and was in fact impossibly fast in such a limited environment. But in space, where planets orbited millions and billions of kilometers apart, even such velocities took a while to cover distances too huge for human instincts to fully grasp. At point one five light speed, the three light hours that separated them from the inhabited world would take twenty hours to cover, but since the planet was itself moving through its orbit at about thirty-five kilometers per second, *Pele* and the troop transport had to aim to intercept the planet as it moved, their paths forming a huge arc through space.

"Kapitan," the comm specialist reported, "we have intercepted a system-wide message from CEO Vasquez ordering a safety stand-down by all Syndicate forces."

"That is certainly the safest course of action for them," Kontos agreed with a smile. Technically, CEO Vasquez was not surrendering to Kontos's demands. She could argue to her Syndicate superiors at Prime Star System that the safety stand-down had left her unable to fight. The senior CEOs at Prime probably wouldn't be impressed by that claim, but Vasquez was making the best of a situation with no good alternatives for her.

Pele and the transport were still a light hour away from the inhabited planet when an alert sounded. The tension level on the bridge immediately jumped as the warning of a warship was accompanied by a bright new warning marker on *Pele*'s combat displays.

Kontos stared at his display, baffled, as the warning symbol appeared where no symbol should appear on the outskirts of this star system. The location was nearly five light hours distant, on the other side of Iwa Star System, so the unknown warship had appeared there five hours ago.

And then vanished as quickly as it had appeared.

"What was that?" Kontos demanded. "What kind of ship was that?"

Pele's sensors had automatically recorded everything that could be seen of the other ship in every frequency of the visual and electromagnetic spectrum, then compared that to the information in its databases. The answer to Kontos's question popped up on his display before he had finished asking the question. "An enigma ship?"

"Yes, Kapitan," the operations specialist replied, sounding worried. "One of their light combatants, about equal in size to our light cruisers."

"How could an enigma ship be at Iwa? The only jump point in a human-occupied star system that they can access in this region of space is at Midway. Iwa is too far from any enigma-controlled star system to be reached by them using jump drives. He must have been hiding from our sensors," Kontos concluded.

"Kapitan," the systems security specialist said, "we are scanning our sensor systems and all other ship systems now. No enigma-originated worms that could have hidden the presence of a ship have been found."

Kontos shook his head, glaring at his display. "You are saying that the ship was not there, then it was, then it wasn't? That could only mean it jumped into this star system, then jumped out again almost immediately."

"Yes, Kapitan," the systems security specialist agreed with clear reluctance.

"How is that possible?" Kontos demanded, turning to look at all of the specialists at their watch stations on the bridge. "There is no jump point at that spot in space."

"That location is nowhere near the jump points that Iwa has, Kapitan," the senior specialist said. "There are only two possibilities. Either the detection was a false one, something produced by a glitch in the sensor systems, or there is a jump point at that location that our own systems cannot identify."

Kontos frowned. "Is that possible? A jump point we cannot detect?"

The operations specialist hesitated. Not long ago, when still a worker under the Syndicate system, he would have done his best to avoid providing any useful answer, instead saying whatever he thought his superior wanted to hear. Workers learned the hard way that Syndicate superiors did not want to hear bad news or unexplained events.

But under Kommodor Marphissa, and now Kapitan Kontos, they had been encouraged to think and to give their best information. The specialist spoke slowly, choosing each word with care. "Kapitan, if the enigma warship did appear there, then we would have to conclude that it is possible for a jump point to be at that location, a jump point that we cannot detect with our sensors. But it is also possible that the warship was not really there, that the detection is a ghost generated by a flaw in the sensor systems which was quickly cleared."

Kontos nodded. "Run checks. Full diagnostics on everything. I don't see how this could be anything but the result of a glitch, but let's check it carefully."

"Incoming call from HTTU 458," the comm specialist reported.

The image of HTTU 458's commanding officer appeared before Kontos. "What was that?" she asked. "That ship that appeared on the edge of the star system?"

Kontos paused before answering. "Your ship saw it, too? Was it over the link with *Pele*?"

"No. My ship's sensors reported a detection independent of that from *Pele*. They identified what they called an *enigma* warship in the same location that *Pele* reported seeing one, then reported that the warship had vanished as if it had entered jump space." The transport's commanding officer shook her head. "But Iwa doesn't have a jump point there."

"No, it doesn't," Kontos said. "Or, rather, it's not supposed to have a jump point there. And we cannot see a jump point in that location."

"I know very little about the aliens, the enigmas. Can they do that?"

It was Kontos's turn to shake his head. "I don't know. Black Jack's people didn't tell us the enigmas could jump to places where we cannot see jump points, but they admitted they were able to learn little about the enigmas."

"Alliance," the transport's captain said, her tone filled with disgust and anger. "They wouldn't tell us the truth." A century of war with the Alliance, a war the Syndicate had finally lost not too long ago, had left a vast reservoir of hatred which might never fully drain.

"It was Black Jack's workers," Kontos repeated. "Black

Jack" Geary, the legendary hero of the Alliance, who had impossibly returned from the dead to save the Alliance and bring an end to the war that seemed as if it would never end. He had been the one to finally defeat the Syndicate. And yet he had also stopped practices such as the bombarding of civilian populations on planets and the execution of prisoners, which during that century of war had become commonplace. He had broken the Syndicate's power and given places like Midway their chances at freedom. "Black Jack is . . . for the people."

The transport's captain grimaced. "The universe seems to be full of impossible things these days. Could the enigmas have used something other than jump space?"

Kontos paused before answering, upset that the possibility had not occurred to him. "We know of only two ways to travel between stars in less than decades. That doesn't mean another one could not exist. But what we saw of this enigma ship matched the behavior of something using jump space."

"How could a jump point be there? Jump points are created because the gravity wells of stars are huge enough to stretch space itself far enough to create thin spots which we can use to enter or leave jump space. Jump points stay in the same spots relative to the stars that created them. They don't come and go."

"Perhaps the enigma ship used a different kind of jump point," Kontos speculated. "Or perhaps the enigmas have discovered a new way to mess with our sensors, and there was no ship there."

"What should we do?"

"We'll investigate both possibilities as well as we can, though neither your ship nor mine has exotic scientific instruments that might be able to see something we cannot already see. Let's get this off-load done as quickly as possible once we reach the planet so we can return to Midway. I want to report this."

He didn't know what the inexplicable appearance of the enigma warship at Iwa meant, but it could not mean anything good. Neither would the chance that the enigmas had discovered a new way to fool the sensors of human ships. The enigmas had refused to negotiate or even openly disclose their existence for decades, remaining invisible to Syndicate sensors as they seized human-occupied star systems and destroyed human spacecraft without warning. The secret of their invisibility had been solved by Black Jack, but the enigmas had nonetheless continued their attacks. If they could now directly jump to human-occupied star systems other than Midway, it would present a serious threat.

President Iceni had to be told. She would know what to do.

THE largest city on the planet known as Midway in the star system that humanity had named Midway had been built to Syndicate standards. Curves were inefficient, so straight lines marked the street grid, and straight lines characterized the buildings that lined those streets. Those designs also meant straight lines of sight in all directions, which helped out another standard feature of Syndicate cities: surveillance systems intended to provide continuous coverage of every square centimeter. Even though the Syndicate Internal Security Service agents (nicknamed "snakes" by the citizens) had been eliminated during the rebellion by President Iceni and General Drakon, the surveillance systems remained, though other watchers now made use of them.

But other standard aspects of the Syndicate were corruption, shoddy work wherever undermotivated workers could get away with it, and shoddy construction wherever corporations could get away with it. Between bribes, badly placed surveillance devices, and poor quality in much of the surveillance gear, the system intended to see everything in fact had cracks in its picture of the city. And in those cracks, crime could still operate, vice could find its outlets, and those who did not want to be seen could remain invisible. The president and the general might be slowly changing how things had been done under the Syndicate, but the nature of the underbelly of human cities had not changed in thousands of years and would not change here anytime soon.

Colonel Bran Malin cautiously eased his way down a short alley, placing each step carefully to avoid noise. A security light intended to illuminate the alley had never worked, but the low-light "cat's-eye" contact lenses Malin was using provided a decent view of the cluttered alley despite the gloom of the night. The suit he wore, similar to that of an average low-level executive, appeared innocent but actually contained a wide variety of weapons and defenses. He thought of it as a hunting outfit, because it had been designed to stalk and eliminate prey.

Human prey, because Malin was determined that anyone who might threaten either Drakon or Iceni would be taken out before they could harm either leader. It sometimes bothered him that he felt no qualms about killing anyone he suspected of being a threat. Perhaps that was because of how important his goals were. Or perhaps he had inherited that lack of conscience from his mother. That thought bothered him as well.

Malin froze in position as one of the screens on his palm pad revealed another flicker of motion as someone slipped from one crack on the surveillance system to another. He had been following that someone for over an hour, a slow-motion game of cat and mouse. This was no ordinary criminal but a highly skilled operative, using the sort of techniques that only someone trained by the Syndicate snakes would know to employ. Malin, who had acquired that same training by means that would have meant his death if the snakes had ever discovered it, had been sorely pressed to maintain contact with his prey.

Was this a surviving snake, operating under deep cover? Or someone like Malin, who was serving other masters?

And where was he or she going? His quarry had at first seemed focused on places and things related to General Drakon and Colonel Morgan, leading Malin to initially believe that this chase might be related to the hiding place of

General Drakon's infant daughter. Drakon wanted to find that girl, to rescue her from whatever planned upbringing Morgan had arranged. Malin always thought of the baby girl as Drakon's, and not as Malin's own half sister. Contemplating the girl's relationship to him too easily brought up emotions that could distract and anger him when focus and cold calm were necessary.

But something about that other's long, careful path across the city had led Malin to think there might be another reason behind his or her skulking journey.

Malin, having waited to ensure the other would have minimum chance of spotting him if his prey was also tapping into the city surveillance network, moved in a sudden, smooth rush from the end of the alley into an adjoining street. Clinging to the side of the building, he slid along until he could twist around the corner where another alley met the street.

Pausing, he studied his palm display again. An itching sensation began between Malin's shoulders, the uncomfortable sixth-sense feeling that someone was aiming a weapon at his back. He leapt across a gap and down a short distance before coming to a halt in a shadowed doorway, a small but extremely lethal weapon in one hand.

He had very little information from the surveillance net to go on, but Malin's instincts warned him that the prey had become tired of the chase and was trying to become the hunter. Malin had spent the last twenty minutes growing increasingly certain that his quarry knew of the pursuit and was not simply trying to remain hidden from chance watchers but was actually hiding from Malin.

A pair of police officers walked by on a nearby street, their casual conversation and the sound of their feet echoing like gunshots to Malin's senses, which were tuned to bare whispers of noise. The police had palm readouts as well, and were doubtless watching them, but would have seen nothing of Malin and his target, and would have seen no alarms or alerts on their pads. The Syndicate had devoted generations to trying to perfect artificial intelligence routines for the surveillance systems, but every AI operated using rules. Once someone knew the rules, it was just a matter of breaking whatever pattern the AI was looking for.

Human minds weren't locked into rules, though. Their ability to think outside of rules and rigid beliefs had allowed humanity to dominate Old Earth, had brought humans to the stars, had brought them as far as Midway, and had brought Malin to this alley.

Malin spotted a minor fluctuation that told him of movement and edged along on a path that would bring him closer to the path of his quarry. Had that quarry actually been moving to ambush Malin? Or had Malin been spooked by the long pursuit and the mental strain of staying to the cracks in the surveillance net during that time?

He paused again, breathing slowly, scanning the darkness for any movement that might not register on the surveillance sensors. The sensor system could be hacked, had been hacked innumerable times, to keep it from noticing someone or some event. Malin himself carried the means to enter the system's controlling software and redirect it. But he hadn't used that tool tonight because of a growing suspicion that his prey had the same capability and would spot Malin the moment he tried to employ it.

A shuttle zipped by above the city, coming down from orbit and heading toward the landing field on the outskirts of the city. A lesser tracker would have been distracted, but Malin kept his senses glued to his readout and spotted the flickers that marked more motion at the same moment as the shuttle crossed directly overhead.

Too easy, Malin thought, frowning. His target had not made any such obvious moves in the hour of pursuit. Was the prey growing tired and careless? Or had those betraying actions been shown deliberately, clear enough and yet subtle enough to lead an eager and also tired hunter into a misstep?

Morgan would have caught them by now. Malin could not block the thought before it taunted him. Morgan had been in a class by herself, but she was almost surely dead. He no longer had to measure himself against her, no longer had to compete with the woman who did not even realize that Malin was her son. But he almost moved quickly then, almost tried to close fast on his prey, almost tried to keep proving he was as capable as Morgan.

More motion, more noise, several flickers along a path.

His prey was running.

A lesser hunter than Malin might have bolted after the fleeing quarry. A lesser hunter might have hesitated, wondering whether to race in pursuit or not.

A lesser hunter would have died seconds later.

Malin hurled himself away from the path his prey had taken. No longer worrying about concealment, he pelted down the alley, trying to put as much distance between himself and his last position as possible.

The explosion came just as Malin rounded a corner and sheltered next to a building.

As the roar of the blast subsided, to be replaced by shouts and screams and the wail of alarms, Malin stood away from the building, brushed off his suit, triggered the software routines that would render him invisible to the sensor net, and walked away. The hunt had failed. A dangerous enemy of General Drakon and President Iceni was still at large. He would have to report this, would have to let Drakon and Iceni know of the threat, and of his failure. It would be up to them to decide on the necessary response. Or, more likely, up to Iceni, because even though they were supposed to be coequal, Drakon had increasingly focused on external security and deferred to her on internal matters. It would probably be Iceni who would decide what to do.

An all-too-familiar self-rebuke echoed in Malin's head. *They wouldn't have gotten away from Morgan.*

KOMMODOR Marphissa had long since stopped expecting to ever again get a full night's sleep. If something major didn't demand her attention in the middle of the "night" aboard the heavy cruiser *Manticore*, then something minor would pop up.

This wasn't minor.

"Dancers, Kommodor! Twenty-four Dancer ships have arrived at the jump point from Kane!"

She sat up on her bunk in her darkened stateroom and rubbed her eyes, trying to make sense of the news, then glared at the image of the specialist who had reported the information. "The jump point from Kane? Twenty-four Dancer ships?"

"Yes, Kommodor," the specialist confirmed.

"Did I miss hearing that twenty-four Dancer ships had arrived in human space? Did this happen while I was at Ulindi?"

"No, Kommodor. I checked the records. There is no report of any Dancer presence here since the ships of theirs that accompanied Black Jack's battle cruisers jumped back toward their own territory."

Marphissa glowered at the comm screen, but she wasn't looking at the nervous specialist anymore. She was running his words through her mind. The Dancers were the only alien species humanity had yet contacted that seemed willing to coexist. The Dancers actually seemed friendly toward humans, which wasn't what people expected of aliens who looked like the result of the mating of wolves with enormous spiders. But the Dancers had saved Midway from a devastating bombardment launched by the enigmas, another alien race, but one that had acted only with hostility toward humans. That alone inclined Marphissa to see the Dancers as allies against a universe her Syndicate upbringing argued was hostile and unrelenting. "How did they get to Kane?"

"Kommodor, I don't—"

The specialist's image was replaced by that of Kapitan Diaz, commanding officer of *Manticore*. He had clearly been awakened, too, but was already on the bridge of the heavy cruiser. "Kommodor, our sensors show that many of the Dancer ships display battle damage."

"Battle damage?" This just got stranger by the moment. "Can we tell what sort of weapons inflicted the damage?"

"The damage is consistent with a variety of weaponry," Diaz said, consulting a screen off to his side. "Something that could be hell lances or a similar particle beam weapon, fragmentation damage from explosions that could be from missiles, some spalling that could mark hits from small kinetic weapons like grapeshot. Because we don't know enough about the precise characteristics of the Dancer hulls, our systems cannot match the damage to exact Alliance or Syndicate weapons. It could even mark damage from enigma weaponry."

Diaz glanced aside, listening to another report. "We have just received a text message from the Dancers, Kommodor. All it says is 'going home.'"

"Going home?" Marphissa repeated, baffled. "From where? Whom did they fight?"

"There is more. Another message." Diaz blinked, looking baffled. "The Dancers say 'watch different stars.' Isn't that what the last group said just before they left?"

"Yes. Maybe we can get this bunch to explain before they leave!"

"That is all we have, Kommodor," Diaz said.

"I will prepare a report for President Iceni," Marphissa said, trying to figure out what to say. Iceni would want more information. Anyone would. But the little available left more questions than answers. Dancer ships arriving from deeper in human space when they had not been seen arriving in human space. Dancer ships that showed many signs of heavy fighting, but whom had they fought? And the repetition of the warning to watch "different" stars, the meaning of which remained obscure.

Hopefully, the president would know what to do about all of this.

CHAPTER TWO

GENERAL Artur Drakon, formerly a CEO in the Syndicate Worlds, watched President Gwen Iceni, also formerly a CEO of the Syndicate Worlds, pacing across the width of her office. One wall of the office appeared to be a vast window looking out on a beach, and Iceni would pause each time she reached that view to gaze at the waves for a moment before turning and pacing back in the other direction. In fact, the office was underground, buried behind layers of armor. Syndicate CEOs took for granted that many enemies would be happy to kill them if the opportunity presented itself, and some of those enemies might well be coworkers and co-CEOs.

"What the hell do I do about this?" Iceni demanded. "How did those Dancers get to Kane? How did they get beyond Kane without passing through Midway after coming in through the jump point from Pele?" Pele had been taken by the enigmas a generation ago, and Black Jack's fleet had been the only human presence to visit that star since then. "We have the only jump point in human space the alien races can access."

Drakon sat relaxed in a chair, watching Iceni. Even at times like this he liked watching her walk, because there was an assurance and a grace to Iceni's stride that naturally generated confidence. "They must have a way of getting to other jump points."

"That is impossible, Artur," Iceni insisted, softening her dismissal of his words by using his first name.

"Is there another explanation, Gwen?" he asked, doing the same to avoid seeming to confront her reasoning. "As far as we know, it's impossible for the Dancers to access other jump points in human space. But here they are, and they didn't come through the jump point from Pele."

Iceni stopped, gazing toward the image of the beach where the waves constantly rose and receded on the sand. "Yes. It's impossible for us. We have little idea of what the Dancers could do."

"Do you think Black Jack would have told us if he knew the Dancers could do that?" Drakon asked.

"I don't know. I think so. He would know how that knowledge would complicate our defense of this region of space against the enigmas. Because if the Dancers could jump to other stars, then the enigmas might also—" She broke off, turning her head to stare at Drakon. "Watch different stars. Are the Dancers telling us that the enigmas might attack somewhere other than Midway?"

"I hope not," Drakon said. "Am I right that our warships are barely adequate to defend Midway itself?"

"Our warships are not nearly enough to be sure of defending Midway," Iceni replied, her voice sharp with anxiety. "Especially when we have to worry about the Syndicate Worlds making another attack on us as well. The Syndicate won't give up just because we've beaten them badly at Ulindi."

The comm alert on Iceni's desk buzzed urgently. She tapped a control. "Yes?"

The image of a watch-stander at the planetary command center appeared before her. "Madam President, we have just seen that *Pele* and HTTU 458 have returned through the jump point to Iwa. Kapitan Kontos reports a successful completion of his mission. He attached to his arrival report a special annex for your eyes only."

"Send it on," Iceni said, then waited a second for the image of Kontos to replace that of the watch-stander. She listened to the brief report of events at Iwa, her expression not betraying her reaction, then looked at Drakon. "An enigma ship detection at Iwa. It looks like you guessed right."

Drakon grimaced, automatically mentally running through options. "I wish I hadn't been right. We could take Iwa easily enough. A single company of Syndicate ground forces wouldn't last five seconds against a battalion of my soldiers, even if the Syndicate ground forces put up a decent fight, which I wouldn't do if I were in their position. But how could we afford to position enough of our warships at Iwa to stop an enigma attack and also provide protection to Midway?"

Iceni called up a display showing the nearby stars, the images floating near her desk. "You have much more military experience than I do. If you were the enigmas, what would you do?"

Drakon studied the stars, rubbing his chin as he thought and not liking what his conclusions were. "If I were an enigma? It would depend how much I knew about what was available to humans to defend Midway and Iwa. How much do the enigmas know?"

"We've had obvious reconnaissance visits," Iceni said, gesturing toward the symbol for the jump point at which ships coming from Pele would arrive. "A single enigma ship jumps in, collects a snapshot of everything that can be seen in this star system, then jumps out within less than a minute. That detection at Iwa could have been the same thing." She brightened. "And they happened to stop by while there was a battle cruiser at Iwa, and a troop transport that for all the enigmas knew could be bringing reinforcements for the garrison."

"What if the enigmas recognized the ships as ours and the ownership of Iwa as still Midway's?" Drakon asked, not willing to make an overly optimistic assessment.

Iceni narrowed her eyes at the display. "It would look like an invasion force, wouldn't it?" she said. "The enigmas would probably interpret what they saw as signs that we have already conquered Iwa." She sighed. "Is that good or bad?"

"In terms of how the enigmas see it?" Drakon asked. "Damned if I know. Assuming the enigmas think we now own Iwa, and assuming they can reach Iwa with an attack, then if I were them I'd try to hit Iwa first. The enigmas can count, and they must know that we don't have enough warships to garrison both star systems in strength. Take Iwa, where they haven't been thrown back twice like they have here, then hit Midway again, maybe with forces arriving from both Pele and Iwa."

She nodded. "If we spread our forces out, we'll be weak everywhere. But if we concentrate our forces here, the enigmas will walk in and take Iwa whether we own it or not. This stinks." Iceni looked around, seeking someone, then sat down with another sigh. "I still keep expecting him to be here whenever I need him."

Drakon fought down a reflexive disquiet and tried to sound neutral as he answered. "Your former assistant?"

"Yes." From the look Iceni gave him, Drakon hadn't been nearly good enough at hiding his feelings. "We still don't know what happened to Mehmet Togo, Artur. Yes, he might have betrayed me then bolted. Or he might have been taken by enemies. We don't know," she repeated.

"He wouldn't have been easy to take," Drakon said carefully. "Can I ask you something?"

"No." But then she smiled slightly. "Go ahead."

"Why don't you think that I or one of my people took out Togo?"

She took a long moment to answer, her gaze on the beach again. "Because you wouldn't do that to me. And if one of your people did it . . . you would have found out and told me."

Drakon grimaced again, feeling a mix of anger and unhappiness. "You know how badly I misjudged how much I knew about my two closest assistants," he said.

Iceni nodded, still watching the waves. "Colonel Morgan died on Ulindi."

"I won't be sure of that until I see a body, and even then

I'll wonder if she cloned one to cover her going deep without my knowledge. Apparently, you still trust Colonel Malin."

Another nod. "As much as I trust anyone." Another pause. "Except you."

He stared at her, wondering why Iceni had said something that Syndicate CEO training and experience insisted no one should ever say. "Um . . . in that case . . . since you need a capable assistant whom you trust, I can lend you Colonel Malin."

Iceni laughed, turning her head to look at him again. "Make *your* agent *my* personal assistant, privy to all my secrets and actions? Exactly how much do you think I trust you?"

"It's not about that," Drakon said, wondering if he was telling the truth. "It's about how much you trust Malin."

"I see." Iceni still looked amused. "And with both Colonel Morgan and Colonel Malin gone, who do you have for a personal assistant?"

"Colonel Gozen."

Iceni's eyebrows rose. She reached out, tapping a few commands, then read from the data that appeared before her. "Former Syndicate Executive Third Class Celia Gozen? *Recently* captured at Ulindi?"

"She wasn't really captured," Drakon said defensively. "She's a fine soldier. And she has been extremely well screened, a process overseen by Colonel Malin."

"I see." Iceni gave Drakon an arch look. "And how does Colonel Malin feel about the elevation of Colonel Gozen to such a position?"

"He's unhappy," Drakon said. "Which is why I know that if he'd found a speck of information indicating that Gozen was problematic he would have pounced on it."

Iceni leaned forward, resting her elbows on her desk, gazing skeptically at Drakon. "But still, Artur. Someone that new getting that level of trust?"

"I have a gut feeling," he said, knowing that he sounded even more defensive and hoping that Iceni wouldn't bring up his misplaced trust in Colonel Morgan.

She did, but not in the way Drakon expected. "Hmmm.

Even the very-probably-late Colonel Morgan didn't betray you in her own eyes. She thought she was helping you. What is it that makes you want Gozen so close to you?"

Drakon shrugged. "She's . . . blunt. She's usually properly respectful, but she has no difficulty telling me when she thinks I'm wrong or that I've missed something. And unless I very much have misjudged her, she cares about the people who work for her more than she cares about the ego of her boss. Someone in my position needs someone like that, and people like that are very hard to find."

Iceni's eyebrows went up again. "She was still an executive in the Syndicate ground forces? Why hadn't Gozen already been executed or sent to a labor camp for telling her boss when she thought the boss was wrong?"

"She had a patron." Drakon waved toward the information Iceni had displayed. "Her uncle, in the same unit. I'm sure you know all about it."

"Yes." Iceni rested her chin on her hand as she looked at Drakon. "I also know that you could have raised the same objections when I quickly promoted Kapitan Mercia to command of the *Midway*, the battleship that is by far our most powerful warship. But you didn't. You trusted my judgment. So I shall trust yours. I don't really have any right to pass judgment on your personal staff, so I appreciate your obvious willingness to discuss the matter with me."

"You're using that word 'trust' an awful lot," Drakon pointed out, grinning with relief.

"I know. I'm going to turn into some bleeding-heart Alliance officer, aren't I? Boasting about my honor and proclaiming my virtue over those scum-of-the-earth Syndics." Iceni looked down for a moment, her expression softening into something like sorrow. "We were, weren't we? Scum of the earth. The things I did to survive, to reach CEO rank—"

"We both did a lot of things that we don't like to remember," Drakon broke in. "We did it to survive, so we could someday do something better. And we are doing something better."

"Something better, hell. I wanted to be in a position so strong I couldn't be threatened, and powerful enough that

I'd be able to avenge myself on some of those who had harmed me. That's what it was about, Artur." She used her arms to lever herself back to her feet. "That's the past. Today, we have a chance at something better, and a star system to defend. I want a meeting with more minds than yours and mine. Agreed? You, me, Captain Bradamont, your Colonel Malin . . . and Colonel Gozen. Anyone else?"

"What about your Kommodor?"

Iceni glanced at the display. "*Manticore* is a light hour from us. Marphissa couldn't contribute in any meaningful way with that sort of time delay. *Midway* and *Pele* are even farther away." She paused in midturn, shaking her head. "I was about to order Togo to set up the meeting. He was with me for a long time."

Drakon nodded, standing as well. "I'll have Gozen set it up. It'll be a nice test of how well she functions off the battlefield." His eyes went back to the display as well, focusing on the images of the Dancer ships. He had once heard old legends about certain birds whose arrival was thought to warn of imminent battle or other woes, and he wondered if those battle-scarred alien ships would prove to be such heralds as well.

GWEN Iceni left the protection of her heavily armored VIP limo, moving between twin lines of ground forces soldiers in battle armor who formed nearly solid walls of protection for her. The security measure irked her, so when she reached the door to the meeting facility she paused to look at the female soldier in an obviously new uniform who was standing at attention. "Colonel Gozen?"

"Yes, Madam C—" Gozen bit off the word just a moment too late.

Iceni smiled without any humor. "A lifetime's habits are not easily forgotten, but you need to work on that. It is Madam President, and I am uncomfortable with a degree of personal security more appropriate to a Syndicate CEO."

Gozen had the look of someone who had just been told

that gravity made things float away. In her experience, of course, CEOs always insisted on every perk they could muster as a means of displaying their importance relative to the citizens and other CEOs. "Ma'am?"

"It's simple," Iceni said. "I'm not a Syndicate CEO." Not anymore, anyway. "I don't play by Syndicate CEO rules, where the more security you get the more important you must be. I don't fear the citizens of this world." She made sure to say that last loudly enough to carry, because every word spoken in public had to be used to reinforce the message Iceni wanted to send. Of course, the statement wasn't strictly true. Some of those citizens were surely gunning for her, and the enthusiasm of the mob scared her since Iceni knew how easily mobs could shift. But most of the citizens of Midway now appeared to genuinely want her as their leader and were not only willing to follow her lead but happy to do so. "I have my bodyguards. That's enough."

Gozen's eyes went to the heavily armored limo, but she was smart enough not to make any comment about Iceni's chosen mode of transportation. "I understand and will comply."

"You're on exceptionally good behavior today, aren't you?" Iceni commented in a low voice as she walked past Gozen and into the building where the meeting would take place. There had been a time when she and Drakon would only meet at neutral locations, directly controlled by neither of them, but the time for those games had passed. Especially since the fortified structures that made up Drakon's headquarters complex offered a comforting sense of security.

Everyone else was already in the conference room. Iceni noticed Gozen avoiding looking at Captain Bradamont, whose Alliance uniform had been a symbol of the enemy for a century, and tried again to get a rise out of her. "You're not used to this sort of company, Colonel Gozen?"

Gozen gave Iceni a bland look in reply. "I'm still getting my feet under me, Madam President. Thank you for your concern."

Iceni raised both eyebrows at her. "You are good at borderline insubordination, aren't you? How did even your uncle manage to keep you out of labor camp?"

"He was an exceptional man," Gozen said.

"Were you able to find which labor camp he was sent to?" Iceni pressed. "We still have covert contacts within the Syndicate that we might be able to use."

Gozen shook her head, revealing no emotion as she spoke. "I'm sorry, Madam President, but records that were captured after the fall of Ulindi revealed that my uncle had been summarily executed when the snakes took over command of my old unit."

Damn. The game of assessing Gozen had just turned dark. That too easily happened when discussing history within the Syndicate. "I'm sorry," Iceni said.

Her sincerity must have come through, because Gozen let a flash of surprise show, then smiled briefly but genuinely. "Thank you, Madam President."

Iceni and Drakon took their seats on opposite sides of the table out of habit, Bradamont sitting next to Iceni, Gozen and Malin sitting on either side of Drakon. "I want candid discussion," Iceni began. "We're facing some unprecedented issues that require an open exchange of ideas."

Drakon nodded, then gestured toward Malin. "Before we do anything else, Colonel Malin has something to report."

Iceni turned a questioning gaze on Malin. As far as she knew, Drakon still wasn't aware that Malin had been a covert source for her for some time. But Drakon knew that she had more trust in Malin than she did in others. Had Drakon figured out the reasons for that? Assigning Malin to her would limit Malin's ability to find out what was going on in Drakon's headquarters. Not that Iceni worried much about that anymore, especially with the fanatical and unpredictable Colonel Morgan out of the picture.

Malin looked as icily correct as usual, sitting straight in his chair, hands clasped before him, speaking with cool dispassion. "Last night there was an explosion in the city."

Iceni nodded. "Cause unknown, I was told. Possibly organized-crime related. Do you know more about it?"

"Yes, Madam President. I was pursuing a suspect. The suspect realized I was trailing him or her, and attempted to kill me with an explosive planted along their path."

"I see." Iceni glanced at Drakon. "I have the impression that Colonel Malin is exceptionally skilled at tracking suspects." Actually, she knew it for certain, but it wouldn't do to betray that knowledge.

"He's very good," Drakon confirmed.

"Whoever I was tracking was better," Malin said, still betraying no emotion that would reveal how he felt about that. "That is of particular concern. I only know of two people on Midway who could have moved so stealthily, detected my own pursuit, and nearly taken me out with an ambush. One was Colonel Morgan. It was not her last night. I would have been able to tell."

"Who is the other?" Iceni asked, feeling her gut tighten because she already knew what the answer must be.

"Your missing personal assistant, Madam President. Mehmet Togo."

Iceni pondered that information while everyone else waited silently. "How confident are you of that assessment, Colonel Malin?"

"Very confident, Madam President."

Togo. Apparently alive, apparently free to move about the city. But not in any contact with her, having disappeared just before Midway had almost fallen apart in a burst of attempted assassinations and social disruptions that had almost led to mass rioting. "What was he doing last night?"

"I was unable to determine my quarry's mission last night, Madam President."

That was vintage Malin. Confessing freely to his failures as if seeking punishment. "All access codes and security arrangements at my offices have been changed," Iceni said. "But I know that would not stop Togo. Are you aware, Colonel Malin, that General Drakon has offered your services to me as a personal assistant?"

"Yes, Madam President."

"If Togo makes it through all of my other security and guards, could you stop him?"

Malin took a moment to answer. "I don't know. It would be difficult. I would have a chance of success, but I cannot quantify it."

"He's the best I have," Drakon said. "There was only one better."

"I wouldn't care to have had Colonel Morgan for a personal assistant," Iceni said dryly. "I would have been more concerned about any dangers posed by her than about any potential assassins. Colonel Malin, alert all security systems to key on Togo's characteristics. If there is even a minor percentage match, I want it followed up. Notify all security forces that Togo is no longer classified as missing but as a potential security threat. Initiate mandatory password changes and security upgrades on all systems. If you, Colonel, find any indications of what Mehmet Togo may be up to, I need to know immediately."

After another brief hesitation, Malin nodded. "Yes, Madam President. I . . . still assess that Togo is loyal to you, so I have had little success in determining his motives."

Iceni waved toward Drakon. "Colonel, I have every reason to believe that the late Colonel Morgan was intensely loyal to your general. But some of the actions she took as a result of that loyalty were not in the best interests of your general."

Malin nodded again, flushing slightly. "I understand, Madam President."

Everyone else at the table carefully avoided reacting to Iceni's words.

"Now," she continued, "there's the matter of aliens. Captain Bradamont, did Black Jack tell us everything that was known regarding the Dancers and the enigmas?"

Bradamont nodded. "Everything that was known as of that time. I don't know if anything else has been learned since, but if it was anything critical I'm sure that Admiral Geary would have passed it on during his brief time at Midway last month."

"He was in a hurry," Iceni pressed. "You've seen copies of the transmissions made during that visit to this star system. What is your impression?"

"I believe," Bradamont said slowly, "that his primary concern was just as he stated, that the longer his battle cruiser force remained at Midway the more likely that the Syndics, excuse me, the Syndicate Worlds, would block his access to the hypernet gate here, preventing him from quickly getting back to a star system much closer to Alliance space."

"His primary concern?" Drakon asked.

"Yes, sir. I had the impression that he also wanted to get back to Alliance space as fast as possible for other reasons, but I could only speculate as to those."

"Please do," Iceni said.

Bradamont looked uncomfortable. "Internal issues. Alliance politics. Possible power struggles. I don't know. But he didn't recall me. Admiral Geary left me here to continue assisting Midway in any way I can. That at least means his wishes continue to have weight."

"Weight?" Iceni asked. "You still maintain that Black Jack is not directly ruling the Alliance?"

"I am certain that he is not," Bradamont said firmly. "He swore an oath to the Alliance. He gave his word of honor."

Iceni barely stopped herself from a reflexive rolling of her eyes, and could see the other former Syndicate citizens at the table also having trouble suppressing their reactions.

Surprisingly, it was Gozen who spoke up. "That might mean something," she offered. "It's Black Jack. He doesn't lie. The Syndicate does all it can to keep people from hearing anything, but in the ranks everybody knew what he'd done."

"Besides," Drakon added, "Black Jack wouldn't have had any reason to withhold critical information from us. He knows we're the front line against the enigmas."

Iceni made a casting-away gesture with one hand. "True enough, but if Black Jack is tied up with events in Alliance space, he's not going to be back here in force anytime soon."

A sudden thought came to her. "Those damaged Dancer ships. Could they have acquired that damage fighting a battle in Alliance space?"

"Black Jack against somebody else inside the Alliance?" Drakon asked. "Why would the Dancers help Black Jack in some internal fight?"

"They would if it involved something they cared about, and they seem to care about Black Jack," Iceni said. She noticed that Bradamont, normally as composed as only a veteran battle cruiser commander could be, looked unusually rattled by the turn in the conversation. "Yes, Captain?"

"I . . . just . . ." Bradamont swallowed and regained her composure. "It could mean some kind of civil war within the Alliance. That's difficult to think about."

"But it is possible?" Iceni asked. "We've been living with various forms of rebellion inside Syndicate space for some time."

"No, that's not the same thing," Bradamont insisted. "The Syndicate Worlds does not allow star systems to leave. You have to fight your way free. But if the people of a star system wanted to leave the Alliance, they would be allowed to go. They wouldn't have to go to war."

"Have any star systems ever actually left the Alliance?" Drakon asked.

"A couple. Usually not, though, because they know they *can* leave if they really want to, and that makes it easier to compromise. And both the Callas Republic and the Rift Federation have distanced themselves from the Alliance since the war ended, though neither has completely severed ties as far as I know." Bradamont looked around at the others. "I can tell that you don't believe me."

Malin answered, his eyes hooded in thought. "It does make sense. If you hold a leash very tightly, the leashed animal will fight against it. As we have against the Syndicate. If you let go the leash, the animal will run. But if you give the animal slack, let it move about, it will not see the need to fight or run. You can work together."

"Nice comparison, Colonel," Drakon said dryly.

"It's important, General," Malin said. "I know that you and President Iceni are still discussing a grouping of star systems. Perhaps we should make that a principle of such an association."

"We have other principles," Bradamont cautioned. "In order to remain within the Alliance, star systems have to abide by basic rules of human rights, and freedom, and representative government. If they break those rules, the Alliance can intervene on behalf of the people. It is rare, but it has happened."

"A leash still implies control," Iceni said. "We will have to handle diplomacy with other star systems very carefully to ensure our offered hand is not perceived to be holding a chain. If they get that impression of us, we'll never be able to depend upon them. We certainly do not have the means to force them to do as we want for extended periods. They might agree under conditions of a major threat like our battleship, but would balk the moment the battleship went elsewhere."

She called up a display over the table, the stars in this region of space winking into life in front of everyone. "All right. We have already sent messages to the Dancers asking for more information. From what we know, and from what Captain Bradamont has told us, it is unlikely that the Dancers will elaborate. But the mere presence of the Dancers here, along with the detection of an enigma reconnaissance ship at Iwa and the warning message the Dancers have twice given us, makes it look very much as if the enigmas will be able to attack other human-occupied star systems. What do we do about it?"

"There have been no reports from other nearby star systems of enigma ship detections?" Bradamont asked.

"Nothing from Taroa or Ulindi," Colonel Malin said. "Those two star systems, along with Iwa, are the closest star systems accessible to the enigmas."

"But Taroa and Ulindi are a bit farther away," Iceni noted.

"From enigma territory to Iwa slightly exceeds the maximum we could manage with Alliance jump drives," Brad-amont said. "But it's close. If the jump drives of the enigmas are similar to ours, they wouldn't need a major breakthrough to manage that jump."

"But there isn't any jump point where that enigma ship arrived at Iwa."

Bradamont frowned, her eyes on the stars floating above the table. "The methods we use to spot jump points are derived from the jump drives. Our sensors, and I assume Syndicate Worlds sensors, basically find any jump point that our jump drives can access. If the enigmas have tweaked the jump drives in a way that makes them more . . . sensitive? Effective? They might be able to spot jump points they can use but we cannot."

"I like rational explanations," Iceni said. "So, for the time being, assume the threat is confined to Midway and Iwa, but might expand to cover Ulindi and Taroa. Recommendations?"

"We must take Iwa," Malin said.

"Iwa isn't worth taking," Drakon groused.

"But if the enigmas turn it into a base, establish a foothold there—"

"What does the Syndicate Worlds have on the other side of Iwa?" Bradamont asked.

"Not much," Malin replied. "They have a shaky hold on Palau and Moorea Star Systems. We have information that Moorea may have already left Syndicate control."

"They've declared independence?" Bradamont asked.

"No. We have not been able to confirm it yet, but it appears Moorea has been conquered by forces loyal to Granaile Imallye, who may be a warlord, or a pirate with a large appetite. Moorea would be the third star system that she has seized control over."

"What does she title herself?" Iceni asked. "You can tell a lot about someone's intentions by the titles they assume."

"She uses no title," Malin said. "She is just known as Granaile Imallye."

"That does not give me a warm and fuzzy," Bradamont commented. "Someone who doesn't think they even need a rank or title to command is someone with a lot of confidence in themselves."

"And a bit of an enigma as well, in the human sense of the term," Iceni said. "But I don't see any alternative to making direct contact with this Imallye and finding out her intentions. If the enigmas establish a presence at Iwa, and her forces are at Moorea, she's going to end up fighting the enigmas, too, and perhaps soon."

"I agree," Drakon said. "We don't have to like Imallye, but we can't afford to be fighting her and the enigmas and the Syndicate. We have to find out if we can live with her, or if we're going to have to get rid of her."

"The Syndicate will take a while to recover from its losses at Ulindi," Malin said.

"I agree with that," Gozen said. "My old unit was the strongest Syndicate ground force in the region. Add in the warships that were lost and the troop transports that were captured, and the Syndicate took a big hit."

"Don't underestimate them," Iceni said. "The Syndicate still controls a lot of star systems with a lot of resources. Even if they can't overwhelm us at the moment, they probably have the means to push us hard. We need to send a ship to contact Imallye, and if I weren't worried about attacks on Midway by either the Syndicate or the enigmas I would send *Midway* or *Pele*. But I want both of those warships on hand. I can't spare a heavy cruiser, either, but I'll have to. I don't want an official contact with this pirate queen or warlord or supreme dictator to be in anything smaller than a heavy cruiser."

"You'll need a high-ranking representative aboard the heavy cruiser," Bradamont cautioned. "Imallye will more likely react positively to contact with a senior official than if someone of lower rank is sent."

Iceni glared up at the stars in the display. "Which means Kommodor Marphissa, doesn't it? Damn. I can't afford to have her gone, either!"

"You have some good commanders in Kapitan Mercia and Kapitan Kontos," Bradamont said.

"Neither of whom has decent experience in commanding formations of warships!" Iceni fixed her gaze on Bradamont. "But you do."

Bradamont shook her head. "I'm not supposed to get directly involved in combat—"

"Oh, hell, Captain! You're here to keep Midway from falling to the Syndicate or to the enigmas!"

"My orders—"

"And if Midway falls to either you know what will happen to Colonel Rogero! He will die heroically, I have no doubt. But he will die. And so would you. Is that really what Black Jack would want?"

Bradamont stared fixedly at the display for several seconds. "I am allowed to use my discretion in emergencies," she finally said.

"Good." Iceni nodded as if the matter was settled. "Then you will go aboard *Midway* or *Pele*, at your discretion, and if we are attacked you will assume overall command of our warships."

Gozen was staring at everyone else. "You're seriously talking about giving command of almost all of your mobile forces to an Alliance officer?"

The laughter from Drakon momentarily shocked everyone. "Yeah," he said. "We are. Can you imagine this a year ago?"

"A lot has happened," Iceni said, smiling thinly in response.

"Hell, yeah, a lot has happened." Drakon looked at Gozen. "Colonel, this Alliance officer is Black Jack's. As crazy as it sounds, she is the best choice for that assignment. We're not Syndicate anymore. Our warship crews respect Captain Bradamont."

"Not all of them," Bradamont muttered. "I'll need to take my bodyguards along if I'm going to be riding *Midway* or *Pele*," she added in a normal voice.

Gozen smiled in turn. "Taking your bodyguards everywhere? So you've become a little bit Syndicate yourself?"

"Please do not say that."

A week later, the war-damaged Dancer warships having crossed the star system and jumped for Pele without ever disclosing where they had been or whom they had fought, Kommodor Marphissa sat on the bridge of the heavy cruiser *Manticore* as the warship approached the jump point for Iwa. Beside her was Kapitan Diaz, who was frowning with clear unhappiness. "Kommodor," he asked in a low voice, "what if the enigmas have already taken Iwa?"

"Then I am to evaluate the situation and either continue on to Moorea," Marphissa answered, "or return immediately to Midway."

"The president gave you that much discretion?" Diaz said, surprised.

"She did. We're not working for the Syndicate anymore."

"That never would have happened if we were," Diaz agreed. "But what if the enigmas have already mined the jump point we'll arrive at, or have some of their warships stationed at it to catch any human ship that arrives?"

Marphissa smiled humorlessly. "In that case, Kapitan, you are to avoid hitting any of the mines, and avoid being hit by any enigma weaponry, until this ship jumps back for Midway."

Diaz stared, then grinned. "Now that sounds like a Syndicate order!"

"Bite your tongue, Kapitan. You may jump for Iwa."

But Marphissa, despite the banter with Diaz, could not help a jolt of anxiety as the stars vanished and were replaced by the dull gray nothingness of jump space. Orders that left her the freedom to decide what to do also meant they left her the freedom to make the wrong choices. And if the enigmas were at Iwa when *Manticore* arrived, even one wrong choice might be one mistake too many.

CHAPTER THREE

"WE need to plan for an attack on Iwa. It might be against the Syndicate presence there, which would be an easy operation." General Drakon looked from Colonel Rogero to Colonel Safir to Colonel Kai. His three brigade commanders. It still felt wrong, it would feel wrong for a long time, to see Safir there instead of Colonel Conner Gaiene. But Conner had died at Ulindi and would never be here again except in Drakon's memories. "Or it might be against an enigma occupation force."

"Which would not be easy," Rogero commented.

"Has there ever been a ground fight with the enigmas?" Safir asked.

"None that we know of," Drakon said. "To the best of our knowledge, some of the star systems they occupied over the last century had surviving Syndicate ground forces. But we have no idea what happened when the enigmas landed."

"Black Jack's information has nothing to offer?" Colonel Kai asked.

"No. They didn't have any ground or ship-boarding operations, either," Drakon said. "The one thing Black Jack's reports emphasized was the enigmas will not surrender and

will try to blow everything to hell before we can learn anything from it."

"Themselves included?"

"Themselves included."

"How much will we send?" Rogero asked.

"Plan on one brigade." Drakon looked over his colonels
again. "I don't know which one of yours will be tapped for
the operation if we go ahead with this. Each of you should
assume it might be your brigade."

"All of the brigades have been pushed hard over the last
year," Kai said.

"It hasn't been as bad as some of the ops when we were
under Syndicate control," Safir pointed out.

"That's not saying much."

"No, it isn't," Safir conceded. Syndicate CEOs had never
shown any worries about casualties, but then neither had
Alliance generals as the apparently endless war had ground
on. With vast populations to draw on, high-ranking leaders
on both sides had developed a tendency to throw endless
bodies into any fight in the hopes that enough deaths would
choke the enemy killing machines.

Black Jack had been different, rumor said. But then, he
was Black Jack.

And Drakon had been different as well, which was why
these soldiers had followed him when he and Iceni rebelled
against the Syndicate.

"We'll get this done if it needs doing," Drakon said.
"We'll do it smart, and we'll do it right."

The colonels could tell when Drakon had ended a discussion and issued an order. They all saluted in the Syndicate fashion, bringing their right fists across to rap their left
breasts.

As Safir and Kai left, Rogero lingered. "General, I'm
going to be escorting Captain Bradamont to the landing
field. She's taking a shuttle up to the light cruiser *Osprey*,
which will take her to *Midway*."

"Good." Drakon gave Rogero a sympathetic smile. "I'm
sorry you two keep getting separated."

"It's not nearly as bad as it was during the war," Rogero pointed out.

"Why isn't she going to *Pele*? Bradamont was a battle cruiser commander for the Alliance. I remember hearing that battle cruiser types in the Alliance looked down on battleships."

"They do," Rogero said. "Swift and agile versus slow and clumsy, attack versus defense, is how Honore explained it to me. But her assignment is to command the entire force, if necessary. *Pele* might have to make some risky attacks."

"So she has to stay on the battleship, so she can survive and continue to command the fight." Drakon nodded in understanding. "We know how that goes. The hardest thing can be standing back and keeping an eye on the big picture when you want to throw yourself into the fight. She's a good officer, isn't she?"

"The Syndicate never could beat them."

"No." Drakon snorted, gazing at one wall, not really focusing on anything as he remembered too many battles in too many places. "They couldn't beat us, either. What do you suppose would have happened if Black Jack hadn't shown up?"

"Both sides would have kept fighting until everyone like you, me, and Honore Bradamont was dead, and then everything would have fallen apart," Rogero said.

"Yeah." Drakon looked at Rogero. "Tell Captain Bradamont good luck from me, and that I expect her to kick the butts of any enigmas or Syndicate warships that show up here."

Rogero grinned and saluted again. "Yes, sir."

But the smile faded before he reached the door and Rogero turned his head to look at Drakon again. "Sir? What do you think they'll find at Iwa?"

"I think," Drakon said, "that you and I are very lucky we aren't at Iwa. The enigmas have never left any survivors."

"Taroa is rebuilding from the damage suffered during its rebellion and civil war, but with Ulindi leaderless it won't be able to contribute any help to us anytime soon."

"President Iceni and I have a plan for Ulindi," Drakon said. "I'm going over to her offices now to see if we can make it happen."

TWO comfortable chairs faced a blank wall. Iceni took one, Drakon the other. "Are you sure about this?" he asked.

"No." She gave him a look. "You have the right to veto it."

"I know." Drakon sat back, trying to relax himself, and trying to decide if he really wanted to exercise that veto. "I saw what things are like on Ulindi. The snakes did their best to gut that star system of anyone who could run things."

"And he can run things," Iceni said. "Our sources in Syndicate space have confirmed his story to some extent. But uncertainties remain."

"Ulindi needs a strong hand," Drakon said. "Let's get this over with."

Iceni tapped a control and the blank wall vanished, turning into a virtual window that covered the entire wall so that the room seemed to have more than doubled in size. Now visible was the inside of a cell designed for VIP prisoners. Not exactly comfortable, but not a living hell, either. The cell boasted a decent bed as well as a chair, both fastened securely to the floor and the chair facing toward where Drakon and Iceni sat, but not much more except for the vast array of sensors that kept continuous watch on the cell's occupant.

CEO Jason Boyens, alerted by the change in light to the virtual window, sat up on the bed, then stood carefully. He looked a little haggard, which wasn't too surprising given that he had spent some time wondering if at any moment he would be taken out and executed. Boyens walked toward the virtual window, facing Iceni and Drakon. "It's nice to have visitors. I'm glad to see you survived the trap at Ulindi, Artur."

"I wouldn't have been in nearly as much danger," Drakon said, "if you'd spilled your guts about the Syndicate trap at Ulindi before I left."

"But I did tell you. Or rather, I told Gwen here." Boyens gestured toward her. "Apparently, my warning came in time. But I don't think you're here to thank me."

Iceni's smile flicked on and off so rapidly that it was barely visible. "No, Jason. We're here to say good-bye."

Boyens stiffened, swallowed, then nodded. "Why the forewarning? To make me suffer as I wait for the end?"

"You misunderstand, Jason," Iceni continued. "We're letting you go."

That was a bit too much even for someone experienced in the often-lethal cat-and-mouse games of Syndicate CEOs. Boyens swayed slightly, then put one hand on the chair beside him. "If you're playing with me, you're doing a good job. May I sit down?"

"Please."

Boyens took his seat, then looked at Drakon. "You were always the straightforward sort, Artur. What's the deal?"

Drakon smiled, too, deliberately letting Boyens see grim amusement. "Just as Gwen said. What you told us about the Syndicate wanting your hide on the wall appears to be true, and since we've let the Syndicate know through various unofficial means that their trap failed at Ulindi because you warned us about it, we can be pretty confident that you won't try to make nice with the Syndicate again anytime soon."

"How nice of you to give me credit," Boyens said. "If the Syndicate gets its hands on me now they'll turn me over to Happy Hua with instructions to make sure my end is painful and prolonged."

"Happy Hua won't serve the Syndicate anymore," Iceni said. "She died at Ulindi."

The smile on Boyens's face was unquestionably genuine. "What a shame. We all do what we have to do, but she enjoyed it. Too bad the Syndicate still has plenty of other cold-blooded killers to employ. What is it you want from me?"

"We want you to go to Ulindi," Drakon said.

Boyens, as skilled at CEO backstabbing as he was, still looked floored by the statement. "Ulindi? Did you tell them I was responsible for what happened there?"

"No." Drakon took a deep breath, remembering things seen at Ulindi. "How much did you know about the trap there? You told us that you only knew it was intended to draw us in and hit us with hidden military forces. Is that all you knew?"

"That's all I knew. It wasn't a plan I was supposed to have any role in, so I wasn't even supposed to know the plan existed. But enough people were gabbing about it that I could make out the outlines."

Boyens could not see the readouts visible to Iceni and Drakon. He would have known his cell contained numerous sensors which monitored every aspect of his body, something useful for maintaining a picture of a prisoner's health but also extremely helpful in determining if someone was lying. The readouts told Drakon that Boyens hadn't lied just now. That wasn't always helpful, because anyone given secrets was also given techniques for outwitting such sensors by phrasing answers in just the right way or simply refusing to answer at all. But in this case Boyens had answered clearly and unambiguously.

Drakon nodded. "It's lucky for you that you didn't know more. As part of their preparations for the trap, the Syndicate wanted to ensure that no one at Ulindi would cause them any problems. The snakes carried out mass arrests."

"Naturally."

"And they murdered everyone they arrested."

"They—?" Boyens inhaled sharply. "That's insane. They must have gutted Ulindi's upper ranks, and middle ranks, and—" He stared at Drakon. "There's a leadership vacuum at Ulindi, and you want me to go there?"

"That's right." Drakon smiled again. "We're giving you the chance to be the person who starts putting Ulindi back together."

"You're putting me in charge of Ulindi?" Boyens didn't seem able to grasp the idea.

"No," Iceni said with a low laugh. "We're not in charge at Ulindi. We couldn't force a ruler on them, and we don't want to. The last thing they need or *want* is another Syndicate CEO." Her expression shifted to a glare. "Do you understand? Anyone who shows up at Ulindi acting the CEO is going to get torn to pieces by the mob, which is very upset by the atrocities the snakes committed before those snakes got a taste of their own medicine at the hands of General Drakon's forces. But the people at Ulindi desperately need someone who can help form a decent government, help the star system get back on its feet, and help establish the means for Ulindi to stay independent of the Syndicate."

"I don't understand." Boyens looked from Iceni to Drakon and back again, as if seeking some answers in their expressions. "What exactly is your goal? What is it I am expected to do? Because I have no doubt that you'll have safeguards in place to ensure that if I do the wrong thing I won't enjoy it for long."

"Our goal," said Drakon, "is a strong Ulindi. That means no dictator diverting resources in order to keep the people in line. No attempts to continue the wasteful and corrupt Syndicate system under another name. But it also means a government strong enough to get things done, a government not dependent on any one man or woman, and able to handle any crisis that comes along, including attacks from more than one source."

"Oh, I thought you were asking me to do something difficult!" Boyens lowered his head, rubbing his face with one hand, then looked back at them. "You really think I can do that?"

"You're good at what you do, Jason," Iceni said. "You couldn't have survived this long while double-crossing and triple-crossing so many people without being a very smart operator."

"But how does anyone form a strong government without just telling everyone what to do and enforcing it with the sort of things the Syndicate does?"

"We can offer you some pointers." She cocked her head slightly to one side, eyeing Boyens. "What's the matter? Is this beyond your ability?"

Boyens laughed. "I'm good enough to spot that simple kind of manipulation, Gwen. So, you're giving me a chance to remake Ulindi and get that star system back on its feet after the Syndicate cut it off at the knees. And if I start murdering my opponents and firing on the mob you'll have me taken out by some of the agents you doubtless have hidden on Ulindi. Or you'll send in a battleship and tell my loyal subjects to turn me over or else, which I'm sure those subjects would do without hesitating if I haven't engendered some loyalty in them. What do I get out of this?"

"Your life," Drakon said.

"And a chance to build something," Iceni said. "What would it feel like to be the founder of a new state at Ulindi? To be remembered for what you built there? You'll get power, and probably wealth, out of the deal. But you'll also get the right to feel a little self-respect again. Let me tell you from personal experience that is not a bad thing."

Boyens didn't reply for a long moment, his eyes on Iceni. "I always thought you were ruthless and clever, Gwen," he finally said, "but I never realized how tough you were. And, you, Artur, always sticking your neck out. I figured Gwen would have you taken out sooner or later, if the snakes didn't get you first. But I didn't realize how smart you were. And now you two are offering me not just freedom but a chance to do something with it. Oh, I know what's going on. For all of your talk about acting differently than the Syndicate, you two are playing the same old game. You're handing me an impossible task, expecting me to fail, so you can blame me. And if somehow I succeed then you'll take the credit for it. But you're right that I can't run back to the Syndicate. Fine. I know that Midway is going to be the big dog in any relationship with Ulindi. I can work with that. I can work with you. You two can be the senior partners. If this is the deal, I accept."

"Then we will arrange your transport to Ulindi," Iceni said, "along with our assurances to what few authorities Ulindi still has that you have been cleared by security."

"We won't tell Ulindi anything else," Drakon said.

"You need to tell them more. People there will know me," Boyens objected. "You rescued those survivors of the Reserve Flotilla. I was in a senior position in that flotilla for a long time."

"That's right," Drakon agreed. "And you were a CEO, but you weren't an awful CEO. You didn't make a good impression when you were here commanding that other Syndicate flotilla, but images from transmissions you made, images that show that snake CEO Happy Hua at your back ready to plunge in a knife, have been popping up in a lot of places, along with comments that she must have been forcing your hand."

"Still manipulating social media, and every other form of media?" Boyens asked sarcastically. "I guess some of those Syndicate habits die hard."

"Those skills are useful and essential for survival," Iceni said. "It is also being noted that when Happy Hua operated that flotilla alone, she acted much more ruthlessly. There were no bombardments of worlds when you were in command, creating the impression that you acted as a check on Hua's natural cruelty."

Boyens straightened in his seat, looking legitimately affronted. "I did act as a check on her. That's not just an impression. I took some serious risks to hold her back. I'm not a butcher, Gwen. Why do you think the Syndicate turned on me? Because Hua's report painted me as the cause of that flotilla's failure, saying I was *insufficiently zealous* in pursuing Syndicate objectives."

"We know," Drakon said. "If you had a history anything like Hua's, you'd never leave that cell you are in. But Gwen and I know that you're actually telling the truth, that you haven't been a cold-blooded killer, that none of the survivors of the Reserve Flotilla have called for your head on a plate, and even Black Jack saw something worthwhile in you. You can go to Ulindi as the man who prevented Happy Hua from doing the sort of thing she did to Kane *after* you were relieved of command of that flotilla, and as the CEO in the Reserve Flotilla who may not have been a hero of the workers but did treat them like they were human."

Boyens shrugged. "Rewriting history is easy. I always

knew rewriting the memories of those who know you is another matter altogether. All right. We have an agreement. Once you let me out of here, I'll let you know everything else I found out in the Syndicate. There's nothing remotely as big as the trap that was being set at Ulindi, that was my trump card and I gave it to you freely, but perhaps you can use some of the other gossip. Oh, one other thing. I have no ambitions to be a general like you, Artur, but if I manage to attain the power I need at Ulindi can I call myself a president as well, Gwen?"

She smiled again. "If you earn it, Jason."

This time, Boyens smiled back. "Then let's get in the same room, raise some glasses, and toast the resumption of a beautiful friendship."

"Just a few minutes, and you'll be out," Iceni said. "We'll see you soon afterward." She closed the virtual window, leaving the blank wall in its place, then sighed. "I hope we're not screwing this up."

Drakon shook his head. "We know Boyens. He's a smart operator, and he can be a decent guy if properly motivated. He's going to be seeing agents of ours around every corner at Ulindi and be constantly worrying about what we'll do if he starts acting like a snake or a Syndicate CEO. Between that and fears of the Syndicate and the enigmas, he might just be what Ulindi desperately needs."

"And what we need," Iceni agreed. "My agents at Taroa report we have enough elected officials in our pockets there to ensure Taroa goes along with reasonable proposals from us."

"My agents at Taroa tell me the same thing," Drakon said. "If we get Ulindi and Taroa tied to us, Kane and Kahiki will do the same. Ulindi, Taroa, and Kane can all support substantial populations and have decent resources, or will once Kane rebuilds. And Kahiki offers us the sort of research labs it would be beyond our means to re-create here. Give us a few more years and we'll have enough strength in these star systems to hold off even the Syndicate and the enigmas."

"But will we have a few more years?" Iceni asked. "Or even a few more months?"

Drakon didn't answer, because he didn't have any answer to offer.

MANTICORE left jump space at Iwa with every weapon fully ready and her shields at maximum strength. As Marphissa shook off the effects of the transition from jump space she stared at her display with a growing sense of dismay.

A low murmuring came from the others on the bridge as *Manticore*'s sensors reported what they could see.

"Is there anything left?" Kapitan Diaz asked the senior watch specialist.

The specialist shook his head, his voice trembling slightly. "No, Kapitan. The city has been totally destroyed by orbital bombardment. All occupied off-planet sites have been destroyed. So have automated sites. Even small satellites have been blown apart."

"But no sign of enigmas, either?"

"No, Kapitan. The ships that must have destroyed Iwa are no longer present."

Marphissa spoke in a low voice that carried across the hush on the bridge. "The enigma ship detected by *Pele* must have been a final check before their attack force jumped here. There are no distress signals from any surviving humans?"

"No, Kommodor. There is no indication that any humans survived."

The recently promoted CEO that Kontos had encountered here had not ruled Iwa Star System for very long.

"Look at that," Diaz said in a wondering voice. "They even flattened abandoned weapons emplacements. There was nothing in those emplacements, but they destroyed them anyway."

"Black Jack told us the enigmas had wiped every trace of human presence from the star systems they had occupied,"

Marphissa said, feeling numb. She had seen worse in her time. Much worse. The war with the Alliance had created scenes of destruction that dwarfed this one. But few that were as complete in their annihilation, and the people here had been totally helpless. They would have been able to do nothing as the enigma bombardment approached. Nothing but wait until nothing was left.

"What should we do, Kommodor?"

Marphissa took a long, slow breath as she considered her options. "Our orders are to warn Iwa and to establish contact with Granaile Imallye. Midway is already aware of a possible threat from Iwa. Moorea is not. Neither is Palau. We will continue on to Moorea, try to speak with this Imallye, and warn everyone that the enigmas have an alternate attack route into human space. And we will not waste time. Proceed toward the jump point for Moorea at point two light speed, Kapitan."

"Yes, Kommodor." Diaz glanced at his display. "That jump point is four and a quarter light hours distant from us. The transit will take a little more than twenty-one hours."

"Very well."

As *Manticore* came about and accelerated toward the jump point for Moorea, Diaz gazed morosely at his display. "Do you think the enigmas will try to establish a base at Iwa, Kommodor?"

"Maybe. Maybe not. Black Jack reported that Pele has remained completely vacant since the enigmas pushed the Syndicate out of that star system. But Iwa would be a toehold in human-occupied space."

"Why, Kommodor? Why do the enigmas do this? Didn't Black Jack tell us they don't want us to know anything about them? Fine. We'll leave them alone."

"They are afraid that we won't stop trying to find out things about them," Marphissa explained. "They must view the entire universe with fear, and fear creates cruelty and ruthlessness."

"It does in people," Diaz agreed.

Marphissa closed her eyes, wanting to block out the vision of what had been done to Iwa Star System. "We are fortunate they could only reach Iwa. This is a tragedy, but there wasn't much here. If the enigmas could have hit Taroa or Ulindi the loss of life would have been much, much greater."

It was cold comfort, but it was the only comfort that Iwa offered.

And it helped distract her slightly from the even colder fear that the enigmas might have also found a way to get the extra jump range they needed to reach Taroa and Ulindi directly.

HABITS taught during Syndicate rule died hard. The ambassadors from Taroa and Kahiki sat apart from each other, uncomfortable with their bodyguards forced to remain outside. A woman who represented what was left of Kane after the civil war and Syndicate bombardment had taken a chair to one side, her eyes shifting rapidly about the room as if expecting ground attackers or a weapon dropped from orbit to strike at any moment. A young man who had somehow survived the snake purge of suspected traitors on Ulindi looked both determined and frightened.

Iceni noticed that the representatives from Taroa, Kahiki, and Ulindi all kept glancing at Drakon as if regarding him as the one who was in charge. Drakon was the one they knew from his time in their star systems. The woman from Kane gave those kind of glances to Iceni, who had herself visited there. All of the representatives gave the appearance not of ambassadors for their star systems but of junior executives facing Syndicate CEOs who could ruin their lives and their worlds on a whim.

"Not much, is it?" Iceni murmured to Drakon where he sat beside her. "Four star systems, and only Kahiki is intact."

Drakon nodded, keeping his eyes on the star system representatives as he answered in the same low tones. They didn't have to worry about their comments being overheard since the security field would hide both their words and the movements of their lips, but still they spoke discreetly because another lesson of the Syndicate was that you never knew who might be listening despite all of your security measures. "None of them can even defend themselves, let alone contribute to defending anyone else."

"Not today," Iceni agreed. "And not tomorrow. But Kane, Ulindi, and Taroa have the resources and the worlds to support decent defense assets someday, and the labs on Kahiki might produce the advances we'll all need to hold off the Syndicate and the enigmas." She reached out one finger to tap a control and negate the security field, then spoke in a normal voice. "We have a matter of great concern to discuss with you, as well as a proposal that should work to all of our mutual benefit."

The suspicious eyes watching her grew even warier. "Madam President," the ambassador from Taroa said, "we have all had far too much experience with Syndicate offers that were supposedly to our benefit. We know that *you* would not make that sort of offer," she finished, sounding hopeful and almost sincere in her belief.

Drakon replied, sounding appropriately gruff and foreboding. He and Iceni had agreed that he would best serve as the bad cop in this negotiation. "With the exception of Kahiki, Midway has taken substantial risks, and combat losses, to aid your star systems. And we have already committed to defend Kahiki. That's in addition to our mutual defense agreements with Taroa."

The woman from Kane shook her head rapidly. "No one would accuse you or President Iceni of not having aided us," she said. "Is the Syndicate preparing another attack?" The question came out with a pleading tone, as if begging them to tell her the answer was no.

Iceni spoke soothingly. "We have no information about Syndicate attack plans, though as you all know the Syndicate will not stop trying to regain control of all of our star systems. After their defeat at Ulindi, it should take the Syndicate a little while at least to muster major new forces to attack any of us, though smaller attacks are possible at any time. I'm afraid the larger threat that concerns us comes from another direction."

"Imallye?" the Taroan asked. "She was threatening Moorea, but that information was over a month old by the time we heard it here."

"We can handle Imallye if we have to," Iceni said, making her flat statement sound confident despite their lack of knowledge of just how powerful Imallye actually was. "No. This threat is not from a human source."

That information hit the four representatives with the force of a blow. They actually all flinched or jerked back as if Iceni had swung a fist their way.

"There were alien ships in this star system recently," the man from Ulindi said.

"Those were Dancers," Drakon replied. "Perhaps not allies of ours, but certainly not enemies. You've all heard that Dancer ships saved this world from being devastated by an enigma bombardment."

"The enigmas? Is that the threat?" The representative from Ulindi looked at the others as if seeking either confirmation or support. "Is Midway asking us for help to stop another enigma attack? We have none to offer."

"We are all too aware of that," Drakon said.

The man from Ulindi flushed with embarrassment. "As grateful as we are for your assistance in throwing off the Syndicate yoke that bound us, we lack any warships. You know that. You took with you every Syndicate mobile forces unit captured at Ulindi."

Drakon's eyes narrowed.

Iceni considered intervening, but decided to let Artur run free a little longer. She wasn't too pleased with the attitude of the representative from Ulindi.

"You mean the Syndicate units that *we* captured at Ulindi," Drakon said, his voice low and powerful. "While *we* liberated Ulindi from the Syndicate. I lost good men and women in that fight."

"So did our warships," Iceni said, more pleasantly than Drakon, which somehow made the point just as effective.

The young man from Ulindi turned even darker with embarrassment, then shook his head, his hands moving indecisively. "I'm sorry, honored—I mean, we lost people, too. The snakes killed so many. Everyone who they suspected might have planned or led or done anything else against the Syndicate. We lost all of the people who should have been here instead of me, all of the people who would have known how to talk to you. I don't know what the hell I'm doing."

"Neither do I," Iceni replied. "This is uncharted territory for us all. All of you know that if Midway had desired to conquer your star systems, we could have done so."

"You might still be trying," the woman from Taroa suggested with a thin smile.

"True," Iceni agreed. "Or we could have done as the Syndicate does, bombarding you into submission." She pretended not to notice the flare of reflexive fear in the eyes of the woman from Kane. "But we have not, and we will not."

"We will not," Drakon repeated in slow and heavy tones.

"The Syndicate taught us to wonder what anyone's motives were," the Taroan noted. "What are yours? We are grateful for the assistance you provided us. But we're still waiting to learn the price."

"We reached mutual defense agreements with you," Drakon pointed out.

"Until we get the unfinished battle cruiser the Syndicate bequeathed us in operational condition, that agreement is pretty one-sided in its demands on you. Why? Why take on that burden?"

"Because someday that battle cruiser will be operational," Iceni said. "And you'll have other warships. And when that day comes, we don't want you as enemies. We'd much prefer to have you as friends."

"But . . . why?" the young man from Ulindi asked in a pleading voice. "What do you get out of this?"

"We get the Syndicate off our doorstep," Drakon replied. "Instead of being a launching point for attacks on us, you are hopefully going to be allies against the Syndicate."

"Allies?" The man from Kahiki spoke for the first time. "As in Alliance?"

"No," Drakon said. He knew that after the century-long war the term "Alliance" was poison anywhere in Syndicate space.

"You have an Alliance officer among your staff. It's widely known."

"I haven't tried to hide it," Drakon said. "Captain Bradamont was assigned here by Black Jack. Personally assigned to Midway by Black Jack, with orders to assist us in defending against the Syndicate and the enigmas. But she has no role in policy and does not interfere with the way we run this star system."

"Does she follow your orders?" the man pressed.

"If they are consistent with her orders from Black Jack," Iceni said. "She's very open about that. You know Alliance officers. It wouldn't be *honorable* to lie to us."

That jab at the reputation of Alliance officers even got a smile from the woman from Kane. The woman from Taroa actually laughed.

"So what does Black Jack get out of it?" The man from Kahiki wasn't going to be sidetracked.

"He gets a hypernet gate on the far side of what used to be Syndicate space," Iceni said. "He gets a stable government here, and we have been stable. I'm certain that your own spies have informed you that the general and I have the support of the people. That matters to Black Jack, too. And, of course, he wants us able to defend human space against incursions by the enigmas. Which brings us back to what General Drakon and I want to warn you of."

She waved a hand over a control, bringing up a star display that floated just to one side of her. "Here are our local star systems, including Midway, Kahiki, Taroa, Kane, Ulindi, and Iwa. Over here you see those star systems occupied by the enigmas over the last century as the Syndicate was pushed back toward Midway."

Iceni pointed. "And here is Pele. One of the reasons the enigmas were held back for a while is that the only human star system they could reach from their own space using jump drives was Midway."

"Was?" The Taroan repeated the word with sudden tension in her voice.

"We have reliable indications that an enigma warship was detected jumping into Iwa recently." Iceni swung her finger across the starscape to indicate that star. "And we have a warning from the Dancers, a warning whose meaning we could not understand until a short time ago. *Watch the different stars,* they told us. Captain Bradamont has informed us of techniques Black Jack knew to get slightly better range out of Alliance jump drives. It appears the enigmas have now done even Black Jack one better."

"If they can reach Iwa . . ." The woman from Taroa put one hand to her forehead, looking shaken.

"They may soon be able to directly reach Taroa," Iceni finished. "And Ulindi."

The man from Kahiki didn't look happy. "Syndicate reports had little information about what happened in star systems taken by the enigmas. You have passed us reports from Black Jack that his fleet found all traces of human presence had been eliminated in those star systems. Do you believe those reports?"

"We have no reason to doubt them," Drakon said. "Captain Bradamont herself witnessed what was in those star systems, and the information is consistent with what little the Syndicate was ever able to learn."

"What about the humans who were prisoners of the enigmas? Can't they tell us anything?"

The woman from Taroa, still rattled, shook her head. "Some of those people were citizens of Taroa. I've talked to them. They were kept inside a hollowed-out asteroid. They never saw an enigma, never talked to one, never saw *anything.* They didn't even know who or what had taken them prisoner."

"But if this is true," the young man from Ulindi said, "then we need you more than ever. Ulindi can't defend itself. Only Midway, or the Syndicate, has forces capable of stopping the enigmas, and after the massacre carried out by the snakes no one on Ulindi would accept the Syndicate even if it was our only hope. What can we give you?"

"That varies by star system," Iceni said. Having seen how her news had frightened the others, she was now doing her best to sound calm and confident, the leader who could protect them. "Kane has valuable resources but must devote what people and industry are left to rebuilding. Kahiki can give us the hope for new weapons and other technology to employ against the enigmas. From Taroa and Ulindi, what Midway needs most is three things. We hope that Kane and Kahiki will also commit to these things in principle."

They tensed again. This was the part of the conversation where Syndicate CEOs would be laying out an offer-that-you-had-better-not-refuse, one that would profit the CEOs and injure the victims.

"Firstly," Iceni said, "agreements to work together, to share what information we have, to allow mobile forces to transit each other's star systems, and to establish a unified command when any of the other star systems acquire operational warships."

"Unified under Midway?" the woman from Taroa asked.

"Yes," Iceni said. "We are the senior partner in the defense of this region of space, and we have officers in command of our warships who have proven their skill and their dedication." No one said anything else, so she continued. "Secondly, to commit to devoting some of your resources to the common defense. We don't know how many more former Syndicate warships we can acquire. I assure you that we have agents spreading the word through Syndicate-controlled space that Midway offers freedom to any crew who brings their warships to us." She paused. "Assuming some more warships show up, we will proportionally share them with other star systems. We *need* you to have the means for your own defense."

"You'd be acting out of self-interest, then," the young man from Ulindi said. That they could all understand. "But we can't help you unless we have the means."

"Exactly. Which brings up the third item." Iceni could see the others brace themselves for the bad news they expected. "Money. Midway is fortunate to have the income from the hypernet gate, but we are not wealthy. The larger our forces grow, the harder it is to pay for them. We would like commitments from you to not only pay for your own defense but to contribute a reasonable sum to our own forces."

"How much is reasonable?" the Taroan asked.

"What can be spared," Iceni said. "And not all of that. You need to have enough to rebuild your economies and to expand. We don't want weak client star systems. We want you all to become strong enough to be partners. Economic partners as well as partners in defense."

Their skepticism was easy to see. Drakon answered the unspoken question. "We've all experienced Syndicate practices, where they milk the cow until it's dead, feast on the carcass, then go looking for another cow. You, and me, all of us, have been in the position of that cow. Now that President Iceni and I have the ability to do things the way we want to do them, we're trying to avoid repeating the mistakes of the Syndicate."

"You want us to be fat cows," the Taroan said.

"That's right," Iceni said. "We're trying to think long-term, despite the very short-term worries about whether any of us will survive for the long term."

"On behalf of the provisional government of Kane," that woman vowed, "I commit us to this. Midway helped us when we had been nearly crushed by Syndicate bombardment. They helped us and asked for nothing in return." She looked a challenge at the representatives of Taroa, Ulindi, and Kahiki. "Because of the damage we have sustained, we will be the least in this . . . this association of star systems. But we will rebuild, and we will be strong, and we will stand with Midway."

"Association?" the young man from Ulindi asked. "Is that what it would be called?"

"No." Iceni smiled, tapping another control. An image appeared next to her, showing a raptorlike bird with spread wings rising from the atomic fires of a star. "We thought we would call it the Phoenix Stars. Strong. Indestructible. Rising from the ashes of what was before."

The Syndicate had never been that big on symbolism. It got in the way of efficiency, it cost extra money, and anyway workers lacked the imagination to understand symbols, or so the bureaucracy thought. They produced crests and insignias for ships and ground forces, but only because that helped identify them. The actual images used, and any accompanying mottos, were always what a long chain of bureaucrats thought looked good. Everyone mocked the resulting symbols except for those who had generated them.

It had never been a smart way of doing business, but it was far from the stupidest thing done in the name of uniformity, conformity, efficiency, and of course in hopes of saving a little money. "Small cuts can make for big costs," one of Iceni's mentors had once explained, and she had never forgotten that. She had also never forgotten how effective well-chosen symbols could be.

No one said anything, but the eager smiles on the faces of the star system representatives told Iceni what she needed to know. This symbol could rally star systems to a single cause.

"Send our offer to your star systems," Iceni directed. "I'll provide you with the proposed text for the agreement of association. Get formal answers from them and be sure they know of the threat from the enigmas. In light of the urgency of the information about the enigmas, we do not want you to have to wait for transport to your own star systems. We will provide each of you with a Hunter-Killer from our mobile forces for transport for yourself or whoever else you want to convey the message." The temporary loss of the use of four HuKs was not a small price, but once again the symbolism was worth the cost.

She looked at the representative from Ulindi. "There will be an extra passenger going to your star system."

"An extra passenger?"

"Another survivor from the old Reserve Flotilla. He wants to emigrate to Ulindi. Perhaps he will be able to render some assistance to you in organizing things there."

"A freighter arrived from Ulindi today," Colonel Malin reported. "We had an agent aboard it who reported that no detections of enigma ships had been seen at Ulindi before the freighter jumped for Midway."

Iceni nodded shortly, glaring at her desk. "But nothing from Taroa yet?"

"No, Madam President."

"If the enigmas hit us again, we may be wishing the Syndicate was back. I'm getting every standard report on events in this region of space. I want you to ensure that I see any important information that doesn't make its way into those reports because someone decided it wasn't worth reporting."

"Yes, Madam President. I did discover some more information about Granaile Imallye which was buried in captured Syndicate files. She is operating under her real name, but once was more widely known by a false one."

"A pirate using an alias?" Iceni remarked sarcastically. "What an amazing development."

"She once called herself O'Malley. As best I can determine, she originally came from Conall Star System and that was the name she used there."

Iceni realized she had stopped breathing, and slowly inhaled. "A woman who went by the name O'Malley? From Conall? How certain are you of that?"

Malin was watching her closely. "Not absolutely certain, but at least eighty percent certain. Do you know of her?"

"Possibly," Iceni said, trying to sound dismissive of the news. "I once knew a woman who used that name, after an ancient pirate she admired." Could it be her? There were surely many, many real O'Malleys in that star system. But if it was her . . .

Iceni needed something to distract Malin from this topic, and fortunately she had just the thing right at hand. "You were out for a while last night, Colonel."

"Yes, Madam President." If Malin had noted her change of the subject, or was surprised that Iceni had been able to discover he had been unaccounted for during the evening, he didn't show any traces of either.

"Did you find anything about Togo?"

"No, Madam President. There has been no trace of Togo. The security forces have found nothing, and system defense experts have not identified any attempted intrusions that could be sourced to him."

"Togo is more than capable of making his intrusion attempts look like someone else's work," Iceni told Malin. "Look at all of the intrusion attempts being detected and see if any pattern exists that could identify a target for Togo's actions."

"That effort is already under way," Malin said. "There has been a slight uptick in attempts against your security systems and those of General Drakon, but the increase is within normal variation levels. No successful intrusions have been detected."

"If Togo manages an intrusion, you *won't* detect it," Iceni said. "I need to know what he is trying to do. Have you discovered anything else?"

This time, Malin paused. "I found indications that may lead me closer to a target General Drakon assigned me."

"Which target?"

"His daughter."

Iceni fought down an angry response before speaking again. She hated being reminded of the girl, and hated that she felt that way. "I was told that Colonel Morgan had placed safeguards around wherever the baby is, and if anyone gets too close the child will die."

"As near as I can determine, what Morgan said is true," Malin said.

"And what were General Drakon's orders in that regard?" Iceni pressed.

"He told me he did not want his daughter to die."

Iceni leaned back in her chair, eyeing Malin. "Suppose I told you to press on in ways that would trigger those safeguards and ensure the child's death. Would you do it?"

Malin did not reveal any emotion as he shook his head. "No, Madam President. I could not obey such an order."

"Why not?"

"Because I believe that it would be a mistake to betray General Drakon's wishes in the matter. He would regard it as a very serious breach of trust. It might sabotage his cooperation with you in the governing of, and defense of, Midway."

"And?" Iceni asked.

"There is no other reason, Madam President."

"No other reason? The girl is your half sister. You refused to kill Morgan for me, without revealing to me that the reason was because she was your mother. Yet now you feel no obligation toward a sister?"

Malin started to speak, paused, then tried again. "We all die, Madam President. Our sacrifices can build important things, great legacies, if we do not hesitate to do what we must."

He sounded sincere. Iceni nodded slowly, then waved a dismissal at Malin. She didn't want to risk anything in her voice giving away how much his reply had disturbed her.

Too many of the people working for her and Drakon were still caught in the Syndicate belief that the ends always justified the means. Worse, they were making their own decisions about means and ends.

Means don't always produce the ends we want. Like "O'Malley" from Conall. Damn. It must be her. And I sent Kommodor Marphissa and Manticore out there to deal with her. The last I had heard, that girl had taken after her father. Of all the pirates out there, why did she have to sail into my region of space? That mess with her father wasn't my worst mistake, but bad enough.

My worst mistake might be pursuing his own goals in this city right now.

Iceni wondered what ends Togo was working toward, and what means he was willing to use.

CHAPTER FOUR

CELIA Gozen had fallen into bed, worn-out from work, only taking time to ensure a ready weapon was close at hand before she fell to sleep. Promotions in the Syndicate sometimes happened because "accidents" befell superior officers, and sometimes workers who spotted an opening went after a supervisor on general principles. Growing up Syndicate meant realizing that you didn't have to be guilty of anything to become a target.

She didn't know whether a noise or simply battle-honed instinct awakened her hours later. Buildings, even a building in the headquarters complex where people worked at all hours of every day, grew hushed at night. Gozen lay in the dark, straining her senses for a clue to what had woken her up. She didn't know why, but she was certain that someone else was in this room. Her pistol was only a few centimeters from her right hand, but she knew the difference between reality and fiction was that in reality someone who had the drop on you wouldn't just stand and watch while you grabbed for a weapon.

And whoever that someone was, they must be very good at what they were doing. In addition to the standard security measures in the building and the door to her room, Gozen had rigged the sort of small, portable alarms that Syndicate executives carried around routinely. But none of them had sounded, so the intruder must have neutralized them all soundlessly.

But whoever it was hadn't yet killed her, so this couldn't be a simple assassination attempt. Gozen spoke into the darkness, her voice very low. "What do you want?"

After a couple of seconds the reply came, in a voice also low, so it was hard to distinguish much about it except for the words. "Someone who is wise. Are you wise?"

"No," Gozen said, unable to avoid the frank reply as she tried to estimate just where in her room the intruder was located. If she rolled to her left as her right hand grabbed her pistol . . .

"You are too modest. I know your record. If you move, I will kill you."

Gozen took a slow breath. "What do you want?" she repeated.

"Drakon is dangerous. He cannot be trusted."

The pause seemed to expect a reply, so Gozen chose a careful response. "Why not?"

"He is Syndicate. A deep plant."

"Must be awful deep. He's killed a lot of snakes."

"The Syndicate does not worry about sacrificing pawns in order to reach the queen."

The queen? "You mean President Iceni?" Gozen asked. The voice was definitely coming from near the door. Whoever it was hadn't gotten very far inside. And it was a man, she thought.

"Yes. I could have killed you before you woke. But I know you hate the Syndicate. They killed your uncle."

The only people she hated more than those who had killed her uncle were those who tried to use her uncle's death to their own ends. Gozen didn't bother trying to hide the quaver of anger in her voice, knowing that the intruder would interpret that as rage at the Syndicate. "And the Syndicate wants the president dead?"

"Yes. They'll use Drakon. All you need to do is watch, and when the time comes, do nothing."

"Nothing?"

"Nothing. Doing something would be . . . a mistake."

"How big a mistake?" Gozen asked, then wanted to slap herself for the flippant reply. She waited for the intruder to say something else, but the silence stretched unbroken.

Gozen brought up her right hand, moving with slow deliberation, then swung it over until it grasped her pistol. She eased her arm around until the pistol was pointed in the direction she had heard the voice coming from, then with her left hand flicked the lights on.

The room was empty.

The door was still locked.

When Gozen got up and checked, her alarms were untouched.

Oh, great.

That guy said he knew my record, then he gave me an order. Is he stupid? I guess I'm supposed to be too afraid to do "something." Screw that.

It's only a few minutes until reveille. Why did my visitor leave so little time before almost everyone in this complex would be waking up?

BY the time she threw on a uniform, ensured her sidearm was holstered and ready to fire, and walked briskly to the command center, the wake-up call had sounded and the passageways were beginning to fill with bleary-eyed soldiers.

Drakon was just entering the command center when she got there.

"General, I néed to talk to you alone," Gozen said, trying not to look nervous. In her experience, senior officers didn't tend to trust juniors who appeared to be jumpy.

Drakon paused on his way inside, giving Gozen a searching look. "How alone?"

"Very, very alone."

"What's the priority on this?"

"Very high." She waited for more questions asking why he should alter his plans for some unstated reason.

But Drakon eyed her silently for a couple of seconds, then nodded. "Come on." To her surprise, he didn't lead on into the command center and his office right off of it. Instead, Drakon led the way through the complex until he reached a small break area with a few tables and a couple of vending machines to one side. A couple of soldiers slumped over coffee cups jolted to attention as he entered. "Keep an eye outside for a few minutes," Drakon told them, waiting until they left before he took a seat and gestured Gozen to one next to him.

"One thing I confirmed when we took snake headquarters on this world," he commented to Gozen, "was that the break areas were all bugged."

"Sure they were," Gozen said as she sat down. "Everybody figured they were."

"But from the snake headquarters I was able to burn out the bugs in some of those break areas." Drakon smiled, sitting back in the uncomfortable chair. The Syndicate bureaucracy, in one of its few truly inspired moves, had deliberately designed break room chairs to be uncomfortable so as to discourage anyone's lingering in break rooms when they should be working for the Syndicate. "This is a place everyone assumes is bugged, so nobody talks about secret stuff here."

"And nobody else will plant a bug here because everyone knows nobody will talk about anything important in this room?" Gozen asked, grinning. "Sir, that is genius."

"It's just thinking sideways. I wanted a place no one would think to bug. Now, you and I know that. Nobody else. Don't share the info."

Gozen's smile shifted to an uncertain frown. "Not even Colonel Malin?"

"Not even Colonel Malin," Drakon confirmed. "From what I saw of you at Ulindi, you don't cry wolf. What's going on? Is Colonel Malin what you want to talk about?"

"No, sir." Gozen took a deep breath, then quickly sketched out the events of the previous night. "There has to be a hidden access to my room, sir."

"Which is supposed to be impossible in this complex," Drakon said, "now that we've sealed off everything we learned about from captured snake files."

"Maybe the CEO who commanded the ground forces here before you had it done," Gozen suggested.

"There's no way of telling now since she was given the opportunity to either die heroically for the Syndicate or watch her family be sent off to labor camps," Drakon said. "She took the hero option. I can get a survey team into your quarters and they'll find that access, but it'll probably lead to somewhere that doesn't give us any clues."

"It'll still make me feel a whole lot better if it's sealed," Gozen offered.

"I'm sure it will." Drakon gave her another appraising look. "It sounds like you handled that situation right. Any guesses as to who the intruder was?"

"No, sir," Gozen said, shaking her head. "I figure it was a male, but I can't even be certain of that."

Drakon frowned at the table's surface, thinking. "I can guess why you didn't do as you were told," he finally commented dryly, looking back up at her. "Why didn't you believe your visitor about me being some deep plant?"

Gozen shrugged. "Snakes are crazy, sir, and I don't underestimate them. But your being a deep plant makes no sense. One word from you, and the snakes on Midway would have nailed the president before she made her first move. You've easily had dozens of chances since then to cause Midway to fall back under Syndic control, but you haven't. You could have let your soldiers get wiped out at Ulindi just by not making a few decisions and come out looking like a hero who miraculously survived the destruction of Midway. But you didn't. How long a game are the snakes supposed to be playing? Are they waiting until you reach Prime and are ready to nail the head CEOs?"

"Good reasoning," Drakon said. "Why do you suppose the intruder tried to get you to believe that was true?"

"Because he, if it was a he, believed it was true." Gozen shook her head at Drakon. "He . . . she, it . . . thinks you're a Syndicate agent, sir. And it sounded to me like they were waiting for a chance to nail you."

"But not President Iceni?"

"No, sir. You're a threat to the president, so you have to be taken out. That's what my visitor said."

Drakon thought again, tapping one finger on the surface of the table. "Have you heard what happened on this world while we were fighting on Ulindi?" he asked. "Someone, maybe a lot of someones, tried to assassinate Colonel Rogero and stir up mobs that would have torn apart a lot of property and shattered the government that the president is establishing."

"I heard about it," Gozen said. "Scared the hell out of a lot of people on this planet."

"It did. But it backfired. President Iceni faced the mob, faced them down without any guards or support, and she won them over. They love her. She's their champion." Drakon glanced at Gozen. "But some of the people who love the president may still figure I'm a danger to her. That love for President Iceni might be what is motivating whoever this intruder was."

"Maybe, General." Gozen felt a thought lurking just around the corner of her brain and tried to coax it out of hiding.

"You handled this right. Don't tell anyone else any details. I'll have a survey team in your quarters within the hour. Anything else?"

Gozen almost said no, then the thought finally leaned out into view. "Sir? You said the plan backfired?"

Drakon had been about to rise, but paused and sat firmly again. "Yes. Why?"

"I've talked to Colonel Rogero, sir, and I have no doubt someone tried to kill him and cut off the head of the ground forces on this planet. But . . ." Gozen paused to make sure she said her next words just right. "We don't know what the plan was for President Iceni. Nobody tried to kill her, even though she exposed herself to danger."

"What else would the plan have been?" Drakon asked, not in a dismissive way but actually trying to draw out her thoughts.

Gozen felt a wave of elation at that. She hadn't guessed wrongly about the type of leader that Drakon was. "If someone believed that the president was a great leader, then they might have thought she would prevail, that she would find a way to get the people under control, and with the ground forces looking to her for leadership, too, she would be totally secure. Just like she is now in terms of how the people think of her, but without you to worry about."

Drakon rubbed his chin. "That's possible. We assumed the plan was to unseat Iceni, to create chaos on this world. But it could have been aimed at forcing her to make the moves she did, which greatly strengthened her position. And you're right that no attempt was made on her life."

"Like tempering metal," Gozen said. "Somebody believed in President Iceni a whole lot, and doesn't believe in you. And from the sound of things, the next plan involves killing you. Why haven't they tried already?"

"They have." Drakon smiled briefly and without humor. "I have very effective bodyguards and assistants."

"Had, sir, in one case. I'm not bad at doing my job, but everybody tells me that Colonel Morgan was in a class by herself."

"She was unique," Drakon agreed heavily. "And you're right about her being a very effective bodyguard. I'll miss . . . that. Thank you, Colonel Gozen. Keep your eyes open and your weapon armed." He got up. "As long as you're here, do you want any snacks?"

"No, sir," Gozen said, standing as well. "I only ever tasted one thing that was worse than a Syndicate food bar."

"You found something worse than a Syndicate food bar?"

"Yes, sir. We captured some Alliance rations. Most of it

was pretty good, but they had these bars. Danaka Yoruk. The name is engraved on my guts." She shuddered at the memory. "They must feed those rations to Alliance workers to punish them."

Drakon grinned. "What did you do with them?"

"Some snakes stopped by and demanded the best of the captured rations, so we gave them all the Yoruk bars." Gozen shrugged. "Either the Alliance killed those snakes later on, or the snakes ate the Yoruk bars and died from that, because we never saw them again."

Drakon's laugh was cut short by the blare of the Priority One Alarm.

"Headquarters complex has been penetrated by a hostile force!" a voice boomed on the general announcing system loudly enough to be heard over the wail of the alarm. "Composition unknown! Headquarters complex has be—"

The voice cut off, but neither Drakon nor Gozen were listening to it any longer. They had both bolted from the break room into the corridor, where the two soldiers that Drakon had told to stand watch were crouching, staring in opposite directions along the hallway. "Where's your armory?" Drakon demanded.

"Down there, sir," one soldier said, pointing to the left.

"Let's get to it." Drakon and Gozen both had their sidearms out, and as the small group hastened down the corridor they watched ahead and behind.

The alarm cut off.

"All clear," a voice announced. "False alarm."

"They've gotten into the base operating system," Drakon told Gozen, his weapon up and sweeping the corridor before them. "If that was an all clear sent by my people they would have also reported that Colonel Oskar was in the command center."

"There's no Colonel Oskar in this unit," Gozen said, keeping her weapon and her eyes on the hallway behind them.

"Exactly. That's our verify code." They rounded a corner and found a hallway where a half-dozen soldiers in battle armor were already in position around the door to the local armory. Weapons swung their way as the soldiers spotted their movement.

"Hey," one of the soldiers with Drakon yelled, holding his hands high and open to show they were empty. "It's me, Taney. We got the general with us."

"Get inside our perimeter!" one of the soldiers ordered. A gap opened in their ranks, and Drakon, Gozen, and the two soldiers ran through it and into the armory.

Inside, a score of other soldiers were hastily donning battle armor and unracking weapons. One of them paused to salute Drakon. "Lieutenant Develier. What's going on, General?"

"What reports do you have?" Drakon demanded, eyeing the available suits of armor. "What's going on?"

"Our armor is reporting multiple hostile software intrusion attempts," the lieutenant replied. "Communications are being jammed. We have line of sight only. No remote data is being relayed."

"Somebody must have gotten access to the primary combat systems and infected them," Gozen said as she shrugged her way into a suit of battle armor. Fortunately, the soldiers already here hadn't taken one that was a decent fit on her. "Got to be special forces."

"Or vipers," Drakon said, naming the elite and vicious fighting component of the Syndicate Internal Security Service. "They must be using stealth gear with some new twists that got past our sensors."

Gozen sealed her armor and watched her heads-up-display come to life on her armor's face shield. There should have been a tactical picture showing what was going on everywhere inside the headquarters complex, but instead the information shown only covered what could be seen by the soldiers in the hallway outside the armory. Bright red warning signs pulsed to signify jamming and software intrusion attempts. "Do we hold here or go looking for trouble, General?"

"What do you think their target is?" Drakon asked in reply, hefting the rifle he had just activated.

"There's only one thing here that can't be replaced, sir," Gozen said. "One person, rather."

"You're probably right." Drakon didn't sound upset by that, merely acknowledging that he agreed. "Which means my best course of action might be to fort up here. Except for the fact that the attackers gained access to our command software to jam it, which means they could have also spotted that I was in the break room when the attack began."

"So they know you're probably here."

"Yes." Drakon paused as he thought. "Our biggest problem is that we don't know where the enemy is and can't spot them if they're in stealth gear that can hide from our armor's sensors."

"Yes, sir," Gozen said. "And if we go running around in this building with the links out, someone on our side might take a shot at us, not knowing we're friendlies."

"So we dig in here. But not all of us." Drakon gestured to Lieutenant Develier. "Send out a few soldiers to try to reach the command center and notify them where we are. We've got twenty-three soldiers here. Send out five of them."

"Yes, sir. I'll send out my best!"

"Not all of them your best." Drakon continued while Gozen puzzled over why he would say that. "Who's the biggest goof-off in your unit?" he asked the lieutenant. "That's here now?"

"Uh . . . that would be Private Pogue, General."

"Make one of the five Private Pogue. Someone who makes a career out of avoiding work is most likely to know how to get around this headquarters without being noticed. Colonel Gozen, get out in the corridor and command the forces there. I'll hold just inside the doorway and try to exercise overall command of the defense forces."

She caught the self-mockery in Drakon's voice and grinned. He was doing the right thing, though. If the attackers would be coming after him, he shouldn't be presenting himself as a target in a hallway without shields or barricades.

Gozen stepped out into the hallway and pointed both ways down the corridor outside the armory. "You heard the general, Lieutenant Develier. We're very likely dealing with the latest stealth tech, which might be too good for our armor's sensors to spot. Get some smoke down so you can see them coming and renew it as needed. I want that smoke kept dense enough to reveal movement."

"Yes, Colonel."

Two soldiers knelt facing in opposite directions and fired smoke charges down the hall. The charges burst five meters down the hall on either side, filling the air with a dense cloud that contained enough particulates of different kinds to not only block vision but also every other wavelength from radar down to infrared. The irony was that something designed to hide those behind it was also the most foolproof means of spotting anyone in stealth armor that rendered the wearer effectively invisible. Nothing could move through the smoke without creating an outline that would reveal its presence.

The five-soldier contact team moved off to the left, Private Pogue in the lead, vanishing into the cloud in that direction.

With six soldiers in the armory watching the interior walls, and Drakon in the doorway, Gozen and the lieutenant distributed the remaining nine soldiers facing both ways down the corridor, then took positions themselves facing in opposite directions. Gozen settled herself comfortably, knowing that distractions caused by an uncomfortable posture might divert her attention at the wrong time.

"Listen up," Drakon said to the defenders. "Anyone who comes through that smoke in regular armor is probably one of ours. Anyone in a stealth suit is probably the enemy. You are weapons free for anyone in stealth armor. If your target is wearing regular battle armor they may be friendly, so wait for either I, Colonel Gozen, or Lieutenant Develier to give a firing order. Does everyone understand?"

"Yes, sir," Gozen replied, waiting as the rest of the soldiers present also answered. She wondered why Drakon had given his order that way instead of simply telling the soldiers to fire on stealth armor and wait for authorization to fire on regular armor. After a long moment of puzzlement, Gozen realized that the general had actually explained *why* the soldiers should treat the two kinds of targets differently. Instead of being given apparently arbitrary commands, Drakon's soldiers now knew the rationale behind them.

It wasn't the Syndicate just-do-as-you're-told way. And it meant these soldiers were far more likely to be effective and carry out their orders properly.

No wonder these guys kicked our butts on Ulindi. Gozen sighted down her rifle at the smoke filling the hallway before her, confident that her choice to join Drakon's forces had been a wise one.

"I'm picking up noise," a soldier to one side of Gozen reported. "It sounded like energy rounds impacting."

"My armor didn't pick up anything," Lieutenant Develier said.

"Check my armor systems, Lieutenant. There's the record. See?"

"Undetermined," Develier muttered. "It could have been impacts. Echoes of impacts."

"Then they're coming from the way I'm facing," Gozen said. "Give us another smoke round down there," she ordered the soldier next to her. "Everybody stay sharp. Lieutenant, keep your people watching the other way even if we start shooting. It might be a diversion, or they could be coming from both directions."

Gozen found watching the smoke through her face shield's gun sight to be a bit disorienting, but she kept her eyes locked on the slow swirls, watching for any sign of a shape.

Shapes appeared, moving very fast, bursting through the smoke so quickly they would have vanished again in moments.

Would have, if Gozen and the others facing that way hadn't opened up the instant the shapes appeared. Solid slugs and energy bolts slammed into the attackers, each one causing a gap in the stealth protection even if they didn't penetrate.

Gozen was firing as fast as she could aim when an object raced overhead from behind. The grenade exploded among the frontmost attackers, knocking two off their feet and slowing those behind them.

She rose to a crouch, ignoring the shots coming at her from the attackers, and put a careful round straight into the face shield of an enemy barely a meter away. The soldiers with her dropped three more who were still charging.

One attacker made it past them, spinning to face the door to the armory then jerking backward under the impact of a shot from Drakon at point-blank range. The attacker hit the wall behind, then before he or she could leap forward again a dozen more hits from the other soldiers riddled the attacker's armor.

"Get your eyes back on sentry!" Gozen yelled, seeing that nearly every soldier was now facing inward toward where the last attacker had fallen. "Comply!"

Under the lash of that command the soldiers hastily took up positions facing outward again.

Gozen checked her display for signs of damage to her own armor and to the other soldiers. "Lieutenant, have one of the soldiers on your side get Private Honda inside the armory and try to patch him up. Medina, how bad are you?"

"I'll live," Medina said. "It hurts and my sensors are degraded, but I'm still combat effective, Colonel."

A warning note sounded inside Gozen's armor, accompanied by a blinking red danger symbol. She was still lining up her rifle when two shots were fired from soldiers near her.

The not-quite-dead-yet enemy who had suddenly swung a weapon toward them jerked under the hits, then lay still.

"Make sure they're all dead," Gozen snapped.

More shots, each one aimed at the helmet of a fallen foe. Then silence again.

"They're vipers all right," Drakon said.

Gozen didn't have to turn to see that he was kneeling to

examine the attacker who had gotten closest to him. Her display showed Drakon's position behind her. "Sir, are you sure that one is safe?"

"Yeah. I used a minipulse to fry her armor's systems. Her systems are all as dead as she is."

"Vipers usually operate in units of twelve," Gozen said. "We only killed six."

"That's a good start," Lieutenant Develier commented, his voice a little ragged. Common soldiers might hate the agents of the Internal Security Service who were nicknamed snakes, but even that hate paled next to their revulsion toward the elite vipers who were often used to execute battlefield discipline on soldiers who were thought to have committed crimes, or who were judged to have been insufficiently aggressive, or who had just been picked at random to be killed as lessons to the other soldiers.

"We don't know which direction the next six will come from," Gozen warned. "Everybody stay sharp. Drop some more smoke in both directions."

They waited again. Gozen, her armor automatically tied in to the command net when she suited up, could see that Drakon was trying to work around the jamming still blocking their longer-range communications and the tactical picture outside their line of sight.

Her display abruptly came to full life and incoming calls began clamoring for her attention. Gozen was trying to grasp all of the new information when she heard Drakon bellow a command.

"Focus on what's in front of you!"

Cursing, she raised her weapon again just as more shapes appeared exiting from the smoke. Gozen and the others on her side pumped out shots, this time joined by two grenades that broke the enemy charge.

As the last attacker fell, Gozen felt a twinge of something wrong. "How many?" she demanded. "Get me a count!"

"Four . . . no five. Five, Colonel."

"We got one viper unaccounted for!" She switched circuits to broadcast that to everyone in the building now that her links were active again. "Eleven vipers dead at my position. Likely one remaining enemy still active!"

Lieutenant Develier spoke again, his voice worried. "I can't spot the five soldiers we sent to link up with the command center."

"Dead zone!" someone called. "We got a dead zone on our sensor displays! It looks active, but it's a dummy picture!"

"It's inside the command center!"

"Get into it!"

"Move!"

As multiple units began to converge on the command center, another order rang out. "All units hold. The command center is secured."

Gozen let out a long breath as she heard Colonel Malin's voice. The guy was scary, but that was good in a situation like this.

"What have you got?" Drakon asked Malin.

"One dead snake, General," Malin answered, his voice cold and precise. "Several dead soldiers and watch-standers. And one portable nuclear device that the snake was prepared to activate. The nuke has been rendered safe."

"Suicide mission," Develier muttered.

"Good work, everyone," Drakon said. "Now, all units, remain on alert. We're going to flood the headquarters complex with smoke and sweep every room and every corridor to make sure there aren't any other attackers hiding in here. Colonel Malin, coordinate the sweeps from the command center. Colonel Gozen and I are moving to join you."

Leaving six soldiers to guard the wounded and watch over the dead vipers, and accompanied by the rest of the soldiers, Gozen and Drakon headed for the command center along hallways that were rapidly filling with smoke. "Cleaning up after this is going to be a chore," Gozen commented.

"It won't be much compared to the cleanup if that nuke had detonated," Drakon replied.

They started meeting other soldiers, most in armor and gathered into larger and smaller groups based on whoever had been closest when the attack started. With the links active again, everyone could track everyone else easily, eliminating surprises that might have led to friendly soldiers firing on other friendlies. Gozen, still not too familiar with the layout of the headquarters, was relieved when they reached the command center.

Standing just outside were Private Pogue and the other four soldiers who had gone with him. "Sir," the corporal in charge of the small group reported, "we got here just as the jamming cleared."

"It takes a while longer to get somewhere if you don't want to be noticed," Private Pogue argued defensively.

"Fall in with us," Lieutenant Develier ordered. "Do you want us to stay with you, General?"

"No," Drakon said. "Report in as available for joining in the security sweep of the building. I won't forget any one of you," he said to the group. "You did well. Damned well. You've got some fine soldiers, Lieutenant, and that reflects well on you."

"Thank you, sir!"

Gozen felt herself relaxing as she followed Drakon into the command center. There were several bodies still on the floor, the watch-standers who had apparently been killed without warning, and a dozen living soldiers present who were checking over the equipment to ensure no other sabotage had been committed by the vipers.

Colonel Malin stood next to what Gozen recognized as a portable nuke. His eyes swept across General Drakon, centered on Gozen, then his pistol came up, aiming straight at Gozen's face shield.

CHAPTER FIVE

GOZEN was smart enough to freeze rather than try dodging to one side or bringing up her own weapon. She knew enough about Malin to know that he could put a shot into the most vulnerable part of her face shield even if she was leaping sidewise when he fired.

Knowing that movement could well mean death, she froze, waiting to see what would happen.

"What is the meaning of this, Colonel Malin?" General Drakon asked, his voice harsh.

"This attack was assisted from the inside," Malin said, still emotionless. "Someone planted worms in our systems that assisted the vipers in reaching this command center without being detected."

"And you have some evidence that Colonel Gozen was involved in that?"

A pause. "Not yet, sir."

"Are you aware that Colonel Gozen was with me when the attack went down and played a major role in defending me against attack when the vipers located me?"

Malin hesitated again, though his pistol didn't waver. "General, they broke into your office immediately after killing the watch-standers. If you had been present, you would not have been able to stop a dozen vipers even with the defenses in your office."

Drakon raised one hand and gestured to Malin to lower his weapon.

After another moment, Malin did so, returning the pistol to its holster with one smooth movement.

"I wasn't in my office because I was talking to Colonel Gozen," Drakon said. "If she had not asked to speak with me, I probably would have been there. Why would she have gotten me out of that office and away from the command center if she was involved in a plot to kill me? Why wouldn't she have killed me herself during the confusion when the alarms sounded, or while the vipers were charging me?"

Malin inhaled slowly, then nodded. "It appears unlikely, sir."

"Colonel Malin, I appreciate your concern for my welfare, but I am getting a little tired of my staff officers pointing weapons at each other. I don't want it to happen again."

Gozen felt herself stiffen at the tone of Drakon's voice. Even though his words weren't directly aimed at her, and even though she hadn't pointed her weapon at Malin, she still had to fight down an urge to come to attention, salute, and promise never to do it again.

For his part, Malin sounded truly apologetic. "I am sorry, General."

"You're sure someone introduced worms from inside this building?" Drakon said, abruptly changing the subject.

"There was no external intrusion, sir. And no indications of any unauthorized person entering the headquarters complex."

"Somebody did," Gozen said. "Maybe that's why my visitor showed up when he did. He or she had just finished inserting the worms. They wouldn't have wanted to do that until just before the attack to limit any chance of the worms being spotted by our security routines. I should have realized that if they could threaten me they could have accessed the security systems in here."

"That didn't occur to me, either," Drakon said. "It's not

like you wasted any time alerting me to the problem. Colonel Malin, there is a hidden access to Colonel Gozen's quarters. Someone used it last night. That access may lead us to other hidden passages."

Malin's eyes narrowed. He nodded, then looked at Gozen again. "Some of the worms employed were the same as those among the snake software we captured on Ulindi. That's why our armor systems were able to block the intrusion attempts."

Gozen felt her face heating with anger. "You're not still thinking that I—"

"No, Colonel Gozen," Malin said. "Because I now recall that among your actions since we returned to Midway was your insistence on ensuring our armor software was upgraded to block everything found among the snake software on Ulindi. You have my apologies for suspecting you of involvement in this attack."

"Accepted," Gozen said. "In a Syndicate command, you would have shot me immediately then when proven wrong apologized for being too zealous in defending the CEO."

"Yes, I would have," Malin agreed.

"We need to find out who did plant those worms to open the path for the vipers," Drakon said. "Are there any leads?"

"None, so far, General. Except for the absence of leads. Whoever did this left no trace of their actions."

Drakon nodded, his expression darkening. "The lack of any mistakes does point in one direction. Colonel Malin, I know you've already been ordered to find President Iceni's former aide Mehmet Togo. You are now authorized to neutralize him at the first opportunity."

A flicker of a smile appeared on Malin's lips. "Elimination of the threat by any means is authorized?"

"Yes. Maybe he does think he's doing this to help President Iceni, but for all we know she would be his next target. Find Togo and kill him."

"I do not believe it will be difficult to convince her of the threat posed by Togo, General, but she may still be reluctant to order his elimination."

"When she hears that Togo assisted vipers in reaching

this planet and staging an attack, I don't think President Iceni will have any reluctance at all." Drakon paused, inhaling sharply, then gave Malin a questioning look. "I'm so used to having you around that I'd forgotten you were supposed to be acting as the president's aide. What brought you to the command center?"

"A hint among security intrusion attempts, General," Malin said. "Something that concerned me even though it is hard to define. I traced it to this headquarters and came over as quickly as I could to follow up."

"You should have issued an alert before you got here," Drakon said. "Why didn't you?"

"I thought such an alert might tip off the enemy and did not put sufficient weight on the possibility that the enemy might be moving so quickly."

"That was a reasonable judgment call," Drakon said gruffly. "But next time put a little more weight on the enemy's moving faster than we expect. How the hell did Togo get vipers onto the planet without anyone spotting it?"

"I will find out, sir."

"Get back to the president and give her a report on what happened here. Turn over the security sweep supervision to Colonel Gozen. Tell President Iceni that as soon as I am convinced my headquarters is secure I will visit her to discuss the matter. Has my office been swept for booby traps and bugs?"

"Yes, sir." Malin waited until Drakon had headed into his office before turning an intense gaze on Gozen. "Do you understand how important both he and President Iceni are?"

She gave him a level look in return. "I've seen other star systems, and I've seen Midway. They freed this star system from the Syndicate without trashing the place in the process, and they've kept it free. Yeah, I understand."

"*Both* of them," Malin emphasized. "It may look at times as if Iceni is the senior partner, but without General Drakon she turns into one more dictator. A currently beloved dictator, it is true, but one person who controls everything and without whom everything falls apart. There must be two, so both have authority and neither one finds it foreign to share that authority with another. That's the only path to long-term stability."

"Long term?" Gozen's gaze at Malin turned appraising. "Not a few years long term? Decades?"

"Longer." Malin, his eyes sparked with fire that contrasted with the coldness of his expression, swept a hand upward as if including all of space in the gesture. "This part of human-controlled space needs a strong alternative to the Syndicate. One that can hold off the enigmas and any other alien threat for as long as necessary and won't suffer from the flaws and weaknesses of the Syndicate."

"There's always the Alliance," Gozen said, probing for Malin's reaction.

"That name is poison in this part of space," Malin said in dismissive tones. "We can use some of their methods, but we can't acknowledge where they came from. This has to be something credited to people here."

"But you don't have any problem with help from Black Jack?"

"Black Jack isn't the Alliance we fought," Malin said, a ghost of a smile appearing. "He's what the Alliance always should have been. We can ally with Black Jack. We can use his help. You accept that, don't you?"

"Yes." Gozen bit her lip, thinking. "I guess that's how I'd been thinking about it. Help from Captain Bradamont was okay because she is one of Black Jack's officers. How closely are *you* tied to Black Jack, Colonel Malin?"

Malin gave another one of his ghost smiles. "Are you asking if I'm his agent? The answer is no. We have similar goals, I think. Do you share those goals?"

"I don't know, yet." Gozen jerked a thumb toward Drakon's office. "But I'm going to back whatever he does."

"That's good enough. Do you have any questions regarding the security sweep?"

Gozen studied the big display where markers indicating individual soldiers and their units moved through a vast 3-D schematic of the headquarters complex. Cleared areas glowed light green. Uncleared areas were yellow. As she watched, several short, small passages appeared and glowed red. "Those are the entrances to the routes used by my visitor last night, I'm guessing."

"Very likely, yes. They are to be searched very carefully. Assume the entrances and the passages are booby-trapped until they have been scanned down to bedrock."

"I figured they'd be rigged to nail anyone who tried a quick pursuit." Gozen faced Malin and saluted formally, her right fist coming across to tap her left shoulder. "I've got it, Colonel."

Malin gazed at her for a long moment, then returned the salute. "I stand relieved. Inform the general that I have left for President Iceni's office." He spun on one heel and walked away.

Colonel Safir showed up ten minutes after Malin had left, walking into the command center along with a squad from her brigade. "They put you in charge already?" she asked, familiar with Gozen from their encounters at Ulindi. "I got word of trouble here, but by the time we could scramble an assist force you guys had put out the fire. Just stopping by to see things for myself."

"We're still picking up the pieces, but it's under control," Gozen said.

Safir was looking at the display. "That's the sort of force dispersal that General Drakon would have set up. Did he do it and hand the task over to you?"

"No. Colonel Malin set it up."

"That explains it." Safir grinned at Gozen. "Are you two pals?"

"Me and Malin?" Gozen shook her head. "Does he have any pals?"

"Not that I ever heard of." Safir's grin turned into a speculative look. "Malin had a long feud going with Colonel Morgan before we lost her on Ulindi. I was wondering if he'd start acting the same way with you."

"No, no trace of going to war on his side," Gozen said. "He is suspicious of me."

"Malin suspects everybody," Safir said with a smile of derision. "If he tries moving on you without good evidence, the general will shut him down."

"The general did," Gozen agreed. "But even when Malin's been accusing me it hasn't come across as heated. Malin's just . . ."

"Cold?"

"Yeah," Gozen agreed. "Cold and driven. I guess he's always been like that?"

Safir paused, looking away, her expression troubled. "Always a bit like that. He's gotten colder and more driven lately though. Especially after Morgan apparently bought it. Like what little human warmth he had went with her." She glanced at Gozen. "It's enough to make someone wonder if they were lovers or something, and all that infighting was just a cover. But if it was a fake, it was the best damn fake I ever saw. There are rumors making the rounds, some of them pretty wild."

"I don't know enough people around here yet to hear the good rumors," Gozen said. "But from what I've heard of Morgan, she and Malin weren't exactly a match made in the heavens. Seems he'd be celebrating, not torn up about her dying on Ulindi."

"She's not confirmed dead," Safir said.

"She was in the snake alternate command center on Ulindi when it was blown to hell."

"Maybe she was still in there," Safir said. "Maybe not. If you'd ever met Roh Morgan, you'd know why the rest of us aren't willing to write her off in the absence of a body. And even if she is dead . . . well, Morgan's exactly the sort who would reach out of her grave to pull down whoever put her there. Know what I mean?" Safir nodded toward Drakon's office. "Is the boss accepting visitors?"

"He didn't tell me otherwise," Gozen said.

"Drakon isn't a micromanager. He expects us to use our heads without being given explicit instructions all the time. But I gather you're picking up on that." Safir gestured to her soldiers, waiting off to one side of the command center, to stay where they were, then strode toward Drakon's office.

Gozen inhaled slowly as she studied the security sweep, now almost complete. A few bugs concealed by the vipers had turned up, but nothing else. The vipers, it seemed, had only one mission, to kill Drakon.

Colonel Malin obviously wasn't the only one who understood how important Drakon was.

JASON Boyens had endured a good many things in his rise to CEO status, including the exile to the Reserve Flotilla, capture by the Alliance, the close personal attention of the deadly Happy Hua, and a prolonged imprisonment on Midway while wondering whether Gwen Iceni and Artur Drakon would forgive his latest twists and turns or choose to get rid of him once and for all. By all rights he should be dead a dozen times over. But he had survived this far.

So he could endure this, too, walking up to a customs checkpoint at the orbital facility where Midway's HuK had dropped off him and the nervous young man named Dingane Paige who had been Ulindi's representative at Midway. The checkpoint bore the scars of fairly recent fighting when Drakon's soldiers had wiped out the snakes who had once controlled this facility. The men and women occupying the security checkpoint wore obviously new uniforms and had the awkward stances of those new to their jobs.

Jason Boyens had to wonder how those new guards, whose world had been the scene of large-scale massacres by the Syndicate Internal Security Service, would take the appearance of a former Syndicate CEO.

He adopted a pose of quiet confidence. Not arrogant. That was the last thing he needed to project. But a sort of comradely assurance that he was part of whatever team Ulindi was trying to put together in the wake of the Syndicate's expulsion.

But his careful effort was nearly undone by a strange

sensation, a chill of fear down his spine as if death itself had passed close by him, known Boyens for who he was, eyed him with interest, then chosen to pass on.

Seriously rattled by the feeling, Boyens looked around hurriedly, trying to spot whoever had produced that reaction in him, but no one in the groups of people arriving or departing appeared to stand out or look out of place. Which only meant that whoever it was could blend in very well, a useful skill for thieves, swindlers . . . and assassins.

Boyens had been eyed appraisingly by assassins before, including those agonizing months with Happy Hua apparently itching for an excuse to conduct a field execution of him for any reason her own superiors might be willing to accept. But this had felt disturbingly familiar. For some reason it called up memories of meetings with Drakon and his two aides, Morgan and Malin, whose gazes could bear an uncomfortable similarity to that of a cat toying with a mouse.

But Morgan had died on Ulindi. And if he screwed up this first encounter with officials of Ulindi he might die here as well.

Boyens regained his poise with a major effort. By the time he finally reached the guards and presented his papers, knowing that he was being scanned by many devices designed to spot signs of fear or deceit, Boyens presented the perfect image of confidence and safety.

The older woman who took Boyens's papers frowned at them, checked the display at her guard post, then frowned at him. "Boyens? Syndicate CEO?"

A cone of silence settled over a wide area around Boyens, conversations and activity halting, everyone turning to stare at him in disbelief that was rapidly turning to anger.

"*Former* CEO," Boyens said, trying to make the CEO title seem like one he was reluctant to claim. Given the circumstances, he wasn't faking that. He spoke loudly enough for his voice to carry, though even a whisper would have been audible in the hush that filled the area. "I came from Midway. You can see the endorsements on my papers, from President Iceni and General Drakon themselves."

"They wanted him to come to Ulindi," Dingane Paige said, sounding more confident as he talked to his peers.

Other guards had hastened over and were examining their readouts. "Iceni and Drakon? Those two really wanted him to come here?" one asked.

"Yes. I'm familiar with this region of space," Boyens explained, doing his best to pretend that he was talking to another CEO rather than to a worker so his attitude would come across well. "I used to serve with the Reserve Flotilla." He remembered conversations he had overheard as well as some Syndicate intelligence assessments and decided to add something else. "I was taken prisoner when the Flotilla was destroyed by Black Jack. *He* brought me back to Midway and released me."

"You expect us to believe that?" a young woman demanded.

"It's true." Two more women had come over. Boyens hadn't noticed them in his focus on the guards, but he saw they wore Syndicate uniforms that had had the Syndicate patches torn off. "We were shuttle pilots with the Reserve Flotilla," the older of the two continued, jerking her thumb at her companion to include her in the statement. "We both saw him with the Flotilla. I flew him a few times."

"I'm glad you survived," Boyens said, trying desperately to recall the woman and wondering how he had treated her. Hopefully halfway decently at least.

"Got transferred off before the Flotilla got sent to Alliance space and hell," the pilot answered. "This guy treated us all right," the woman added. "He was a CEO, but he wasn't an arrogant ass."

"Everyone knew that Boyens wasn't half-bad," the other pilot commented, "for a CEO."

"That's not saying much," one of the guards grumbled, staring at Boyens's papers as if searching for a single comma out of place that could be used to justify arrest and interrogation.

"President Iceni asked me to come here," Boyens repeated.

"He's telling the truth," another guard commented, eyes on the readouts.

"That's a first for a CEO," another added, bringing a ripple of angry laughter.

"Iceni was a CEO once, too. Why did President Iceni ask you to come to Ulindi?" the older pilot asked. "Last I heard, you were attacking Midway in command of a Syndicate flotilla."

"Because I escaped," Boyens said, phrasing his words carefully. "The snakes commanded that flotilla, not me. I had snake CEO Hua Boucher at my back every moment. I managed to prevent some actions by the snakes and kept it from accomplishing the Syndicate's goals." The first part of that sentence was true, but the second half was shading the truth considerably. Hopefully, the way he had phrased it, thinking of what Boucher really had accused him of doing, would keep the statement from showing up on the security sensors as deceptive. "I had to run when it became obvious I was going to be blamed for the flotilla's failures. I brought important information to Midway. I wish I could have killed Boucher myself before I left, but the attempt would have been futile." He didn't have to worry whether that last statement would come across as true.

The commander of the checkpoint scratched his head, then shrugged. "I have to admit to a strong desire to just go ahead and shoot you now, but that'd be a snake thing to do. We're going to, uh, take you into custody, though. Take you down and let the interim government talk to you. They'll decide what to do."

"That's fine," Boyens said, trying not to look too relieved. If he could get in the same room with the inexperienced people trying to run this star system he was certain that he could convince them that he would be useful to Ulindi. It would take some time to unobtrusively shift from being a source of advice to becoming someone in authority, but he had time. Only fools tried to rush things.

The two guards assigned to him weren't deferential, but they weren't rough, either. A lifetime in the Syndicate had left them with a residual dread of CEOs that held them back even now. Boyens saw that the pilots on the shuttle taking him down to the planet were the two women who were also survivors of the Reserve Flotilla. He took that as a good sign for the future.

"We're all survivors, aren't we?" Boyens commented to his guards and Dingane Paige as the shuttle fell away from the orbital facility and began dropping toward the planet below.

"So far," one of the guards commented in tones that made the implied threat obvious.

Paige was gazing morosely at the display near him, which showed an image of space outside the shuttle. "We can't defend ourselves. How long can we survive like that? We don't even have one Hunter-Killer like the one that brought us back to Ulindi."

"Get one," Boyens said matter-of-factly.

Paige and the guards stared at him. "You mean buy a mobile forces unit?" Paige asked. "We don't have the money."

"No, no!" Boyens protested. "Even if you could buy a warship, that's what President Iceni calls them instead of mobile forces, you know," he added in an aside to the guards to emphasize that he knew Iceni, "there are better ways. You have jump points to Maui and Kiribati, right? And the Syndicate is posting warships at Maui and Kiribati to keep those star systems from revolting, and to protect against attacks by Midway's forces. You need to get word to the workers and any right-minded executives on those warships that if they are sick of the Syndicate they can find a safe home here at Ulindi. For them and for their families!"

"Encourage them to mutiny?" Paige asked, then shook his head. "There must be snakes all over those units . . . um, warships. They couldn't mutiny."

"Even the Syndicate doesn't have unlimited numbers of snakes," Boyens advised. "How many snakes died here at Ulindi? On the planet where we're going and in warships that were destroyed during the fighting in space? And that's on top of all the other losses and all the other demands for snakes that the Syndicate has faced lately. They are spread thinly, I tell you. We have a window of opportunity in which mutinies have a higher chance of success, and we should use that to convince as many of those warships as possible to come to Ulindi for a new home where they can be free of the Syndicate. A new home that they can help defend against the Syndicate and all other threats!"

The two guards exchanged smiles, and even Paige managed to let some excitement and hope overcome his apparently habitual anxiety. More importantly (from Boyens's point of view), none of them had objected when Boyens had used "we" to include himself with them.

And it wasn't a bad plan at all. Some of the executives and sub-CEOs on those Syndicate warships at Maui and Kiribati might be men and women he knew. That wouldn't be a positive in every case, but as a rule, Boyens had tried to avoid leaving vengeful victims in his wake. He had seen too many examples of unforgiving subordinates tripping up (or worse) those who had harmed them to not realize that generating living enemies on the way to the top made for a bad long-term strategy. Now Boyens's attempts to ensure he wasn't personally blamed for misfortunes that befell others might help bring Ulindi exactly the sort of muscle it very badly needed.

And if it led to more than one snake like the late-and-unlamented snake CEO Hua Boucher being shoved out an air lock by angry workers, so much the better.

HEAVY cruiser *Manticore* dropped out of jump space at Moorea to the accompaniment of combat system alarms warning of danger nearby.

"A Hunter-Killer," Kapitan Diaz said as he shook the lingering effects of leaving jump from his brain. "Two light minutes away. It's holding an orbit near the jump point. It is *not* broadcasting Syndicate unit identification."

"A trick?" Marphissa asked.

The senior watch specialist answered. "Kommodor, the

communications we are picking up indicate that Moorea has been occupied by the forces of Granaile Imallye. The HuK guarding this jump point is specifically identified as belonging to her forces."

"So. A sentry posted at the jump point. That implies a decent level of organization and discipline." Marphissa gazed at her display as new information appeared. Moorea was a fairly well-off star system, with five inner planets and six larger ones in the outer reaches. One of the inner planets was not merely inhabitable by humans but pleasant, orbiting its star at seven and a half light minutes out, while a second at ten light minutes out was cold but livable.

Orbiting near the primary inhabited world were two light cruisers, two more HuKs, and a single battle cruiser. While clearly of Syndicate origin, none of those were broadcasting Syndicate unit identification either.

"Imallye has some serious firepower here," Marphissa commented. But the jump point from which *Manticore* had arrived was nearly six light hours from where that planet and those other warships now orbited. She waved one hand toward the comm specialist. "Set me up to contact the HuK on sentry duty."

"Yes, Kommodor," she replied. "It will take one moment. Done. Channel Two, Kommodor."

Marphissa sat straight and tried to look authoritative but not hostile. "Unknown warship at the jump point from Iwa, this is Kommodor Marphissa of the Free and Independent Midway Star System aboard the heavy cruiser *Manticore*. I have been sent to Moorea by our President Iceni to contact Granaile Imallye and to pass on warning of a new and serious threat from the alien enigma species." She paused. "We have just come from Iwa, where all Syndicate installations were recently destroyed by an enigma attack. There were no survivors. I must speak with Granaile Imallye and the leaders of Moorea as soon as possible. Moorea may be the next target of the enigmas, and their next attack could come at any time. For the people, Marphissa, out."

"That should get their attention," Diaz commented.

"Why leave a single HuK on sentry duty? It could only deal with the smallest level of threat arriving here."

"Perhaps Imallye wants to see if whoever arrives immediately attacks the HuK or tries to talk," Marphissa said. "Put *Manticore* in an orbit that holds us near here until that HuK answers us. President Iceni was very clear that we must not provoke combat with Imallye's forces."

Diaz was still maneuvering *Manticore* when a reply came from the HuK. The man whose image appeared before Marphissa wore what had once been a Syndicate executive's suit, but one bedecked with numerous extra decorations and jewelry. Under the Syndicate, that suit would have been kept pressed and immaculate, but the current owner didn't seem bothered by the wrinkles and sags in it. "I am Mahadhevan, commander of the *Mahadhevan*," he announced, "a unit obedient to Granaile Imallye and to no one else."

"He says that like he expects us to be annoyed," Diaz commented.

"He's a worker," the senior watch specialist declared. "A former worker." The other specialists nodded in agreement.

It wasn't too hard to figure out how a former worker would come to be wearing the uniform of a Syndicate executive. When the workers on Syndicate warships mutinied, there was little mercy shown to many of their former supervisors. Marphissa, herself a former executive, was grateful that Iceni had maintained control over the crews of the ships on which she had fostered rebellion against the Syndicate. "He's not using a title," Marphissa observed. "Maybe that's how Imallye runs things."

Mahadhevan, after pausing to let his audience presumably have time to be outraged by his attitude, spoke again, sounding unconcerned. "You will wait here, in the orbit I give you, while I pass on your request to Imallye. That is all."

The image vanished.

"Are you certain that we cannot provoke hostilities?" Diaz asked, his voice angry now.

"I'm supposed to avoid it if possible," Marphissa said, trying not to become equally angry. "That ass is too busy showing off his new status to listen to what I told him. He might delay sending on a message just to emphasize his current exalted state."

"What will we do, Kommodor? He has sent us the orbit we are supposed to remain in."

Marphissa thought, the image of the devastation at Iwa filling her mind. "I cannot risk this fool's slowing down the warning I must give. Comm specialist, set up a signal tagged for military and civilian leaders here in Moorea, no matter who they are loyal to. I want the signal aimed to intercept the orbit of the primary world and those warships orbiting near it. Kapitan Diaz, while I send my message out, you are to take *Manticore* toward the primary inhabited world at a velocity of point two light speed."

Diaz grinned. "Yes, Kommodor! And if Mahadhevan and the *Mahadhevan* react in a hostile manner?"

"That HuK does not have sufficient firepower to hurt us on a single firing run. We will see, Kapitan, if Mahadhevan has enough brains to realize that. If he does not, we will have to show him that attacking warships of Midway without provocation is a serious mistake."

Surely President Iceni would want her to act quickly, and to refuse to be easily intimidated by a single ship far weaker than her own. But Marphissa still waited, outwardly calm but inwardly tense, to see what the worker-turned-commander would do when his orders were ignored.

Manticore could easily handle a single HuK. But that battle cruiser could smash *Manticore* if Imallye decided to back even a foolish decision by one of her subordinates.

And she knew almost nothing about Imallye.

"Shields at maximum strength," Marphissa ordered. "Do not power up weapons."

Manticore accelerated out of orbit, heading down the long path to where the primary inhabited world of Moorea would be in sixty hours.

CHAPTER SIX

"THE *Mahadhevan* is changing vector," the senior watch specialist announced.

Marphissa eyed her display, watching the HuK accelerating and coming around, using her experience to guess its path even before it had settled out. "An intercept. The man is a fool."

"Power up weapons?" Diaz asked hopefully.

"Not yet." She slouched back a little in her command seat, then tapped the control to contact the HuK again. "*Mahadhevan*, I am happy to accept your offer to serve as our escort while *Manticore* heads to a meeting with Imallye." Marphissa could only guess that the pirate queen would be aboard the battle cruiser, but Imallye's forces couldn't include that many ships of that size. Imallye would almost certainly be riding the battle cruiser, and perhaps was acting as the warship's commanding officer.

"Just let me know if *Mahadhevan* requires specific stationing instructions relative to *Manticore*," Marphissa continued with cheerful confidence. "It would be very unfortunate if any accidents occurred while your ship was close to my heavy cruiser. For the people, Marphissa, out."

Diaz looked from Marphissa to his display and back again. "May I ask what you are doing, Kommodor?"

It was an exceptionally bold question for anyone trained in the Syndicate system of absolute obedience. Marphissa gave him a stern look, then laughed. "I am responding to Mahadhevan on his own terms. Do you not recognize what he was doing? Trying to overawe me and dare me to dispute his status and his orders?"

"I saw that," Diaz said. "And now you are going back at him in the same way?"

"Exactly. You must have seen the same game played a thousand times or more when you were in school."

"Yes." Diaz looked at his display again, where the HuK *Mahadhevan* was continuing on a course to intercept *Manticore*. "But I have never seen that schoolyard game played with warships carrying arsenals of deadly weapons."

"The ball is in his court," Marphissa said. "He must decide whether to throw a punch or take advantage of the out I gave him and pretend that it was always about his escorting us to his superiors. That's what he'll do if he's smart."

"And if he's stupid?"

Marphissa gave Diaz a serious look this time. "He is in command of one of the warships of Granaile Imallye. What intelligence we have on Imallye says that she has amassed a significant fighting force and established control of more than one star system. We see evidence here at Moorea supporting that intelligence. Would such a capable commander allow a reckless fool to command a warship? The Syndicate may see HuKs as throwaways, warships that last only moments in most combat situations, but neither we nor Imallye have so many warships that we can afford to think that way. So, if what we have been told of Imallye is right, if what we see here at Moorea before us is as it seems, then for all his posturing Mahadhevan must have some intelligence and skills. I tell you this to explain my reasons for acting as I am. I am not simply responding to a schoolyard bluff with another bluff, but made my decisions based on analyzing this particular situation."

"Thank you, Kommodor," Diaz said. "Even after serving with you for a while I am still surprised, and grateful, to have you explain your reasons and plans to me."

"If worse came to worst for me, you'd have to carry out this mission," Marphissa said, waving away his words to cover her inner embarrassment at Diaz's admiration. "And you may command a force on your own someday. I hope to provide you with good training for that." She smiled. "Despite my own lack of experience."

The combat systems specialist broke into their conversation. "The HuK *Mahadhevan* will be within our weapons range in seven minutes, Kommodor. He will be close enough to fire on us in eight and a half minutes."

On Marphissa's display a translucent globe appeared around the Hunter-Killer, depicting the effective range of its weapons. Another, larger, globe centered on *Manticore* showed the longer range of the missiles and more powerful hell lance particle beams that the heavy cruiser carried. After the heavy cruiser had changed vectors to accelerate toward the inner star system, the HuK had been positioned slightly above and just forward of *Manticore*. As the HuK dove toward an intercept with the heavy cruiser, its relative position did not change, but the other warship drew steadily closer.

Marphissa watched the edges of the globes approaching each other as the minutes passed.

"Kommodor," Diaz said respectfully, "the *Mahadhevan* will be within range of our weapons in three minutes. I recommend targeting the *Mahadhevan* at this time but holding fire until the HuK fires upon us."

"Do not target the other ship yet," Marphissa said. "We must allow Mahadhevan the man to pretend that his actions are not driven by fear of us."

Diaz nodded, biting his lip as he watched the distance between the two warships dwindle. "You appear to have an insightful knowledge of the workings of the male mind, Kommodor."

"One of the benefits of an unsuccessful dating history,"

Marphissa replied dryly. "Ah," she added with satisfaction as her display showed new movement. "Here he goes."

"*Mahadhevan* is altering vector," the combat systems specialist reported. "Rate of closure has dropped . . . rate of closure has come to zero. *Mahadhevan* has taken up relative position just ahead of us, proceeding along the same vector toward the primary inhabited world."

"As if he is escorting us," Diaz said scornfully. "But he is staying just outside of our weapons range. That's foolish. We could put on a burst of full acceleration, get him inside our missile engagement range, and launch at him before he could accelerate out of reach again."

"Yes," Marphissa agreed. "But Mahadhevan the man is not experienced enough in command to know that. We won't tell him. With any luck, we won't have to engage any of the forces of Granaile Imallye."

"How close are we going to get to that battle cruiser?" Diaz asked.

"No closer than I have to in order to carry out a real-time conversation," Marphissa said. "We'll see whether Imallye contacts us before we get that close." It would still be about fifty-nine hours before *Manticore* intercepted the planet along its orbit and the warships near it. Plenty of time for Imallye to hear Marphissa's message, which, traveling at the speed of light, should arrive in about five more hours, and send a reply, which would take almost five hours on top of that to be received by Marphissa. Light was very fast, but in the immense distances of space it often felt very slow as well.

It actually took nearly twelve hours before Imallye's reply came in. In the interim, Marphissa had worked for some hours, ate, slept, had a breakfast, then returned to the bridge to work on some more of what was still called "paperwork" even though little of it was ever printed out on paper.

Imallye, sprawled in the fleet command seat on the battle cruiser, wasn't wearing a cast-off Syndicate CEO's suit. She was in a skin suit meant to be worn under battle armor, the suit's dull, black shade set off by gold insignia that glittered at her neck and on her sleeves. A large sidearm in a worn-looking holster was on one hip. A big, standard-issue Syndicate close-combat knife was sheathed on her other hip. It was, Marphissa had to admit, a very effective image.

"I have received your message, Kommodor Marphissa," Imallye said without any indication of how she felt about the warning it contained. "Proceed to a rendezvous with my flagship *Vengeance* so we can conduct a real-time conversation about these critical matters." Imallye paused, then smiled. "Please proceed. We will speak again when you are less than one light minute from *Vengeance*. Imallye, out."

"*Vengeance?*" Diaz said. "That's not a very reassuring name for a battle cruiser."

"No." Marphissa called up a still from the message and studied Imallye. "What do you think of her?"

"She looks . . . strong," Diaz said. "Confident. Powerful. Dangerous. Overtly so."

"Yes," Marphissa agreed. "It's a show, but a very good one. That skin suit she's wearing. Maybe Imallye is former Syndicate ground forces. No one else wears those."

"Vipers do."

"Mutinous workers following a former viper? I don't think so. They would rip her into pieces no matter how dangerous she looked." Marphissa scowled at the image. "What's her game? How did she get her hands on that battle cruiser? I admit to being worried about getting too close to that warship, but we need to find out more about Imallye. I need to talk to her, and I am certain if we try to talk again from any distance farther out than one light minute, she will refuse to answer."

"Notice what we can see of the bridge of the *Vengeance*?" Diaz added. "It looks neat and well kept. The bridge of *Mahadhevan* had some signs of sloppiness, but what is visible inside *Vengeance* shows a tight ship."

"She knows her business," Marphissa agreed. "Let's hope she is willing to work with President Iceni. I have no doubt that Kapitan Kontos and *Pele* could take apart *Vengeance*, but *Pele* might take a lot of damage in the process. We couldn't afford that, not with both the Syndicate and the enigmas to worry about."

She could not share with Diaz the confidential words of President Iceni before *Manticore* had left Midway. Marphissa had replayed that private message again just a few hours ago, studying the somber expression on Iceni's face as she spoke. *"Kommodor, be wary of Imallye. What she has accomplished already indicates that Imallye is both resourceful and driven. She could be an important ally. Or an implacable enemy. Do all you can to convince her of the need to work together against the enigma threat to this region of space. But just because she is an enemy of the Syndicate does not mean that she will be a friend to us. General Drakon and I are former CEOs, and if Imallye is driven by a desire for reprisal against senior Syndicate officials, our prior status may be all she cares about."*

In light of that warning, the name of Imallye's battle cruiser, the *Vengeance*, felt even more worrisome.

Point two light speed worked out to about sixty thousand kilometers per second, an almost unimaginably fast velocity for humans to contemplate. But the distance to cover to reach the primary inhabited planet along its orbit was about six light hours, which came to nearly six and a half billion kilometers. A distance so great that even light required six hours to make the journey did not quickly yield to velocities measured in mere thousands of kilometers.

And so it was nearly two and a half days later that *Manticore* reached the vicinity of the planet, swooping in from the outer star system on a curving path that intercepted the world as it raced along its orbit about the star Moorea at a piddling twenty-eight kilometers per second.

"I want us brought into an orbit exactly fifty-nine light seconds from Imallye's battle cruiser *Vengeance*," Marphissa directed. "Make certain we are at a dead stop relative to *Vengeance*. Do not use more than seventy-five percent power on your main propulsion when braking. I want to conceal our maximum capability."

Manticore's automated maneuvering systems could handle that kind of challenge fairly easily. Pivoting under the push of thrusters so that her bow faced backward and her main propulsion forward along their path, *Manticore* began firing her main propulsion, fighting momentum and slowing her progress through space. The ship's inertial dampers ran their stress readings up toward the red danger zones, but stayed well out of trouble as the heavy cruiser braked.

It took a while to kill such immense velocity, but eventually Diaz smiled triumphantly as *Manticore* came to a halt relative to *Vengeance*. Both ships were still moving through space along their orbits, but their vectors matched exactly, so they were apparently sitting still compared to each other. "Exactly fifty-nine light seconds from *Vengeance*, Kommodor," he announced.

"Thank you, Kapitan," Marphissa said. "Well done. Now, let us see what Granaile Imallye will say to us."

This time, Marphissa sat straight and tried to look as professional as possible. She couldn't match the informal deadliness of Imallye's outfit and posture, and so did not even try. Imallye would see that Midway's Kommodor was no slacker.

"Honored Granaile Imallye," Marphissa began, "I have come to Moorea on orders from President Iceni of the Free and Independent Midway Star System. I am to convey to you and everyone else the dangers posed by our discovery that the alien enigma species has developed enough range on their jump drives to reach Iwa Star System directly. I am also to offer our willingness to reach peace agreements, trade agreements, and even mutual defense agreements with the star systems under your control."

It would only have taken two minutes for a reply (one minute for Marphissa's transmission to reach *Vengeance* and another minute for the return journey of Imallye's reply), but more than ten minutes elapsed before the answer came. Imallye was clearly trying to establish herself as superior in status to Marphissa.

The pirate queen was wearing the same outfit and was in nearly the same pose as before. But her expression was harder as she gazed out at Marphissa. "So, you came to offer us deals and favors, Kommodor. And a peace agreement. On behalf of CEO Iceni."

The reference to Iceni's Syndicate past brought up worrisome memories of Iceni's warning. Marphissa tried to look unruffled and to keep her voice even. "*President* Iceni sent us here. She has renounced the Syndicate and their ways, and governs Midway Star System by the will of the people. We do not wish hostilities with your forces. The Syndicate is a threat to us all, and so are the enigmas. I have sent you our records of what the enigmas did to Iwa Star System. Moorea may be their next target. A mutual defense agreement would serve us all well."

When her response came two minutes later, Imallye did not appear to be impressed by Marphissa's argument. "I know nothing about the so-called enigmas except that the Syndicate claimed that they existed. Since the Syndicate lied about so much else, that means little to me. I also know the damage your records show at Iwa, if those records have not been manipulated, could have been inflicted by weapons fired from ships such as yours, Kommodor. And I know that no matter what she calls herself or what flattery her minions offer up in describing her, CEO Iceni is fully capable of ordering such an attack. I do not see grounds for peace in such a situation."

That sounded very much like personal animosity toward Iceni. Where had that come from?

Before she could touch the transmit command to answer, Kapitan Diaz halted Marphissa with an urgent gesture. "My systems specialists inform me that there are intrusion attempts being made against our software. At least one of Imallye's ships is trying to use the Syndicate unit net to break into our systems."

"Is there any danger of their succeeding?" Marphissa asked.

"My specialists are certain they can maintain the firewalls. They say the intrusion attempts are using Syndicate-origin malware which is a few revisions behind that which our forces captured from the snakes at Ulindi, so our systems can easily spot it and stop it."

"Good. I won't let Imallye know that her efforts have been detected and neutralized." Marphissa composed her expression once more before touching the transmit command and kept her reply even in tone as if nothing untoward had occurred. "Honored Granaile Imallye, I know little of President Iceni's past. Like all of us who were forced to serve the Syndicate, she doubtless has her share of skeletons in her closet. I can only speak to who she has been since arriving at Midway. As a CEO, she worked for the people. As soon as a good opportunity arose, she rebelled against the Syndicate and destroyed the snake presence in Midway Star System. Since then, she has overseen reforms of the election system and the legal system at Midway to grant real rights to the people, and to protect the people and their rights from those in power. Whatever has led to your skepticism regarding President Iceni's nature and motives, I ask that you become familiar with her record at Midway."

Imallye smiled without visible humor. "I will become very familiar with it when I sift through the rubble of her headquarters in that star system."

That sounded more like a promise than a threat. *To hell with diplomacy.* Marphissa drew herself up and gazed sternly at Imallye. "The only wreckage that will be produced if you attack Midway will be the debris from the remains of your ships," she said coldly. "We have already driven off multiple attacks by the Syndicate. We have substantial forces, very capable commanders, and the loyalty of our crews. They will fight for their homes and their families and destroy anyone who endangers them. We would, however, much rather fight alongside your ships against those mutual threats we face."

"Indeed?" Imallye displayed that grim smile again. "I can't help but wonder why such a powerful foe would come to me begging for peace and support against her enemies. Is Iceni trying to buy time to set up defenses at Iwa against me? Does she fear that Iwa will fall to me before she can snatch it up?"

Marphissa blinked, surprised by the statement. "There is nothing left at Iwa to fall, nothing to conquer. No defenses. I sent you the records of what we saw there. You know that every aspect of the human presence at Iwa has been devastated."

"What I know is that, if your records are accurate and not manipulated, then Iwa is unoccupied, and therefore easily available to me as a base," Imallye said.

"A base?" Marphissa failed to hide her incredulity. "When the enigmas can hit it again at any time? Iwa is a death trap!"

"And yet you are working so hard to keep me from going there." Imallye's image glared at Marphissa. "I don't believe you. You work for Iceni, so you'll say anything. And I know that if I leave myself exposed to Iceni at all I will end up with a knife in my back."

"President Iceni does not want hostilities with you! Midway wants to free star systems from the Syndicate. We threaten no one!"

"As long as Iceni has a flotilla of warships, she is a threat," Imallye said flatly.

And *Manticore* was part of that flotilla. Marphissa made sure her comm control was off before flinging an order at Diaz. "Kapitan, head for the jump point back to Iwa. Now. Maximum acceleration."

She faced forward, composed her expression, then hit transmit again. "Honored Granaile Imallye, you are mistaken. I ask again that you familiarize yourself with the situation at Midway before you reach a decision. The enigmas are real, and they are resolved to destroy any human presence. Please accept President Iceni's offer of peace."

Manticore was pivoting around under the push of her thrusters putting out their full force, her bow nearly lined up with the vector back to the jump point.

Forty seconds into the maneuver the combat systems

specialist called out a warning. "*Vengeance* began altering vector fifty-nine seconds ago!"

"He started maneuvering before he could have seen our moves," Diaz said.

"I had a hunch that conversation was at an end," Marphissa replied.

"All hands brace for full acceleration!" Diaz warned a moment before *Manticore*'s main propulsion lit off and hurled the heavy cruiser out of her orbit. High-pitched whines of complaint issued from the inertial dampers as they tried to keep the strains on the crew and the ship's structure from tearing both apart.

"*Vengeance* lit off her main propulsion fifty-nine seconds ago! Estimate the battle cruiser is accelerating on an intercept with our previous orbit."

Diaz, back pressed against his seat by the acceleration, still managed to shake his head. "Anticipating what *Vengeance* would do bought us a little advantage starting out. But we can't outrun a battle cruiser. They've got a higher thrust-to-mass ratio than we do."

"Maybe we got enough of a head start," Marphissa said. "And we were already fifty-nine light seconds ahead of them. Maybe that will be enough." She didn't believe that, but she still nursed an irrational hope.

"We'll know for sure when the vectors steady down," Diaz said. But from the way he said it, *Manticore*'s captain didn't expect to see good news when that happened.

Caught flat-footed by the sudden maneuvers, the nearest of Imallye's warships, the HuK *Mahadhevan*, had been left behind when *Manticore* bolted. The HuK began pivoting to join in the chase, then abruptly stopped.

"None of Imallye's light cruisers or HuKs are pursuing us," Diaz said. "It looks as if *Mahadhevan* started to but then received orders to stay in orbit."

"Imallye doesn't need the HuKs or light cruisers if that battle cruiser catches us," Marphissa said angrily. "And a prolonged chase would run through the fuel cell supply on the HuKs and leave them in trouble. She's probably leaving the light cruisers here to keep an eye on that planet, which may not be as securely under her control as she implied."

An alarm pulsed on Marphissa's display, accompanied by a red flashing symbol. "Hull stress is exceeding safety parameters," the senior specialist reported.

"Kommodor?" Diaz asked.

Marphissa took a moment to think, breathing deeply, and weighing the need to maintain the highest possible acceleration against the certain disintegration of both ship and crew if the hull or the inertial dampers failed. She nodded to Diaz. "You may reduce acceleration to stay within safe limits, Kapitan. Do not reduce it even a tiny amount below that level."

Rather than order a specialist to do it, Diaz brought up the thrust controls on his own display and carefully lowered the output from *Manticore*'s main propulsion until the red symbol shaded into a cautionary yellow. "We can hold this as long as our fuel cells hold out, Kommodor."

Both the heavy cruiser and the pursuing *Vengeance* had steadied out on their vectors. *Manticore*'s projected course was a very long, shallow curve that would bring her back to the jump point for Iwa, the time until that arrival still slowly diminishing as the heavy cruiser continued to accelerate. Behind her, *Vengeance*'s projected path was another shallow curve, this one aimed to intercept *Manticore*'s course far ahead of where both ships were now located, and far short of the jump point that would allow the heavy cruiser's escape.

"Assuming both units continue operating main propulsion at their current rates, maneuvering systems project intercept of *Manticore* by *Vengeance* in fifteen point three hours," the senior specialist reported in an admirably calm voice.

Marphissa tried to relax even though the acceleration leaking past the inertial dampers was still pushing her back against her seat. Her display showed the same information the specialist had reported. Her attempt to stay as far from

Vengeance as possible while meeting Imallye's demands, and her anticipation of the battle cruiser's attack, had bought some time and space, but not nearly enough.

It wasn't a wildly difficult problem for the automated systems to calculate. The most complex aspect of it was how much acceleration would slow as the velocity of both ships climbed ever higher. Relativity was unforgiving. As *Manticore* moved at ever-higher fractions of the speed of light, the warship's mass would inexorably increase as well, making it harder for the same amount of thrust to push the ship even faster. If *Manticore* could somehow get close to the speed of light, the ship's mass would grow so huge that it became impossible for any amount of thrust to keep accelerating her.

But such an effort would burn far too much of the heavy cruiser's fuel cells, and in any event, *Manticore*'s velocity would be limited by another consideration. A ship could only enter jump if it were going at point two light speed or less. *Manticore* would have to limit her maximum velocity so that she could brake back down to point two light speed by the time she reached that jump point.

But *Vengeance* wasn't planning on jumping, so the battle cruiser wasn't worried about braking his velocity. And this was exactly the kind of situation that battle cruisers were built for, with massive main propulsion that let them accelerate faster than any other warship despite the large mass of a battle cruiser. The price for that was in far less armor than battleships, and not as many weapons as a ship that size could have carried. But battle cruisers carried plenty enough weapons to annihilate most of the warships they could chase down.

Diaz leaned close to Marphissa and spoke in a very low voice. "What is our plan, Kommodor?"

"Right now, I am praying for a miracle," she murmured in reply. "Captain Bradamont taught me how to do that."

Kapitan Diaz hesitated, licking his lips nervously. "Kommodor, Captain Bradamont has also instructed me. She told me that the situation is never hopeless as long as you can still move or fight."

"I agree. But I am not seeing any alternative at this point to moving until we are caught by *Vengeance*, then fighting until we are destroyed. Help me find an alternative, Kapitan. We have fifteen hours until we are within range of the battle cruiser's weapons." Marphissa nodded to herself. "And if that happens, I intend engaging *Vengeance* and inflicting so much damage that Imallye's battle cruiser will pose no threat to anyone afterward. *Manticore* will be destroyed, but Imallye will deeply regret the price of her victory."

Diaz nodded as well. "Yes, Kommodor. My ship will not fail you."

Marphissa turned her head to look at him and forced a smile. "Not your ship, nor its commander, nor its crew, have ever failed me, Kapitan Diaz, and I am certain that they never will." She had let her voice rise in volume so the words carried, wanting the specialists to hear them as well. Word would have already spread through the ship of *Manticore*'s apparently helpless situation. Anything that would help morale, no matter how little, was important right now.

And Diaz deserved the public praise as well.

He flushed slightly, nodded again, then sat back and began tapping in internal comm connections. "I will speak with all of my officers and senior specialists to let them know that recommendations would be welcome."

The next several hours passed with increasing slowness, as if relativity had already placed an iron grip of time's rate of progression on the perceptions of those aboard *Manticore*. Marphissa had to use a down patch to get some sleep so she would not be exhausted when *Vengeance* finally caught *Manticore*. The rest of the time she spent running simulations of different attempts to avoid that intercept, each attempt only succeeding in bringing about the clash a little sooner. After a while, Marphissa abandoned that effort and began gaming out the battle between her heavy cruiser and *Vengeance*, trying to work out the best possible means of inflicting maximum damage on the battle cruiser before *Manticore* was destroyed. The results of those simulations were also discouraging, but she worked away at them stubbornly.

"Kommodor?"

Diaz's voice roused Marphissa from a dark reverie of dying warships. She glanced around the bridge, noticing that everyone was quieter than usual as they contemplated the apparently inevitable, then focused back on Diaz. "Yes, Kapitan?"

"Senior Specialist Beltsios has an idea, Kommodor."

Marphissa roused herself fully, tapping her controls to bring up a virtual window showing Beltsios. "What do you have, Senior Specialist?"

"Kommodor," Beltsios said, speaking clearly and carefully, "I understand that you were informed of attempts by Imallye's forces to plant malware in our systems."

"Yes. I was told such attempts were all blocked."

"They were, Kommodor! Are you familiar with the standing instructions we software specialists have always had when encountering non-Syndicate ships?"

Marphissa shook her head, frowning. "You mean standing instructions under the Syndicate? You are still following those?"

"Some of them, Kommodor, that do not conflict with the orders of our president," Beltsios hastened to assure her. "One of those instructions is that when we encounter a ship not under Syndicate control, we are required to test its software defenses to see if it is vulnerable."

Relieved, Marphissa nodded. "There is nothing objectionable about that. It is a good policy. You tested the defenses of Imallye's ships, then? Just as her ships tested ours?"

"Yes, Kommodor, and Imallye's ships were found to have effective defenses against any intrusion attempts on our part." Beltsios paused, concentrating on his next words. "But, I thought, we have copies of the snake software captured at Ulindi. We have employed it defensively against intrusion attempts. The software we were given after Ulindi does not identify itself as offensive. It self-describes as defensive. But could it nonetheless be used offensively against Imallye's ships despite their firewalls and other software defenses?"

Marphissa felt a stirring of hope. "And?"

Beltsios smiled triumphantly. "It is possible, Kommodor. I went into the menus and the code and I dug, looking for eggs and rocks and land mines and treasure chests," he explained, giving the nicknames for various hidden software features, some good, some bad. "And I found something that calls itself Blindfold."

"What does it do?"

"From what I and my coworker can tell, it is an attempt to use our kinds of software weapons to mimic what the enigma worms did to our sensors."

That took a moment to sink in, then Marphissa gave Diaz a startled look. "The enigma worms selectively blinded our sensors so our systems could not see enigma ships. If we can get that into *Vengeance*'s systems—"

She faced Beltsios again. "Can we get it into the battle cruiser's systems?"

"I do not know, Kommodor. I can tell that Blindfold contains the very latest snake tunneling worms. If Imallye's ships do not have defenses against those, they can tunnel through the firewalls."

Diaz gazed at the depiction of *Vengeance* on his display. "Doesn't that require our systems to shake hands with the systems on the battle cruiser? Why would they do that instead of rejecting our attempt to link?"

"It does not require a handshake, Kapitan," Beltsios said confidently. "The tunneling worms and Blindfold itself are contained in the initial contact attempt. When we knock on the battle cruiser's firewall, the firewall's defensive responses will give the worms the openings they need to exploit."

"How did you think to look for that hidden program inside the snake software?" Diaz asked.

"It is a trick used by code monkeys," Beltsios explained. "Hiding something inside another piece of software. Officially, it is never supposed to be done. Under Syndicate instructions," he added quickly. "It is something that software inspectors were always searching for when they audited our systems. So no one thought that snakes would employ it. But, I thought, the snakes always had a visible presence, and a hidden presence, so we would never know when we were being watched. Maybe they would also do that in official software, have an open function and a hidden one, even though their own rules prohibited it."

"Good thinking," Marphissa said. She checked her own display. "Imallye's battle cruiser is twenty-three light seconds from us and closing at an ever-faster rate. Send that software to knock on *Vengeance*'s firewall, and let us see what happens."

"*Vengeance* could have defenses against that generation of tunneling worms, Kommodor," Beltsios said. "It is possible our intrusion attempt will fail."

"It is still a far better option than any other we have," Marphissa said. "Kapitan?"

Diaz nodded. "Senior Specialist Beltsios, attempt the intrusion as soon as possible."

"I understand and will comply!"

As Beltsios's image vanished, Diaz looked suddenly startled and gazed at Marphissa again. "It just occurred to me that even if we manage to blind *Vengeance*, Imallye will still know that we have to leave this star system through the jump point for Iwa. She can keep heading that way while working to clear her sensor systems of the snake worms. She'll get there before us and wait for us like a cat at a mouse hole."

"Damn! Couldn't you have mentioned that thirty seconds ago?" Marphissa demanded. "Call that senior specialist and tell him not to send that knock yet!"

Diaz hastily conveyed the order. "It had not been sent. Senior Specialist Beltsios will hold it ready to send on our command."

"Good." Marphissa frowned, doing the thinking she should have done before too-eagerly ordering the employment of the malware. "Even if we get it into *Vengeance*'s systems, there is no telling how long it would take the code monkeys on the battle cruiser to neutralize the malware. It might take them hours, or only minutes. More likely minutes, if they are any good."

"Then no matter when we send it—"

"Now you are being too pessimistic," Marphissa chided him. "Kapitan, you were quite right that we could not send that malware too soon. We must wait until just the right moment."

"But it might not work, Kommodor," Diaz pointed out.

"Then we are no worse off than before," Marphissa said, thinking that there probably weren't a lot of ways in which they could be worse off. "But if it works, it can give us a small window of opportunity. Thank you for realizing that we must wait to try it and giving us that chance."

"Senior Specialist Beltsios should have told us how limited the effectiveness of that snake malware is," Diaz grumbled, his expression dark.

"Do not blame him," Marphissa said, shaking her head. "He knows nothing of tactics and maneuvers and combat. Not our kind of combat. His job was to provide us with a weapon to use, and he did that. We are the ones who are supposed to know how to best employ that weapon."

She checked her display, focusing on not only the position of *Vengeance* and the battle cruiser's rate of closure but also on *Manticore*'s fuel state. "We're burning through fuel cells, Kapitan. Cease accelerating. Hold our current velocity."

"Kommodor?" Diaz looked and sounded bewildered by the command. "If we cease accelerating in order to conserve fuel cells, the battle cruiser will overtake us quicker."

Marphissa nodded. "And without having built up as much velocity, so our relative speeds will still be fairly close. I want an extended opportunity to engage that battle cruiser, Kapitan. Our hope lies in that."

"You want to be within weapons' range of the battle

cruiser longer? Yes, Kommodor." Though clearly not understanding why, Diaz gave the orders, and *Manticore*'s main
propulsion units cut off with what almost felt like a collective
sigh of relief after the extended period of acceleration. "You
have a plan?"

"I have a plan," Marphissa announced assuredly, knowing that the specialists on the bridge would hear and convey
the news throughout the ship so that *Manticore*'s crew would
feel hope.

Diaz shrugged and smiled. "We all have confidence in
you, Kommodor."

Marphissa smiled herself and leaned back in her seat
again, the very picture of poise on the outside. Inside, she
felt fortunate that no one else aboard the heavy cruiser knew
just how tiny were the odds of success.

But if *Manticore* was destroyed, she would go down
fighting.

CHAPTER SEVEN

"WE will be within range of the battle cruiser's weapons in ten minutes," the senior specialist on the bridge reported.

Marphissa waved an acknowledgment, her hand now encased in the glove of the survival suit she had donned in preparation for battle. Everyone else was wearing a suit as well. The suits were nothing like the heavy battle armor of soldiers, being just strong enough to protect a human from the dangers of space and minor physical hazards if the hull of the ship was pierced by enemy weapons. "Kapitan Diaz, is your ship at maximum combat readiness?"

"Yes, Kommodor," Diaz replied. "All shields at maximum, all crew at combat stations, all weapons ready."

"Good." Marphissa took a long look at her display, trying to estimate when to act given all of the uncertainties that existed. "Order your senior software and systems specialist to transmit the snake software when we are five minutes from being within range of the weapons on *Vengeance*."

"Yes, Kommodor." Diaz passed on the order, then gestured toward his display. "This marker will indicate when the software has been transmitted. Senior Specialist Beltsios has set it to show red if the knock fails, yellow if its status is uncertain, and green when the tunneling worms send back a pulse indicating success. It will remain green as long as the malware is active aboard *Vengeance*."

"Understood." Marphissa reached out to wave an extended finger through her display. "Pivot *Manticore* to face *Vengeance* bow on."

Diaz didn't question that command. It was an expected move prior to combat. Thrusters fired, swinging the heavy cruiser's bow up and over in a smooth arc until more thrusters fired to halt the swing. *Manticore*'s bow, carrying most of her weapons and her strongest shields, now faced the enemy even though the heavy cruiser's velocity in the other direction had not changed. *Vengeance* had been overtaking *Manticore* from both behind and a bit above and to starboard, hanging off that flank of the heavy cruiser and growing steadily larger as the remaining distance between the two warships dwindled.

As she waited through the next minute, Marphissa wondered why, after all her time in space, it still felt odd for the ship she was on to be racing backward at such incredible velocity. As long as the ship was going forward, that felt all right. But backward? It didn't feel right at all.

The symbol marking the status of the snake malware came to life, glowing yellow.

Marphissa kept moving her gaze from the deadly threat of *Vengeance* drawing ever closer to the malware marker that continued to stubbornly display a yellow hue. Was it darkening to red? No. Maybe. No.

"One minute until we are within range of the battle cruiser's weapons," the combat systems specialist announced with a voice that somehow remained steady.

"Kommodor?"

"Wait."

Somewhere aboard *Vengeance*, a different sort of battle was being fought between weapons and defenses carefully crafted by humans from coded pulses of energy. The battle was taking place at an incredible pace as the snake software attacked and the battle cruiser's software tried to parry and block in a fencing match at the speed of light.

"Kommodor," Diaz said urgently, "thirty seconds before *Vengeance* can open fire on us."

"Wait." Was the color of the marker altering yet? No. Yes. Darkening? But which way?

Green.

"Kapitan! Brake *Manticore*'s velocity enough to quickly bring us directly astern of *Vengeance*, then pivot one hundred eighty degrees again and target his main propulsion!"

"Yes, Kommodor!"

Manticore's main propulsion surged to life once more, slowing the ship this time and allowing *Vengeance* to overtake her more rapidly.

Marphissa could not help smiling fiercely as she thought of the scene that must be playing out aboard *Vengeance*. Imallye would have been preparing to give the order to unleash a devastating volley upon *Manticore*, only to see the heavy cruiser suddenly disappear from her display. Imallye would be screaming at her crew right now, demanding that they find out what had happened, demanding that they find out how their target had completely vanished, ordering them to—

Vengeance fired her forward-facing hell lances, a lattice of deadly particle beams that speared through space.

The salvo tore through the spot where *Manticore* would have been if she had not reduced her velocity, then subsequent shots from *Vengeance* began working their way through space farther ahead along that track.

"They think we're trying to accelerate away from them while we're hidden," Diaz said with a laugh. He was wearing the same sort of ferocious grin as Marphissa.

Manticore's main propulsion had cut off as *Vengeance* slid by off to starboard and slightly above the heavy cruiser like a huge shark sailing past a smaller cousin. Usually, space engagements took place at combined velocities so great that the actual combat occurred within a tiny fraction of a second when the opposing forces were within range of each other. But despite the great speed that both *Vengeance* and *Manticore* were traveling, they were going in nearly the same direction, making their relative speed as slow as that of two ground vehicles passing each other.

Diaz brought the heavy cruiser back around so she was once more facing the same direction as she was going, her bow facing toward the stern of the battle cruiser as it came into view at close range. "Main propulsion on full," Diaz ordered. "We want time to put a lot of shots into his tail! All weapons, fire!"

Manticore unleashed a barrage from her own hell lances, launching missiles and, this close to her target, also firing the ball bearings called grapeshot. "Continuous fire!" Diaz called out. "Maintain attack!"

The battle cruiser's stern had the weakest shields and the least armor because of the main propulsion units clustered there. The bow was always supposed to be pivoted to face an enemy. But that couldn't be done when the enemy couldn't be seen.

The hits registering on the stern of *Vengeance* were a clear sign of *Manticore*'s general location, however. Even though the battle cruiser did not yet have a precise target to engage, *Vengeance* ceased hurling hell lance shots into empty space, cut off main propulsion completely, and began firing thrusters to pivot around and face toward the attacks.

But as the battle cruiser's bow began to swing up, the stern remained clearly in sight of *Manticore*. The heavy cruiser's weapons impacted on *Vengeance*'s stern shields with brilliant flares of light that blazed and faded with every blow as the merciless barrage continued. Marphissa, checking the time, was startled to see that barely a minute had passed since *Manticore* opened fire. For those used to typical microsecond-long firing engagements, this one felt incredibly prolonged.

"Enemy shields are almost down," the combat systems specialist reported.

"Their turn rate is increasing, but we'll still be able to hit his stern for another two minutes before it swings out of our line of sight. How much longer do we have before *Vengeance* can see us again?" Diaz wondered, his eyes locked on his display to monitor the attack.

"We won't need much longer," Marphissa said.

"Hell lance batteries are beginning to overheat," the weapons systems specialist warned.

Marphissa breathed another one of the prayers that Bradamont had told her. Designed for fights of very short duration, the particle beam weapons could not sustain firing for long periods. If they overheated enough and shut down too soon *Manticore* would lose critical weapons capability.

That was just one of her concerns. Was the green malware marker changing color? Not yet. Marphissa blinked rapidly, trying to spot the first trace of change in hue.

The stern shields on the battle cruiser collapsed. *Manticore*'s shots began impacting the ship, slamming into *Vengeance*'s main propulsion units and in some cases triggering secondary explosions.

"Hit them!" someone on the bridge whispered exultantly.

Marphissa stared intently at the malware status marker. Had the green shade flickered? There it was again. "Kapitan, continue your attack with any weapons that can bear on the enemy but get this ship turned and start braking hard!"

Diaz clearly wanted to keep landing blows on the enemy, but hesitated for only a fraction of a second before calling out orders. *Manticore*'s main propulsion cut off again. *Vengeance*, though pivoting now as fast as the thrusters could bring the battle cruiser around, was still rocketing forward at undiminished velocity. The distance had already opened enough that *Manticore*'s grapeshot was no longer effective, but the heavy cruiser kept throwing out missiles as fast as the launchers could reload and firing any hell lance whose projector could bear on the enemy as *Manticore*'s bow swung through another half turn.

Facing away from her foe once more, *Manticore* lit off her main propulsion and began reducing velocity as fast as the ship and crew could endure. The inertial dampers shrilled protests again as red stress warnings pulsed on displays and the heavy cruiser's structure groaned under the conflicting forces that threatened to shatter it.

Marphissa, her head once again pressed against the back of her seat by momentum forces leaking through the inertial damper fields as *Manticore* labored to slow down, saw the malware marker abruptly turn as red as the stress warnings. Seconds later, *Vengeance*, bow pointing straight up relative to *Manticore*, began firing the hell lances that could target the heavy cruiser astern, following those with a stream of missiles that rolled and spun onto intercepts aimed at the heavy cruiser.

With the distance between the two warships now increasing rapidly, *Manticore* dropped out of range of the battle cruiser's hell lances after only a few shots had been fired, flaring against *Manticore*'s shields and weakening them but not breaking through. Marphissa breathed a sigh of relief as the chance of a full volley of *Vengeance*'s hell lances slamming home vanished. But the missiles were another matter.

"Target incoming missiles with hell lances and grapeshot," Diaz ordered, his face reflecting the strain that the entire crew was feeling as *Manticore* continued to brake velocity at a rate that was producing increasingly urgent warnings from the ship's systems.

With *Manticore*'s stern facing toward the rapidly receding *Vengeance* as the heavy cruiser reduced speed, few weapons could engage the oncoming missiles. Diaz opened his mouth to give a command.

"Hold your current vector and propulsion settings," Marphissa ordered.

Diaz gulped as if swallowing his unspoken command before replying. "Yes, Kommodor."

"Stand by for maneuvers, Kapitan. Keep your combat systems targeted on those incoming missiles, and remember that maneuver that Captain Bradamont showed us against the Syndicate warships."

Marphissa waited for the right moment, watching as the missiles tore closer, hoping she had learned enough from watching and listening to Bradamont. "Main propulsion off!"

Diaz repeated the order, but Marphissa's command was already being carried out. *Manticore*'s propulsion units ceased laboring to lower her velocity. Her speed unchecked now, the warship was moving faster than if she had kept slowing down. The incoming missiles, aiming to hit the heavy cruiser where she would have been if she had kept braking, were now aiming for a point behind where *Manticore* was.

Two missiles passed close enough to *Manticore* for their proximity fuses to detonate. The warship shuddered as the shock waves of particles and shrapnel slammed into her shields, but the shields held. The rest of the missiles shot past the heavy cruiser and labored to turn fast enough to reengage their target. Most of those missiles disintegrated as their structures failed under the stress of the too-rapid maneuvers. The few that survived were almost at a standstill relative to *Manticore* when they came out of their turns, and having raced past the heavy cruiser were now facing *Manticore*'s heavily armed bow. Hell lances tore into them and wiped out the remaining missiles.

"We are out of range of *Vengeance*'s weapons," the combat systems specialist announced, sounding dazed.

Marphissa could see the battle cruiser on her display, the massive warship still pivoting under the push of her own thrusters to face back fully toward *Manticore*. "I need an assessment of damage to *Vengeance*'s main propulsion units."

"Preliminary estimate from our sensors is that *Vengeance* has lost eighty percent of her main propulsion," the senior watch specialist said.

"Eighty percent?" Marphissa felt herself finally beginning to relax. "And he got his velocity up to nearly point three five light speed before we clipped his wings. With that much momentum, that much mass, and only one-fifth of his normal propulsion working, it's going to take *Vengeance* a long time to slow down again."

Diaz was working on his maneuvering display. "Our systems say *Vengeance* won't be able to get his velocity down to reengage us before overshooting the jump point. We can just keep going, following *Vengeance* at a distance, until we reach the jump point after he overruns it. Imallye's light cruisers and HuKs back at the planet's orbit are so far out of position they couldn't catch us unless we dropped our velocity to the pace of a CEO going to hand out bonuses to workers." He put up one hand to rub his forehead, smiling in disbelief. "Your plan was a good one, Kommodor."

"I'm certain that you never doubted me," Marphissa replied dryly, then smiled as well to take any sting out of the words.

Diaz squinted at his display again. "Our engineering specialists are saying that while we did extensive damage to the main propulsion on *Vengeance*, none of it was extreme because the battle cruiser was able to shift her stern out of a direct line with our incoming fire. They believe that the damage can be repaired without wholesale replacing of those units once the battle cruiser reaches an orbital dock. That won't be until long after we leave Moorea, of course. Granaile Imallye is going to be very unhappy."

"I imagine she is already very unhappy."

The message that arrived from *Vengeance* several minutes later confirmed Marphissa's guess. Imallye wasn't sprawled in her seat this time but sitting rigidly, her eyes lit with a cold fury that chilled Marphissa even across the many thousands of kilometers already separating the two warships.

"I underestimated you, Kommodor," Imallye said, her voice as frigid as the breath of space. "I will not do so again. Your tricks will not save you the next time I encounter you. Nor will tricks save CEO Iceni. When you get back to Midway, tell your *president* that the fate she long ago earned by her actions will soon be visited upon her and *anyone* who dares to follow her orders."

The transmission cut off. *That was rude,* Marphissa thought, then almost laughed at the absurdity of that characterization of the message after the brutal threats contained in it. *What the hell.* She did laugh, drawing surprised looks and then smiles from Diaz and the rest of the crew on the bridge. "Get us back on a clean vector to the jump point for Iwa, Kapitan. We don't appear to be welcome in Moorea Star System!"

Even with the long acceleration, chase, and a battle in which everyone had continued to head at very high velocity in the direction of the jump point, it still took two more days of travel, including the time spent braking *Manticore*'s velocity down to point two light speed, to reach the jump point. The sensors on the heavy cruiser had been able to spot a lot of activity on the outer hull of *Vengeance* as her crew labored to repair enough main propulsion to allow another fight. But Syndicate warships were designed efficiently, which meant not enough crew to repair battle damage, little repair training for a crew expected to simply swap out broken black boxes with new ones, and not enough spares or other parts aboard to do such extensive repairs even if the necessary men and women had been available. Surprisingly, *Vengeance* did manage to get one of the damaged main propulsion units working again despite all of those hindrances, but by the time that happened *Manticore* was on final approach to the jump point and *Vengeance* had already rocketed helplessly past that point despite all attempts to reduce velocity.

In the privacy of her stateroom, Marphissa prepared a final transmission aimed at *Vengeance*, ensuring that there was no trace of gloating or amusement in her expression or her voice. "Honored Granaile Imallye, I regret that our first encounter has involved hostilities. On behalf of President Iceni, I once again extend the hand of friendship to you and urge you to contact her peacefully for negotiations. Whatever past events lie between you, I assure you that President Iceni is no longer the person who did you such a wrong. I also assure you that should you come to Midway Star System with hostile intent, neither you nor any of your warships will survive. Iwa Star System offers a clear and ugly example of what the enigma race intends doing to every human-occupied star system. You can see it for yourself and know that the threat is real. We can face that threat together, to the benefit of all. For the people, Marphissa, out."

She relaxed as the transmission ended, leaning back to gaze at the hatch to her stateroom. As was common with Syndicate warships, that hatch was both armored and outfitted with alarms, because their own subordinates were feared by Syndicate bosses almost as much as the enemy. But the defenses increasingly felt to Marphissa like anachronisms, souvenirs from another time, no longer needed when the crew was motivated by belief in what they fought for and loyalty to their leaders rather than terror of the consequences of failure or insubordination. Imallye's grudge against President Iceni, no matter how well justified it might be, was also an anachronism, rooted in the past.

The past could not justify destroying the future Iceni was creating.

"Kommodor?" Diaz called down from the bridge. "*Manticore* will reach the jump point for Iwa in five minutes."

"You have permission to jump when ready," Marphissa said. She activated her stateroom's display and sat watching it until the stars disappeared and were replaced by the gray nothingness of jump space.

MARPHISSA had *Manticore* once more at full combat readiness when the heavy cruiser left jump space. But there was no sign anywhere in Iwa Star System of the enigmas. Iwa was still a lifeless graveyard whose markers were debris floating between worlds and the craters pockmarking the surface of those worlds. If the aliens had returned, they had apparently departed again already.

"Head straight for the jump point for Midway?" Diaz asked.

She paused to consider the question, studying her display.

Nothing visible. But . . . "Do you remember that the humans captured by the enigmas were confined inside an asteroid?"

"Yes." Diaz gestured to his display. "But we would spot that. There would be waste heat that could not be hidden."

"Maybe." Marphissa shook her head, not sure why she was feeling uncertain. "But the enigmas hide themselves. They hide everything. We can't take time to tour this star system looking closely at every object, though. President Iceni needs to be informed about what has happened here and at Moorea. Take us to the jump point, but route our path through the star system instead of skirting along the edge. That will bring us closer to many of the objects orbiting Iwa, though still a long ways from many others. Make sure our sensors look over every object in this star system as best they are capable for any signs of anything amiss."

"Yes, Kommodor. I will ensure the specialists are alert."

Another long transit through space, this one longer than necessary because of Marphissa's orders to take a more lengthy transit that swung through the inner planets and past the star, but unmarked by any events or tension except for the need to get home. Marphissa checked at random intervals on the specialists on watch and found them always attentive to their displays, but no one reported anything and none of the automated scans reported anything unexpected.

Until they were an hour from their closest point of approach to the world where most of the Syndicate presence had been before the enigmas destroyed everything.

"Kapitan?" One of the specialists spoke with growing worry evident in her voice. "There is something happening on that planet where the Syndicate city was located."

"Something?" Diaz prodded. "Show me."

"What our sensors are seeing is very subtle, Kapitan."

"Show me."

"Yes, Kapitan."

Marphissa watched as Diaz studied his display with a frown of puzzlement. "What am I seeing?" he finally asked the specialist. "What do these indications mean? They are barely detectable by our sensors."

"Show me as well," Marphissa ordered.

The data that appeared on a magnified image of that world didn't mean anything to Marphissa, either. But she did see that it clustered near the large craters that were the grave markers for the mostly buried Syndicate city which had been totally destroyed by enigma bombardment.

"We haven't had a good look until now at that location on that world during this transit because of the planet's position relative to our track," the specialist explained. "But we are now only about ten light minutes from the planet, which is approaching our track as it orbits Iwa, and we can get a clear view of the planet as it rotates."

"What are we seeing now that we can see it?" Marphissa asked.

"I believe," the specialist said cautiously, "that this data indicates substantial subsurface activity. From this distance, with our sensors, we would only detect large-scale events deep beneath the surface of the planet."

"Large-scale events?" Marphissa questioned. "Do you mean earthquakes? Triggered by all of the impacts of enigma bombardment projectiles on that world?"

"No, Kommodor." Some of the data reports glowed a little brighter. "These indicators show regular variations. That would mean they are artificial."

"Artificial?" Marphissa felt a glow of hope. "Some of the people here survived the enigma attack by going deep? I didn't think Syndicate shelters could have ridden out impacts of the size that struck that area."

"No, Kommodor," the specialist said. "They should not have. Any Syndicate shelters, even deep ones, should have been pulverized."

"Then who is digging—" Diaz began irritably. He stopped speaking, his face going rigid. "Or should I be asking *what* is digging very deep on that planet?"

"We may be detecting enigma subsurface activity," the specialist said in a rush. "A very large amount of subsurface activity."

Marphissa exhaled slowly, feeling a coldness that was

not born of any life support fluctuation. "Just as we feared. They're establishing a base. In a place where we couldn't see any trace of it, their work and any excavated materials hidden by the devastation where they tore that part of the planet to hell."

"No surface facilities at all?" Diaz asked, bewildered.

"I told you. It's consistent with what Black Jack's fleet saw in enigma space. Captain Bradamont and I have talked about it," Marphissa said. "She said the enigmas hide *everything* as much as they can from any possible observation."

Diaz nodded, rubbing his chin as he gazed at the apparently innocuous data. "I once saw the Syndicate base at Kure. An entire moon hollowed out. If the enigmas want to construct a major base deep beneath the surface of that planet, and if they have automated construction capabilities anything like ours, they could do it. Any surface accesses, even ones big enough for a battleship, could be concealed."

"And that fool Imallye is planning to set up shop here as well!" Marphissa said. "If they don't check things out thoroughly, or if the enigmas have finished their major excavations by the time Imallye's forces arrive, Imallye might be oblivious to the fact that she's sharing this star system with an enigma force that could wipe out her base at any time with no warning!"

She spun to look at the specialist who had spoken up and was still watching Marphissa and Diaz to see how her report would be received. "Well done. Very well done. You spotted that subtle data and you interpreted it well. Kapitan Diaz, this specialist deserves a promotion."

"I understand and will comply," Diaz said, making the old, fearful Syndicate response sound like a pleasant tasking. "Can we bomb that enigma base out of existence?"

"We can't, not with the bombardment projectiles that *Manticore* carries. They're not big enough to get at something as deep as the enigmas apparently are. And I don't want to tip off the enigmas that we've spotted their work by tossing some futile rocks their way. As for whether any of our mobile forces can do the trick, I don't know. We might need a big asteroid to do enough damage, and that would require a while to divert and reach the planet. We will inform President Iceni. She will decide."

Marphissa gazed at her display, morose. She perfectly understood the uncertainty of the specialist who had reported the indications of enigma activity on that planet. No one wanted to be the one to inform the boss of a problem. Sure, Marphissa had survived Imallye's attack at Moorea, but she would be returning with news that the Syndicate presence at Iwa Star System had been wiped out by the enigmas, that Granaile Imallye had refused offers of cooperation, threatened Iceni herself, and attacked *Manticore*, and that the enigmas were busy constructing a major base at Iwa. *If I was bringing this much and this kind of bad news back to a Syndicate superior, I'd be expecting to be sent to a labor camp for being the bearer of unwelcome information. President Iceni won't do that. But I have let her down. Instead of returning with good news, I am going to be a herald of many dangers.*

She was roused from feeling sorry for herself by an urgent tone that drew Marphissa's attention back to her display. She stared at it in disbelief. "Is that a pickup signal?"

"Yes, Kommodor," the senior specialist confirmed. "It is coming from the same planet on which the enigma construction is under way, not too many kilometers from the craters that mark the former site of the Syndicate city."

"An enigma trick," Diaz scoffed. "It must be."

"Why would they be calling our attention to that planet?" Marphissa wondered. "How directional is that pickup signal?" she asked the comm specialist.

"It is aimed at us," the specialist said. "They are highly directional signals."

"How would someone on that planet, assuming they survived, know that we were out here?" Diaz demanded.

"Sir, if it is standard Syndicate ground forces armor, then it would automatically scan overhead for any visible activity. The visual sensors on ground armor would be capable of spotting the movement of this ship across the heavens when we drew close enough."

"Could that armor identify us?" Marphissa asked.

"No, Kommodor. Not from that range. It would only know that we were an artificial object. A ship."

She rubbed her chin and stared at her display, knowing that the next move was entirely up to her. A human might have survived on that planet and be signaling for help. Even if he or she or they had access to extra power supplies for their armor they must be near to exhausting those, and once their armor was out of power they would surely die on the surface of what had always been an inhospitable world. Their armor had seen a ship in space and, desperate, they had signaled for help, assuming or hoping that it was a human ship.

If she were still Syndicate, Marphissa knew exactly what would be expected of her. Do not risk the unit by heading into what might well be a trap. Do not risk the mission by risking loss of the ship. Whichever workers had survived on that planet were not worth diverting her ship's track. Maybe they had important intelligence, but if so she could send a signal back ordering their battle armor to automatically upload all information their systems had accumulated. With that information in hand, she could proceed on her way without risking *Manticore*.

But she wasn't Syndicate anymore, and never had been in her heart.

"What do you think?" she asked Diaz in a quiet voice.

Diaz inhaled deeply, blew out the breath, then answered in the same low tones. "Odds are it is a trap. No one has ever been recovered from a world occupied by the enigmas."

"But the Syndicate could never mount recovery operations," Marphissa said. "Eventually, any humans left on an enigma-occupied world would be run down and killed, but they could have remained hidden for a while. Planets look tiny from up here, but to someone on the surface a world is a very big place."

"It would be dangerous to get close to that world," Diaz pointed out. "We don't know what sort of hidden defenses the enigmas might have already installed."

"Shouldn't we try to find out? That would be very important to know."

"It would," Diaz agreed. "But how do we lift anyone off the surface? We don't have a shuttle. I can take *Manticore* into atmosphere, but there is no way of landing a heavy cruiser on a planet's surface unless you crash it."

Marphissa pondered that problem, feeling relieved that there seemed to be no way to save that person, but also feeling guilty to be relieved about it. "If there's no means of—"

"Wait." Diaz grimaced. "My pardon, Kommodor. I just thought of something. The tow cable."

"The tow cable?" Marphissa took a moment to understand what he meant. Heavy cruisers, battleships, and battle cruisers were all equipped with long cables that could be hooked to other warships that had been crippled by enemy fire, allowing those damaged ships to be towed back to a repair facility. Even the efficiency-obsessed Syndicate bureaucracy had decided that the costs of tow cables were more than offset by the savings from recovering warships that otherwise would have had to be abandoned. "We could hover low enough for the cable to be just above the surface . . . How long is it?"

"Half a kilometer."

"Half a kilometer," she repeated, thinking of a heavy cruiser coming within half a kilometer of a planet's surface. "Is that idea even technically feasible?"

"I'll have to have my specialists run the numbers on it," Diaz said. "The atmosphere on that world is thin, so it might be possible if we cut our velocity down to a crawl. But it would be very risky, Kommodor."

"I know." She looked past her display to the blank bulkhead beyond it, thinking. "When Black Jack's fleet went into enigma territory, they learned that Syndicate citizens were prisoners inside an asteroid and they rescued them. At great risk, they rescued Syndicate citizens and brought them home."

"It was Black Jack," Diaz said. "He is for the people, even though he is Alliance."

"Can we do less than an Alliance fleet?" Marphissa asked. "Can we abandon whoever is on that planet, when Black Jack would go there and somehow rescue them? We are no longer Syndicate. There are people there who need our help."

"Would you risk this entire crew to save one man or woman?" Diaz asked.

"Yes!" Marphissa nodded firmly. "Have your specialists analyze the proposal, Kapitan. While they are doing so, alter our vector to intercept that world in its orbit."

"Yes, Kommodor. We will have to brake as we near orbit, so it will take two and a half hours to reach a point above where that recall signal came from."

Two and a half hours to second-guess her decision. As *Manticore*'s thrusters and main propulsion pushed her into a new vector, Marphissa looked at the depiction of the planet they were now directly approaching. If the enigmas deep under that world's surface were keeping track of events above it, as surely they must be, then they would know that the human warship was now heading their way.

"They are hiding," she said to Diaz. "The enigmas don't want us to know they are there. Even if they detected the pickup signal sent to us, they will not want to do anything to tip us off that they are digging inside that planet. So they will stay quiet, watching, and waiting for us to go away."

"I hope you are right, Kommodor," Diaz said.

Half an hour later, the specialists rendered their verdicts on the plan. "It is possible," Diaz reported to Marphissa. "My specialists recommend that we program in the task and allow our automated maneuvering systems to handle everything inside atmosphere, because no one on this ship has experience with maneuvering so close to a planet's surface."

"The idea of hovering half a kilometer from the surface

of a planet terrifies me," Marphissa confessed. "It is within safe operating parameters for the ship?"

"Yes, Kommodor." Diaz checked his display again where the report was visible. "Our main propulsion is so powerful it can easily hold the ship in a hover above a planet of this size. The main fear is making some imprecise adjustment from which we would not have room to recover, but that should not happen with the automated systems controlling the approach to the surface and the hover."

Marphissa pointed to part of the report. "This is the only way to do it? Have them latch on to the tow cable, haul everything back out of atmosphere, then bring in the cable?"

"Yes, Kommodor. We can't bring in the cable while main propulsion is going, and we can't shut off main propulsion until we get back into orbit."

She sighed heavily. "Let us hope that citizen, or those citizens, have intact armor or survival suits. Can we rig anything on the cable to make it easier for them to hang on?"

Diaz nodded. "My people are putting together a . . . well, it's a cage. We'll fasten it to the end of the cable. Whoever is down there will have to grab the cage and climb inside."

"This is crazy," Marphissa said. "You're thinking that, too, aren't you?"

"I would never tell a superior officer that her plan is crazy," Diaz said. "I would tell her if I thought it could not be done. We will be sitting ducks, though. If the enigmas choose to attack us while we are inside atmosphere, our velocity will be limited to speeds far below what we normally use."

Marphissa frowned in thought. "When we reach the planet, I want to do some orbits before descending into atmosphere. Do some high passes, then some low ones, as if we are looking for any sign of the enigmas and *want* to provoke a reaction."

"Then when we go into atmosphere they will think that's just another attempt to get them to show themselves?" Diaz shrugged. "That might work. But it assumes the enigmas think like humans."

"Captain Bradamont told me that staying hidden was the number one priority for enigmas," Marphissa said. "I don't pretend to know why that is, but as long as I know that is how they tend to act, I can use it."

Manticore reached the planet and went into high orbit, swinging around the globe as if conducting an intensive search. And, indeed, that was happening, as the warship's sensors strained to spot any sign of whoever had sent the pickup request.

"Let's go closer in," Marphissa ordered. "Is the cage ready?" she asked Diaz.

"Yes, Kommodor. It is securely attached. I inspected the cage myself. It will hold under expected stress conditions."

Manticore slowed and dropped lower, skimming the upper atmosphere of the planet. As the heavy cruiser passed over the region where the pickup signal had originated, an alert sounded.

"We have the signal again," the comm specialist said. "A burst transmission. Our systems have localized its origin within a twenty-kilometer radius."

"Can we see anything?" Diaz asked, chewing his lip.

"No, Kapitan," the senior specialist reported. "There is dust and atmospheric interference."

"What about the indications of subsurface activity?" Marphissa asked.

"They ceased while we were still approaching the planet, Kommodor. We are detecting nothing artificial on the planet at this time except for the pickup signal."

"The enigmas are hiding, as we hoped, trying not to betray any sign of their presence. Take us around one more time," Marphissa ordered Diaz. "Then begin descent into atmosphere, aimed for a point at the center of the estimated position of that signal."

CHAPTER EIGHT

DIAZ nodded, eyeing his display as one of his hands moved to set the location for the descent. "I will transfer full control to the maneuvering systems in twenty minutes, Kommodor."

"Comm specialist," Marphissa said. "Be prepared to contact the source of the pickup signal."

"Yes, Kommodor," she replied. "I have the necessary commands already loaded and ready to transmit, but it is likely the Syndicate battle armor will refuse to link with our systems, and the people down there may not know how to override that. But we will be able to establish a voice link and use that to precisely establish their position."

"Excellent."

Marphissa leaned back, trying to look relaxed and confident, as *Manticore* finished most of another orbit and began braking, lowering her velocity to levels her hull would withstand inside the planet's atmosphere. The heavy cruiser dropped toward the planet, her path a long curve heading downward and around the globe toward the point where the signal had originated.

Kapitan Diaz sat, both hands gripping his seat's arms as if trying to ensure he would not reflexively enter a manual maneuvering command. "If I pretend our display is just zooming in on the planet's surface," he said, "it's a lot easier to handle than if I think about us actually going this deep into atmosphere."

"We're barely moving," Marphissa heard one of the specialists whisper to another. "Look. Our velocity is being measured in *hundreds* of kilometers per *hour*."

"Try the link," Diaz ordered the comm specialist.

She entered the command. "We're not getting a link back, Kapitan. Request permission to go to voice comms."

"Permission granted."

The specialist began sending. "Whoever is requesting pickup, we need you to establish your position by answering our transmission. Comply. We require a signal to find you. Comply."

After several iterations, an answer came, weak and riddled with static. *"Almost out of power,"* the reply murmured. *"Three of us. Where is shuttle?"*

"Three," Diaz said in amazement. "Give me the comm link. This is the commanding officer of the heavy cruiser. We do not have a shuttle. We are bringing our unit down to within half a kilometer of the surface and extending a cable. You must go to where that cable reaches the surface and climb into the cage attached to the end."

"Cannot go far . . ."

"Continue to transmit and we will drop that cable as close to you as possible."

"We are ten kilometers from the surface," the senior specialist reported. "But the distance readings are fluctuating."

Marphissa checked them and laughed slightly. "That's because we're traveling over the surface of a planet and what you're seeing are altitude readings. Whenever we pass over a higher part of the planet the distance to the surface gets shorter for that reason alone, and past that high part the distance gets longer on its own."

"That . . . is odd to see, Kommodor. Distance to surface now seven kilometers."

Marphissa looked at the image of the surface below and

was surprised by the sensation of speed as the ship dropped lower with a velocity still in the hundreds of kilometers per hour. The mostly desert terrain beneath the warship appeared to be whipping past below at a disconcerting rate.

"Three kilometers."

"I really hope we don't have to go to manual maneuvering," Diaz said, holding his hands back and away from the controls. "I'm afraid to touch anything."

"Tow cable is being payed out. One point four kilometers remaining to surface."

"Huge . . . fire . . ."

"That must be what we look like to them beneath us," Marphissa said, trying to keep her breathing even. "They're looking up and seeing our main propulsion pointed almost straight at them."

Thrusters fired on automatic, gently nudging *Manticore* to try to position the end of the cable at the same point where the signal was now pinpointed.

"Half a kilometer," the senior specialist said, his voice a little unsteady. "End of cable has made contact with the surface."

"Get to the cable!" Diaz transmitted. "Can you see it? Get to the cable and get inside the cage. We can't hold this position very long."

"Understand . . . comply . . ."

"We've got visual," a specialist announced. "Three figures. Syndicate ground forces armor. They are moving toward the cable."

The motion of the three figures below, stumbling over broken ground and rocks, felt glacial. "How long are they going to take to get there?" Diaz grumbled.

Marphissa tore her eyes from the three figures and scanned her display for any sign that the enigmas were reacting. But this close to the surface *Manticore*'s sensors could observe only a tiny part of the planet. "With any luck, the enigma sensors are focused on objects in orbit and can't see us when we're this low."

"One in." *Manticore* shuddered, thrusters firing again. "Something shoved us."

"Wind," Diaz said. "Let's hope it doesn't pick up."

The remaining two figures were racing after the cage, which dragged along the surface as *Manticore* was blown around. They caught it, and a second one boosted into the cage.

The warship lurched again, sliding sideways, the motion transmitted to the cable below. Once again, the third figure ran after it, stumbling over rocks, the other two reaching out and down.

"Come on," Diaz breathed. "Do it!"

One of those in the cage got an armored hand locked onto the third figure and began pulling it in, assisted by the second.

A bigger gust of wind hit, twisting and pushing *Manticore*.

Down below, the third figure clung desperately to the outside of the cage as it skittered and bounced over rocks. Either by accident or design, one bounce brought the soldier up and over to fall on top of the other two inside the cage.

"Get us out of here, Kapitan," Marphissa ordered.

Diaz reached with great care to touch the control that would start the automated maneuvers for bringing *Manticore* up out of atmosphere.

Marphissa, accustomed to the heavy cruiser leaping under the thrust of her main propulsion, had to grit her teeth in frustration as the warship rose at what felt like an incredibly gentle rate. But she could see the hull stress and temperature readings that told her that even at this apparently slow acceleration the heavy cruiser was going as fast as could be dared inside even the thin atmosphere of this planet.

After what felt like an eternity but was only a few minutes, the sky around *Manticore* changed from a disturbing shade of blue to the familiar black of space.

"Anything from the planet?" Marphissa demanded as the

ship rose high enough to view a large chunk of the world once more.

"Nothing, Kommodor. No indications of enigma activity."

"Coming into orbit," Diaz said. "Not stable yet, but the thrusters can handle any problems."

"Good. Shut off main propulsion and bring in that cable."

Once again, a fairly quick process felt like it took forever. As the cage at the end of the cable neared *Manticore*, crew members in survival suits went out to collect the three soldiers and disconnect the cage. The soldiers were hauled along the hull to the nearest air lock, while the cage was shoved down toward the planet to vaporize during an uncontrolled descent to the surface.

"They're inside," Diaz reported. "Air-lock outer hatch sealed. Towing cable recovered and locked down."

"Get us out of here, Kapitan," Marphissa said. "Take us to the jump point for Midway, and don't waste any time getting there. I'm going to see our new guests."

"Yes, Kommodor!"

Marphissa, bracing herself against the surge of acceleration as *Manticore* whipped out of orbit and headed for the jump point, walked carefully off the bridge.

To her surprise, she heard cheers breaking out through the ship. No words were identifiable, just sounds of jubilation. A group of specialists on their way to their watch stations saluted her, grinning broadly. "We did it, Kommodor! Thank you, Kommodor!"

She could not help smiling back as she returned the salutes. It did feel good right now.

The rescued soldiers were packed into the small compartment that served as a medical office aboard the heavy cruiser. They were still being helped out of their armor by unusually solicitous crew members who commonly expressed disdain for their ground forces counterparts. But now there was none of that rivalry.

The three soldiers, two men and one woman, were thin,

with haunted, confused eyes. "They look like hell," Marphissa said to the senior medical specialist who was examining them. All three had already had med packs slapped on their arms, the packs providing intravenous nourishment, fluid replacement, and antishock drugs.

"They're in awful shape, Kommodor," the medical specialist paused to report.

"Keep working," Marphissa said. "Brief me as you work."

"Yes, Kommodor," the medical specialist replied gratefully, maintaining the formal tones of an official report as he continued working. "Living in battle armor for so long is stressful under the best of conditions. They were also conserving energy, and their available food and water, and running their armor life support on filters that should have been cleaned or replaced long before."

"Are any of them in danger?"

The specialist paused to consider the question. "No, Kommodor. Not now that they are receiving proper care. They will require extensive recovery time."

The soldiers, though dazed, had slowly shifted their gazes to Marphissa and appeared to have realized that she was a superior. All three began trying to rise from their seats and come to attention. "Sit down!" Marphissa ordered, and the three instantly dropped back down. "Report."

One of the men blinked, then began reciting a standard Syndicate accounting for himself. "Capek, Katsuo, Worker Third Class, First Squad, Eighth Platoon, Third Company, Nine Hundred Seventy-First Ground Forces Brigade. Immediate Superior Worker First Class Adalberto Horgens. Unit Commander—"

"Enough." Marphissa looked at the other two. "Your names and ranks, only."

"Dinapoli, Mbali, Worker Fourth Class," the woman said.

"Keesler . . . Padraig . . . Worker Fourth . . . Class," the second man managed to recite. He was in the worst shape of the three, his eyes having trouble focusing on Marphissa.

Marphissa looked at Capek, who was watching her with a bewildered expression as he tried to figure out her rank from her uniform. "What happened?"

"Honored, um—"

"Do not worry about titles. Just tell me what happened."

Capek blinked again, but with a clear order to follow he managed to rally his thoughts. "We were on a wide patrol . . . checking out areas far from Iwa City Complex. Our orders were to search for . . . for . . . anything out of the ordinary. My supervisor told me that we were searching for . . . infiltrators. On the third day of our patrol, we received an emergency alert that hostile forces had entered the star system. We were ordered to . . . return to Iwa Complex to defend the city. Two hours later, we were ordered to hold positions and . . . prepare to ride out orbital bombardment."

He stopped, his gaze on Marphissa growing troubled. "Are we prisoners, honored . . . ?"

"No," Marphissa said. "My ship, our forces, did not attack Iwa. What happened after you received orders to dig in?"

"Our unit commander told us to head away from the city. Get as far away as we could, he said. All units were . . . dispersing." Capek paused, trying unsuccessfully to swallow and continue his report.

"We got far enough out." The woman took up the tale, her voice thin with exhaustion. "We saw the rocks come down and felt the impacts, saw the flashes and the debris clouds even from as far away as we were. All comms lost. We could not contact anyone. Worker First Class Horgens ordered us to head back toward the city." She paused, her face twitching. "Toward where the city had been. We would fight to the death, he said."

Capek managed to start speaking again. "We traveled for over a day, on foot. It got very hard when we hit the bombardment zone. Very hard." He appeared to be about to cry. "They destroyed . . . everything. We saw their ships coming down. Not like ours. Not Alliance."

"Like turtles?" Marphissa prodded. "Big turtle shapes?"

"Yes," the woman soldier agreed. "Different sizes. They came down. Worker Horgens led us toward them."

"Dispersed column formation," Capek said. "Standard dispersed column formation. Horgens was in center. Then . . . his head exploded. We went to ground. Others dying. We could see. I realized our links . . . were . . . being . . . targeted. I told Di—Dinapoli and K—Keesler, only two near to me, to kill links. Total elec . . . tronic silence." He stopped again, staring at nothing but clearly seeing the slaughter of his comrades.

"You three survived," Marphissa said, "because you went totally passive. Did you see the enemy?"

Capek focused back on Marphissa as if momentarily uncertain of where he was, then shook his head. "Long-range smart rounds . . . I think. Nobody close to see us. They came much later, we are certain. To take away bodies."

The woman spoke once more. "We didn't move for . . . an hour? Then Worker Capek said we should get spare power packs and rations off the dead. We would need them. But don't take packs already plugged in. If the enemy saw armor had been looted . . . they would come looking for us."

"That was smart, Worker Capek," Marphissa said. "You've been hiding since then?"

"Hiding, watching their ships come and go. No ships for a while, though." Capek's eyes went distant again for a moment. "Long time. Lying quiet, conserving power. Not transmitting. Cold. Air getting bad. Not enough water, food. Make it last. Someone will come. Someone will come."

She thought about how many days those soldiers had spent suffering and in fear, nursing a wild hope that rescue would arrive. Marphissa looked over them again, seeing how thin they were, their badly cracked lips, the bleeding skin sores from their long time in Syndicate armor, the eyes that twitched around as if expecting to wake and discover that this was a dream. "How did they manage to run to the cage?" she asked the medical specialist.

He shrugged. "In extreme conditions, people find strength

sometimes. They knew if they didn't get in that cage they would die."

"But they will be all right now?"

"It will take some time, Kommodor. I will soon sedate them and strap them down, because"—he tapped his head—"nightmares come, you know. After this sort of thing. Nightmares come."

"I know." She stood up, stopping with a stern gesture the automatic attempts by the three soldiers to rise again as well. "You will rest now. You are safe. I will speak with you again when you are better."

Capek tried to stand yet again despite his unsteadiness, and shakily recited the standard Syndicate Acceptance of Responsibility. "This worker is responsible for the failure. My coworkers did not—"

"There was no failure," Marphissa said.

"You came," the woman said. "You came for the CEO. We failed to—"

"We came for you."

"But . . . we're just workers."

"You are our comrades," Marphissa said. "We do not leave anyone behind."

As she walked back toward her stateroom to try to get some rest, Marphissa realized that was why the crew had cheered. It wasn't simply that they had plucked three soldiers away from certain death, it was that those soldiers were "just workers." They hadn't been saved because they were high-ranking executives or CEOs. The risk had been run, the chance taken, even though the objects of the rescue were "just workers."

The Syndicate never would have approved such an operation, Marphissa knew. It wouldn't have been cost-effective. The risks would have been out of proportion to the possible gains, as precisely calculated in spreadsheets that assigned the same sort of carefully calibrated values to human beings as they did to pieces of equipment. The workers would have been left to their fates, slowly dying as they waited in vain for rescue.

It surprised her to realize that it had never occurred to

her that the person or persons who needed to be picked up from the planet might be "just workers." That simply hadn't mattered.

She reached her stateroom and closed the hatch, falling gratefully onto her bunk fully clothed, and thinking that maybe, perhaps, it would be possible to overcome much of the toxic influence she and everyone else aboard *Manticore* had inherited from their years as servants to the Syndicate.

MARPHISSA could not really relax until *Manticore* finally entered jump en route Midway. They had only been intermittently able to see the portion of the planet where the enigmas had been working, but during those periods no activity could be detected. Either the enigmas were continuing to lie low until the human warship was gone, or the distance to the planet had grown too great to spot the small surface indications of the work deep underground.

"I tell you," Diaz commented, "I was expecting some enigma warships to pop up at any moment while we were inside atmosphere and simply blow us apart."

They were sitting in Marphissa's stateroom, Diaz having stopped by after leaving the bridge. Being in jump meant he could relax somewhat as well, and the stateroom offered far more privacy for candid talk than did the bridge.

"I was expecting that, too," Marphissa confessed. She ran one hand through her hair, sighing. "I am guessing that what we did was so unexpected that the enigmas were still arguing over how to react by the time we were done. They had never seen a human warship do what we did, so they had no idea what to do about it."

"Doing the completely unexpected does sometimes help you out," Diaz admitted. He stretched slowly. "Damn. I think I've been tensed up every minute we were at Iwa. And at Moorea. It's a good thing the crew can't tell how scared we are at times."

"I think they may figure out a lot more than we give them credit for," Marphissa said. "Speaking of figuring things out, did your people finish downloading and copying the data from those soldiers' battle armor?"

"No." Diaz made a helpless gesture with both hands. "They were going to try, since we told them to do it, but fortunately before they started I asked the right question, and they admitted that they were not familiar with ground forces' software, so there was every chance that the access and download attempt would have triggered an autowipe of all the data by Syndicate-installed security subroutines."

Marphissa clapped a hand to her face, exasperated, then slowly lowered it. "Every time I think we're getting the workers past their Syndicate training . . . and look I just called them workers instead of specialists, so I'm also defaulting to that . . . they start to mindlessly obey an order instead of letting us know there might be a problem."

Diaz shrugged. "Under the Syndicate, telling a supervisor there might be a problem with an order could get you shot. They learned to obey first and think not at all. Anyway, I told them not to touch the armor. We can turn it over to Drakon's ground forces when we get back. They'll know how to access that data. What are we going to do with the three soldiers?"

"Give them to Drakon, too, I guess." Marphissa saw the look that Diaz couldn't quite hide. "President Iceni trusts him. He's backed the president in every way. And Honore Bradamont says that General Drakon is a good man who never really acted like a CEO."

"I believe Bradamont," Diaz admitted, "even though her judgment might be a little influenced by her involvement with that ground forces colonel. I just hate the thought of those soldiers thinking that we betrayed them after all. My medical specialist is keeping them asleep to aid their recovery, but he says every time he lets them wake a little they always look terrified until he can remind them that they were rescued. In their heads, those soldiers keep going back to that hellhole." He grimaced and looked down. "I wonder if they'll ever leave it, or if they'll spend the rest of their lives feeling like they are still there."

"You know how it is for us," Marphissa said softly. "There's a battleship I served on soon after becoming a junior executive. We got on the wrong end of a nasty battle. Everything knocked out, then the Alliance Marines came aboard. I don't know how many times I've woken out of a nightmare where I am still fighting that battle in the darkened passageways of that doomed ship, blood and death everywhere, all my friends dying, some of them dying slow so they had plenty of time to know it—"

Her voice choked. Marphissa breathed in and out slowly, blinking back tears, aware that Diaz was conspicuously not looking at her.

"I know," he finally said, still looking away. "There are two kinds of people in the Syndicate service. Those who died horrible deaths, and those who survived to remember. How did you survive?"

"The Alliance got driven off. Their Marines pulled back off the ship before they could take our defensive citadels." Marphissa rubbed her eyes irritably. "Then those of us who were still alive were ordered to handle the casualty detail, collecting the bodies of our former friends and comrades, and getting the battleship into good enough shape to be hauled back and scrapped for parts and materials."

"Nobody ever accused the Syndicate of being sentimental. It's not good business."

"True." Composing herself, Marphissa nodded to Diaz. "We are the lucky ones, you know. Yes, we remember those who did not live, we remember how they died, but we can still try to make things better, try to save those that we can."

Diaz smiled briefly. "Like three ground forces workers who expected to die?"

"Like them. It matters," she insisted. "They matter. That's why we must win—because we believe that."

Diaz nodded, then smiled again. "But also there is this. We must win because if we lose, you and I will surely be killed in a very painful and public fashion."

"That is another good reason," Marphissa agreed.

CAPTAIN Honore Bradamont had mostly gotten over the occasional ugly flashback caused by being aboard Syndicate-design warships crewed by men and women in what were still basically Syndicate-style uniforms despite minor changes and new rank insignia. She had grown familiar with having bodyguards watching her to ensure none of the crew decided to act on their long-nurtured hatred of the Alliance and everyone who wore its uniform, even though that very familiarity with the practice disturbed her. And she had been able to accept that these men and women were not the "Syndic" monsters she had been taught to hate, who had killed many of her friends, and whom she had spent much of her life killing and trying to kill.

But to be riding a former Syndicate battleship, poised to assume command of a flotilla of former Syndicate warships if necessary, felt too bizarre to be real. To be sharing meals with former Syndicate officers whose own warships she had fought, and destroyed, at places like Varandal Star System, and who were supposed to follow *her* orders? If not for the orders that Admiral Geary had given her to do everything she morally could do to ensure the survival of the new regime on Midway, and her own belief that anyone who could win the loyalty of Colonel Donal Rogero as General Drakon had done must be a person worth following, Bradamont might have felt too disoriented to command at all, let alone well.

Manticore should have been back by now. Where the hell was Kommodor Asima Marphissa anyway? They had become friends, giving a strong personal aspect to Bradamont's worries. But she would be relieved once Asima made it back to Midway not simply because it would mean she had survived her mission, but also because Bradamont could then gracefully return the role of flotilla commander back to Midway's own Kommodor.

Five minutes ago, Midway's sensors had spotted the battle cruiser *Pele* altering vector and accelerating toward the jump point for Lono. What was Kapitan Kontos doing and why was he doing it? Since *Pele* was nearly three light hours away, the action had been taken that long ago, and any message sent by Bradamont demanding explanation would require a six-hour round-trip.

Her impatient thoughts were interrupted by a call from the bridge. "Two light cruisers arrived at the jump point from Lono three and a half hours ago," Kapitan Freya Mercia reported. "They are accelerating toward the inner star system at the best rate they can manage."

Bradamont frowned at the image of the battleship *Midway*'s commanding officer. "That's a very small attack force."

"Ridiculously small," Mercia agreed. "Our sensors have spotted combat damage on both warships."

A tone sounded, drawing Bradamont's attention to an incoming message. "Kapitan Kontos is hopefully informing us of his intentions. Are you copied on this message?"

"Yes," Mercia replied.

The image of Kapitan Kontos appeared before Bradamont. He was seated on the bridge of *Pele*, and still looked impossibly young for his rank and for being assigned to command Midway's only battle cruiser. But she had seen him in action and knew that Kontos was a brilliant tactician with an instinctive grasp of space combat.

"Honored Captain Bradamont," Kontos said, his tone and bearing formal and respectful. "I have sighted two light cruisers arriving from Lono and am proceeding to intercept their track. A message sent by them to my ships asks for asylum and indicates they were pursued by Syndicate warships when they entered jump at Lono. Main propulsion on both ships has suffered damage, limiting their ability to accelerate. Unless otherwise ordered, I will join up with the two light cruisers and escort them to a safe orbit. For the people, Kontos, out."

"He attached the message sent to his ships," Kapitan Mercia noted. "Shall I play it?"

"Yes, please, Kapitan." Bradamont had early on sensed Mercia's unease with her, but the former Syndicate officer had done her best to accept Bradamont, so she did her own best to deal respectfully in turn.

The image this time was of a dazed-looking executive on the bridge of a standard Syndicate light cruiser. The small bridge of the light cruiser was marked by signs of combat, a few bodies still sprawled within sight. "We have killed all of the loyalists and Internal Security Service agents aboard and are seeking to join forces with those of Midway. But we took damage fighting our way free of our flotilla. There were two heavy cruisers in close pursuit when we jumped from Lono. Both of our ships have suffered damage to main propulsion. We urgently require escort. Please save us! For the people, Kavistan, out."

It seemed like a pretty much straightforward situation. Bradamont took a quick glance at the display in her stateroom, but she was already familiar with the arrangement of Midway's warships. The battleship *Midway* that she was riding, along with heavy cruiser *Basilisk*, light cruisers *Falcon* and *Osprey*, and three Hunter-Killers were orbiting together to cover both Midway's hypernet gate, the most likely place for another Syndic attack to arrive, and the jump point from the star Pele, from which any enigma attack would come. That put them three and a half light hours from the jump point from Lono, far too distant to reach the new arrivals quickly.

Another heavy cruiser, *Kraken*, the remaining light cruisers *Hawk*, *Kite*, and *Eagle*, and six Hunter-Killers were orbiting far around the edge of the star system, covering the jump points from the stars Kahiki, Kane, Laka, and Iwa. They were more than five light hours away from the new arrivals.

The remaining three Hunter-Killers that Midway's small navy boasted were still gone, returning representatives to the star systems of Ulindi, Taroa, and Kane.

That left the battle cruiser *Pele* and a single heavy cruiser, *Gryphon*, who had been orbiting to cover the jump points from Lono and Kahiki. *Pele* and *Gryphon* had been only about one light hour from where the new ships had arrived.

She shouldn't have to do anything. By the time any of

Midway's other warships could get to the vicinity of those two light cruisers, *Pele* and *Gryphon* would already have long since engaged and driven off a pursuit force consisting of only heavy cruisers. Even a far-less-capable officer than Kontos could handle that.

The virtual window showing Kapitan Mercia was still open. Bradamont noticed that Mercia was frowning. "What's the matter?"

"I don't know." Mercia's frown grew deeper. "Something doesn't feel right, but I'm not sure what." She studied something off to one side of her. "From our own look angle we can't see much of the main propulsion on those light cruisers, so we can't confirm their reports of damage."

Bradamont checked her display again and did a quick appraisal. "*Pele* and *Gryphon* can see less than we do. The light cruisers are almost bow on to them. Why would the light cruisers lie about the damage they had sustained? Two of them can't threaten a battle cruiser."

Another alert tone, this one urgent. "The Syndicate heavy cruisers pursuing those light cruisers arrived," Mercia noted. "Two of them, just as we were told to expect."

Bradamont gazed at the display again; the two heavy cruisers had come in from the same jump from Lono, and had quickly steadied out on intercepts aimed at the light cruisers that had shown up earlier. The damaged light cruisers were limping toward *Pele* and *Gryphon* as fast as they could accelerate, and Kontos was bringing his two warships toward those light cruisers at a considerably higher rate. "About three hours until they meet up," Bradamont murmured. "Damn. Even if we sent a message it wouldn't get there until they were almost . . ." She gave a sharp look to Mercia. "Why do I want to send a message? This doesn't look like anything that Kontos can't handle."

"He's very good," Mercia said. "He does lack experience, but that shouldn't matter here. The light cruisers have killed all of the snakes aboard and—" She stopped speaking, looking unhappy. "That's part of it. Why did that executive call the snakes ISS agents? He used the formal title."

"What was his Syndicate rank?" Bradamont asked.

"Executive Second Class, what you would expect to find in command of a light cruiser." Mercia paused. "The commanding officer survived the mutiny. That's unusual, but I understand some of the commanding officers survived when President Iceni led the mutinies on warships here, so it can happen."

"How many days in jump space from Lono to here?" Bradamont asked.

"Lono to Midway? Seven days." Mercia sat straighter, suspicion lighting her eyes. "Seven days. At least seven days after the mutiny, and there are still bodies lying around the bridge?"

"It looked staged, didn't it?"

"I'm not too familiar with such things," Mercia said, "but, yes, it looked like . . . exactly what I would expect to see if I was watching a vid. What are they up to?"

"I don't know." Bradamont hit her comm control. "Kapitan Kontos, myself and Kapitan Mercia are concerned that there is something wrong about those two light cruisers. Verify the damage they claim to have suffered and do not let them approach you too closely. We need to confirm that they are who they say they are." She paused to consider adding more specific instructions, but that was foolish when she was observing events from three light hours away. Kontos would have to react to events as they developed. "Proceed with caution. Bradamont, out."

"You didn't say 'for the people,'" Mercia chided her, smiling crookedly to show it was meant humorously.

"I almost said 'to the honor of our ancestors' out of force of habit," Bradamont admitted. "But I know you don't believe in the same things that we do."

"Do you mean me personally?" Mercia asked. "Or everyone out here?"

"Everyone, I guess."

"Some of us do share that belief. Others believe in other things. And yet others accepted the belief in nothing that the Syndicate worked so hard to convince us all of." Mercia shrugged. "Not . . . what do you call it? Atheism. But denying even a belief in that. Only the Syndicate was supposed to serve as a guide and a purpose, because there was supposed to be no other possible guide and purpose."

"I'm not sure I understand what you're saying I should say," Bradamont said. "Does it look bad that I'm not saying 'for the people'?"

Mercia smiled very briefly. "I am saying that for all our lives we were told what we had to say. Now we can choose what to say. I don't think anyone will deny you the right to say what you wish. But you are probably wise not to flaunt your differences from us. Thank you, by the way."

"For?"

"Taking my concerns seriously. I worry about Kontos. When someone is as naturally good as he is, it is far too easy for them not to realize how much they have to learn."

"Agreed." Bradamont shook her head as she looked at her display. "And all you and I can do is watch and see what he does."

For the next three hours, she had to watch as events unfolded too far away for her to have any control over them. The heavy cruisers chased after the light cruisers, which were racing to meet *Pele* and *Gryphon*, which were in turn charging to intercept the light cruisers. The tracks of the various warships all converged toward one point in space.

Bradamont's unease kept growing as she watched. The Syndicate heavy cruisers in pursuit of the light cruisers were accelerating at a rate that would catch the smaller warships just after they joined up with *Pele* and *Gryphon*. There were plausible explanations for that, but it was odd that the heavy cruisers were continuing their pursuit when their own projections must have shown them that they would reach their prey too late to destroy them. And every meter the heavy cruisers drove toward *Pele* was another meter into a fight with a battle cruiser that the heavy cruisers could not hope to win.

It felt increasingly wrong. Kontos should see that, too. But she knew how easily a ship's captain could be caught by such a lure, not seeing the problems or potential dangers and focusing on the chance to not only save two newly friendly warships but also to destroy two enemy warships. What an opportunity! Exactly what someone would wish for. Admiral Geary had often made a point of warning against situations that seemed too good to be true.

Half an hour remained until they would see *Pele* and *Gryphon* meet up with the fleeing light cruisers. Bradamont stood up abruptly and left her stateroom, trying to ignore the bodyguards, who fell into place behind her. The walk to the bridge wasn't too long since the command spaces and the highest-ranking officers' staterooms were all located near the center of the battleship in the most well-protected part of the ship.

Mercia looked over at Bradamont as she walked onto the bridge and sat in the flotilla commander's seat next to Mercia's own ship commander's seat. "It stinks worse with every minute," Mercia said.

"It does." Bradamont brought up her display and pointed an angry finger at the two heavy cruisers. "Look at them. Coming on straight toward *Pele*. Kontos has to see that it's a trap of some sort!"

"But what kind of trap?" Mercia asked herself as much as Bradamont. "I've heard that the Syndicate has employed some suicide attacks, but those used small ships, courier ships with small crews."

"They have," Bradamont said angrily.

"Ah. Apologies. You were with Black Jack when they did that? It's an ugly way to fight, but the snakes always fight ugly."

Fifteen minutes remained until they saw what had happened when Kontos had met up with the light cruisers. "How much longer until he receives my message?" Bradamont asked, gazing at the unfamiliar Syndicate Worlds controls.

"Here." Mercia leaned over and tapped a control. "There's the count. About five more minutes. If Kontos hasn't already started wondering about this whole setup, that message should wake him up."

Midway's bridge usually had only a low level of noise. Kapitan Mercia ran a tight ship. But it was quieter than usual now as everyone watched the events on their displays, knowing that no matter what happened, they were far too distant to influence events that had taken place three hours before.

If no other maneuvers had occurred, Kontos's force would have passed through the two light cruisers at close range, continuing on to hit the pursuing Syndicate heavy cruisers.

"He's detaching *Gryphon*," Mercia noted at the same moment that Bradamont spotted the movement. Battle cruiser *Pele* had turned and was braking, while *Gryphon* had accelerated toward the oncoming light cruisers. "It's not a direct intercept. *Gryphon* is going to pass to one side of the light cruisers."

Bradamont felt herself smiling. "He's going to have *Gryphon* take a good look at the main propulsion on those light cruisers before *Pele* gets to them. And *Pele* is swinging out and down to pass clear of the light cruisers as well."

The results of those moves had come quickly. Three hours ago, as *Gryphon* and *Pele* split, the two fleeing light cruisers had also begun diverging, one aiming for *Gryphon* and one for *Pele*.

"Smart!" Bradamont said. "Kontos did exactly the right thing to force the hands of those light cruisers!"

A tactical feed from *Pele* appeared alongside the other data, relaying the communications that had passed back and forth three light hours away. Kontos had warned the light cruisers to continue onward, saying he would deal with the heavy cruisers. The same executive on the same light cruiser had called back, pleading for protection. "Our units will be very valuable to Iceni!"

As one light cruiser continued to close on *Gryphon* and the other on *Pele*, Kontos's messages grew sharp. "You will remain clear of my ships!"

The executive had kept pleading. "The Syndicate heavy cruisers are right behind us! We need protection! Our main propulsion has been damaged!"

Mercia indicated another set of data on the displays.

"*Pele* and *Gryphon* have two sets of firing solutions ready, one set aimed at the heavy cruisers and the second at the light cruisers. Kontos is ready for anything."

At that point, three things had occurred almost at the same moment.

Kapitan Third Rank Stein on the *Gryphon* had suddenly altered vector, getting a clear look at the main propulsion on one of the light cruisers. "Kapitan Kontos! Only minor cosmetic damage is visible!"

An alert appeared, showing that the sensors on both *Pele* and *Gryphon* had picked up unusual fluctuations from the power cores on both light cruisers.

Simultaneously, the two light cruisers leapt forward as their main propulsion kicked in at full, one cruiser homing in on *Gryphon* and the other aiming for *Pele*.

CHAPTER NINE

MISSILES tore away from Midway's warships, the ones fired by *Gryphon* having such a close target that they impacted within seconds as *Gryphon* hurled a full volley of hell lances and grapeshot at the light cruiser. One moment that light cruiser was trying to bend its vector fast enough to hit *Gryphon*, and the next its entire forward section had been blown to dust, the stern section rolling wildly up and off to the side.

Pele had a slightly longer time to shoot, but the light cruiser aiming for her was already lined up for intercept. Kontos didn't take any chances, pivoting *Pele* to ensure every possible weapon could come to bear on the attacker. The light cruiser was hit by a barrage that immediately collapsed its shields, tore through the light armor on its bow, then ripped down the length of the ship.

Pele continued onward, a field of small debris and dust passing astern and beneath her marking the remains of the second light cruiser.

The heavy cruisers which had been pretending to pursue the light cruisers had also altered vectors, swinging through an arc as they aimed to hit *Gryphon* before she could rejoin *Pele*.

"They weren't planning to ram," Mercia said, her eyes intent on her display. "The light cruisers were going to get right next to our ships and detonate their power cores. *Gryphon* would have been destroyed and *Pele* crippled, then the heavy cruisers would have finished her off."

"There haven't been any escape pods coming off what is left of the light cruiser that went after *Gryphon*," Bradamont noted. "I wonder how large the crews were on those light cruisers?"

Kapitan Stein on *Gryphon* hadn't done the instinctive thing and tried to evade the heavy cruisers, which would have only slowed down *Gryphon* and made her an easier target, instead charging right into the attack. The three ships had rocketed past each other at a combined velocity of nearly point three light speed, so fast that even their automated fire control systems could not compensate for the relativistic distortion that warped the ships' views of each other. Every shot fired missed.

With *Pele* now bearing down on them and *Gryphon* swinging in a vast arc to intercept again, the two Syndicate heavy cruisers bolted back for the jump point. The Syndicate warships had not finished their own turn back when *Pele* raced past above them and hammered one of the heavy cruisers so badly that it began sliding off to one side, unable to maneuver.

The second heavy cruiser abandoned its comrade, accelerating all out, as *Gryphon* swung in from one side and below to hit it in another swift pass. *Gryphon* rolled out and began a huge, graceful arc aimed this time at the crippled Syndicate heavy cruiser, while *Pele* settled onto a stern chase of the fleeing cruiser.

Bradamont watched as *Gryphon* had hit the damaged heavy cruiser again, suffering some hits herself but taking out some of the Syndicate warship's weapons and inflicting some damage to its main propulsion. Hurt as it was and trapped inside an enemy star system, the Syndicate heavy cruiser was doomed. Bradamont waited to see escape pods begin to launch as the Syndicate crew abandoned ship.

Instead, before *Gryphon* could finish swinging up and around for another firing run, the heavy cruiser had abruptly dropped its remaining shields and shut down its weapons.

The transmission from that ship resembled the earlier ones from the light cruiser, but did not have any feeling of having been staged. An Executive Fourth Class with blood running unheeded down one arm of his suit spoke in halting words. "We surrender to you. All snakes aboard this unit are dead. We swear it! This isn't a trick. We won't fire on you again. We heard that Iceni and Drakon are for the people. We surrender."

The second heavy cruiser kept fleeing despite the very small lead it had, firing on *Pele* as the battle cruiser finally overtook it. With a fairly small relative velocity to the heavy cruiser, *Pele* was able to methodically smash the heavy cruiser from stern to bow as the Syndicate warship made futile attempts to outmaneuver its foe. Only a few escape pods launched before the second heavy cruiser's power core overloaded because of the damage, and blew the battered warship into fragments.

Bradamont, realizing she had been sitting on Midway's bridge for a long time watching the battle that had played out hours ago, stretched and smiled. "Kapitan Mercia," she said loudly. "Black Jack would be proud to have such ships and such men and women fighting alongside his own."

Mercia's eyebrows went up. She knew that Bradamont almost always referred to Admiral Geary by his name and rank, not using the Black Jack nickname that Syndicate and former-Syndicate personnel always employed. Then Mercia gave Bradamont a genuine smile, different from her usual stiffness toward the Alliance officer. "One of his own would know."

Another alert, this one a mild tone. Mercia gestured toward the symbol that had appeared at the jump point from Iwa. "*Manticore* has returned. Your chance for glory has passed."

"You don't know how glad I am to know that."

Moments later, the first transmission from *Manticore*

arrived. As she watched and listened to Marphissa's report, Bradamont felt any sense of relief fading rapidly.

DRAKON studied Kommodor Marphissa's report, knowing that his expression was falling into grim lines. "Which major problem are we going to discuss first?"

"Oh, why not the enigmas and their secret base," Iceni said. She looked tired and unhappy, which wasn't too surprising considering the matters that needed to be addressed.

"Their deep underground secret base," Drakon said, knowing that Gwen Iceni wouldn't want him to soft-pedal anything. "Deep, deep underground. Probably designed for defense, with a lot of angles to hide behind, choke points to funnel attackers into, and materials that will block sensors and communications by enemy forces."

Gwen Iceni had called a meeting when Marphissa's report came in. They all sat in another conference room at Drakon's headquarters. With at least one potential assassin running loose on the planet, it made sense to avoid using the same rooms or the same routes or the same routines. Predictability made a killer's job much, much easier.

"The corridors would very likely be designed as a maze," Colonel Malin added.

"And," Drakon continued heavily, "we would be attacking enigmas, who, according to Black Jack's reports, prefer to blow things up rather than have them captured." He looked toward Captain Bradamont, who had returned to the planet just in time for this meeting.

Bradamont nodded. "Ships, installations, you name it. It seemed everything we encountered was rigged with self-destruct capability. The enigmas don't want anything left that could provide any information or clues about them."

"You're saying an assault by ground forces would be a suicide mission," Iceni observed, looking steadily off to one side.

"Effectively, yes," Drakon said, wishing he knew what Gwen was thinking.

"Do you think that those ground forces workers who were rescued by *Manticore* will be able to provide any useful intelligence?"

Drakon nodded. "They already have. *Manticore* is still a ways from reaching this planet, but my ground code monkeys were able to walk the space code monkeys through accessing and downloading the data in the battle armor. Most of the data is a lot of nothing as those soldiers lay low waiting for rescue, but they got some decent data on the enigma attack that killed most of their unit."

Iceni gave him a look. "That attack employed distance weapons, I understand. What did you learn from it?"

Colonel Malin answered. "Madam President, we were able to confirm from the battle armor status and records that the ground forces unit they were in was not leaking electronic signals when they were targeted by the enigmas. All of their emissions were extremely low power and extremely short-range, to tie their armor into a single tactical net."

"Which means," Drakon said, "that the enigmas are very, very good at spotting even tiny indications of comm and active sensor activity by our forces. But when those three soldiers went totally passive, nothing went after them. That might mean the enigmas don't routinely employ active seekers."

Iceni raised an eyebrow at Drakon. "Why would it imply that?"

"Because our own distance strike weapons are at least dual-seeker systems. If they don't spot anything using the passive seeker that is looking for electronic signals, they automatically switch to active, or infrared, or visual. Visual can be movement triggered or look for shape matches."

"If they don't use active seekers," Bradamont commented, "that's consistent with the enigmas' desire to remain hidden. Active paints your position loud and clear for anyone watching."

"But what about IR?" Colonel Gozen asked. "That's passive. But if the enigma weapons had automatically shifted to IR targeting they would have nailed those three soldiers."

"IR might be a blind zone for them," Drakon agreed. "I

wish those three soldiers had gotten even a long-range look at some enigmas operating on the surface so we'd have at least a basic idea of what kind of protective suits or armor they use, and what sort of weapons they carry." He shook his head ruefully. "I used to be unhappy about Syndicate intelligence reports that couldn't tell me little details about new Alliance ground threats. I never realized how much basic and very important information I already knew as a matter of course."

Colonel Malin frowned. "It is possible that the enigmas try to do all of their ground fighting at long range, beyond line of sight, so as to minimize any chance of being seen by a foe."

"Even other enigmas?" Iceni asked. "Surely they don't worry about other enigmas seeing them."

"Such a strong motivation cannot operate in a vacuum," Malin said. "The enigma desire for privacy, for remaining hidden, must influence their interactions with each other."

Bradamont called up some images on her data pad, studying them. "When Admiral Geary's fleet was in enigma-owned star systems we got long-range looks at enigma towns, but those looks were obscured by privacy fields over the towns. The fields appeared to be a routine thing. About all we could tell was that the towns were almost all coastal and were about half in the water and half along the surface of the coast."

"The enigmas certainly live up to their names," Gozen commented. "Could Black Jack's ships have spotted deep underground installations like the enigmas are building at Iwa?"

"No," Bradamont said. "Maybe if we had gotten in close we could have spotted traces, but getting in close would, we thought, lead the enigma population on the surface to commit mass suicide. Admiral Geary did not want to commit genocide."

"Good for him," Drakon commented. "But is it genocide if the other guys decide to kill themselves?"

"They're dead either way," Iceni said. "Even if it is second-degree genocide instead of first-degree. But after seeing those images of Iwa, I'm not sure I would have been as restrained as Black Jack was. Let me summarize. We know very little of enigma ground combat capabilities, except that they have signal detection capabilities markedly superior to our own and highly effective distance weapons. We know that they are building a base of some kind deep underground on that planet at Iwa. And we know, from what they did at Iwa, that the enigmas have not altered their basic approach to humanity."

"Wiping out all trace of humans might be described as an approach," Drakon said, wondering why he found the phrasing comical. "Here's something else we can be sure of. Even if we overcome their defenses against ground attack, which I think we could do, but that has to be a guess since we know so little about the enigmas' ground combat capabilities or how many enigmas are at this base, then from all we know the enigmas would have dead-men switches built into their gear to ensure their installation, and all of our troops, were blown to hell on the heels of our victory."

"Dead-enigma switches," Iceni said.

"What?"

"You said dead-*man* switches." Iceni moved her head slowly to look at everyone else. "We've gone over the difficulties. Can any of you tell me how we can do this?"

"Why not just drop a big enough rock on the planet to reach however deep the enigmas are?" Drakon asked, unhappy at the idea of sending his soldiers against a foe of essentially unknown capabilities and strength.

"That would be one hell of a rock," Bradamont said.

"It would take time," Iceni said. "We would have to round up a local asteroid or minor planet that was big enough and boost it toward the target planet. It would take a while to get there. Besides that, we *need* to capture some enigma technology. Maybe some records that we can exploit. We still know almost nothing about them."

"We know they keep attacking us," Drakon said.

"But we don't know why!"

"General Charban, who accompanied Admiral Geary's fleet," Captain Bradamont explained, "thought that it was pure paranoia in human terms. The enigmas may think that as long as we inquisitive humans are close enough to the enigmas, as long as we exist, we will keep trying to learn about the enigmas, keep trying to penetrate the screen of secrecy they maintain. We tried to use that as basis for establishing a peace agreement, promising that we would never violate their privacy if they did not attack us, but they never responded."

"Except with more attacks," Malin pointed out. "Paranoia would cause the enigmas to conclude that we will always violate any agreement and always be a threat to them."

"I said paranoia in human terms," Bradamont corrected. "Whatever drives enigma thinking and actions appears to have common elements with what we'd call paranoia, but they're not human, and their ways of thinking may have major variations on how a human with paranoia would perceive things."

"Captain," Malin said, his words precise and cold, "while both General Drakon and President Iceni have expressed distaste at the idea of genocide, we may eventually be forced to engage in a war of elimination with the enigmas. We will have no choice."

Drakon felt a reflexive tightening in his gut at Malin's words. "We've spent the last century in a war that became more and more a war of elimination, Colonel. I'm personally sick of that kind of thing."

"But if it is our only option—"

"You know I always ask for at least two options," Drakon interrupted. "There are always at least two options." He paused, then gave Iceni a sidelong look. "Just like our beloved President asked for more options a minute ago. And one option to beginning a genocidal war is learning enough about the enigmas to figure out what else might work, which takes us back to capturing that base. Colonel, can we come up with a way to take that enigma installation that doesn't involve suicide for our soldiers and the enigmas alike?"

Malin hesitated, frowning in thought.

"What are they going to expect us to do?" Bradamont said. "That's one thing Admiral Geary always tried to work out. What does the enemy expect to happen?"

"Because then you can do something the enemy doesn't expect?" Iceni said, smiling slightly.

"More than that," Bradamont said. "It also tells you what kind of defenses the enemy will have, what kind of plans. If they are anything like humans in terms of thinking, they are going to configure their plans around what they expect us to do, and their defenses will be focused on countering our expected weapons and tactics."

Colonel Gozen spoke up for the first time. "Like those long-range weapons that hit the soldiers at Iwa, targeting them using their battle armor net. I've been told the enigmas had been secretly watching us fight the Alliance during the whole war? So they know our standard tactics, and they've seen our ground force weapons in use."

"Alliance tactics, too," Bradamont said. "But Admiral Geary still figured out ways to outthink the enigmas and frustrate their plans."

"Admiral Geary isn't here," Iceni pointed out. "It would be wonderful if Black Jack showed up with his fleet, ready to lead the charge against the enigmas, but all indications on that front are that he is tied up at home."

"Captain Desjani told me that the Admiral always insisted he was not special, that it was just a matter of learning from mistakes, anticipating enemy moves, and trying new things."

"Captain Desjani?" Gozen asked.

"The captain of the Admiral's flagship," Bradamont explained. "She said Admiral Geary was always listening to others' ideas, and always asking advice. I've been able to watch you in action. Kommodor Marphissa, and Kapitans

Mercia and Kontos, Colonel Rogero, and you, General Drakon. You've repeatedly succeeded because you've outthought the Syndicate Worlds forces and done things they did not expect."

"Luck played a role, too," Drakon pointed out. He had felt an unexpected burst of pleasure at hearing Bradamont implying that he and his officers were the equal of Black Jack, but he wasn't about to let the unanticipated praise go to his head. "How do we know what the enigmas will expect?"

"You said it yourself!" Bradamont pointed to Gozen. "Or, rather, your new colonel did. The enigmas will expect any ground attack from you to match what they have seen Syndicate Worlds ground forces do during the war."

"A head-on attack with everything we've got, heedless of casualties," Drakon said. "Preattack bombardment, by orbiting warships and any artillery we have landed on the planet, followed by combat engineers breaching outer defenses, then systematic overrunning of the entire complex."

Malin nodded. "A mix of energy and projectile weapons in the hands of the soldiers, employed along with smoke to screen our attacks, and localized electromagnetic pulses to neutralize enemy systems within limited areas."

"Stealth armor and special forces," Gozen added.

"We used those last two in enigma space," Bradamont said. "To rescue the human prisoners inside that asteroid."

"Then the enigmas will be doubly on guard against that threat," Drakon said, leaning back to think. "I bet we can come up with something those guys don't expect. But how do we neutralize the dead-ma—I mean, the dead-enigma switches that are certain to be in place?"

"Offensive software and hackers are out," Malin said. "The enigmas know how our systems work because of all of the human ships and ground facilities they have captured over time, but we know nothing about theirs. They probably have defenses against the most sophisticated weapons we could put together, including jammers focused on every aspect of our weapons, communications, and sensors."

"Too bad we can't just hit them with rocks," Gozen said. "Not big ones dropped from orbit. Just one-on-one, look them in the eye, then whap them in the head and anywhere else that hurts. You can't jam a rock."

Iceni raised one hand to stop the conversation. "What did you say, Colonel Gozen?"

Gozen looked startled. "You can't jam a rock, Madam President."

"You said more than that."

"Um, yes. Too bad we can't look them in the eyes and hit them close-up."

Drakon suddenly understood what Iceni was driving at. "You're thinking we should fry the whole installation? Knock out every piece of equipment, every circuit, everything that isn't a manual brute-force-operated widget? Is that possible?" he asked Malin.

Malin shook his head. "The enigmas know we use EMPs tactically. And they are a spacefaring race who has had to deal with radiation in that environment. They will have their equipment well shielded, and their critical equipment very well shielded."

Bradamont laughed. "Oh. Yeah. And I know what they'll use." Everyone looked at her. "Water," Bradamont explained. "The best natural radiation shield that exists, and still one of the best radiation shields period. The enigmas are semi-aquatic from what we saw of their worlds. They would need a lot of water in that underground facility."

"Where would they get all that water on a rock like that planet?" Gozen wondered.

Iceni checked her data. "The same place the Syndicate colony used to get it. Underground reservoirs. Oh, hell. What do you bet they partially drained one of the big, deep reservoirs to flood their excavations, and fixed up the partially drained void to take advantage of it?"

"They are apparently digging deep enough that could work," Malin said.

"How do we fry something on the bottom of a swimming pool that is beneath a hell of a lot of rock?" Gozen demanded. "And even the best stealth battle armor can't hide something moving through water."

The ensuing silence stretched for more than a minute before Iceni rubbed her eyes with one hand. "All right. What about the other big problem?"

Drakon chose his words carefully. "Imallye seems to have a grudge against you."

"You think?" Iceni glared toward a vacant corner again. "I didn't know the name Granaile Imallye. I had no idea she was the same person in my own past as the one who called herself Grace O'Malley after an ancient hero of hers. But it seems she is."

"She hates you," Bradamont said.

"Yes." Iceni inhaled deeply before saying anything else. "I must share one of the things in my past that I regret the most. You all know that I was exiled to Midway because of my involvement with reporting an illegal scheme by another CEO. What you don't know is that I actually fingered the wrong person when I reported it."

"Why did the Syndicate exile you for that?" Drakon asked, realizing he was probably the only person in the room who would dare to ask for more information.

She lowered her head, avoiding his gaze. "The Syndicate didn't care that I had accused the wrong person. That's because the CEO actually behind the scheme had planted extensive evidence implicating a sub-CEO. I admit that I thought I was safe reporting on malfeasance by a sub-CEO, but I also believed that he was guilty of a plot that was diverting important money and resources away from the tasks the Syndicate had ordered me to undertake.

"But that sub-CEO had been set up to take a fall by a very powerful CEO, who also set me up to take a fall. Like a fool, I reported the sub-CEO, who was conveniently executed before he could provide any information about the powerful CEO. Then evidence of the sub-CEO's innocence miraculously appeared, and the powerful CEO used it to brand me as a loose cannon who might cause problems for other CEOs in the future. The powerful CEO went on making lots of money in various legal and illegal schemes, I got exiled to Midway, the sub-CEO was dead, and . . ." Iceni paused, raised her head, and finally looked at Drakon. "The sub-CEO's daughter swore that she would make me pay for the death of her father."

Most of those present simply absorbed the information, but Drakon noticed that Captain Bradamont appeared to be baffled. "I'm sorry," she said. "I can see how hard it is for you to speak of this, Madam President, but how did the sub-CEO get executed so quickly that he couldn't even give testimony?"

Iceni shifted her gaze to the Alliance officer. "He was accused of a serious crime."

"But—" Bradamont looked around at the others for enlightenment, even more confused. "There wasn't any trial?"

"Of course there was a trial. It took five minutes. The sub-CEO wasn't allowed to testify because, of course, a criminal wouldn't tell the truth, his lawyer had been appointed by the Syndicate and did nothing, the judge who was appointed by the Syndicate and controlled by the Syndicate pronounced the sub-CEO guilty, and ten minutes after that the sub-CEO was executed for his crimes."

Bradamont's mouth had fallen open. She closed her eyes and looked away. "I'm sorry, I—"

"That's the sort of thing we revolted against," Drakon said, feeling both upset by her reaction and defensive because he had, after all, been a part of that Syndicate system.

"That's how the Syndicate works," Gozen added. "Same thing happened to my uncle. It doesn't matter if you're innocent. The system assumes that you wouldn't have been accused if you weren't guilty, and anything you say to defend yourself is just proof that you're refusing to admit to your guilt. If you confess to your crimes, maybe they'll go a little easier on you and send you to a labor camp instead of executing you. Or maybe you'll accuse someone else, someone they want to nail, and that might help make things a little easier for you."

"And I knew all that," Iceni said, her voice tight. "Yet I accused that man anyway. I am responsible for his death."

"You've made extensive reforms to the justice system on

Midway," Drakon insisted. "To prevent just that sort of thing from happening. Sorry if this all shocks you, Captain Bradamont."

Bradamont shook her head, looking embarrassed. "No. It didn't shock me. The reason I reacted as I did was because . . . because the Alliance was well on its way down that same road. Not for every crime. But for some. There were a lot of people, a lot of political leaders, saying that if someone was accused of certain crimes then trials weren't necessary. We should just punish them as if certain of their guilt because they had been accused, because they were suspected of having committed crimes or planning to commit crimes. It went against every legal principle that the Alliance was supposed to stand for, but it happened. Admiral Geary, after he awoke from his century in survival sleep, he told us that we had become too much like our enemy. That we had let the long war change us, so that we were willing to do the same things the Syndicate Worlds did. It is difficult to be reminded of just how true that was.

"However," she added, looking at Iceni, "if this Imallye is going to pursue a vendetta against you, when both the enigmas and the Syndicate Worlds threaten this region of space, then she's being an idiot. Nothing she does to you will bring her father back, but what she does can end up causing the deaths of countless more people."

"Thank you," Iceni replied. She looked away again, staying silent for a moment. "Unfortunately, as you have seen from Kommodor Marphissa's report, Granaile Imallye doesn't want to listen to reason. The question is, will she try to set up her own base at Iwa? Or will she launch an attack in the near future against us here, coming in either from Iwa or the longer way around through Laka?"

"From what the Kommodor says," Gozen offered, "Imallye is as mad as hell right now. People with that kind of mad on don't take detours on their way to revenge."

"That would be my assumption as well," Drakon said. "Imallye not only wants her revenge on you, now she also wants to get even with the Kommodor for embarrassing her in her own backyard and messing up her battle cruiser."

"How long do you think it will take to repair the damage to Imallye's battle cruiser?" Iceni asked Bradamont.

Bradamont shrugged. "It depends partly on what repair capabilities exist at Moorea. From the data that *Manticore* brought back, I agree with her engineers that the damage to the battle cruiser's propulsion was widespread but didn't penetrate to require propulsion unit replacement. That's not a criticism," she added. "*Manticore* needed to knock out as much propulsion capability on that battle cruiser as she could in a very short time, and was highly successful at that."

She frowned in thought. "I'd estimate it would have taken Imallye at least a week to get that battle cruiser back to a repair facility, and after that anything from three weeks to six weeks to repair the damage that *Manticore* caused. That's assuming that Imallye does a good job of motivating the repair workers."

Iceni smiled thinly. "You do know what *motivating the workers* means in the Syndicate, don't you?"

"I've seen enough to guess," Bradamont replied in dry tones. "Unfortunately, we have only a vague idea of what Imallye's forces add up to. She certainly has more than were at Moorea, but how much more, and how long will it take her to marshal them at Moorea, and how much will she have to leave behind to ensure none of the star systems she controls decide to change their allegiance?"

"We can preempt whatever move Imallye is planning," Colonel Malin suggested. "Move into Iwa, ensure that Imallye knows we have set up a base there, and wait for her to react."

"Why would she come to Iwa?" Bradamont asked. "If Midway places enough forces at Iwa to deal with Imallye, then Imallye could just go around through Laka and hit Midway."

"Imallye wants President Iceni," Malin said calmly. "If she is at Iwa, personally supervising our forces—"

"I don't like that idea," Drakon growled, feeling angry at Malin for suggesting it. "President Iceni is not bait for a trap."

"She would be commanding a substantial portion of our warships, sir. If she were aboard the battleship *Midway*, she would be both well protected and able to strike back."

Drakon shook his head. "That's what the Syndicate thought when they set up their ambush at Ulindi. I'm sure Happy Hua felt completely safe aboard that Syndicate battleship, but there's nothing left of her except dust floating in a debris field orbiting Ulindi."

Iceni had given him a sharp look. "General," she said, "I have to admit that Colonel Malin's plan has merit. Our biggest problem is that we face two major threats, the enigmas and Imallye, and have to worry about splitting our forces to defend against them. But if we can suck both the enigmas and Imallye into Iwa, the enigmas by attacking their hidden base and Imallye by offering my presence, then we will be able to maximize the forces with which we can confront those threats."

"You're forgetting the Syndicate," Drakon grumbled. "That's a third threat."

"The Syndicate wouldn't have tried an attack with four cruisers if they had something more substantial on hand or expected soon. We hurt them badly at Ulindi, and we are but one of numerous star systems that are rebelling against the Syndicate, whose forces are stretched thin."

"Or it was an attempt to wear us down before a bigger force hits us," Drakon said, wondering himself if he was arguing plausible threats or simply trying to dissuade Iceni from considering Malin's idea.

"Perhaps," Iceni commented. "Captain Bradamont, as the closest thing to a neutral observer available to us, what do you think of the way the Syndicate tried to take out *Pele* and *Gryphon*?"

Bradamont made a face. "The crew of the heavy cruiser that surrendered said the light cruisers were not crewed at all, operating on automated targeting and attack routines.

The transmissions coming from them were animated on the fly by routines designed to react as well as they could to whatever was happening. That could mean that after all of their losses the Syndicate Worlds is so short on trained crew members that they couldn't afford to lose even skeleton crews on a suicide mission. Or it could mean that they didn't trust a human crew to carry out the planned attack."

"What did they tell us about other Syndicate forces in this region?"

"They didn't know of any," Bradamont said. "But, since the senior officers on the heavy cruiser died, and one of the snakes aboard managed to fry most of the classified data before he was killed, that might just mean the few junior officers who survived the battle and the mutiny were not given that information."

"Junior officers are rarely told about the big picture," Gozen said.

"What do you think of Colonel Malin's suggested plan?" Iceni asked.

Bradamont cast a wary glance at Drakon but spoke without hesitation. "I believe it is a promising concept, and perhaps the best option available if the problem of how to capture the enigma base can be addressed."

Iceni looked at Drakon. "You're unhappy with the idea, though. Do you consider it too risky?"

Drakon took a long moment to answer as he considered possible replies. But the real reason for his objection, one he had only fully realized when everyone else was talking, was one he did not wish to discuss in front of others. "I would like to speak to you about my reasons in private. Just the two of us."

"Certainly." Iceni waved the others present toward the door. "Wait for us outside and see that we are not disturbed unless there is an emergency."

Bradamont, Malin, and Gozen left, closing the door behind them. There wasn't anything unusual about two high-ranking individuals holding a private conference. Iceni waited until the security lights above the door glowed green to indicate a secure environment before she turned an inquiring look on Drakon. "All right. We're alone. What are your reasons?"

Drakon found it unexpectedly hard to speak. "I don't like the plan."

"Artur," Iceni said with a sigh, "I can't work with that. I need reasons."

"My reasons are difficult to explain," Drakon said, frowning at the surface of the desk in front of him.

She sounded frustrated. "Do you dislike the strategy? Do you think there's another, better approach?"

"I don't—" Drakon set his mouth in an angry line. "I admit that the strategy has potential. But I do not like it."

"You've made that clear. But we have to evaluate this idea on its merits," Iceni insisted. "Impartially and purely in terms of its likelihood to succeed."

Drakon met her eyes, struggled with himself, and with every bit of *don't expose yourself, don't trust anyone, don't admit to any potential vulnerability or weakness* that he had been taught by the Syndicate, then finally said it. "I can't do that."

She eyed him in return, puzzled. "You can't do what?"

"Evaluate it impartially. This plan involves a serious threat to you."

"And I'm your most important ally," Iceni said patiently. "I understand that you would face some difficulties maintaining order at Midway if I was killed, but—"

"Dammit, Gwen, I'm not talking about you as an ally! I . . . don't want to see you hurt! I don't want to face a universe without you."

She seemed perplexed, then revealed growing astonishment. "Artur Drakon, was that your idea of an avowal of affection?"

He looked away, not sure what to say. "Call it what you want. I thought you might also . . . Sometimes it seemed that you . . . that you wouldn't mind if I . . . felt like that. But you don't seem to be happy about it."

"I'm . . . surprised. I thought your tastes in women ran a lot more exotic than a beat-up run-of-the-mill type like me."

Drakon stared at her, trying to figure out if Iceni was joking. "No. And that's not how I see you."

"Really?" She leaned her head on one fist, watching him. "Something must be wrong with your vision, and since I know you're physically all right, the problem must be mental or emotional or both. Just what is influencing how you see me, Artur Drakon?"

He struggled for words again. "I . . . care about what happens to you."

"You already said that. Now, you are blocking a perfectly viable plan for dealing with serious threats to this star system. I think I deserve to know exactly why you don't want to consider that plan."

She sounded absolutely serious. Had all the times he thought she might have been interested in him just been misinterpretations on his part? One CEO could never trust another CEO. That was a basic rule of the Syndicate, a rule both he and Gwen had seen proven by the treachery and double-crossing actions of other CEOs while they were still part of the Syndicate, a rule that had kept them at arm's length from each other for some time. But he had come to trust Gwen, to more than trust her, and he had thought she might feel the same way. He wasn't going to back down without finding out for certain. Drakon steeled himself and said the words. "It's because . . . I . . . want to form a permanent joint venture with you, Gwen."

Iceni's eyes widened. "You do?"

"I'm . . . pretty sure I do." He couldn't tell how she took that. "I just . . . it's . . ."

She held up a restraining hand. "You know, Artur, if I didn't like you, I'd keep forcing you to try to be articulate when discussing your feelings regarding . . . my value as a partner. But I'm going to have mercy on you."

"Meaning what?" He was feeling cross now, upset by his inability to speak clearly. He had led forces in combat, calling out orders without hesitation as enemy forces rained death all around, but now he found his tongue tied and words sticking in his throat.

She smiled. A genuine, affectionate smile. "You big oaf. I've been trying to avoid feeling the same way about you. Unsuccessfully trying. You are an exceptional man, with enormous potential as a partner, as well as being exasperating and difficult at times. But I know I am also exasperating and difficult at times. Let's have dinner tonight, just you and me, no one else, no recordings of anything by anyone, and talk about not just threats and strategies and problems, but about each other and what we expect from the deal. If we're going to make this cooperation between us into a long-term, binding deal, we need to have a chance to discuss it."

He could not help smiling back at her. "Like any other business deal, huh?"

"Oh, hell, no. A very special business deal. We'll have dinner at my headquarters and see how it goes. All right? And even if it all goes well, that plan may still have to be on the table, Artur, unless we can come up with a good alternative. I had to see you off to Ulindi. You may have to see me off to Iwa." She stood up, then took two quick steps and kissed him quickly before stepping back again. "Don't disappoint me. Please don't disappoint me."

Drakon stood as well, still smiling and still feeling the touch of her lips on his. "I don't let anyone down, Gwen."

She laughed. "Ah, yes. My loyal knight, his armor a bit worn and torn, but still determined to fight to the last for what he believes in. Do you really believe in me?"

That one was easy. "Yes."

Iceni looked away, still smiling. "I'll see you at dinner."

She left, head high and a bounce in her step. Colonel Malin, waiting outside, gave her a speculative look before following her.

Drakon walked out of the conference room and saw both Bradamont and Gozen watching Iceni leave. Both women switched their gazes to him, neither revealing anything in their expressions. For some reason that irritated Drakon.

"I'm going to be having dinner with President Iceni tonight," he told Gozen. "To . . . discuss the proposed plan. You won't be needed. It'll be a private dinner."

"Yes, sir," Gozen said, poker-faced. "Is it possible the meeting will run late?"

Drakon's gaze on her sharpened, but Gozen wasn't betraying any hint of what she was thinking. "Possibly."

"I'll arrange transportation, sir," Gozen said.

"Thank you." Drakon walked toward his office, fighting off a temptation to look backward suddenly to see if Bradamont and Gozen were daring to crack smiles.

CHAPTER TEN

COLONEL Bran Malin stood silently in a slice of shadow just large enough to cover him, trying not to move and breathing as shallowly as possible to avoid giving off any signs that someone could spot. The city was unusually active this late at night, but there were still many areas where silence and stillness reigned.

President Iceni had told him to take the night off without explaining why, but it had not been difficult to find out that General Drakon was to be her guest this evening. Malin had long wanted to encourage such a relationship, but had been at a loss for how to do so. He knew that physical intimacy by itself was unlikely to produce any good results, and that in theory a strong relationship between Drakon and Iceni would involve emotional ties and intimacy.

In theory. Malin gazed into the darkness, remembering the woman who had raised him as her own. She had loved him, and he had thought he loved her in return. But then he had learned of his real mother and sought her out. Roh Morgan. A woman who knew a great deal about anger and pain, but seemingly nothing about any softer emotions except as tools to wield against the targets of her plans. And Malin had found he had a natural skill at the same sort of machinations. Inherited, apparently, along with who knew what else.

He had walled off his feelings as much as possible, trying to bend his work toward some greater goal that might prove he had overcome his mother's legacy. There was an irony in the fact that both he and Morgan had fixed on Drakon as the means to achieve their ends, though those ends differed hugely.

Was she dead? Malin stayed motionless, gazing into the night, wondering why he felt a conviction that Morgan had somehow survived the destruction of the snake alternate headquarters on Ulindi.

Neither Drakon nor Iceni trusted him as much as they once had, but that was fine. It wasn't about him. What mattered was that the two former CEOs seemed to have finally reached out to each other in a way that should help preserve this experiment at Midway, this attempt to build a government and a society that were both strong and free.

Malin inhaled slowly and deeply, repeating in his mind a mantra he had recited countless times. *I have been a slave to my past, but I will free myself by freeing others from their pasts.*

His instruments registered a flicker of motion in an area half a block down and to the left, an area that should have been empty at this time of night. Malin moved like a wraith through the darkness, determined that this time he would run his quarry to earth.

Move. Hide. Pause. Move. His prey was moving with great care as well. Did the prey know of the hunt this time? Probably not. There had been no moves so easy to spot that they were obviously intended to draw Malin on. And though the path his prey wended through the dark areas of the city veered in direction to remain well concealed, that path kept coming back to a course centered on the region near the main spaceport.

A rat skittered away through the trash, causing Malin to freeze once more while waiting to see if the movement had attracted attention. Part of him mentally noted the state of this back alley and the need to direct that those responsible clean it up, while another part wondered at the absurdity of being concerned about trash in an alley while engaged in a deadly pursuit, and yet a third part pondered the symbolism of the fact that humanity had brought rats to the stars.

And, somewhere inside, part of Malin wondered if Morgan had experienced those kinds of complex, cascading thought streams. It had always been impossible to ask her, and the question might have led Morgan into a line of investigation that would have had her discovering that Malin was her son. Morgan's reaction to that might have rivaled a nova in its destructive fury.

Malin moved cautiously again as he spotted more traces of his quarry on his sensor readouts. Still tending toward the spaceport. Interesting. Were more snake agents expected, slipping in among cargo shipments and passengers?

But as he neared the spaceport itself, Malin gradually became aware of a third player in the stealthy pursuit. Somewhere, there off to his left, someone was pacing both him and his target. That someone moved like a ghost, the signs of their presence so subtle that Malin saw them as much by instinct as by indications on his sensors. Was the third party an ally of Malin's quarry? Or another agent of Drakon's or Iceni's pursuing the same target as he? But Malin knew of no other agent with that level of skill.

The path finally led to a large warehouse near the security boundaries of the spaceport. The walls, lights, and defenses around the spaceport glowed with a riot of data on Malin's sensors. He realized with grudging respect that this location had been chosen because the noise from those systems, as well as the fairly high levels of foot and vehicle traffic, helped mask those who did not want their presence noted.

A link using the highest level of security override disarmed the lock and alarm on one of the doors. Malin studied the pingback from that command, seeing that the security software had distinct signs of snake coding. Sloppy of them to leave that kind of clear sign, but snakes sometimes underestimated the intelligence and capabilities of their opponents, or were so rushed in carrying out a command that corners were cut.

He glided inside the warehouse, every sense alert and every sensor built into his clothing at maximum sensitivity. Cargo containers were stacked in neat rows, each container bearing security stamps from dozens of star systems.

The barest noise reached Malin, something out of place in this warehouse. His weapon in hand, Malin ceased moving and crouched next to a stack of cargo containers.

He waited. Often, in this kind of life-and-death game, waiting was a winning tactic. Someone would get impatient. Someone would move. The one who waited as if turned to stone would eventually see the one who could not wait long enough.

Whoever else was in here was not linked in to the city's official security software as warehouse guards or police would be. It was always possible that they were nonetheless innocent of any crime, but Malin waited with grim resolve, willing to kill the innocent if necessary to ensure he got the guilty. President Iceni would not approve. Neither would General Drakon. Which was why Malin took the burden of the action on himself. He would pay any price demanded by fate for his actions, and spare the others that guilt.

There. Two of them, one covering the other as they eased through the warehouse, checking out each lane between rows of cargo containers. The warehouse security scanners should have spotted any intruders, but the searchers were smart enough to know that anyone who could get inside without triggering any alarms was also likely smart enough to have blinded the security scanners to his or her presence.

They were getting close. Malin tried to spot any other movement in the warehouse, but failed. Moving with glacial slowness, he lined up his pistol on the figure who was farthest from him. Then he waited some more.

The lead searcher, gliding closer and closer to Malin, suddenly made a tiny, betraying movement. He or she had spotted some indication of Malin.

Malin fired, slamming a shot directly into the searcher to the rear. The lead searcher, unaware that their companion had already been dropped, swung a weapon around rather than seeking shelter first. That gave Malin time to twitch his own weapon to one side and fire again.

The second searcher was still falling when another shot tore through the warehouse behind and to one side of Malin.

He dropped, rolled, and sprinted into a location that offered some cover from that direction, then paused, breathing slowly and deeply, straining his senses for signs of whoever had fired.

They were moving. Two of them. Racing from cover to cover, never exposing themselves for more than brief moments, not to pin down and kill Malin, but along the edge of the warehouse and then, before he could react, out into the streets beyond.

The warehouse felt dead now, no one present except Malin himself. He stood up and walked to the two he had shot, carefully checking over the bodies from a few meters away in case of booby traps they could be wearing that their deaths might have activated.

Finally getting to one of the bodies, Malin searched it carefully and dispassionately, moving gently because he didn't want to trigger anything else and not out of respect for what was no longer a living foe. He found identification documents that looked completely legitimate but did not explain at all why this person had been in this warehouse at this time with a weapon. Malin felt sure this had been a snake agent, perhaps recently arrived, and that the other dead searcher was as well.

He called General Drakon's security forces, not wanting to turn this matter over to the police who were still tainted by their long history enforcing Syndicate laws. The security specialists would sweep this warehouse and the bodies for any signs of who they really were, what their plans had been, and who else might be helping them.

While Malin waited, he searched for and found the impact point for the shot that someone else had fired. It had been nowhere near him or any line of sight to him. Turning and locating the spot where he had awaited the searchers, Malin could see that anyone who had been aiming from here would have had a clean shot at him. Someone else, then, had fired at a person who was about to shoot Malin. Then pursued that someone through and out of the warehouse.

He was still standing there, going over questions to which he had no answers, when Drakon's security forces arrived. "See if there is any trace at all of anyone else having been in this building," Malin ordered them, then headed back toward Iceni's headquarters.

DRAKON stifled a yawn, determined not to betray by any signs how little sleep he had had the night before. Before him, virtual windows showed his three brigade commanders, Colonels Kai, Safir, and Rogero. "That's what we're facing at Iwa," Drakon concluded. "I want you to get with your best people and see if anyone can figure out how to take that alien base without it and everyone in our force getting blown to hell. Are there any questions?"

"We are to concentrate on attack scenarios?" Kai asked. "A long-term siege to starve out the enigmas is not on the table?"

"That's correct," Drakon said, not surprised that Kai had raised that question. Kai, slow and methodical, thought in defensive terms. Which could be a very useful mind-set in certain conditions. Just not this one. "We don't have the luxury of that much time."

The windows disappeared, leaving him alone, and Drakon did yawn this time. He cut the yawn short as a message came in from Colonel Malin outlining his activities of the night before. Attached was a summary of the results of the security search of the building where the fight had occurred. The two killed by Malin had both been wearing some special surveillance and security equipment that no one but a snake should possess, confirming their identities. But nothing on them or in the building offered any clues as to who their contacts were or what their mission had been. That wasn't what bothered Drakon the most, though.

Drakon called Malin. "Why wasn't I notified of this last night? You're acting as the president's aide right now, but you are still supposed to report security incidents to me directly as well as notifying President Iceni."

"There was no need for immediate notification, General," Malin replied. "The incident was over."

"According to your report, two other unknown individuals were involved and escaped," Drakon said. "That doesn't sound like *over* to me."

Malin paused before answering. "The snake site has been neutralized and shut down. The two unidentified individuals are a long-term issue, General. I will pursue that matter to its conclusion."

"That's not the point."

"No, sir. I understand. I should have informed you immediately."

It was only at that point that the real reason why Malin hadn't informed him right away popped into Drakon's head. He had been with Iceni last night, and Malin had interpreted that as a Do Not Disturb sign. "Colonel, I want it clearly understood that I should be informed of important developments at any time. That has not changed."

"Yes, sir. In the future, I will do so."

"Do you think one of those people you encountered was President Iceni's former assistant Togo?"

Malin nodded with every sign of confidence. "I have no doubt that the one who was preparing to kill me was Togo, sir."

"What about the other one? The one who apparently saved your life?"

This time Malin took several seconds to answer. "I have

no idea, General. I was only aware of that second person for a few brief seconds, not enough time to form any impressions."

"Yet, whoever it was, was better than you, and at least as good as Togo?" Drakon pressed.

Malin nodded again. "I realize that may narrow the list of possible suspects a great deal, sir."

"Roh Morgan could have gotten back to this star system, and back onto this planet, without being spotted," Drakon continued. "But if she is alive, and she did come back here, why is she hiding her presence?"

"I could only speculate, sir."

"Then speculate, dammit!"

"Yes, sir." Malin hesitated, a hint of distress crossing his features. "Colonel Morgan knows that her status in this unit has been compromised. Before she left for Ulindi, she was confined to quarters. If Colonel Morgan believes that she has some task to complete that revealing herself to you would hinder, then she would remain hidden from you in order to complete that task."

"Why not at least drop me a message? If Morgan is trying to stay hidden, there's no way anyone could find her."

"Yes, sir," Malin agreed. "But if you knew she was here, and you instituted a search for her, it might tip off her target."

"You think she's hunting Togo?"

"The events of last night would seem to imply that, General."

Drakon leaned back, eyeing Malin. "So you think Morgan is hiding her presence from everyone because she thinks that's the only way she could track down and nail Togo." What had his last orders been to Morgan regarding Togo? He had told her more than once not to go after him, but had he ever modified that order in a way that Morgan could interpret as authorization to hunt Togo now? No. He was sure he had not allowed that sort of exception, not before Togo vanished while Drakon himself was still on Ulindi and unaware of the desertion of Iceni's aide.

That must be why Morgan was staying hidden, if it was her. She was acting against his orders, and would expect him to tell her to stop. But, this time, Morgan didn't want to stop. She thought Togo had to be taken out in order to protect Drakon, and she was going to do it without any interference by him.

But that still left a puzzling question. "Let's say you're right, that Morgan has been hiding that she's still alive, and hiding her presence here because she wants to kill Togo. Why did she take that shot last night, then? If it was Morgan. Why did she take a shot that was likely to miss and alert her prey?"

"I don't know, General," Malin said, his expression harder than usual.

"Bran, you already admitted that shot saved your life."

Malin shook his head. "Sir, that cannot have been the reason, if it was Colonel Morgan who fired. My life was never anything to her but a—" He choked off the words, his face rigid with unstated feelings.

Rubbing his forehead, Drakon looked away, trying to imagine once again how it would feel to discover that Roh Morgan was your mother. "I'm sorry, Bran. I didn't mean to push you there."

Malin, looking and sounding composed once more, nodded a single time. "It is not as if she ever knew, General. Not consciously, anyway."

"Right." She had felt something, though. It had been hate at first sight when Morgan met Malin. Morgan had treated most men, with the notable exception of Drakon himself, with amused contempt. But not Malin. He had pushed her buttons just by existing. Why, if it was her, had Morgan not let Malin die in that warehouse, then nailed Togo when he let his guard down, thinking he was safe? It would take reading Morgan's mind to get an answer, and no one had ever proven good at that. And if she was pursuing Togo from deep undercover, that wasn't a bad thing. In fact, if Morgan did show up now, Drakon would probably order her to do exactly what she was doing. If that was all that she was doing. "Let me know the moment you learn anything else about either of those two mystery people. And if, somehow, you establish contact with the second one and it turns out to be Colonel Morgan, tell her I urgently need to speak with her and will assure her of safe status if she contacts me."

After ending that call, Drakon rubbed his face, straightened himself, then called Iceni. "Good morning, Gwen."

She was in her own office, looking considerably more rested than he felt. Iceni smiled. "You already told me that a couple of hours ago."

"I liked saying it," Drakon admitted. "Have you seen Malin's report?"

The smile was replaced with a businesslike expression. "I have. What is your take on it?"

"Three things, the first being the obvious that neither the Syndicate nor whoever is helping it have given up." Both he and Iceni suspected that person aiding the Syndicate to be her former assistant Togo, but neither knew what Togo's motives really were. Drakon didn't want to bring up the next topic, but knew he had to. "The second is that the two people who escaped the warehouse could have been your former aide Togo and my former aide Colonel Morgan."

Iceni gazed steadily back at him before replying. "She's alive?"

"I don't know. This incident last night is the first thing I know of that might indicate Morgan is still alive." The last person he wanted to talk about to Iceni was Morgan, especially after last night.

After several more seconds, Iceni nodded slowly. "You didn't have to tell me your suspicions of who that second person was, Artur."

"Yes, I did. I wouldn't keep something like that from you."

"Do you think Morgan is a danger to me?" Iceni asked coolly. "If she hears that you and I have become more than co-rulers of this star system?"

Drakon shook his head in reply. "No. She thinks that daughter of hers is going to become some sort of super warlord who will end up conquering every star system in what used to be the Syndicate Worlds. Morgan can play the long game very well. And, with one possible exception, she has always obeyed firm orders from me. One of those firm orders was not to harm you or let you be harmed."

"Would that possible exception be her sleeping with you despite your clearly expressed orders that subordinates shouldn't do that with superiors?" Iceni asked.

"That was my fault for getting so drunk," Drakon said. "I should have said no. I didn't."

"I won't belabor that point," she said, "because I agree with you. However, there have been lasting consequences. Morgan's daughter, wherever she is currently concealed, is not just hers. She is also your daughter." Iceni waited to see how he would react.

Drakon bit his lip. "Yes. That's true. Gwen, that baby girl hasn't done anything. I can't punish her for who her mother is. Or was, if Morgan is indeed dead."

Iceni smiled slightly. "Did it ever occur to you that I might feel the same way? Oh, I don't care for Morgan at all. And for a long time I didn't care to think about you and her and the offspring that resulted. But you've owned up to your mistake, accepting full responsibility. What you say is true. None of us get to choose our parents, and none of us should be blamed for who those parents are. The stars above know that I have often sneered at the claims of those who consider themselves special because their parents are powerful and wealthy. It makes no sense for me to condemn that child because I don't care for the mother."

"Thank you, Gwen." Drakon paused, trying to think what else to say.

"You said there were three things," Iceni prompted.

"Oh, yeah. The last thing is that we should have been told right after the incident in the warehouse happened."

"Agreed," Iceni said. "Since under the Syndicate it is simply assumed that any CEO is sleeping around, I don't understand why our subordinates felt a need to be so discreet. I've been trying to figure that out. But I think the problem will be solved if we openly acknowledge the relationship, even if we don't formalize it." She cocked her head slightly to one side and eyed him closely. "Do you have any objections to that?"

"You don't?" Drakon asked. "I mean, you're still interested? Even after talking about . . . ?"

"I could always change my mind if you hesitate too long or keep bringing up unpleasant subjects." Iceni's gaze on him grew more intense. "Do you have any objections?"

"To acknowledging the relationship or formalizing it?" Drakon asked.

"Take your pick."

"No, I don't have a problem with that."

Iceni raised an eyebrow at him. "With acknowledging it or formalizing it?"

"Take your pick," Drakon said, wondering how she would respond.

She laughed. "Serves me right after I teased you yesterday afternoon. I personally favor acknowledging the relationship, but holding off the formalities until we resolve the situation at Iwa."

"That could take a while," Drakon pointed out.

"I know. But I don't think we need the distraction, and I don't want anyone thinking we've rushed things because of a belief that I might not come back from Iwa." Iceni paused, waiting for a response from him that did not come. "You're not arguing with that? Are we agreed that I will need to accompany our forces to Iwa?"

Drakon nodded, feeling a heaviness inside. "You actually convinced me yesterday afternoon when you pointed out that you had sent me to Ulindi. It was necessary that I go there, but it must have been difficult for you. Seeing you off to Iwa will be hard, but I can't expect a partner of mine to live by a different set of rules than I follow."

She smiled again. "That's why I remain interested in you. You keep passing your tests, General. I will admit to you that I won't be thrilled to be going, but as you say necessity must rule our actions. Speaking of actions, there's another decision coming up. *Manticore* will reach orbit around this world today and those three soldiers from Iwa will be shuttled down to here." Iceni gave Drakon an inquiring look. "What are you going to do with the three soldiers?"

He shrugged. "Let my medical people check them out and fix them up, while my intelligence people find out everything they saw at Iwa and try to learn anything they might have observed but didn't realize was important. Then do what I usually do. Security screen them, and if they pass ask if they want to join my forces. I have no idea from the Kommodor's report whether any of those three are hardcore Syndicate, or have strong family ties that they wouldn't want to imperil by joining us."

Iceni looked pensive, putting her hand to her mouth and looking off to the side. "They were rescued from an enigma-controlled world. Black Jack's fleet rescued humans from the enigmas, too. But now *we* have. That is going to give us important standing with everyone who hears of it."

"I love it when you talk like that," Drakon said, amused and relieved that the conversation had gone so well despite the need to talk about Morgan.

She gave him a sidelong look. "We have enough challenges facing us that we need to make use of every possible resource."

"I was thinking about that," Drakon said. "Every possible resource. What are you going to do with that heavy cruiser we just captured?"

"Something that big isn't just my decision," Iceni said. "You get a say even though this is a mobile forces unit. The obvious thing to do is to add it to our forces, and screen the surviving crew to see which ones we can trust. But . . ."

Drakon nodded, "What's the hitch?"

"Money," Iceni said. She spread her hands in the age-old gesture of helplessness. "We've had enough discussions about this, especially before mounting that operation to Ulindi. Midway is one star system. We're not particularly wealthy, though thanks to the hypernet gate and transit fees on merchant ships using our many jump points we rake in more money than most star systems like ours. We've been collecting more warships, and using up expendable weapons and fuel cells, and recruiting crews, and . . ." She sighed. "In a perfect world we'd keep adding more warships until we matched Black Jack's fleet. But money is getting tight. We can borrow, we can delay, but we have to think of the future as well as right now."

It felt good to hear her talking about "we" and knowing that Iceni really meant it. "Are you thinking of scrapping that heavy cruiser because we can't afford it?"

"No! It's too valuable. But it will require a lot of repairs, and a crew that has to be paid. I haven't decided." Iceni waved one hand toward him. "What do you think?"

Drakon returned the gesture. "You brought this up before. If we can't pay for it, why can't we get someone else to pay for it?"

She laughed. "I don't— You're serious?"

"We handed a battle cruiser over to Taroa," Drakon pointed out.

"A battle cruiser that was not even half-built," Iceni protested. Then she fell silent as she considered Drakon's words. "We've already reached out to surrounding star systems to form a tighter relationship for self-defense and trade. They're concerned that we're just going to use that as a step for eventually establishing full control over them by building a new, mini-Syndicate."

"But," Drakon said, "if we give one of them something as substantial as a heavy cruiser, even one that needs repairs . . ."

She nodded quickly. "I wasn't actually ready to start offering warships to other star systems. Mentally, I know the importance of that. Emotionally, I still want every warship here at Midway that I can get my hands on. But you are right. And there are still some survivors of the Reserve Flotilla who haven't found new jobs. Some of them would surely want to go to that heavy cruiser, no matter whether it ended up at Taroa, or Ulindi, or Kane, or— Who gets that cruiser, Artur?"

"Taroa." Drakon leaned back and explained. "They're finishing building that battle cruiser that the Syndicate started. According to the status reports that I'm getting, in another few months that battle cruiser will be well enough along that other people might decide it's worth trying to steal it, or the Syndicate might get wind of it and decide to send in a small force to sabotage it if they can't steal it. Taroa needs the heavy cruiser to protect the battle cruiser, until that battle cruiser can protect itself."

She nodded to him, smiling. "I can't find any flaws in that reasoning. Taroa is also, aside from Ulindi, the best positioned to actually be able to pay for repairing and operating that warship. As soon as the heavy cruiser is fixed up enough to safely jump to Taroa, we'll gift it to them as a sign of our deep commitment to the security of neighboring star systems, and that we meant what we said to them. And you know what else, Artur?"

"What?"

"I just realized that during this whole conversation I never once found myself wondering what other game you might be playing, what cards you were holding back, or how you might be maneuvering to position yourself against me."

He gazed at her, surprised to realize the same of himself. "Damn. Saves a lot of time when you're not worried about a knife in the back, doesn't it?"

Iceni's smile broadened. "We're going to do it, Artur. You and me. We're going to beat the enigmas, and Imallye, and the Syndicate, and we are going to make this star system and those around it into something that will stand against every danger."

He smiled back and nodded, trying not to show the fears he felt about her facing both the enigmas and Imallye at Iwa. "How about discussing it over dinner?"

"Yes," she said. "I'd love to . . . discuss more with you tonight. Your heavily defended place or mine?"

THE next morning, she and Drakon went together to the ground forces medical wards to see the three rescued soldiers. Iceni wanted to make it publicly clear that the relationship was not a one-night thing and that it was not considered a secret by either her or Drakon. She also wanted to see those soldiers.

The three had obviously benefited from the medically imposed sleep aboard *Manticore* as well as from all of the intravenous and regular nourishment that could safely be pumped into them. Their bodies showed substantial recovery from the hardships that the three had endured. But their eyes still held that trapped-animal look which would take longer to heal than the damage done to their bodies. "I want to thank you for a job well done, and assure you that you will be welcome in this star system should you pass the security screening," Iceni told them.

The three, lying in three adjacent med units, stared at her with varying degrees of incomprehension and disbelief. Finally, the most senior spoke up hesitantly. "Honored CEO—"

"President," Iceni corrected.

"Honored . . . President, we failed in our mission."

"Your mission," Drakon said, "changed. The moment it became clear that you had no chance against the aliens and the rest of your unit died, your mission became to survive so that the records in your armor and your own personal observations could be of use to us in retaking Iwa for humanity."

The woman's eyes grew dark. "You are going to retake Iwa? Avenge our fellow workers?"

"Yes," Drakon said.

"I will give you all you wish. Ask me! I will . . . I will even go back! I will go back there and fight them again!"

"I will, too," the senior of the three added after a brief hesitation.

The third averted his eyes, shivering as he stared at nothing. Drakon, well aware of how stress could break anyone, spoke to all three of them. "I appreciate your volunteering. None of you will be required to go. All of you would need medical clearance before you can go, and that may take more time than we have before the assault force leaves here. Your observations, your experiences, anything you saw on Iwa, could be immensely valuable to us. When my people come by to ask you about them, be as accurate and complete as you can."

"Yes, hon— Sir?"

"General. General Drakon."

"You are no longer Syndicate?"

"No," Drakon said. "We are free. And we will free Iwa."

"KOMMODOR Marphissa has shuttled down to the planet for a conference on the Iwa operation," Iceni told Drakon as she prepared to leave his headquarters. "We're going to be discussing how many warships to send. Do you want to attend?"

Drakon shook his head. "Not unless you want me there. I'd just endorse whatever you decided."

"How sweet." Iceni shook her head back at him. "That's not a requirement for being in a relationship with me."

He grinned. "Good thing, since I wouldn't always do it. But in this case, I don't know much about mobile forces. You do, and you'll be talking to the mobile forces commanders, who seem to be very good at their jobs. Is Bradamont going to be there?"

"Of course."

"Then I'd just be taking up space and consuming oxygen other minds might be needing." Drakon gestured back toward the inside of his headquarters. "What I do need to be doing is figuring out how to take that underground enigma base."

"You deal with your area of responsibility, then, and I'll

deal with mine." Iceni blinked and looked away. "How many are going to die this time, Artur?"

"I don't know, Gwen." He sought for the right words. "If we don't do this, if the enigmas dig into Iwa and fan out from there, they'll take down Imallye and every star system in this region. How many would die if that happens?"

"Too damned many." She sighed, then forced a smile as she looked back at him. "Isn't it odd to feel superior because you want to limit how many people die because of your orders? But we are better than the Syndicate, and whatever their reasons are we are better than the enigmas who would kill so ruthlessly and give us no opportunity to make a deal both sides can live with."

"I think we're better than Imallye, too," Drakon said.

"That just leaves Black Jack, doesn't it?" Iceni asked sarcastically. "We can't claim to be better than him, can we?"

"We'll have to try to better him," Drakon said. "That's the only way we'll beat Imallye, the enigmas, and the Syndicate if they decide to throw in, too."

ANOTHER conference room, this time in Iceni's complex. Just outside was the star system command center, with a truly awesome and immense display that sometimes seemed capable of showing entire planets at one-to-one scale. Iceni had learned that such displays were traps, though. Looking at them, it was far too easy to believe that they showed everything, in perfect detail. What was far harder to realize was that anything the sensors could not see, anything unknown, would not be shown on the display. As capable as they were, the automated routines running the displays were incapable of conceiving of the possibility that their image of the universe was incomplete. Of course, they weren't capable of conceiving anything, just processing known data as they had been programmed to do, but that was very easy to forget when gazing at the godlike perspective a command center display offered.

She entered to find Kommodor Marphissa and Captain Bradamont already waiting, standing beside their seats. Two other places at the table were actually empty, but apparently occupied by the virtual presences of Kapitan Mercia and Kapitan Kontos also standing at attention. "Take your seats," Iceni directed.

Marphissa and Bradamont sat down at the same time as Iceni, but the two officers attending by virtual means remained standing.

Iceni glanced at the time delays glowing beside the two images. Mercia aboard *Midway* was several light minutes from the planet, which would mean an annoying but endurable level of delay in any inputs she had to the meeting. Kontos, though, was nearly a light hour distant aboard *Pele*. This meeting would very likely have been over for a while before Kontos's image finally sat down in response to Iceni's direction. But even though he would not be able to provide his own opinions and advice, Kontos would get to see the deliberations and send onward later any suggestions he might have.

She nodded toward Marphissa. "You did a very impressive job at Iwa and Moorea. I regret not being in the command center to greet you in person when you arrived, Kommodor."

Marphissa hesitated in her reply. "I . . . understand . . . that you were . . . otherwise occupied, Madam President."

Iceni frowned at Marphissa, puzzled by the vague wording. "General Drakon and I have established a personal relationship. There is nothing remotely odd about CEO sleeping arrangements changing. Why is everyone tiptoeing around the matter?"

"I don't know," Marphissa confessed. "It just doesn't feel appropriate with you and the general. Talking about it, I mean."

Bradamont looked amused. "Congratulations, Madam President. You're transcending your previous role as a Syndicate Worlds CEO."

Iceni switched her frown to focus on the Alliance officer. "What does that mean?"

"They don't see the rules for a CEO applying to you," Bradamont explained. "They're treating your personal life with respect, not because it is demanded of them but because they think you deserve it."

"I will never understand workers," Iceni muttered, lowering her gaze to the table. Yet the implied compliment, if Bradamont was right, did make her feel very good. She composed herself, raised her eyes, and pointed to the two women who were present and the images of Kontos and Mercia. "We're here not to talk about my love life, but about how to handle the operation at Iwa. I am open to opinions as to how many warships to take to Iwa and how many to leave here to defend Midway, and as to who should remain at Midway in command of that defense force."

"The basic problem with the command question," Bradamont said, all business now, "is that your best two possibilities are both commanders of your two strongest assets. I would nominate Kapitan Mercia, but you will want the battleship *Midway* at Iwa, so if she stays behind to command the defense that would require passing command of *Midway* to someone else not long before an extended combat operation."

"I could leave Kommodor Marphissa here and command the flotilla at Iwa," Iceni prodded, wanting to see how they would respond.

Bradamont exchanged a single glance with Marphissa before replying. "Madam President, I have reviewed the operations that you have commanded. You have some skill. But Kommodor Marphissa is very much your superior at commanding warships in battle. I would strongly urge you to assign her in command of the forces at Iwa."

"A very blunt reply, Captain," Iceni said. "Also, I believe, a truthful one. I need to be at Iwa to provoke an attack by Imallye there, but I agree that the Kommodor should command our warships against Imallye. Kapitan Mercia, reply with your suggestions as to who might serve as commander of *Midway* if you remain here to oversee the defense of this star system."

"What about the heavy cruiser captains?" Marphissa asked. "Would any of them be acceptable as commanders of the defense at Midway? If we are taking both *Midway* and *Pele* to Iwa, then any defensive force here will be built around one or more heavy cruisers."

Kapitan Mercia's virtual image finally sat down. None of the others paid attention to that, being used to the way that virtual conferences could involve significantly staggered response times.

"*Manticore* has Kapitan Diaz," Bradamont said. "*Gryphon* has Kapitan Stein, and *Kraken* has Kapitan Seney. Kapitan-Leytenant Lerner on *Basilisk* is too junior, and Seney is the least experienced of the full Kapitans. Either Diaz or Stein might be able to handle it."

"Might be. Why would we have to leave Kapitan Mercia here? We have you, Captain Bradamont. You have ridden *Manticore*," Iceni pointed out. "You, Captain, are known to *Manticore*'s crew, and you know Kapitan Diaz. Would you ride *Manticore* again, and give him the benefit of your experience at flotilla command if he were assigned to defend this star system?"

Bradamont only paused for a moment before nodding. "Yes, Madam President. Such a task would be fully in keeping with my orders from Admiral Geary."

Kapitan Mercia's reply finally arrived. "I will have to consider a list of possible replacements for command of *Midway*, Madam President, but I am hesitant to recommend assigning a new commanding officer to my ship so soon before what will likely be a major engagement."

"Not to worry, Kapitan Mercia," Iceni said, waving away her words. "As you will see before you see this reply, we have resolved that matter. You will remain in command of *Midway* and Kapitan Kontos in command of *Pele*.

"How large a force do we leave with Kapitan Diaz?" Iceni continued. "At least two heavy cruisers, surely."

"*Manticore* and *Basilisk*," Marphissa suggested. "One or two light cruisers, and four Hunter-Killers."

"Make it two light cruisers," Bradamont said. "That way

Diaz will be able to split his force into two equal formations if necessary to guard against more than one threat vector. And I would suggest *Gryphon* instead of *Basilisk*. If Diaz does decide to split his force, the commander of the other group will need to be as experienced as possible."

Marphissa nodded. "*Manticore* and *Gryphon*, then. Light cruisers *Osprey* and *Kite*. Hunter-Killers *Guide*, *Vanguard*, *Picket*, and *Watch*. That is my proposal for a defensive force for Midway, Madam President."

Iceni looked toward the images of Mercia and Kontos, knowing that only Mercia was close enough to respond in any reasonable time. After a few more minutes, Mercia nodded. "I concur with my Kommodor."

"Presumably, Kapitan Kontos will have no objections," Iceni said, drawing grins from Bradamont, Marphissa, and a little while later from Mercia. Kontos had a firmly established reputation as someone who would respond to any order with enthusiasm and a sincere belief in the wisdom of both Iceni and Marphissa. "That means our force at Iwa will consist of *Midway*, *Pele*, the heavy cruisers *Kraken* and *Basilisk*, light cruisers *Falcon*, *Hawk*, and *Eagle*, and Hunter-Killers *Sentry*, *Sentinel*, *Scout*, *Defender*, *Guardian*, *Pathfinder*, *Protector*, and *Patrol*."

"We will take Imallye with that flotilla," Marphissa predicted. "And the enigmas if they dare to show their faces."

"Even if they show up, the enigmas won't show their faces," Bradamont pointed out.

"Madam President," Marphissa asked after wincing at Bradamont's joke, "have you made any determination regarding the heavy cruiser captured during the latest Syndicate attack?"

"Yes," Iceni said. "I have already been informed that repairs sufficient to return that heavy cruiser to combat status are unlikely to be concluded in less than a month, so odds are it will not be available to add to our forces during this operation. In any event, I do not intend to fully repair the heavy cruiser." She paused to let that sink in and watched surprise appear on both Marphissa's and Bradamont's faces. "The heavy cruiser will be offered to Taroa. They require a strong unit to protect the battle cruiser under construction there."

Bradamont smiled. "That is an impressive gift, Madam President, one that will surely convince the Taroans and other star systems of the sincerity of your offers of alliance."

Iceni shook a reproving finger at Bradamont. "We never use the word *alliance* to describe our association of star systems, Captain. It has bad connotations everywhere that was touched by the war, and in a century of war no star system was left untouched even if the losses were confined to young men and women sent to battle who never came home."

Her smile gone, Bradamont nodded. "I understand, Madam President. My apologies."

"You need not apologize, Captain," Iceni said. "I am certain that no one in Alliance space ever calls themselves part of a Syndicate. We just need to be careful to avoid using terms that will prejudice those we want to view us with favor."

"I understand," Bradamont repeated. "I suppose if I were a politician I would have known how to say things, but if—" She stopped speaking.

Iceni gave her an exaggeratedly inquiring look. "But if?"

"I was unthinkingly repeating a common saying in the Alliance," Bradamont said.

"I'd like to hear all of it."

"Very well." Bradamont finished the sentence she had earlier broken off. "If I were a politician I would have known how to say things, but if I were a politician you wouldn't be able to believe what I said."

"You were embarrassed to say that?" Marphissa asked.

"To the president, yes!"

Iceni smiled. "Any president who can't handle people speaking frankly around her isn't cut out for the job. I assure you that the vast majority of people who live under or have lived under the Syndicate would agree with that saying."

"They wouldn't admit to it out loud," Marphissa said. "Not if the Syndicate is still in charge where they are. But they all think it."

"I'll still watch my words," Bradamont said with a re-lieved smile. "Out of respect."

"Hmmph," Iceni scoffed. "I'll remind everyone that Granaile Imallye does not have any love or respect for me, and as a result is threatening this entire star system. Make the necessary arrangements for dividing the mobile forces and preparing them for these operations," Iceni told Marphissa. "I want every warship going to Iwa to be at maximum combat capability. Captain Bradamont, I am again indebted to you for your assistance. You are autho-rized effective immediately to communicate directly with Kapitan Diaz and Kapitan Stein to discuss the defensive operations here. I will speak with General Drakon about his planned force so we will know how many of our troop trans-ports to employ on this operation."

Iceni saw the flicker of reaction in Bradamont's eyes to her last statement, and knew why. Drakon would almost certainly assign Colonel Rogero to the task of taking the enigma base, meaning that Bradamont would be seeing her lover depart on another extremely risky mission. Iceni nod-ded silently to Bradamont in recognition of the burden that she and Rogero shared with Iceni and Drakon. Go they must, but some of those who went to Iwa would not come back.

CHAPTER ELEVEN

THE suite where Iceni lived, once designated by Syndicate laws and regulations as the Star System CEO Operations and Accommodations Suite and now simply called the President's Suite, was one of the most heavily alarmed and protected places on the planet. The bedroom where Iceni slept in that suite was *the* most alarmed and protected place on the planet, with the possible exception of the bedroom in Drakon's headquarters where he normally slept.

However, for a canny Syndicate CEO, even that level of security was not sufficient. After all, any alarm installed could be broken into by enemies, or the Syndicate Internal Security Service snakes, and rendered useless. Redundant and overlapping layers of alarms merely made the process of doing that more challenging. As the old inside joke went, there was a name for CEOs who underestimated the resourcefulness of their rivals, or the snakes, or embittered workers, and that name was "dead."

And since her former close assistant Togo had gone missing, and apparently rogue, Iceni had been uncomfortably aware of how many codes and secrets he had been privy to. Even if he had supposedly not known some of the access codes, he could have found out what they were from his position on Iceni's staff.

So Iceni had acquired other alarms, rigged up independently of the installed systems, and set them up. They were among the highest tech alarms available on Midway.

She had also set up a few other alarms, using perhaps the oldest such systems in the book, reasoning that someone focused on defeating the sophisticated threats might overlook the simple ones. A metal tray leaned against one door, ready to fall with a clatter if the door opened a little. A breakable glass object, hard to acquire in these days of enduraglass and permaglass, teetered on a ledge above another door, certain to drop and smash if that door began to open. And scattered on the floor in front of every other possible access were small contact caps, toys that would explode with a loud snap under the slightest pressure, something which delighted children, drove parents to distraction, and might trip up anyone clever and skillful enough to penetrate every other alarm.

She had spent the last two nights at Drakon's headquarters, enjoying the comfort of having someone so close without worrying about how that someone might use her or betray her. And with only about two weeks left before the expedition left for Iwa, she wanted to spend as much time as possible with Drakon, knowing that there was a chance it might be all the time they would have. But he was elsewhere on the planet tonight, inspecting one of his brigades, so Iceni slept alone. She had paused before scattering the contact caps, tired and not feeling like the effort, but had forced herself to do it as a small voice of experience or paranoia warned her that during her absence someone might have been able to test the defenses of her living area.

The pop of one of the contact caps in the darkest hour of the night jolted Iceni awake. She rolled out of her bed on the far side from the door, the wall at her back, one hand grasping the weapon she always kept handy and the other hand slapping the emergency alarm pad above her.

She hit the floor on her knees, the bed between her and the door to her bedroom, her pistol lined up on that door.

The blare of the alarm covered up any more sounds from outside, but activating it had also summoned many guards, granted access for the guards into her suite, and alerted the entire building.

Iceni waited, tense, her pistol centered on the door. She breathed slowly and carefully, trying to calm the pounding of her heart. Who could have made it past every obstacle and into her living area? Even if Morgan was still alive she shouldn't have had access to enough inside information to be able to pierce the layers of security around Iceni's quarters. Only one other name came to mind, and if it was Togo out there, and he was determined to get in here, then Iceni knew that she would need not only great accuracy but also skill to take him out before Togo could get to her.

Yet even while focused on the need to ensure she hit Togo with her first shot and every shot, Iceni could not help wondering what his goal was, what his purpose was, and why someone who had been so loyal to her would now be threatening her.

The sound of the alarm ceased, telling Iceni that her guards had entered her suite and were now advancing toward her bedroom. She listened intently, her hand growing sweaty as she gripped her pistol tightly and kept it aimed at the door.

The clatter of the metal tray could be heard outside, followed by the crash of breaking glass. So much for those improvised alarms. Now people would talk about them, and she would have to come up with something else unknown to anyone but her.

The comm pad next to Iceni's bed lit up, showing the senior watch supervisor at the star system command center that was located near Iceni's headquarters. "Madam President, your guards have searched the outer living area and found nothing. They are poised outside of your inner living area and can see your door. There is no threat apparent on our sensors, but after you sounded the alarm a string of doors and accesses that should have immediately sealed instead remained open, and there were indications of movement near them."

Iceni breathed out slowly, relaxing herself. "Full search. Nothing by remote, all eyes-on and hands-on. All rooms in this building, all doors and accesses. Find out how those open doors were hacked. I want to be absolutely certain that whoever got into my living area has not faked a retreat and is still hiding somewhere, waiting until things calm down to make another try."

"I understand and will comply," the supervisor said, saluting and beginning to issue the necessary orders.

Iceni slumped back against the wall of her bedroom, then realized that anyone who knew where she slept and that she would roll out of bed in this direction and have her back to that wall might be able to set a trap on the other side. She jerked herself away from the wall and moved in a crouch to another location in the bedroom, her weapon now aimed between the door and the area where she had previously been.

She settled herself comfortably, resting the pistol on one knee so it remained up and pointed in the right direction. The sort of search she had ordered would take considerable time. It was going to be a long night.

EVEN when warships could zip across thousands of kilometers of space in seconds, it took a while to cover planetary distances when hindered by atmosphere. By the time General Drakon arrived at midmorning, Iceni was behind her desk and sipping hot tea. "You are all right, Gwen?" he asked, knowing that she might have concealed an unpleasant truth for the sake of political stability.

"I'm fine." She offered him a seat, trying to act more casual than she felt. "I am also tired, and achy, and more than a little annoyed."

"Annoyed." Drakon, reassuring in his presence and his strength, sat down and smiled slightly. "I'm a little more than annoyed."

"Colonel Malin's suspicions must be correct," Iceni said. "Only Togo could have gone undetected as far as that intruder did last night."

"We can't be certain it was him," Drakon said. "I understand that you've ordered Malin to review your security systems and make some changes."

Iceni nodded, taking a slow drink to steady her jumpy nerves. "The access codes had already been changed, of course, but they're going to be changed again. I suspect all redundant versions of my security software are infected by worms that my intruder activated. My software specialists swear that the activations will leave footprints that will allow them to find and neutralize those worms."

Drakon snorted with derision. "If there was one undetected set of worms in that software, there could be more."

She nodded, feeling a flash of the old anger. "I want to punish someone, Artur. Order some supervisors to be shot for failing in their duties. I know that would be stupid, that if I get rid of trained, experienced personnel before I even know who if anyone has actually made a mistake, that I will be just weakening my own security instead of strengthening it." Her voice trembled slightly with fury. "But the part of me that is still stuck in the Syndicate really wants to kill someone right now."

"I'll help."

For some reason that matter-of-fact offer helped cool her rage. "Thank you." Iceni sighed and took another drink. "You haven't asked, but I am screening everyone in my building again to ensure none of them have turned traitor on me."

"If they had," Drakon pointed out, "they would have already bolted."

"I know. But I still have to check out the possibility."

"Malin will find anyone who let you down," he said.

She gave him a quizzical look. "Why aren't you angrier about this? I don't want you to be. I need a stable anchor right now. But why aren't you stomping around threatening to kill whoever threatened me?"

Drakon smiled, but it wasn't a happy smile. It was the sort of smile that gave Iceni a pleasant shiver up her back. "I am angry. But anger makes me more focused. It makes me want to ensure I make the right moves, that I get whoever is responsible, and not whoever makes a handy scapegoat."

"That's a nice talent," Iceni approved. "I should have realized that about you before now. You've shown plenty of signs of it before this. No wonder you managed to survive the Syndicate. The more they screwed with you, the more focused you must have gotten."

"That's right." He looked grim once more, then nodded upward. "Maybe it would be a good idea for you to take up residence aboard the *Midway* sooner rather than later. Not that I want you up in space instead of down here with me, but if you're on that battleship it will be a lot harder for anyone to get to you."

"It's supposed to be impossible for anyone to get to me *here*," Iceni said, her voice getting sharp again. "But I see your point. I'll miss seeing you in person, but I can handle my presidential tasks from orbit, and it will make it easier to oversee the preparations for the expedition to Iwa if I am up there." She bent a crooked smile at Drakon. "You tried to talk me out of going to Iwa, and now here you are urging me to get going. Is that what you do with all of your lovers?"

"No," he said.

"I'm just teasing, Artur. To help calm myself. Bear with me." Iceni thought about what it would take to move herself up to the battleship today, but then another thought intruded. "What if my intruder goes after you once I'm no longer available?"

"I'm hoping he or she does," Drakon said, showing that smile again.

She wagged a finger at him. "Don't underestimate the danger."

"I'm not. Like you said, getting through your defenses to this point was impressive. But I have a few tricks even he, or she, might have trouble with."

Iceni found herself smiling, feeling calmer in the face of Drakon's steady assurance. "Good. When I get back from Iwa, let's make this relationship formal."

"Limited time or open-ended?" Drakon asked.

"Open-ended, if you're good with that." She kept her voice casual, but felt tension inside as she waited for his answer.

"Yeah," Drakon agreed. "I'm good with that. When you get back."

"It's a date." After he had left to personally speak with Malin, Iceni sat at her desk for a while, pretending to work. It had been important not to hurry to make the commitment before she left, to not project any image to the citizens of appearing to fear whether or not she would return. She could tell that Artur had understood that. But it now left her worried whether, with her promise to handle that important task when she returned, she had just jinxed both of them.

AS much as he disliked meetings, Drakon realized that occasionally there was no substitute for them. As long as whoever was in charge kept the discussion moving and worthwhile instead of meandering into endless blind alleys.

And this time his brigade commanders had asked for the meeting, which hopefully meant that someone had thought of something useful.

To Drakon's surprise, it was Colonel Kai who led the discussion about plans for Iwa. But Kai soon provided the reasons for his role.

"After careful thought," Kai said, as if he did not always think carefully before acting and speaking, "I believe that a certain tactic employed during the second and third decades of the war with the Alliance might give us insight into how the enigmas might defend their installation."

Kai brought up a virtual window that was visible to not only Geary and Colonel Gozen, but also to the other two brigade commanders who like Kai were attending this briefing virtually. The relatively tiny distances involved on the surface of a planet meant that there were none of the time delays that Drakon had heard bedeviled virtual conferences in space. "At the time," Kai explained, "the Alliance was rebounding from initial setbacks and threatening to seize

Syndicate installations in several star systems. Having bled out its own ground forces in a series of futile offensives, the Syndicate could not adequately defend those installations. Therefore, a policy of calibrated self-destruction was adopted."

Drakon studied the new window and the images on it. "The installations were wired for self-destruct, but not so the whole place would blow at once."

"Yes, sir," Kai said. "As Alliance forces seized one portion of the installation, that portion was destroyed. When another portion was captured, it too was destroyed."

"Along with any Syndicate ground forces or citizens left in those portions?" Colonel Safir asked in amazement. "That's harsh even by Syndicate standards."

"But it worked," Kai said. "The Alliance realized what was happening after suffering serious casualties every time a newly captured or almost-captured area blew up around the victorious Alliance forces. The Alliance had to pause its offensives in various star systems in order to develop new attack methods and tactics."

"But the Syndicate stopped using that tactic when its own ground forces were able to get back up to strength?" Drakon asked.

"Yes, sir. By accessing highly classified files previously restricted to snake CEOs, I was able to determine that the negative morale aspects of the tactic were threatening to undermine Syndicate defenses as badly as the lack of ground forces had."

Colonel Rogero nodded, smiling bitterly. "Of course. Once the soldiers figured out that the place they were defending might blow up at any moment, instead of standing their ground they started retreating as fast as possible to avoid being killed by their own side. Is that correct?"

"That is correct," Colonel Kai said. "However, from what Black Jack's fleet saw of the enigmas, individual enigmas rarely appeared to balk at suicidal tactics aimed at protecting their privacy. That would make this a plausible tactic for them, and, again according to Black Jack's reporting as well as our own observations of the aftermath of space battles in this star system, the enigmas have a tendency to employ self-destruction to avoid any compromise of their secrets."

"Good job," Drakon said. "I bet you're right. Ground tactics built around blowing up an entire installation as soon as it was attacked would just lead to quick defeat of the enigma race. But holding out until the entire installation was nearly occupied would give away too many of their secrets. Blowing up their bases in segments would allow them to tailor the self-destructs to match the situation, and discourage any attempts to capture those bases."

"For those reasons, General," Kai added, "I believe it is safe to assume that the enigmas will have developed a flexible self-destruct capability in their ground installations that can be tailored to meet requirements. They can probably quickly and easily designate exactly which portions of the installation to destroy and immediately carry out the task."

Drakon sat back, one hand to his mouth, still looking at the old diagrams and thinking. "How do we beat that?"

"If we simply want to destroy the installation piece by piece," Kai suggested, "then send in robotic scouts. We would need a lot of scouts, though, as we must assume the enigma defenses would inflict serious losses on anything trying to enter their base."

"We don't have that many, not even close, and the enigmas must have watched humans try to employ robotic combatants often enough to have seen all of the countertactics the Syndicate and the Alliance have used over the last century," Drakon said. "The command and control links are too easily severed by jamming, or intruded upon."

"The enigmas have demonstrated extensive capabilities to mess with software on our warships," Safir said. "They can surely do the same to our battle armor and other ground forces software."

Drakon stared at her as Safir's words penetrated and he realized the implications. "Where is the armor those three soldiers from Iwa were wearing?"

"Still on that ship, I think," Rogero offered. "It was going to be brought down on a routine shuttle run."

"The code monkeys on that ship can scan for enigma quantum-coded worms in their own software, right? Did they do any scans like that of the battle armor software that came off Iwa?"

Everyone else finally understood. "Our system software might also already be laced with enigma worms?" Safir said, horrified. "If we went into a fight against them like that—"

"They'd wipe us out," Rogero finished. "Maybe that's what happened to that unit the three soldiers were in. Maybe enigma worms provided the long-range targeting. But then how did going passive save the three soldiers from death?"

"Let's see if we can find out," Drakon said. "Colonel Kai, what tactics did the Alliance ultimately develop to use against the Syndicate's calibrated self-destruction?"

Kai spread his hands. "I could find nothing in the files available to us that speaks specifically about Alliance countertactics. There are just general statements that such tactics had been or were being developed."

Drakon turned to Gozen, who had been sitting silently to one side of Drakon's office, listening to the discussion. "Colonel Gozen, take the lead on working with the space apes to check the armor of those three soldiers for enigma worms. Let me know if any are found. If that battle armor is infected, we'll have to check every set of armor and every system down here as well." He turned back to face the others. "Colonel Rogero, check with Captain Bradamont on whether she ever heard anything about Alliance counter-tactics against that calibrated self-destruction. I'm not expecting her to have ever heard of it, but maybe somebody mentioned something."

"Would Black Jack know anything about it?" Safir asked. "He's from back around then, right?"

Rogero shook his head. "Black Jack was lost in survival sleep after one of the first battles of the war. All he knows of the first decades of the war is what he might have read in old reports. But I will ask Captain Bradamont."

Hunching forward over his desk, resting his arms on the surface, Drakon eyed his colonels. "This job keeps getting more difficult. I know that can be discouraging. However, we have never met a challenge we could not overcome. I have the utmost confidence that together we will figure out a way to kick the enigmas out of their underground base at Iwa and not lose our own butts in the process."

When Gozen reported back two hours later, her eyes were wide. "Those space code monkeys say the three sets of battle armor from Iwa are pumped full of so many enigma worms that they feel like fishing bait buckets."

"Great." Drakon considered his first response, then repeated it in more enthusiastic tones. "Great. We've discovered some of the enigma weapons that would have been used against us. Those warships know how to scrub out all the worms, right?"

"Yes, sir," Gozen said. "It's sort of weird. Instead of anti-malware software like we're familiar with, the stuff the warships use scans the operating software for stable, persistent patterns at the quantum level, and if it finds any it cancels out the patterns using quantum wave interference. Whoever thought of that was a genius."

"So I understand," Drakon said. "She was an Alliance battle cruiser commander. Someone whom Captain Bradamont knew."

"Knew?" Gozen asked.

"She died at Varandal, fighting our own Reserve Flotilla."

Gozen shook her head. "More waste. How much human potential did that war grind into dust? And our side, the Syndicate, killed the person who might provide a critical boost to our efforts to beat the enigmas?"

"Yeah," Drakon said. There really wasn't any need for more words than that.

She sighed, then saluted him. "I've already arranged through Colonel Malin for warship code monkeys to come down here and run our people through the drills so they can scan all of our stuff. Colonel Malin gave it priority from the president's office, so it should only take three hours for the shuttles to get those monkeys to us, then an estimated hour longer for scans to start."

"Good."

"And Colonel Rogero asked me to tell you that when he asked Captain Bradamont about an obscure aspect of Alliance ground forces tactics eighty years ago he received in reply a quote blank stare unquote."

Drakon couldn't suppress a grin. "That's what I expected. Anything else?"

"The docs say that one of those three soldiers from Iwa is broke too bad for him to get back into combat condition," Gozen reported. "From what they got out of him and the other two, his unit had been chewed up fighting a rebellion-suppression mission at some star about two dozen jumps from here. Instead of sending the survivors in for treatment, the Syndicate broke up the unit and sent the survivors out piecemeal as replacements to units that needed the warm bodies."

His smile vanished as Drakon clenched a fist. "Already nearly broken and the Syndicate just sent him out again, without even the support his former comrades could have offered. He's the one who couldn't talk to me? I suspected something like that. Tell the docs to see what they can do and to take their time. Maybe they can pump enough happy pills into him to help him be functional again in some non-combat job."

"Already told them that, sir."

"What about the other two?"

"Not nearly as settled as they ought to be," Gozen said. "But good enough if you want to take them along with the assault."

"I'll get a final appraisal on them just prior to the assault force leaving before I make that decision," Drakon said. "You do realize that I am not going to Iwa?"

Gozen nodded. "Permission to ask a question, sir?"

"In my headquarters, officers do not have to ask permission to ask questions, Colonel. What is it?"

"Why not, sir? It's going to be one tough fight, and, well, you're pretty damned good."

"Thank you," Drakon said dryly. "I'm not happy about it. But President Iceni has to go to Iwa. Between you and me, I'm not happy about that, either. That means I have to stay at Midway as leader of the government in the president's absence."

Gozen grinned. "Is that going to make me some kind of high-ranking government official who can take her pick of any guy who catches her eye?"

"No, it's going to make you a colonel with a smart mouth, which is what you already are," Drakon added. "Let me know what we get from the software scans of our systems."

ONE of the things that Drakon had vowed never to do if somehow he ended up in charge of everything was to rush through preparations for an operation in the name of sticking to a timeline, even when critical questions remained unanswered. Critical questions such as just how his ground forces would take an installation very deep beneath the surface of a planet and defended by fanatical paranoids willing to die in massive explosions rather than permit a glimpse of themselves.

But this operation was being driven as much by the need to lure Imallye into an attack at Iwa as it was by the need to cut off at the roots the attempt by the enigmas to establish a base inside human-occupied space.

So it was that Drakon found himself riding in an armored VIP limo toward the spaceport. Gwen Iceni, who had always sat on the opposite side of the vehicle, now sat with him. On the virtual windows on both sides of the limo, crowds of citizens could be seen lining the streets.

"They look worried," Drakon said.

"I noticed." She tapped the control to talk to the driver. "Stop the vehicle. The general and I will be walking from here."

"Walking?" Drakon said.

"Yes. The people have to see me confident as I go off to fight the ogre. Or the dragon. Or whatever we want to characterize Imallye and the enigmas as. And we want to be absolutely certain that Imallye knows that I am going to Iwa. The best way to do that is to make a big event out of it and announce our intentions to everyone, as if we were totally confident of the outcome. So you and I will walk and wave and look completely certain of victory as we proceed on foot the rest of the way to the spaceport." She gave him a sad look. "This will be our last private moment. Before I return. Take care of yourself, Artur."

"You, too." He found himself tongue-tied again, so Drakon just held her very tightly for a long moment before Iceni sighed, broke away, and released the locks on the armored doors to the limo's passenger compartment.

The people cheered when Iceni stepped into sight. She smiled and waved, offered her hand to Drakon as he also left the limo, and the cheers redoubled.

Bodyguards got out of the armored escort vehicles ahead and behind them on the road, but Iceni gestured to them all to maintain their current distance rather than closing in tightly around her and Drakon as the bodyguards normally would have done.

The several blocks left to be walked to the spaceport were nothing in terms of physical exertion, but Drakon found them stressful all the same. The need to conceal his worries for Gwen, and the need to constantly scan the masses of citizens for anyone who looked dangerous, wore at him.

But it was heartening to see that Gwen had been right about how much the people had taken her to heart as their leader. Mixed in with the approval was clear concern for her welfare.

At the entrance to the spaceport, where security loomed to block the crowds from entering, Iceni stepped up onto a security barrier and turned to face the crowd that filled the entire street behind them. "Thank you!" she cried loudly. "I am going to Iwa to personally deal with threats to this star system. To deal with threats to *you*. Our warships will depart within a few weeks, with me leading them. I will leave this star system in the capable and dependable hands of my partner, General Artur Drakon, who has always been my close coworker in liberating this star system from the greedy grasp of the Syndicate and in making it a place that is *for the people*!"

The cheers echoed and reechoed from the surrounding buildings. Drakon, still accustomed to the staged enthusiasm of Syndicate mandatory celebrations, felt his breath catch at experiencing the real thing at such an intensity. "The people of Midway really do love you. You're their champion."

"That's the problem, Artur." Iceni waved again, her smile remaining fixed in place, as she spoke in a voice just barely audible to Drakon. "I know how to deal with being hated, with being feared. I know how to make people do things that they don't want to do. The Syndicate taught us how to do that. But these citizens . . . they believe in me!"

"So do I," Drakon said.

"It's not quite the same thing. I didn't worry about letting down the citizens when we were all still Syndicate. I was expected to let them down. But now I have this awful power and responsibility."

"Gwen," he said, turning to face her fully. "You always cared about them. You always worried about them. You just pretended not to. The only thing that has changed is that now *they* know it. Just keep being who you always were."

"Damn." She searched his eyes, her smile becoming genuine again. "You are good. I want them to know that, too." She bent down and leaned in close, her kiss lingering to show real affection and not just duty, and the crowd responded with another roar of approval.

After her shuttle had left, leaping upward to meet the battleship *Midway* which had come into orbit about this world, Drakon watched the dwindling shape of the shuttle until it vanished. He had long since lost track of how many times he had vowed to stop caring about people, because he didn't want to keep feeling the pain that followed when something bad happened to them. Maybe it was time to stop pretending that he could ever stop caring.

General Artur Drakon walked out of the spaceport to where the vast crowd of Iceni's people, who were his people as well, awaited him.

LIKE anyone else, high-ranking or not, Drakon had a hierarchy of callers loaded into his private comm. The tones assigned to the different groups told him instantly whether a call was from a watch center, or one of his brigade commanders, one of his aides, or Gwen Iceni. Once, there had been a special tone to alert him to a call from whoever was the local snake CEO, but he had with great pleasure deleted that after snake CEO Hardrad had his brains blown out by Colonel Roh Morgan just before Hardrad was able to detonate the nuclear weapons once buried under the cities on this world.

He had kept some tones even after the people they were assigned to had died or apparently died, though. Drakon would never delete the tone he had assigned to calls from Colonel Conner Gaiene. Nor had he deleted the tone assigned to Morgan despite all of the evidence pointing to her death on Ulindi.

So when his private comm suddenly shrilled in the hours before dawn, Drakon woke instantly, recognizing Morgan's call. He had the comm in his hand, responding, within seconds, but the call had already terminated. As was to be expected from Morgan, she had hacked her own comm so there was no hint on Drakon's comm of exactly where the call had originated from.

That seemed to settle decisively the question of whether Morgan was still alive. But why would she have called him at such an hour and then hung up the instant he answered it?

To wake him up.

To warn him.

Drakon lunged out of his bed, weapon in hand. He took

up a position that allowed him to cover most of his outer office, waiting for some sign of whatever Morgan had intended to warn him about.

The sign came from an unexpected source. His comm chirped, indicating that its sensors had picked up traces of something bad in the air.

Drakon didn't think he would have time to don battle armor, so instead he yanked out the survival suit kept in a special hidden alcove and shoved himself into it, activating the seals. His comm chirped again, more urgently as the canary app warned of dangerous gas, until he silenced it.

He waited, weapon ready. He could call the command center on the survival suit's comm, but if the intruder was half as good as Drakon expected that would tip him off, and Drakon was pretty sure whoever was coming was a him.

The outer door to his office opened. It had been locked, sealed with his personal physical characteristics, and alarmed in multiple ways. But he could see it open noiselessly, and as easily as a simple sliding partition.

Drakon didn't see anyone entering, though. That was not a good thing.

His shot was aimed at the fire sensor in the ceiling. It went off with a wail and misters began filling the room with water which outlined the shape of someone in stealth armor.

That someone was already turning toward where Drakon had fired. Shots tore through the mist as Drakon fired rapidly at the revealed figure, and as that figure moved with incredible speed to fire back.

Drakon had already flung himself to one side, behind a substantial chair that bore substantial hidden armor under its comfy exterior. The assassin's shots tore into the chair, but none penetrated.

Other alarms were sounding now in the headquarters complex. On-call guards would be racing toward Drakon's office, and other guards taking up positions to seal off every possible way into and out of the complex. "The attacker is wearing a stealth suit," Drakon sent to his command center, abandoning comm silence now that all hell had broken out.

"He is in my outer office. Be aware that there are atmospheric contaminants in this area."

The shots aimed at Drakon ceased. He launched himself across the office toward another chair, catching out of the corner of his eye a glimpse of something flying in a low arc toward where he had been sheltered. Drakon rolled behind the second chair to put it between him and the first chair a bare second before a thunderclap and a flash of light marked the grenade's detonation.

He rose fast, weapon lined up, but there was no longer any shape visible in the water mist. "Intruder has left my office. Flood hallways and rooms with smoke and find him!"

"I understand and will comply," the duty officer responded. "Sir, what are our engagement parameters?"

"Shoot to kill. If you don't, the intruder will. I want him neutralized."

Squads of soldiers were racing into position, some of them cautiously checking the area just outside Drakon's office and then the office itself. Drakon changed into his own battle armor, monitoring developments throughout his headquarters.

"The intruder is definitely no longer in your office or anywhere nearby," the lieutenant in charge of the nearest unit reported to Drakon.

Togo must be running, trying to get clear to fight another day. Drakon checked his display, seeing that every access that could be used by someone wearing stealth armor was physically blocked by soldiers. It should only be a matter of time before they ran Togo to ground, and then—

"General, we have locked doors and escape hatches opening in a line leading out of the complex," the duty officer reported. "Another worm is overriding our security software. We'll kill that worm, but in the meantime the opened doors are being blocked by our soldiers."

It was too obvious. "He's not going out that way. It's a diversion."

"Yes, sir! We're maintaining security everywhere while more soldiers are activated to conduct wall-to-wall searches."

But as time wore on no one reported any contact with the intruder. Drakon watched the progress of the search with growing impatience. He was missing something. He had to be. What was it? After Gozen's late-night visitor, every wall, ceiling, and floor had been painstakingly swept to ensure that any hidden ways into or out of the complex were found and sealed so completely that using them again would require major excavation work.

Gozen called him from the command center. "Sir, I've ordered an inventory of battle armor in our armories."

"Why?" Drakon asked.

"Just a hunch, General."

Half an hour later, as the search was grinding to a halt without results, Gozen called again. "Sir, we've got an extra set of armor. Full stealth. With some very recent damage to it."

Realizing what that must mean, Drakon took a moment to rap his fist against the side of his own head. "The intruder got to an armory, removed his own armor, then left through some series of accesses just big enough for a person not wearing armor."

"Or mingled with soldiers who hadn't armored up yet," Gozen agreed. "I've got our people searching for human-sized accesses that should be sealed but aren't."

Drakon confirmed that the air inside his living quarters was safe again and pulled off the survival suit with quick, angry movements. Not only had Togo, because it must have been Togo, nearly succeeded in killing him, but Togo had then escaped despite everything thrown up to stop him.

They found the intruder's escape route eventually. A series of vents and ducts that were barely big enough for someone to have slid through, their governing mechanisms and status sensors all hacked.

"He's real good," Gozen commented, then noticed the glower from Drakon in response. "In a bad way, I mean."

Drakon blew out an angry breath and made a fist, relaxed it, then tightened it again as he looked at his hand. "I underestimated him, even though I was warned not to. How long was he planning to go rogue on President Iceni? There is no telling how many worms and other malware he planted in how many systems, and how many other plans he has already done all the preparations for."

"He did fail, though."

"Not on account of me, Colonel," Drakon admitted.

"But . . . what alerted you, sir?" Gozen asked.

Drakon tapped his comm unit. "I got a call that woke me up, then the canary routine in my comm reported something bad in the air."

"Yes, sir. An incapacitating agent. I am raising hell with our security folks to explain how someone was able to introduce that into your living area without setting off a million alarms." Gozen looked puzzled. "Why not just use a lethal agent if he wanted to kill you?"

"Because," Drakon said heavily, "*he* wants to kill me. Not by remote means or by using some agent, but by lining up a weapon on me and firing it himself." He paused. "But I am increasingly accepting your suggestion that Togo does not mean harm to President Iceni. He wants me out of the way and her completely in charge. I don't know what he intended when he broke into her living quarters, but there was no incapacitating agent used that time."

"Maybe he was going to explain to her what he was doing," Gozen said. "Maybe he was planning on getting to her in a way that no one else would know he had been there, so he could sit down and monologue to the president about his reasons and everything."

"I suppose that's possible," Drakon said. "If Togo does consider himself still loyal to President Iceni, it must bother him that she considers him a dangerous traitor. But that sort of why-I-am-doing-this talk usually only happens in stories, not in real life. Usually all anyone can do is guess at the motivation behind acts by others, because someone willing to do what Togo is doing is also very willing to lie even to himself as to why he's doing it."

"We'll get him, sir," Gozen vowed. "Who was it that called, by the way? Good timing on that."

"That's because it was a deliberate warning," Drakon

said. "The call was from Colonel Morgan. She is indeed also after Togo and must have spotted him entering this headquarters and guessed his target."

"Did Colonel Morgan say why she didn't tell us she didn't die on Ulindi?" Gozen asked.

"She didn't say anything. I can only guess at her motivations right now, too."

"Is Colonel Morgan a threat?" Gozen asked in the tones of someone who didn't really want to know the answer but knew she had to ask.

"Not to me," Drakon said. "But I have no idea who else she might decide to go after."

"Maybe it was her, not Togo, who broke into the president's quarters."

Drakon stared at Gozen. "I hope you're wrong." Two trained killers who had both slipped their leashes and were now seeking out targets on their own. It was the unstated worry of everyone who employed assassins, that such deadly weapons would turn upon their former owners, or would simply begin choosing their own victims.

When he was assured of total privacy, Drakon gazed at his comm, remembering not only how lethal Roh Morgan was but also the many times her talents had proven extremely valuable. Arguably, Drakon had long owed his own life to Morgan, since it was she who had successfully deleted any information that might link him to the escape of a subordinate whom the snakes wanted to arrest. The snakes had seen Drakon exiled to Midway anyway, but they had chosen to wait for him to trip up again, and perhaps expose other disloyal Syndicate personnel, rather than nail him immediately.

He owed her. Even now.

Drakon tapped the comm to call Morgan's number. The comm waited patiently for an answer, finally informing Drakon that no one had acknowledged the call and that, for reasons unknown to the comm unit, the location of the comm called could not be determined at all. But he could leave a message. "Roh, whatever you're doing, please contact me. I want to talk. I promise no attempts to trace your location. If you are hunting Togo, that's what I would order you to do if I could speak with you. But no other targets, Roh. No. Other. Targets. President Iceni is not to be harmed. Oh, and thank you. You saved my life. Again. I have not and will not forget how loyal and capable you are. But no other targets, Roh. Call me. Drakon, out."

If Morgan did go after Iceni out of some twisted sense of loyalty, he would have to kill her.

CHAPTER TWELVE

"SO, what's the plan?" Colonel Safir asked as she formally took over responsibility for the areas of the planet where Colonel Rogero's brigade normally provided security.

"We're still working on that," Rogero admitted.

"If we were still under the Syndicate," Safir reminisced, "they'd order us to send in a worker to make the aliens blow a segment of their installation, then send in another worker to blow up another segment, and so on until either the aliens ran out of segments or we ran out of workers."

"I have a feeling the enigmas have a way of dealing with a tactic like that," Rogero said. "They must have a way, because according to Black Jack's people the enigmas have likely fought among themselves. They have to have developed a means of fighting a ground opponent that doesn't guarantee victory to the commander most willing to send someone in to die."

"Yeah," Safir agreed. "Because from all we know the enigmas don't have any problem with dying in the line of duty. Hey, you know what might work?"

"If this is a new idea, I'd love to hear it."

"If they had some way to blind attackers," Safir said.

"Not just what we think of as jamming. I mean, block every-thing. Visual, infrared, radar, comms, sound. You're fighting them, you're in the installation, but you can't see anything or hear anything, so the enigmas wouldn't have to blow a section until they actually lost control of it."

Rogero stared at her. "What made you think of that?"

"I used to explore caves when I was a kid. One time my light failed and . . . it was dark." Safir shuddered. "I just re-membered that, and how I could have been surrounded by stobor or fuzzies or anything and I wouldn't have known."

"I think you figured it out. Now all I have to do is figure out how to counter whatever means the enigmas have for full-spectrum blinding and sound suppression."

"Your transports won't be pulling out for a little while yet. I'll talk to Kai and the general and see if we can't come up with some ideas." Safir made an ancient sign, the sort of thing that would have been prohibited under Syndicate rule. "Good fortune."

"Thank you. Take care of things around here while I'm gone." Rogero returned the gesture that his own family had secretly passed down, then headed back to his unit to oversee their lift up to the troop transports waiting in orbit.

IT only took two of the big troop transports captured from the Syndicate at Ulindi to carry all of Colonel Rogero's brigade. The brigade's soldiers, who had stayed at Midway to provide security during Ulindi and had since endured considerable taunting for "missing the hard fight," were in generally good spirits despite the rumors about the difficul-ties of their impending mission. That was at least partially because the troop quarters on the transports, which were of the usual Syndicate bare-bones type for workers, were still much superior to the cramped accommodations on con-verted freighters which the soldiers had endured on earlier missions.

Rogero stood on the bridge of troop transport HTTU 332 along with Leytenant Mack, the commanding officer. Mack, like HTTU 332, had been Syndicate before being captured at Ulindi. Mack and his crew had been happy to change allegiances, but he appeared to be far from enthusiastic about taking the soldiers to Iwa to confront an alien enemy. He had nonetheless handled every part of the embarkation efficiently enough to impress Rogero.

"Can I ask you something, Colonel?" Mack said during a pause in shuttle arrivals.

"Of course," Rogero said.

"These aliens I'm hearing about. They control space beyond Pele Star System?"

"That's right," Rogero said. "The Syndicate had expanded into that region a century ago, but then started getting rolled back by a mysterious opponent whose ships were invisible to Syndicate sensors. The Syndicate ended up being pushed back as far as Midway over the next several decades, then not long ago what we call the enigma race tried to take Midway as well."

"And you guys stopped them," Mack said, visibly impressed.

"Black Jack's fleet stopped them," Rogero corrected. "He'd just ended the war with the Syndicate, and came here to save Midway from the enigma attack."

Mack called up a small display of nearby space and pointed to one of the stars beyond Pele Star System. "Some relatives of mine were among those sent by the Syndicate to colonize this star system. All my family ever knew was that they stopped getting messages back. The Syndicate never told anyone anything."

"What had happened was inconvenient for the Syndicate to admit to," Rogero said, "so the Syndicate just rewrote history again and wrote that part out of it."

"But now I've got some idea what happened." Mack gazed at the display, his face grim. "They never got anybody back?"

"No. Not once the enigmas had taken a place. Not until we pulled those three soldiers off Iwa. Every place the enigmas have taken they have eliminated every trace of humans once being there."

"My people are long gone, then. No descendants to try to contact." Mack gave Rogero a determined look. "We'll get you to Iwa and get you and your ground forces down to that planet. Take a piece out of those enigmas, for my family, all right?"

"We'll do our best," Rogero promised.

ONE week later, the expedition to Iwa was ready to depart.

It was the largest force Midway Star System had ever assembled. Small by the standards of the immense war with the Alliance that had ended not long ago, or by comparison to the fleet that Black Jack had brought through Midway more than once, the flotilla was nonetheless impressive when measured against the forces now operating in this region of space that had once been firmly under control of the rebellion-wracked Syndicate Worlds.

The flotilla resembled a school of disparate predatory sea creatures moving in unison. Instead of the standard Syndicate box formation, Marphissa had arranged the flotilla in a flattened sphere. In the center were the whalelike shapes of the two troop transports. Just above them moved the battleship *Midway*, even larger than the transports, shaped like an immense, fat shark. Ahead of and below the transports the battle cruiser *Pele* swam through space, also shark-like but leaner and more lithe than the battleship. Ranked behind the largest ships were the two heavy cruisers, *Basilisk* and *Kraken*, dwarfed by the battle cruiser and battleship but still lethal-looking as they protected the rear of the flotilla.

Three light cruisers ranged ahead like barracudas, small by comparison to the major warships but long and slender and dangerous-looking. Ranged all around the formation were seven Hunter-Killers, sized and shaped like deadly young offspring of the light cruisers.

President Gwen Iceni sat in the fleet command seat on the bridge of *Midway*, smiling as she viewed the spectacle on her display. "I have been part of Syndicate flotillas much larger than this," she commented to Kapitan Mercia, "but I have never been as impressed as I am by these warships."

She looked around the bridge. "I haven't been back here since we captured this ship from the Syndicate at Kane. Have you been told of Kapitan Kontos's stand inside the bridge citadel on this ship?"

"I have heard of it," Mercia said. "Not from Kontos himself. He dismissed that action as not worth discussing."

"That doesn't surprise me. It was an heroic stand, the sort of thing anyone could boast about, but Kontos seems to have no ego. I didn't think that was possible in a man." Iceni ran her right hand down the arm of her seat. "I have been very fortunate in the quality of those men and women who have chosen to accept my orders."

"Good fortune had little to do with it," Mercia said. "We follow you because you have given us all good reason to do so. I cannot believe that Imallye's commanders are so well-motivated."

"I wish we knew more about them," Iceni said. "We have agents out, but the distances and the time lags are such that we have heard little back from any of the agents in the short time we had before having to act." She rested her elbows on the arms of her seat, clasping her hands together and placing her chin on them as she gazed at her display. "We did get a report from Moorea that came by a roundabout means. Apparently, Imallye isn't instituting any big changes where she takes control. She just changes the titles. Her representative is installed as star system CEO in all but name and uses the existing Syndicate infrastructure."

"I can see that working in the short term," Mercia said. "The citizens would be waiting to see if anything changed for them. But once they figure out that it's the same game with different bosses, and without the entire Syndicate backing those bosses, they'll push back. You know how they can do that."

"Oh, yes, I know how they can do that," Iceni agreed, smiling crookedly. "Theft, slowdowns, diversions, so-called mistakes, so-called accidents, and many more tricks and games. The citizens can make the system grind almost to a halt without ever overtly going on strike." She looked over at Mercia. "That's one thing the Syndicate succeeded at. Teaching workers how to sabotage a system in ways that can't be pinpointed or proven."

"Those of us who realized that always knew the importance of respecting our workers," Mercia commented. "But we always seemed to be working for idiots who thought threats and punishment would fix any problem."

"We've come such a long way," Iceni said, letting the irony sound in her voice. "Here we are going to Iwa to fix our problems with massive amounts of firepower."

"That's not a path you chose."

"No." Iceni glanced at Mercia again. "We'll have to ensure that Imallye knows I am aboard *Midway*. Once Imallye knows that, she will focus her efforts on destroying this ship."

"I look forward to it," Mercia replied with her own small smile.

Iceni looked at the image of the planet Midway, realizing that she had not left this star system since the expedition that had resulted in the capture of this battleship. A lot had happened since then. "Someday . . . no, right now . . . Midway Star System must be as a battleship itself, a fortress that all attacks break upon, and that protects those inside it. What I have risked all to create must not be lost."

"It will not be, if the citizens have any say in the matter," Mercia replied.

"Did I say that out loud?" Iceni asked, embarrassed.

Fortunately, she was saved from any further comment by the appearance of Kommodor Marphissa's image before her. Marphissa was in the fleet command seat aboard *Pele*, looking perfectly at home there despite the responsibilities that seat implied.

Marphissa saluted. "Madam President, I request permission to take the flotilla out of orbit and begin the transit to the jump point for Iwa."

Returning the salute, Iceni nodded. "Permission is granted, Kommodor. One more thing. You will command this flotilla. That is not my function here. From this point forward, you are to issue all commands that you deem needed without first requesting permission from me."

"Yes, Madam President," Marphissa said. "Does that include the order to jump for Iwa?"

"That includes *all* orders, Kommodor. Just ensure that I receive a copy of them so I am aware of what is happening." Iceni smiled at her. "You have my confidence. You are more than welcome to ask my opinion if time permits, but do not hesitate to command this flotilla as you see fit."

"Yes, Madam President. I understand and will comply." With a return smile she could not quite suppress, Marphissa's image vanished.

Iceni tapped a control, and a moment later the image of Colonel Rogero appeared. "Yes, Madam President."

"Are you as fully prepared as possible, Colonel?"

"Yes." Rogero gestured with one hand as if casting a die. "There are a number of uncertainties remaining, but we will confront them and deal with them."

"I want it clearly understood, Colonel," Iceni emphasized, "that if you confront something that appears to be beyond your soldiers' abilities to deal with, that you inform me so we can make any necessary alterations in our plans. I want that enigma facility captured if at all possible. But if it becomes clear that that is impossible, if our planned tactics do not work as hoped, then I will not hesitate to order the withdrawal of your forces and the bombardment of that base with a rock big enough to split the planet. You are not to destroy your brigade attempting to achieve the unachievable."

"I understand and will comply, Madam President." Rogero saluted. "And, thank you. If the task can be done by human effort, the men and women in my brigade will succeed. General Drakon asked me to ensure that you knew that two of the soldiers rescued from Iwa are with my brigade. They were insistent on going back to Iwa to fight the aliens who killed their comrades."

Iceni sought for words, then simply nodded. "I hope those two don't expect to find peace inside themselves by seeking vengeance."

Rogero smiled slightly. "But are you not seeking *Vengeance*, Madam President?"

It took her a moment to get the joke. She could not help a snort of laughter at the wordplay. "Tell your Captain Bradamont that I will do my best to bring you home, Colonel. For the people. Iceni, out."

ABOARD *Pele*, Marphissa looked around the battle cruiser's bridge, which felt ridiculously large after all the time she had spent on a heavy cruiser. Next to her seat was that of Kapitan Kontos, who still appeared so young that Marphissa felt an irrational urge to mother him even though she wasn't that much older. But Kontos was already a veteran of some very demanding battles, and had proven himself not only daring enough for command of a battle cruiser but also the sort of leader whose crew would strive to do anything for him.

Kontos noticed her look and grinned. "This should be an adventure, Kommodor."

"That's one way of looking at it," Marphissa agreed. She tapped a control to talk to Kapitan Diaz aboard *Manticore*. "We're about to begin our transit to Iwa. Take care of this star system until we get back, Kapitan."

Diaz nodded back, his expression serious. "We will die defending this star system, Kommodor."

She shook her head at him. "I don't want you to die defending this star. I want you to kill anyone who attacks it. Are you clear on that?"

Diaz's sober face split into a grin. "Yes, Kommodor. They are to die, not us. I understand and will comply."

"See that you do. The defense of Midway Star System will be in your hands once this flotilla jumps for Iwa, but we'll be out of position to stop attacks coming in from some vectors well before that. Listen to Captain Bradamont, but also listen to your gut. You've got good instincts."

"Thank you, Kommodor. Give Granaile Imallye my respects when you kick her butt back to Moorea."

"I'll do that." Marphissa ended the call and tried to relax, feeling suddenly small and far too inexperienced for this command. That sensation only lasted a moment, though. She had fought and beaten the Syndicate. She had fought and beaten Imallye. She had outwitted the enigmas and snatched stranded ground forces soldiers from right under their noses. If they had noses. And she had the confidence of not only Captain Honore Bradamont, one of Black Jack's own battle cruiser commanders, but also that of President Iceni. *I will not be overconfident, but I think I have every right to feel qualified for this command!*

She touched the flotilla command circuit control. "All units in the Midway Offensive Flotilla, at time two zero come port three five degrees, down zero four degrees, and accelerate to point one five light speed. Marphissa, out."

The small multitude of warships swung around under the push of their thrusters, lining up on the same vector, then accelerated together toward the jump point for Iwa Star System. Every ship maintained its position relative to the battleship *Midway*, which formed the physical guide of the flotilla as well as its figurative heart.

The cruisers and Hunter-Killers of the Midway Guard Flotilla split away from the others, one group heading to an orbit guarding against attacks from the hypernet gate or the jump point from Pele Star System, and the other group moving to take up position to guard against Syndicate attacks from most of the other jump points that Midway boasted. In terms of commerce, those many jump points were a major blessing. In terms of defense, they were a major headache. But Kapitan Diaz would be able to handle whatever came up, Marphissa was certain. And if he needed any advice, Captain Bradamont would be there with him.

But, still, she worried. The Syndicate had surprised them

more than once already, and the Syndicate wanted Midway back very badly. If the CEOs running the remnants of the Syndicate had heard that most of Midway's warships were heading to Iwa, they might make another attempt at reconquering the star system.

Though any reconquest would also require getting past General Drakon and his ground forces. That thought reassured Marphissa quite a bit.

TWO and a half days later, Captain Bradamont saw the Midway Offensive Flotilla vanish as it had entered jump space about three hours before. In the seat next to her sat Kapitan Diaz. On most of the warships in Midway's fleet, she would still be eyed with suspicion and even hatred by many in the crew, but not on *Manticore*. Bradamont had become theirs, by that odd process of comradeship that forged bonds where none ought to exist. She knew it, too, acting calm and cheerful around the specialists instead of tense as she usually was on other ships.

But Bradamont was all business at the moment. "Assume that they're going to come," she warned Diaz.

"The Syndicate or the enigmas?"

"The Syndicate," she said. "From what we've seen of the enigmas, they focus on one objective at a time. Right now, that would be Iwa. Once they have that installation working they'll be able to bring in warships. I warned Kommodor Marphissa to expect enigma ships to conduct reconnaissance of Iwa so they'll know if humans try to retake the star system. Hopefully, she'll have finished with Imallye before any more enigmas show up. So what we have to worry about is Syndicate Worlds attacks coming in either through the hypernet gate or one of the jump points from stars they still control. I would advise telling Kapitan Stein to patrol closer to the hypernet gate so she can intercept whatever comes out of it faster."

"And if the enigmas do show up?" Diaz asked, then answered his own question. "I can't defend every possible entry into this star system with the warships I have. I have to prioritize. That's what you mean? So if Kapitan Stein takes *Gryphon* and her other ships nearer the hypernet gate, where should I prioritize do you think?"

"In my experience fighting the Syndics—Damn, sorry, I mean the Syndicate Worlds," Bradamont corrected herself, angry that she kept slipping up by using the insult when talking to the people it had once been aimed at, "they tended to keep using the same lines of attack."

"That's so," Diaz agreed, showing no sign of offense at Bradamont's gaffe. "It wasn't official doctrine, but in practice we would often be ordered to repeat attacks using the same approach and tactics. Syndicate CEOs think that if they make you do the same thing over and over, sooner or later the results will be different."

"Then would the next Syndicate assault come through the jump point from Lono?"

"Very likely," Diaz said. "Not just because of pursuing the same approach, but because the Syndicate can route forces to Lono through Milu Star System. That's a pretty easy hop from the hypernet gate at Rota Star System. I could have figured all of that out by myself, couldn't I?"

"You could have," Bradamont agreed. "All I did was walk you through the steps to get there so you'll know how to work it out by yourself next time."

That's what she was supposed to be doing, preparing these people to stand on their own once the orders Admiral Geary had given her were changed and she was ordered to return to Alliance space. Bradamont had no doubt that would happen sooner or later, and little doubt that when she got back to the Alliance whoever had threatened to blackmail her would once again threaten her. She had never been a spy for the Syndicate Worlds, never wavered in her loyalty to the Alliance, but the Alliance's own intelligence services had ordered her to play at that in hopes of using her relationship with Rogero to get secrets from the Syndicate. And the relationship with Donal Rogero had always been true, even if neither of them had ever expected any opportunity to pursue it.

She had given her adult life to serving the Alliance, and had fought hard on its behalf. Once, there had only been two real options, either the Alliance or the Syndicate Worlds, and Bradamont would never have turned to the enemy. But now there was Midway, which had been the enemy but was now working very hard to become something much more like the Alliance. Midway, which had good leaders, citizens happy with those leaders, men and women willing to fight for their freedom, and Donal Rogero. The taint of the Syndicate Worlds would take a long time to fade, but these people were trying. They were already partners of the Alliance in every way that mattered.

Could she go home when ordered, pursuing the same paths that duty had once demanded?

She still wore the uniform of the Alliance, but her loyalties were shifting. Not against the Alliance, but to include something else as well.

JUMP space should have been tailor-made for meditation, Asima Marphissa thought. However wide across jump space was, the entirety of it was composed of gray nothingness. No human had ever detected anything else. In jump space, there was no external world to distract the senses.

There were the mysterious lights that came and went without any detectable pattern. The lights would flare into existence amid the gray nothing, then fade again. Human instruments could detect the visual light coming off them, but nothing else, no heat or radiation or other hint as to what caused the lights.

Marphissa had heard from Bradamont that Alliance sailors considered the lights to have religious meaning. The Syndicate, of course, had no use for metaphysics, so the Syndicate had officially declared the lights to be just illusions created by human senses.

Marphissa sat in her stateroom aboard the battle cruiser *Pele*, watching her display where the outside view showed grayness and the occasional flare of a light that could be a million light years away or within touching distance. No one knew. All she knew for certain was that the view of jump space brought with it no sense of peace or harmony.

Her living area aboard *Pele* was a ridiculously large and well-appointed stateroom intended for someone of CEO rank. Marphissa, rapidly promoted from a midgrade executive rank, thought it far too pretentious. She thought she had grown accustomed to her rank as Kommodor, but that had been mostly within the confines of the heavy cruiser *Manticore*. Nothing aboard *Manticore* had this much luxury to it. She felt out of place.

Maybe her discomfort wasn't rooted in the fact that jump space made humans increasingly uncomfortable and uneasy as days went by. Maybe it was because she still did not feel qualified for her responsibilities. The fate of Midway Star System rested in her hands. It was not a comfortable feeling, no matter what kind of stateroom she might be occupying or what kind of space existed outside the hull of this battle cruiser.

"Kommodor." The image of Kapitan Kontos appeared next to her display. "I wish to inform you that we will leave jump space in one hour. My ship will be at full combat readiness when we arrive at Iwa, per your instructions."

Marphissa tried to rouse herself from her reverie. "Thank you, Kapitan. I will be on the bridge in one half hour."

"Yes, Kommodor. I am sorry to have disturbed your planning for our actions upon arrival."

She couldn't help smiling at that. "All you disturbed, Kapitan, was my attempt to understand something."

"Something related to this battle cruiser?" Kontos asked.

"No. Something related to us. To humans." Marphissa took another glance at the outside display as another mysterious light bloomed. "Why is it, Kapitan, that no matter how long the journeys we humans take, no matter how strange the places we go, we always manage to take all of our baggage along with us?"

Kontos looked baffled, then his expression cleared. "You mean emotional baggage. Even the Syndicate never figured out a system inefficient enough to allow us to lose that in transit!"

"Well, I fully intend losing some of mine at Iwa," Marphissa said. "I'm going to unload it on whatever is waiting for us there."

A half hour later she was on the bridge, waiting through the final minutes before arriving at Iwa.

Marphissa had expected to find at Iwa Star System either a flotilla of Granaile Imallye's warships laying claim to the star, or a force of enigma warships ready to defend their own possession of the star.

But as she shook off the mind-blurring effects of leaving jump space, Marphissa saw something else on her display, which was rapidly updating as the sensors on *Pele* and the other Midway warships tried to spot every change at Iwa since *Manticore* had left.

"Syndicate," Kontos commented in wondering tones. "They didn't care enough about Iwa to defend it when they controlled it, but now that they've lost it, they want it back."

"Apparently they do," Marphissa agreed. "And that is just like the Syndicate. The bureaucracy screws up and then they send citizens like you and me out to fix things."

The Syndicate flotilla, which was about three light hours from the newly arrived Midway flotilla and barely twenty light minutes from the formerly inhabited world that was now the site of the hidden enigma base, contained an impressive mix of warships for the overextended Syndicate. Two battle cruisers, five heavy cruisers, a light cruiser, and nearly twenty Hunter-Killers, plus three troop carriers and four freighters.

"Kapitan Kontos, the Syndicate flotilla came in from

Palau Star System," the senior watch specialist on *Pele*'s bridge announced. "Their vectors track right back to that jump point."

"Why so much for Iwa?" Marphissa wondered. Before Kontos could reply, a call came from Iceni. "We have company, Madam President."

"Yes," Iceni said, looking unruffled by the unexpected development. "I doubt this was originally intended for Iwa. The Syndicate was probably marshaling forces at Palau to strike at either Midway or at stars controlled by Imallye's forces. They might have even come here along a planned attack route to hit either Midway or Moorea, but are now moving to reestablish a Syndicate base on that planet."

"How would they know about the underground enigma base there?" Marphissa asked. "Our sensors have been studying the planet and we can't detect anything now even though we know where it is."

"I seriously doubt that the Syndicate forces know about the alien facility," Iceni said.

"Kommodor?" Kontos interrupted. "The Syndicate flotilla is maneuvering. It can't be in response to us. They won't see us for another two and a half hours."

Both Marphissa and Iceni fell silent as everyone waited to see what the Syndicate forces had done. "They're coming around hard," Marphissa finally murmured.

"Maximum push on their thrusters," Kontos agreed. "They must have seen something that we haven't yet."

"The Syndicate flotilla is accelerating at the maximum rate the freighters with it can manage," the senior watch specialist advised.

"Heading back toward the jump point for Palau," Kontos said. "Something scared them. Imallye?"

"I hope not," Iceni said. "If Imallye has brought a big enough force to Iwa to scare a flotilla of that size, we're going to have some trouble dealing with it ourselves."

The image of Kapitan Mercia appeared beside that of President Iceni. "If the Syndicate flotilla had seen some force of Imallye's arriving from Moorea, then we should have seen it by now as well. Whatever they saw is way on the far side of the star system from us."

Kontos sucked in a sudden breath. "The enigmas. The jump point we saw that ship of theirs using is over there."

Marphissa quickly ran some data through her display, using one hand to draw vectors through the images of planets and ships. "If the enigmas have come in at the same place you saw that one ship . . ." She shook her head. "The Syndicate battle cruisers can outrun them and jump back to Palau. The others won't make it."

"Are we close enough to intervene?" Iceni asked. She paused for a moment to let her words sink in before adding more. "They may be Syndicate, but they're people like us, or like we used to be."

Kontos nodded, smiling. "If we can hit the enigmas while they are engaging the Syndicate flotilla, we might be able to inflict enough damage to ensure victory."

"See if we can do it," Marphissa said.

"Kommodor?" The senior watch specialist gestured toward her display. "The Syndicate flotilla changed vector again."

Everyone focused on their displays, waiting to see what the Syndicate flotilla had done hours before. "They're coming back around," Mercia said, puzzled.

"Back onto their original vectors," Kontos confirmed. "They are heading for the planet again."

Marphissa felt a heaviness inside. "The CEO commanding that flotilla did the math. They know the troop transports can't get away, so they're going to land the ground forces on the planet to give them a chance."

"And the battle cruisers will stay with their comrades and fight the enigmas together." Kontos was smiling again, his enthusiasm and admiration for the Syndicate flotilla's actions obvious. "Kommodor, we must help them."

"They are still the enemy," Marphissa reminded him. "As much as a quarter of the men and women aboard those units may be snakes. Remember what Syndicate mobile forces did to Kane."

"I have not forgotten," Kontos said, the smile and admiration disappearing from his face. "But, still, in this they are doing the right thing."

"They are," Marphissa conceded. "I would like to know why the snakes are permitting it. Work up a vector toward that planet. We don't know yet where the Syndicate ships will go once they have dropped off the ground forces, so we will head for that world so we can also drop off our ground forces before proceeding into battle with the enigmas." She would have to call Colonel Rogero and tell him that, and did not for a moment imagine that he would be thrilled by the news.

"Here is your vector, Kommodor," Kontos said a few seconds later. "Assuming you wish to limit our velocity to point two light speed?"

She felt an urge to check with Iceni, but decided this was as good a time as any to see if the president had meant it when she granted Marphissa full control over the mobile forces. "Yes. I don't want to go any faster until I know more about what the enigmas are doing. We should see them within a couple more hours and at least be able to tell if they were also heading straight for that planet as of several hours ago."

Marphissa forced herself to study Kontos's proposed vector, taking her time to look it over. The urge to act quickly, to maneuver now, was a human one, but very mistaken in space. Just because you could see the enemy did not mean that the enemy was a threat. In fact, the enemy might be days away from being able to engage your forces. But still the instincts passed down to Marphissa from primitive humans hunting on the plains and forests and tundra of Old Earth insisted that she must act immediately against an enemy that could be seen.

"Good," she finally said. "All units in Midway Offensive Flotilla, immediate execute, come starboard five seven degrees, down zero six degrees, accelerate to point two light speed."

Pele swung around under the push of her thrusters, nimble and fast, then waited as the other warships matched the movement. The HuKs and the light cruisers moved almost as quickly as the battle cruiser, the heavy cruisers were noticeably slower, the troop transports were about as agile as the heavy cruisers, and the battleship *Midway*'s thrusters brought the vast mass of that warship around with ponderous deliberation.

With everyone lined up in the right direction and main propulsion lit off on every warship, *Pele* and the other warships keeping their acceleration slow enough to match that of *Midway*, the flotilla dove into Iwa Star System, heading for the orbit of the planet where humans and enigmas would soon clash again to determine the fate of everyone in this region of space.

CHAPTER THIRTEEN

"MADAM President, what can I say to the Syndicate forces?" Marphissa asked.

Iceni was sitting back, her lower face covered by one hand as she thought. Finally she answered, her eyes meeting Marphissa's. "*I* should say this to them. I will send a broadcast to the Syndicate flotilla that we may be enemies to each other, but we can work together to defeat the enigmas. I will say that we are willing to suspend hostilities against Syndicate forces until the aliens are defeated."

She paused, waiting for Marphissa's reaction.

"That is . . . pragmatic," Marphissa said. "They might accept it. I do not think they would believe any offer that did not obviously benefit both our force and their flotilla. What about the enigma base? Will you tell them of that?"

Iceni brooded over that question for several seconds more, then nodded. "Yes. Those Syndicate ground forces may be massacred before we can get there to help them, but I will not let that happen without at least trying to warn them. I'll transmit from *Midway*, Kommodor. If I receive any reply from the Syndicate forces, I will ensure you are aware of it."

It took another two hours, as they watched the hours-old movements of the Syndicate flotilla toward an unseen enemy, before the light showing the enigma ships finally reached the Midway flotilla.

"There they are," Kontos said as a new set of symbols appeared on the displays accompanied by an urgent alert sound.

"Forty-four of them," Marphissa said. The largest of the enigma warships was larger than human heavy cruisers but significantly smaller than human battle cruisers or battleships. But there were a lot more enigma warships than there were human warships. "Seeing those numbers, I'm even more surprised that the snakes in that Syndicate flotilla haven't ordered the battle cruisers to run and leave the rest to their fates."

"It will be very hard for them to win," Kontos conceded.

"Kapitan," Marphissa said patiently, "it is impossible for the Syndicate flotilla to win. They are choosing to die here. I do not understand that. You know how the snakes think. There is nothing here that they would consider worth the sacrifice of those two battle cruisers in addition to the other warships in that flotilla."

"They would abandon the ground forces to their fates," Kontos agreed. "Perhaps the snakes have firm orders to stop the enigmas from taking this star system, and would face death from the Syndicate even if they escaped from Iwa."

"That is possible," Marphissa agreed. She was looking at her display, where the vectors from the two human flotillas and those of the alien armada were now visible and made obvious an unpleasant future. "We can't get to them in time to help. Not if they hold to what they're doing."

"They won't even know we're here for another hour," Kontos said. "And they won't receive the president's message until then, either. They don't yet know any alternative exists."

Marphissa pressed her back against her seat, glaring at her display. Another hour before the Syndicate warships finally saw that the Midway flotilla had arrived, then almost another three hours before she saw what they did with that information. And about another twelve hours of travel at point two light speed after that before this flotilla neared the planet where the Syndicate ground forces were probably landing at this moment. "The enigmas were coming straight for that planet's orbit as well, and as we guessed the Syndicate flotilla was heading to meet them." The long, long curved tracks of the two forces met a light hour from the planet. "The enigmas and the Syndicate flotilla will engage each other while we're still too far away to do anything but watch what happened hours earlier."

"If the Syndicate flotilla turns back to meet us—" Kontos began.

She shook her head firmly. "They're obviously trying to protect those troop transports and freighters. Unless they know the enigmas are going to chase them, turning away and running toward us would just leave those transports and freighters completely open to attack. Unless something else happens, I don't see any chance of the Syndicate flotilla changing its vector."

As if triggered by her words, a new alert sounded and new symbols appeared on her display.

Marphissa stared as the display reported that yet another flotilla had appeared in this star system, this time at the jump point from Moorea. Two more battle cruisers, three heavy cruisers, a light cruiser, and eight Hunter-Killers.

Granaile Imallye's flotilla had arrived.

Before getting to Iwa, Marphissa had anticipated fighting a couple of two-way battles, her forces against Imallye and her forces against the enigmas. But now there were four flotillas at Iwa, and each one of those flotillas regarded the other three as hostile. "Imallye's forces, the Syndicate forces, and the enigmas, will all attack us at the first opportunity. The only good part of that is they will also attack each other at the first chance that offers itself."

"A four-way fight?" Kontos asked in disbelief.

The image of Kapitan Mercia appeared before Marphissa. "Well, Kommodor, we have three different enemies to choose from. Which do we attack first?"

Put that way, the answer wasn't too difficult. "The enigmas. We'll continue on our approach to intercept their armada."

Mercia nodded. "I am obligated to point out that it is possible Imallye's forces will ignore us, the Syndicate, and the enigmas, and proceed straight to the jump point for Midway while the rest of us kill each other."

That was an ugly possibility. Marphissa remembered the implacable woman she had exchanged messages with at Moorea. "That could happen. We must give Imallye a reason to come after us." She knew that Iceni would be listening in to this conversation, and would know what that reason would have to be, but Marphissa did not feel comfortable telling her president that it was time to broadcast her presence as bait.

President Iceni's image appeared as well, looking both resigned to her fate and determined. "I will transmit a message to Imallye. A long message, so she can confirm that it is coming from *Midway*."

"Thank you, Madam President," Marphissa said. "May I suggest that you also include some recent details of events here so that Imallye will not think the message is just a recording."

"I'll do that." Iceni glanced to one side, studying the situation on her own display. "What are your intentions, Kommodor?"

Marphissa took a deep breath, then spoke clearly. "I intend continuing onward to engage the enigma armada, splitting off our troop transports to land our ground forces as we pass closest to the planet. If any Syndicate warships still survive when we reach them, I will not target the Syndicate units but allow them to continue engaging the enigmas as well. Once the enigmas are destroyed, I will evaluate the state of any surviving Syndicate warships before turning to engage Imallye's flotilla. After destroying Imallye's forces, I will bring our flotilla back to the planet to support our ground forces in their assault on the enigma base."

"That's as good a plan as any at this point," Iceni said. "How does Colonel Rogero feel about it?"

"Colonel Rogero is . . . not happy," Marphissa said, choosing her words carefully.

"I'm not surprised. But as bad as things may be on the surface of that planet, they will certainly be a lot better than if his soldiers stayed on those transports with that many enigma warships on the loose." Iceni paused to rub her forehead, revealing for a moment beneath that not-quite-concealing-enough gesture the concerns she was otherwise hiding very well. "I approve of your plan of action, Kommodor. Proceed. Remember that the enigmas often try to surprise their opponents, so take nothing for granted."

"Yes, Madam President."

As Iceni's image vanished, Marphissa gazed once more at the situation in Iwa. The Syndicate flotilla was still nearly three light hours distant and just to the starward side of the bows of Marphissa's ships and slightly beneath them. The Syndicate forces should have reached the planet holding the enigma base a short time ago, and would have probably dropped off the transports and freighters while proceeding onward to meet the enigmas. Marphissa's own flotilla was heading into the star system, aiming for that planet's orbit as well. Two light hours beyond the Syndicate forces was the enigma armada, which was visible just to port (away from the star) of Marphissa's flotilla and several degrees above Midway's ships. As of five hours ago, the alien armada had been on a vector aiming to meet that of the Syndicate flotilla.

Imallye's flotilla had arrived from Moorea a little over four hours ago, and was coming in from far to port and just aft of amidships relative to Marphissa's force. Because of where the jump point from Moorea was located and the times the other flotillas had arrived at Iwa, Imallye would have seen the other three groups of warships as soon as her ships left jump space.

The vector for Marphissa's flotilla curved into the star system, aiming to intercept not just the orbit of the planet but also the Syndicate flotilla that was moving to meet the aliens. As Marphissa watched her display, the projected track of Imallye's force shifted only slightly, aiming to swing past the stern of Midway's flotilla. Mercia had apparently been right about Imallye deciding to hit Midway while the bulk of its forces were tied up in the fighting at Iwa. Hopefully, President Iceni would either persuade Imallye to join in the fight against the enigmas, or goad Imallye into chasing Marphissa's force as it raced to meet the Syndicate flotilla and the enigma armada.

It was all already complicated enough. What sort of hidden strike could the enigmas also manage when their forces were clearly visible?

"Kapitan Kontos," Marphissa said, slumping back and gesturing at her display, "if you were an enigma, how would you surprise us or anyone else in this star system?"

Kontos shrugged. "Reinforcements."

"If more enigma warships arrive at their new jump point, we'll have plenty of time to see them coming," Marphissa pointed out. "And our path isn't coming closer than twenty-three light minutes to any other planet in this star system, so even if the enigmas are hiding behind one of the planets we'll still have time to react."

"We will come much closer than twenty-three light minutes to our objective," Kontos said, pointing to the world they were heading toward. "We are currently tracking to be within a few light seconds of that planet."

Marphissa gave him a cross look. "It's a buried installation. Deeply buried. Even if the enigmas have installed defenses on the surface we'll be too far away for those weapons to threaten us unless we change our track and go into orbit about that planet."

Kontos nodded, then turned a questioning look on Marphissa. "How do the enigmas supply that buried base, Kommodor?"

She looked back at him, thinking about the question. "There isn't any landing area visible on the surface," Marphissa said slowly. "The enigmas have to have some sort of capability to transfer bulk cargo from orbit to that base."

Another nod from Kontos. "I would guess very large

access tunnels covered with camouflaged doors of some kind. At least one, maybe more."

"Hidden ways in and out of their base." Marphissa smiled admiringly at Kontos. "That's consistent with what Black Jack's ships learned of the enigmas. They hide everything. I am impressed, Kapitan. How did you think of that?"

He actually appeared to be embarrassed by her praise. "I just thought, if there are insects underground like ants, you can always see how they get in and out. And buried human facilities as well. But we can't see any accesses to the enigma base that we knew was being built. So . . ."

Marphissa nodded, eyeing the planet on her display. "Warships, maybe, already in deeply buried hangars, ready to leap out as human ships pass by. But if that is their plan, they won't strike when the Syndicate gets there. They'll wait for them to pass and plan to hit us or Imallye's ships after the main enigma force has wiped out the Syndicate flotilla."

"Is it that certain?" Kontos asked in a low voice. "The destruction of the Syndicate flotilla?"

"Yes," Marphissa said without mercy. "You have seen the enigmas in combat, how fast and maneuverable their warships are, and how they attack without letup or concern for their own survival. The commanders of the Syndicate flotilla's units do not have the benefit of having seen the enigmas in action, but even if they had it would make no difference. They know that. The Syndicate is badly outnumbered."

"Why didn't they run?" Kontos asked. "I respect that they turned to fight, but—"

"There must be a powerful reason. Perhaps we'll find out what it is before the Syndicate forces are wiped out."

THERE were times when it made no sense to try to manipulate others. When the truth should be laid out plainly. When an appeal to reason was infinitely better than any mind game or play on emotion.

This was obviously not such a time.

Gwen Iceni had gone to her stateroom aboard the battle-ship, the sort of grandiose quarters that suited a Syndicate CEO and thus were more than adequate for a star system president. She sat back in the large, comfortable chair that dominated one corner of the suite, resting her chin on one hand as she thought. Just to one side floated a display showing the entirety of Iwa Star System and the four groups of warships vying for control of it.

It was ironic, she thought, that a star system so poor in resources that the Syndicate hadn't bothered to defend it properly was now being fought over by four separate powers who all wanted it.

Of course, Imallye only wanted the star system because she thought that Iceni wanted it also.

The enigmas wanted it as a springboard to begin wiping out the human presence.

The Syndicate wanted it back because someone else had taken it.

And herself? Iceni didn't want Iwa. She just wanted Iwa Star System to be in the hands of someone who did not pose a threat to Midway Star System. Unfortunately, everyone else involved was a threat to Midway.

An ideal solution would have the enigmas, the Syndicate flotilla, and Imallye's forces annihilating each other and leaving Midway's flotilla unscathed.

No. That wasn't an ideal solution. Iceni scowled at the image of Iwa's star. *I don't want to have to worry about defending Iwa when I have my hands full defending Midway. But I also don't need a vacuum here. I don't want a vacuum here. I need Iwa in the hands of someone I can work with, so they can be responsible for keeping the enigmas out of human space at this location.*

But I sure as hell can't work with the enigmas even though Black Jack said they had political divisions among themselves. And the Syndicate doesn't play well with others.

Which leaves Imallye, who hates me. I have to convince her that she can hate me and still work with me.

If Imallye learned anything from the Syndicate she must have learned how to work with people she hated. Everybody had to learn that survival skill.

Iceni composed herself, trying to look concerned but confident, mentally rehearsed what she wanted to say, then touched the message control. "Granaile Imallye, this is President Gwen Iceni. We have met before, some years ago. I freely admit that I have done you and your family a great harm. I was fooled into accusing your father of a crime, an accusation that not only resulted in his death but my own internal exile. I cannot ever adequately compensate you for my action, and I am aware that my own expression of deep regret is unlikely to bring you any real comfort."

Iceni firmed her voice and her expression as she continued. "But our personal quarrel is of little importance at the moment. Every human in this region of space faces a serious threat from a foe who has no interest in coexistence with humanity. I understand that you have expressed skepticism regarding the existence of the enigmas. The warships you captured from the Syndicate possessed the security software needed to scrub enigma worms from your sensor systems, and you can now see for yourself that the enigmas are real. Soon, long before my flotilla can reach them, the enigmas here will attack the Syndicate flotilla without mercy. I know this because I have seen them in action before. They will not hesitate to die rather than allow us to win or to learn anything about them. Since you have seen them, they will pursue you until they have destroyed every ship you possess and every trace of humanity in every star system to which you flee.

"Your vendetta with me has endured for more than a decade. It can wait a little longer, until we deal with this threat to everyone.

"Or, you can choose to attack me as my forces attempt to deal with the aliens. If I am victorious against them, I will not hesitate to destroy you afterward. If they defeat my forces, they will not hesitate to destroy you next."

Iceni gestured with one hand, a reaching out and a casting away in one movement. "The choice is yours. As you have doubtless realized by now, you are no longer responsible for just your own welfare. You have many men and women depending upon you to lead them well and lead them wisely. You have many lives depending upon your decisions. You and I can resolve our issues once the threat to those who follow us is dealt with. Or you can be as foolish and stupid as I was over a decade ago and do what your enemies want you to do.

"For the people, Gwen Iceni, out."

She sat back again, satisfied that there would be no doubt in Imallye's mind that Iceni was here and that she was aboard the *Midway*.

Go ahead, Iceni thought. *Chase me. Because I'm on a warship headed straight for the enigmas, and if you follow me you'll find yourself mixed up in a fight with the alien armada whether you want it or not.*

And then, maybe, you'll forget about vengeance on me long enough to help us stop the enigmas, and finally be the woman your father surely wanted you to be.

The situation was complicated, but Iceni was pleased with herself as she returned to the bridge to make an appearance. It wouldn't do for the president to be lounging in her stateroom while events were still developing.

As she sat down, Mercia gave her a troubled look, then spoke cautiously. "Madam President, there is something I do not understand."

"What is that, Kapitan?" Iceni asked, certain that she could easily deal with whatever question Mercia had.

"Why did the Syndicate commit these forces to retaking Iwa instead of retaking Moorea or the other star systems that Imallye has taken from them?"

"Because—" Iceni began, then halted speaking as the implications of the question sank home. Why hadn't the Syndicate hit Imallye first, then moved on to reoccupy Iwa?

"I have been wondering," Mercia continued, "how Imallye accumulated so many warships so quickly, and seized three star systems just as quickly. I thought, perhaps, the Syndicate has focused its energies on retaking Midway."

Iceni frowned at Mercia. "And yet we know that Moorea, at least, was restive as well and threatening rebellion, encouraged by our example. And we have learned that Imallye is not wiping clean the Syndicate structure in the star systems she has captured, instead substituting her choices for whichever Syndicate CEOs were ousted."

"A false flag?" Mercia suggested.

"Damn." Iceni no longer felt any sense of satisfaction. "They outthought us again, didn't they? The pirate queen Imallye is operating at the Syndicate's sufferance, giving a fresh face and a false face to the Syndicate system while also continuing to support it."

"It explains a great deal."

She paused, thinking again, remembering Imallye's father, and what she had heard of Imallye herself. "But I find it hard to believe that Imallye would stooge for the Syndicate like that. There is something missing in that explanation."

Mercia hunched forward, eyeing Iceni. "How much do you know of her?"

"Imallye? Both too much and too little." Iceni considered the question before saying more. "Her father was ambitious and smart. Clever, too. He tended to think a step or two ahead of his opponents and held his own cards close to his chest. He didn't hide any of that, which earned him some admiration but also a lot of enemies."

Iceni glanced at Mercia. "The problem was, no one knew what he would do next. Who would benefit from knowing him, and who would turn out to be a step to be trod over on his ladder to the top. I was far from the only junior CEO worried about what he might spring on me. That made it much easier to believe what I heard he was doing and reported him for."

"So the question is, what are the cards that Imallye is planning on playing?" Mercia said.

"And what game it is that she's playing," Iceni agreed.

COLONEL Donal Hideki Rogero glared at the image of the planet that was his objective, wishing that the offending world would somehow spontaneously explode before he and his soldiers were landed there.

He still didn't have a decent plan for assaulting that alien base. What he did have was an assortment of equipment which had been jury-rigged to perform in slightly different ways than designed. Whether that could defeat the assumed enigma capability to inflict full-spectrum blinding on attacking enemies was anybody's guess.

But now he had to worry about not just the alien installation, but also a large force of Syndicate ground troops that were probably being dropped onto the same planet at this very moment. And those Syndicate ground troops might be human, but they would regard Rogero and his soldiers as enemies, so Rogero would have to worry about dealing with two different threats at the same time.

And what had the Kommodor said when Rogero had pointed that out? *"I've got* three *different threats to deal with."* Which was certainly true, but not at all helpful.

He had less than a day to figure out how to win a fight that had just gotten worse after already being nearly impossible.

IT required another three hours for the reply to President Iceni to come in from the Syndicate flotilla.

Marphissa was surprised at the image she saw before her. Syndicate CEOs were required to maintain "standards," which was a fancy way of saying that they had to always look perfect as spelled out in a multitude of rules, some of them written down and others unwritten but understood by anyone who dealt with CEOs with any frequency. Because of the political games and posturing among Syndicate CEOs, they could also be counted on to present a haughty and confident face to anyone of lesser or equal rank whom they dealt with.

However, the CEO commanding the Syndicate flotilla did not look arrogant or comfortable. His suit, instead of being freshly pressed, looked rumpled. He bore on his face and in his eyes the marks of too little sleep and too many worries. As he spoke, his voice carried not the whiplash of orders or demands, but the quiet fatalism of someone who needed help that he knew would not be coming.

"President Iceni, you know that I cannot agree to the deal that you have proposed," the CEO said. "I am under orders to attack and destroy your mobile forces whenever and wherever I encounter them."

His lips twisted in a sardonic smile. "But you know that my units are soon to be engaged with another foe. Our chances are . . . not very good. I fully intend to carry out my orders by confronting and destroying all enemy forces in this star system, but there is a high probability that my flotilla will not be . . . one hundred percent successful in that effort when we engage the enigmas. And so I must ask of you a favor even while I refuse to work with you in defeating a common foe."

The smile slipped away from the CEO's face. "You have seen that we have troop transports and freighters accompanying my flotilla, and that these units have been left at the planet to off-load their passengers and as much cargo as possible before the enemy reaches them. Those passengers are partly ground forces, and partly the families of our crew members and of the ground forces personnel. The Syndicate ordered them to accompany us, to ensure that we fought our hardest to defend this star system."

Marphissa stared at the CEO's image in disbelief as his words hit home. Families. The Syndicate had sent citizens, men, women, and children, into a war zone to stiffen the spines of the military units tasked with holding Iwa against any more attacks.

Iceni's image appeared next to Marphissa. "That's why the Syndicate mobile forces are acting the way they are.

Look at that bridge shot from the Syndicate flagship. Not a snake in sight. That's how the Syndicate is handling the losses of so many snakes in recent battles. There aren't any snakes on the warships. The snakes are with the families of the crews, ready to enforce the will of the Syndicate without risking themselves on the warships. And the warship crews are going into a hopeless fight to try to save their families."

The Syndicate flotilla commander struggled with his words as he continued. "I . . . ask . . . that you take what measures you can to . . . save anyone from the transport units who is . . . still alive after we have done our best to stop the enigma force. I cannot compel your aid in this matter. I cannot promise anything to you in payment. I can only . . . ask."

He straightened, regaining some composure. "My flotilla will do its utmost. For the people, Juvenale, out."

Marphissa sighed and rubbed her face with both hands as the message ended. "He said the last phrase as if he meant it."

Iceni nodded in agreement. "If he was thinking of the people on those transports and freighters, I am certain that he meant it. He and his crews are preparing to die for those people, for *their* people. Can we save them, Kommodor?"

"The CEO and the crews of his ships?" Marphissa asked doubtfully.

"I can read a display," Iceni said, her voice short. "There is no possible way for us to save them. I meant the people who will be left on the planet. Can we save those citizens?"

"I do not know, Madam President." Marphissa gazed at her display with a fierce determination growing inside her. "If it can be done, we will do it. I will notify Colonel Rogero of the new complication in his mission."

Rogero listened with a deadpan expression as Marphissa passed on the information, then looked quickly to one side, inhaling deeply before answering. "Aliens and snakes and citizens."

"And Syndicate ground forces," Marphissa added.

"Have any flying monkeys shown up yet?"

"Not yet," Marphissa said, wondering again why and how "flying monkeys" had become an expression to describe the worst possible development. "That's one thing to be thankful for. Should we call off the ground operation?"

"No." Rogero looked at her, his eyes hard. "The citizens will be trapped down there, caught between the snakes and aliens. They need someone on that planet who is on their side. Request permission to attempt direct communication with the Syndicate ground forces."

"Permission granted," Marphissa said. "President Iceni will probably agree to any deal that keeps either the aliens or the snakes from massacring those citizens."

"If the enigmas pop up and hit them before we get there, nothing we can do will prevent them all from dying," Rogero pointed out.

"I don't think they'll act that soon," Marphissa said, remembering her discussion with Kontos. "As far as the enigmas know, we are unaware that they have a buried installation on that planet. If they're going to spring a surprise attack, they'll wait until it will have the greatest possible impact."

His eyes narrowed in thought as Rogero nodded. "That's a real possibility. As alien as they are, the enigmas have demonstrated a skill at tactical surprise that matches what capable human commanders would do. They will have seen that we also have troop transports with us, so they will wait until we have also dropped our soldiers, or hit while we are dropping and too committed to pull out of the operation. Is it acceptable for me to reveal the presence of the enigma facility to the Syndicate ground forces?"

"Yes," Marphissa replied immediately. "From what I know, the Syndicate soldiers cannot take that base themselves."

"No. That won't happen. It'll probably turn out to be impossible for us, and we've been trying to plan and prepare for exactly that mission."

She felt an odd sense of disappointment. "Colonel, I have to confess that I am surprised to hear you say that about our own chances. I guess I have become too used to seeing General Drakon's forces do the impossible."

Rogero grinned. "A reputation like that is a two-edged sword. It's useful against enemies, but can result in your own side telling you to do the impossible one time too many."

"I worked for the Syndicate, too, Colonel," Marphissa said wryly. "We are all very familiar with being given those sorts of orders. Perhaps the Syndicate ground forces will recognize that they face exactly such an impossible mission and will eliminate the snakes among them knowing that no matter how bloody that battle it will still be preferable to any alternatives. If they do get rid of the snakes among them, they may be willing to cut a deal with us. Let me know how it goes."

A couple of hours later, as Marphissa's flotilla headed toward an intercept with the enigma armada, the light showing Imallye's reaction finally arrived.

"She's changing vectors on her ships," Kontos observed. "Coming starboard and climbing slightly. They're accelerating, too."

"Aiming for us," Marphissa said without waiting for the course projections to steady up.

"Yes," Kontos agreed. "Our president appears to have motivated Imallye in the way we wanted. We did want her to attack us, right?"

"Better that than forcing Bradamont and Diaz to deal with Imallye's flotilla with what we left at Midway."

"Kommodor," the comm specialist said. "We have an incoming message to President Iceni, but it is also addressed to our entire flotilla."

"I might as well see it, then," Marphissa replied, knowing that the specialists on every ship in the flotilla would already be finding ways to view the message as well.

There was Imallye again, garbed just as Marphissa had seen her at Moorea. The black skin suit and weaponry were the same, the only difference being a large, bloodred jewel clipped to Imallye's left earlobe. The earring looked unsettlingly like an actual fat drop of blood hanging on the pirate's ear.

"You're making this easy for me, Iceni," Imallye said with casual menace. "I'll finish you off here, then wipe out the other contenders for Iwa before I move on to deal with your general at Midway. Oh, and say hello to your Kommodor for me. I have unfinished business with her as well. This time I am the one springing the surprise on you. Out."

Whatever plea Iceni had made to Imallye had obviously fallen on deaf ears. Marphissa didn't say anything for a long moment as she looked at her display, counting up the odds facing Midway's flotilla.

Kontos broke the silence, his voice sounding . . . intrigued. "This should be interesting," he commented.

"Interesting?" Marphissa bent a skeptical look his way. "That's one word for it."

"We'll take our opponents out one by one? Or all at once?"

Kontos couldn't be that oblivious. She took a closer look at him and realized that he wasn't. He was putting on an act of his own to counteract the performance that Imallye had just shown them. The specialists witnessing this little conversation would pass it around to their friends in the flotilla, and morale among the crews would not be as badly affected by Imallye's threats.

"One by one," Marphissa said with tones whose confidence matched that of Kontos. "Getting them all together at once would be too much trouble."

"I see. Good idea. Just wait until our battleship gets a shot at them!"

Marphissa managed a smile she thought would look real to those watching. It was true that the battleship *Midway* packed a punch that none of their opponents could match, but the massive warship was also too sluggish compared to their enemies to force a fight. She would have to lure the faster warships within range of *Midway*'s firepower, which meant limiting the maneuvers of her own more nimble ships like this battle cruiser.

It was the sort of problem that made for challenging simulations, and very tough real battles.

I may not have a big jewel stuck on my ear, but I'll show Imallye just how tough I am before this is over, Marphissa vowed to herself.

CHAPTER FOURTEEN

CAPTAIN Honore Bradamont had spent about a decade in the Alliance fleet, which made her an old-timer in a force that for a century had been losing ships, men, and women at a rate matched only by their equally stubborn and equally bloodied opponents, the Syndicate Worlds. She had survived her first years through sheer luck, managed to learn enough to help her survive the next few, gotten captured by the Syndicate Worlds, gotten rescued by the Alliance several months after that, gained command of the battle cruiser *Dragon*, and had spent the final months under the command of Admiral John "Black Jack" Geary, who had been the sort of leader who could win victories that did not demand mass sacrifices on his own side.

And then, with peace having been declared, she had found herself fighting first through vast reaches of unexplored space inhabited by a couple of intelligent and hostile nonhuman species, as well as the ambiguously friendly Dancers, then assigned to Midway to help fight battles here.

"What exactly is *peace*?" Kapitan Diaz asked her.

Bradamont, her seat next to his on the bridge of heavy

cruiser *Manticore*, shrugged. She had long since gotten used to those who had grown up under Syndicate rule asking her about things that Bradamont thought common knowledge. But this particular question dealt with a topic she wasn't familiar with, either. "It's supposed to be when someone isn't at war."

"So there isn't any fighting? There is no need for ships like this?" Diaz waved around to indicate his cruiser.

"There is fighting," Bradamont said. "As far as I know, the fighting isn't all that different, and people die just as surely in peace as in war. And there are still fleets of warships and armies of ground forces."

"Then what is the difference?"

"I don't really know." Bradamont gazed off to one side, remembering. "Admiral Geary knows. He used to try to explain it to us. After the Syndicate Worlds finally signed an agreement to end the war, we all waited for everything to change. But none of us can see any difference. None of us know how to be different. Maybe that's the problem."

"How can you stop someone from attacking you?" Diaz wondered.

She focused back on him. "Do you want to attack Admiral Geary?"

"Black Jack?" Diaz shook his head, a gesture mimicked by all of the specialists on the bridge. "Why would I? He is for the people."

"He is an admiral in the Alliance fleet," she reminded him.

"But . . . he's different. He only does what he must. No more. He doesn't war on those who can't fight back, or demand more than we can give, or . . ." Diaz screwed up his face as he thought. "He fights only those who force him to fight. Is that right?"

"That's right." Bradamont spread her hands. "So, Admiral Geary has stopped you from wanting to attack him."

Diaz frowned in thought. "We need more Black Jacks, don't we?"

"You have President Iceni and General Drakon. That is no small thing."

Whatever Diaz would have answered was interrupted by an alert. He looked quickly at his display, the frown changing into a scowl. "The Syndicate is back. At the jump point from Lono, just as you predicted, Captain."

It wasn't a big Syndicate flotilla, but big enough to be a serious problem. Three heavy cruisers, a light cruiser, and ten Hunter-Killers. "Whatever peace is supposed to be," Bradamont commented sarcastically, "it still looks like war from here."

KOMMODOR Marphissa wasn't sure whether she was racing her flotilla to intercept the Syndicate flotilla at Iwa, or to intercept and battle with the enigma armada to help the Syndicate flotilla. In any case, her intentions didn't matter. The distances were too great, the time too short, and the odds against the Syndicate flotilla too dire. Marphissa could only watch as the Syndicate flotilla charged toward the enigmas.

One of the worst parts of space combat was born of the sheer size of space. With light requiring hours or days to cover the distances between formations of ships, it was all too easy to be in a situation where a badly outnumbered flotilla of friendly forces faced certain doom, and to be so far away that there was no means of intervening even though the action could be viewed with perfect clarity. What was being seen was both history, events that had already taken place hours or days before, and immediate, because what was viewed was not a record of past tragedy but the actual moments when ships and crews were dying.

The Syndicate warships had arranged themselves into the standard box formation, with one broad side facing toward the enemy. Leading the formation were the Syndicate light cruiser and fifteen of their Hunter-Killers, arrayed in the rectangle forming the side facing the enigmas. Behind them came the two battle cruisers and two of the heavy cruisers, arranged in a diamond inside the box, and in the rectangle making up the rear side of the box were the other three heavy cruisers and remaining four Hunter-Killers.

Swooping in to meet the Syndicate box head-on were the enigmas, who had arranged their many more warships into a nearly flat box with one narrow side facing the Syndicate. The arrangement of alien warships bore an uncomfortable resemblance to an immense axe head, with the leading edge swinging toward the Syndicate box.

Kapitan Kontos was watching as well, his expression gloomy. "Why can't their deaths mean something?" he murmured to Marphissa.

"They will mean something," she replied. "Every enigma warship they destroy will be one less that we have to defeat in order to save the people the Syndicate transports and freighters have been shuttling down to the planet."

He glanced at the time/distance marker next to the representation of the Syndicate formation on their displays. "One hour and forty light minutes away. We're seeing them when they were two minutes from contact."

"The enigmas will take time to finish off the Syndicate warships," Marphissa said, her voice sounding harsh even to her. "That will give us the time we need to intercept the enigmas before they can reach the Syndicate people on the planet." It felt ugly, spending human lives like some perverted form of money to buy time, but that sort of trade-off was familiar to them all. She sighed. "Trade lives for time. I used to think that was something only the cold-blooded business minds of the Syndicate would do. Then I saw the Alliance fight and realized that they would make the same choice. There are two kinds of people in war. The kind who are willing to sell their lives to defend their people or their homes or their beliefs, and the kind who aren't willing to pay that price. The first kind always beat the second kind."

Kontos gave her a troubled look. "What if both sides are of the first kind?"

"Then they kill each other until one side wins or both

sides are bled white and collapse." She met his gaze. "Unless someone on both sides is smart enough to realize that there need to be limits on what they ask people to die for."

"We're still willing to die," Kontos said. "Not for the Syndicate, though."

"No." Marphissa pointed to her display. "They're not going to die for the Syndicate, either."

The time to engagement between the Syndicate flotilla and the alien armada scrolled downward. One minute. Thirty seconds. Ten seconds.

They saw what had happened one hour and forty minutes ago.

The Syndicate commander had been brave, but not smart. He held his vector, but the enigmas used their superior maneuverability to tilt their formation upward in the last seconds before contact. Instead of slicing through the center of the Syndicate box, the enigma axe went in near the top at a slight angle.

Marphissa tried not to wince as the sensors aboard her ships reported with emotionless precision the outcome of the first engagement.

The light cruiser and ten of the Hunter-Killers along the upper edge of the Syndicate box had all been blown to pieces. One of the Syndicate battle cruisers had also been hit so hard that nothing was left but fragments. Three of the heavy cruisers were out of action, one blown apart by a massive number of hits, another broken into several large pieces that were tumbling away from the remnants of the Syndicate flotilla, and another still intact, still fighting, but heavily battered.

The enigmas had taken some losses, but not nearly as many as the heavily outgunned Syndicate warships. "Only six," Kontos murmured. "They only took out six."

"They damaged some others," Marphissa said. "They could have done better!" she growled, feeling anger and frustration. "He just ran right at them instead of trying last-minute maneuvers himself!"

The surviving Syndicate warships were bending their courses up and around. They weren't fleeing, but were maneuvering to make another pass at the aliens.

The enigmas were whipping about as well. At the incredible velocities the human and alien warships were traveling, their "tight" turns swung through many thousands of kilometers, but the enigmas were able to outturn even the human battle cruisers.

Forty minutes later, the two forces clashed again. The enigmas came in under the surviving Syndicate warships, their axe head this time slashing at a high angle upward through the human formation.

The enigmas lost another four warships as they overwhelmed the rest of the human formation, but only one Syndicate warship had survived the second encounter. The heavy cruiser badly damaged in the first pass had lagged enough behind its comrades that the enigmas had not been able to target it as well. Most of the enigma ships cleared the debris field that marked the remains of the last Syndicate battle cruiser, two heavy cruisers, and nine HuKs, then turned to head for the Syndicate transports and freighters orbiting the planet. They had a great distance yet to cover, almost two light hours as they chased the planet around its own orbit. But a dozen enigma craft had peeled off from their formation and angled around to hit a much closer target, the sole surviving Syndicate heavy cruiser.

"Why isn't he launching escape pods?" Kontos wondered. "That unit doesn't have a chance. Why not save as many of the crew as possible?"

"The enigmas will just target the escape pods," Marphissa said. "They don't want any humans watching them, even humans who couldn't possibly hurt them."

"I guess the enigmas believe that being watched does hurt them," Kontos said, bewildered. "Why?"

"The enigmas have probably said the same thing about us while they watched humans butchering other humans for a century. They're aliens. They don't think like us, they don't care about the same things as us. We have no idea why they're so obsessed with privacy, and they aren't about to explain it to us." Marphissa narrowed her eyes as she studied her display. "That cruiser doesn't have a chance, but he's maneuvering to meet those enigma warships. At least they're going down fighting. I wonder if he—"

The answer to her question came before she finished the sentence. An hour and a half ago, the distance now lessened as Marphissa's warships raced toward the scene of battle, the heavy cruiser had met a dozen alien warships racing close by to ensure the destruction of the human warship. The doomed cruiser's commander had not chosen to die futilely, though.

Instead, the heavy cruiser had detonated its power core at the precise moment when the enigma warships were darting in to administer a death blow.

Wrathful cheers erupted on the bridge of *Pele* as only six enigma warships staggered out of the field of destruction created by the heavy cruiser's deliberate sacrifice.

"He got six of them," Kontos breathed. The Kapitan turned to sweep the bridge with his glance, silencing the celebration. "That leaves twenty-eight alien warships for us," he reminded his crew.

Marphissa drew in a long, slow breath. As the tracks of the enigma warships steadied out, she could see the projected track for her own flotilla intercepting them before they could reach the planet. "And all of those who died bought the time their people needed. We will honor their sacrifice by completing the task they could not, and ensuring the safety of those they died to protect!" It sounded like something an Alliance officer would have said, full of idealism and honor. Maybe she had spent too much time around Captain Bradamont.

But none of the crew seemed surprised or unhappy at what Marphissa had said. Instead, they appeared ready to cheer again, but cast worried glances at Kontos. He made a small affirmative gesture, and then they did cheer.

Because she was leading them into battle with a force that had just annihilated a flotilla similar to their own.

Kontos must have been reading her thoughts. He shrugged. "Humans are crazy, too."

"Yes," Marphissa agreed. "But it's our crazy. We were willing to leave them alone to their crazy; they wouldn't take the deal, so we're going to show them what happens when you push people too far."

She took another look at the planet looping about its star. Above the planet were the symbols marking the three Syndicate troop transports and four Syndicate freighters. From the over-an-hour-ago images visible, the troop transports were still busy landing every passenger they carried, while from their movements the shuttles servicing the freighters must have been dropping their cargo haphazardly to save time. It was past time for her to make another decision.

First she made another call to Colonel Rogero. "I can detach our troop transports at any time, Colonel. Do you wish to proceed with the landing?"

"Yes," Rogero replied without visible enthusiasm. "I'm not in the habit of giving up before trying, and staying on the transports wouldn't give my soldiers any chance of fighting back. I haven't heard back from anyone with the Syndicate ground forces. If what we were told by the Syndicate flotilla commander is correct, there must be a lot of snakes enforcing Syndicate loyalty on the surface of that planet. There's a chance that when we get close enough to the planet my people will be able to find a way to contact some of the Syndicate soldiers through circuits the snakes aren't watching. That's my best hope at this point. I'll also be able to get a better look at the enigma presence by using the sensors on the transports to scan the planet."

"Good luck, Colonel." There wasn't anything else to say. As soon as that message was over, Marphissa called Leytenant Mack on HTTU 332. "Leytenant, you are hereby placed in charge of both troop transports, subject to the orders of Colonel Rogero. You are to detach from our formation and proceed on a direct vector to meet the planetary objective in its orbit at the best velocity you can manage. Are there any questions?"

Mack did not look particularly thrilled at the assignment. "What will our escort be?"

"You'll have a distant escort, Leytenant," Marphissa said dryly. "This flotilla. Nothing I could detach to go with you would be strong enough to stop any of the three enemy warship formations in this star system, so instead I will keep them occupied while you land our ground forces."

"Yes, Kommodor," Mack said. "I understand and will comply."

"We will do our best to cover you," Marphissa said. "Once you get the soldiers landed you won't be nearly as attractive a target for enemy attack."

She ended the call, feeling extremely guilty.

Kontos gave her a sidelong look. "What if the enigmas spring their ambush as soon as the transports get close to the planet?"

"Then we couldn't stop them from reaching the transports anyway! The transports' track will diverge slowly from ours," Marphissa insisted, gesturing to the projected courses arcing through space on her display, "so we're not going to be far from them when they reach the planet."

By the time the transports finished braking into orbit and landing the soldiers, though, Marphissa's formation would be well past and going very fast away from them. She knew that, Kontos knew that, Mack knew that, and very likely Colonel Rogero knew that. It just couldn't be helped. "If I had twice as many ships . . ." Marphissa muttered.

Kontos nodded wordlessly, his mouth a thin line. He knew just as well as she did that the transports would have a very small chance of survival when they had finished doing as she had ordered, and that any other course of action she might have ordered would have been even worse for the chances of everyone in the flotilla.

She tried to find some satisfaction in knowing that the situation had simplified a bit with the destruction of the Syndicate flotilla. Now it was only a three-way fight in space, as well as a looming three-way fight on the planet.

ONLY a down patch had sufficed to get Colonel Rogero some rest in the hours leading up to the assault on the planet. His stateroom on this troop transport, having been intended for at least sub-CEO rank in the Syndicate, was actually comfortable, but that hadn't helped. He slept only intermittently, and was awake an hour before his alert time, feeling anything but alert.

He had every reason he could wish for to cancel this operation. No one would blame him in the least if he pulled the plug right now. Not General Drakon, not President Iceni, not the Kommodor, not Honore Bradamont whose worry had been ill concealed when they parted, and certainly not his own soldiers, who knew enough about combat operations to know how ugly this one was.

But he couldn't do it. He couldn't give up without trying. It wasn't pride, he told himself. Partly it was the knowledge that more than once seemingly impregnable enemy positions had proven to be surprisingly vulnerable. There was no way to be certain until you actually tested the defenses, especially in a case like this where practically everything they knew about the enigma base was pure speculation.

Partly it was knowing that his soldiers, relieved or not at the cancellation, would wonder if he had lacked confidence in them.

Partly it was knowing how many enemy warships were already in this star system, and how many more the enigmas might have concealed if the Kommodor's guess was right, and what those warships would do to these transports if they got a shot at them.

Partly it was thinking of those poor bastards already on the surface. Not just Syndicate ground forces but also who knew how many civilians who had been dragged into this mess by the Syndicate. Rogero didn't care whether or not the snakes who were holding guns on everyone were themselves massacred by the enigmas. He actually liked the idea.

But there didn't seem to be any way to make that happen without the civilians also being wiped out.

The civilians. That was mainly it, wasn't it? He and so many others had kept fighting for the Syndicate because they wanted to protect their families from both an Alliance that didn't care who died in their bombardments, and from the Syndicate that would retaliate against anyone who failed to follow orders. But now the Syndicate had brought the families into the war zone. Hostages to keep the mobile forces and the ground forces in line.

He didn't know how many snakes the Syndicate still had. But if word of this got around, it wouldn't be enough. Not anywhere.

Rogero donned his battle armor, then clumped glumly through passageways large enough to accommodate him in that heavy outfit. He passed parts of his brigade, the soldiers all suiting up with the careful efficiency of those who had done this plenty of times already. That was an odd thing to think about. They had taken losses since revolting against the Syndicate, but not nearly as many as had been the norm during the war. He had a growing proportion of veterans in his unit, men and women who had accumulated experience in the grim art of war.

He reached the bridge, where the transport's commander awaited him.

Leytenant Mack saluted with rigid precision. "My ship and HTTU 643 are ready to land your ground forces upon your command, Colonel."

"What are the Syndicate transports doing?" Rogero asked.

"They took off when we reached the planet. Them and the Syndicate freighters." Mack pointed off in a direction that meant nothing to Rogero. "Running. I don't know where. They're heading along the track their flotilla took, which means they're running toward the enigmas. I don't know what's up with that."

"They're staying together?"

"No, sir." Mack shook his head, looking uncomfortable. "The transports have been pulling steadily away from the freighters. Leaving them behind."

Rogero looked at Mack, knowing even with his helmet visor up he still appeared very menacing in combat armor. "Why does that bother you, Leytenant?"

Mack glared back at Rogero. "Because it's not right. I understand running to try to live. But those Syndicate transports haven't a chance in hell anyway. Somebody or other is going to blow them apart before they can jump out of this star system. They should have at least put on a good show and stood by the others."

"At least," Rogero agreed. "Now, what about the planet? I've got the data from your sensors showing what they can see of the Syndicate position, but not anything on the enigma base."

"Yeah," Mack said reluctantly. "That Syndicate ground position is a mess, huh? Looks like they just dropped people and stuff any which where. Panic, seems to me. I bet those freighters still have some critical stuff on board that anyone on a rock like that will need to live long-term."

"Long-term living requirements are the least of their worries," Rogero said. "Why don't we have anything from our ground-penetrating sensors on that buried base?"

Mack brought up an image that floated before them, a segment of the planet below lit up in various colors to enhance the information. "You have everything that we can see," Leytenant Mack advised, waving at the display. "We've tried every trick, every sensor for remotely seeing what's on the surface and what's beneath the surface, and that's all we get."

Colonel Rogero scowled at the image. One of the advantages of real assault transports was that they came equipped with active sensor systems that could penetrate objects like the surface of a planet to map underground installations. When aboard warships he had asked for that kind of support and been met with blank stares. The warships depended so heavily on passive sensors that collected everything that could be seen across every band of the spectrum that they were shocked at the idea of sending out energy using active systems like the advanced radars on a troop transport.

But this time the transports' sensors weren't helping much. "It's just a blob covering a huge area," Rogero complained.

Leytenant Mack nodded. "That's all we can see," he repeated. "There's something in the surface soil blocking our scans across every frequency and wavelength. At least we know whatever the enigmas are hiding is somewhere under that."

"What could they seed across hundreds of square kilometers that blocked everything?" Rogero wondered. "They must have a way to vent heat, at the very least."

"You could do it underground," Mack said. "My sister's a geologist. Did I ever tell you that? We were talking once and she said you could either dump the heat into an underground river or into a really big underground reservoir. That would get rid of the heat and disperse it so much that the source couldn't be pinpointed."

"We should have brought a geologist," Rogero said. "Despite knowing these are aliens, I keep expecting them to do things like we do. To have the same capabilities that we do. But they are obviously a lot better at camouflage."

"Where do you want to drop?"

Rogero gazed at the display. To one side of the underground blob that marked the enigma's masking efforts were a cluster of symbols that marked the Syndicate personnel and equipment that had been hastily landed. They might be directly over part of the alien installation. Or not. "I might have to fight those Syndicate ground forces as well as the aliens, but I am supposed to protect the citizens with those ground forces from the aliens."

"I wouldn't come down too close to them," Mack cautioned. "Keep a few kilometers off, at least outside the range of their hand weapons. Odds are they've already been targeted."

"Odds are so has this transport." Rogero took a slight,

perverse pleasure from seeing Leytenant Mack's anxiety when that was pointed out. "I think the enigmas are going to wait and see if we and the Syndicate ground forces start fighting before they attack either of us."

"Why would they do that?"

Rogero sat back, folding his arms and frowning as he spoke. "That's been their usual tactic. From what Captain Bradamont told me, the enigmas might have tricked the Syndicate into starting the war with the Alliance, and once it was going the enigmas apparently leaked to both sides the hypernet technology that ensured we would keep fighting longer. The Alliance thinks the enigmas expected humans to eventually figure out that the hypernet gates could be used as nova-scale bombs to destroy the star systems where they were placed, and then to use the hypernet gates against each other until both the Syndicate and the Alliance had been totally gutted by the mutual destruction."

Mack's mouth had fallen open in shock. "Seriously?"

"Yes. Why waste time and effort killing enemies who were willing to kill each other with a little encouragement?" Rogero nodded firmly. "I am certain that they will wait here to see if we are attacking the Syndicate ground forces. If so, they will wait until one side or the other has triumphed, then hit the survivors with enough force to wipe them out."

"That would be smart," Mack conceded. "Ugly as all hell, but smart for them. That sounds like we should at least mimic a combat drop aimed at the Syndicate ground forces. But if the Syndicate troops see you coming like that, they'll open fire on you."

"The snakes will order them to do so," Rogero agreed. "I am hoping we can fool both the snakes and the enigmas."

"Too bad the snakes and the enigmas won't kill each other off while we watch," Mack commented.

Rogero started to smile politely at the weak joke, then paused. What if . . . ? "Leytenant, I advise you to leave orbit and chase after the flotilla once you have dropped off my people. There's no telling what kind of antiorbital weapons the enigmas might have or how long their range is. I want to start the landing in one hour, when we're in the best orbital position for the shuttles. In the meantime, I need to send another message."

There were always at least two levels in any system of communication. The openly used and officially controlled level that was supposed to be the only one that existed, and the backdoor or hidden level that workers quickly improvised for informal communications among themselves. Internal security devoted immense efforts to trying to shut down every backdoor system as quickly as possible, but no matter how many were uncovered and blocked, more popped up. The complexity of comm systems and unit networks created a huge number of places where potential back doors could be cobbled together by the sort of software manipulations that left no fingerprints for frustrated snakes to trace back to a source.

General Drakon had lent Rogero the services of Sergeant Broom, the most devious hacker available to him. "Sergeant, I need a way into whatever back door those Syndicate ground forces are using."

Broom scratched his head, grimacing slightly. "That back door will still have virtual barricades to any intrusion attempts by us, Colonel. Workers learned the necessity for those the hard way a long time ago."

"This isn't for an intrusion. I want to be able to talk to those ground forces without any chance the snakes will intercept it."

"We're close enough I might be able to find their net now," Broom murmured, his hands racing across virtual controls as he gazed at information flows on his specialized display. "It depends how much they're talking and . . . aha. The snakes are making this easy."

"What did they do?" Rogero asked, peering at the cascade of unfamiliar data.

"Constant pingbacks on all command circuits," Broom explained. "The snakes are maintaining constant checks on the comm nets to spot anything that shouldn't be there."

Rogero shook his head. "I don't understand. I thought our systems did automatic checks for intrusions."

"They do, Colonel," Broom advised. "But the checks are randomized and not continuous so they don't overload the comm net and send out enough noise to make it possible for someone on the outside to spot the net parameters. The snakes have set the net down there to do the checks constantly. I will guarantee you that the tactical data feeds for those ground forces soldiers are being slowed significantly. And . . ." His frown changed to a grin. "Oh. That is tray dough!"

"Dough?" Rogero asked, raising both eyebrows.

"It's an old expression where I come from," Broom explained. "It means really great, or something like that. All that snake activity is lighting up their net perfectly. I know exactly what to look for, so I should be able to find any back doors pretty fast."

"We're pressed for time, Sergeant," Rogero said. "How fast?"

"Ten minutes, Colonel."

"Make it five."

"Yes, sir," Broom answered.

The reply came quickly and confidently enough to make Rogero certain that Broom had deliberately overstated how long the task would take, just as General Drakon had warned he might do. "Let me know when you have it. Have the other code monkeys put together a burst transmission package containing the means to sweep the Syndicate ground systems for enigma quantum worms."

"Yes, sir. We're on it."

Four minutes later, a new symbol appeared on Rogero's comm display. "That's your door, Colonel," Broom advised cheerfully. "And here"—another symbol appeared—"is your link to the burst. Just tap it when you want to send through that door."

"You are invaluable, Sergeant Broom," Rogero said. "General Drakon asked me to remind you to not do anything unauthorized that will require him or me to have you shot. It would be a great loss to us."

"It would be a great loss to me as well," Broom said. "But it would be useful to have it spelled out clearly as to exactly what actions by me would result in execution and which would merely involve lesser punishments."

"I think it's better to leave that a bit vague," Rogero said.

He paused, ordering his thoughts, then tapped the back-door symbol. The symbol pulsed several times, then steadied as it established a firm link to the back door being used by the ground forces workers. "I am with the Midway ground forces preparing to land near you," he said, deliberately avoiding identifying himself as an officer. Syndicate workers had learned the hard way not to trust executives or CEOs without solid evidence that they could be relied upon. "You have already seen that the aliens called enigmas have destroyed the mobile forces that escorted you to this star system. Our mobile forces will stop the enigma warships from destroying you, but there is also an alien base hidden deep beneath the surface of the planet you are on. Your forces are standing over the area where the base is located. We are landing to capture or destroy that base, but once the aliens have both of our forces on the surface they will try to destroy us all. If you want to live, your only chance is to use the software package I will be sending after this message. That package won't harm your systems. It will sweep them for worms planted by the aliens. You can verify that is what it does, and that is all it does."

Rogero inhaled deeply, then spoke with the best conviction he could. "We believe that the aliens use the worms they have planted in our systems to allow them to target individual workers and supervisors with pinpoint precision. If you don't sweep your systems, you will die without any chance of survival as soon as the enigmas open fire using distance weapons. Share the sweep software with anyone who can be trusted, even executives. That will mean the initial enigma attack will take out the snakes and any supervisors whom you cannot trust. We want to save the people with you. This is your only chance to survive. Get the word around. Get the citizens with you under whatever cover exists. We will begin landing soon. It will look like a combat drop, but we will not drop close enough to fire on you and will not fire upon anyone who does not fire on us. For the people."

He tapped the second symbol, watching as it flickered once to mark the transmission.

Rogero checked the time, then touched another control. "Get the remaining soldiers loaded for the first drop," he ordered. "I will be boarding my shuttle now. We will drop as scheduled."

One way or another, he had to get his troops on the ground, and give the troop transports a chance to run before the enigmas sprung whatever surprise they had in store.

He was about to board his shuttle when the backdoor symbol pulsed. "Why should we believe you?" The voice was so heavily disguised by software tricks that it was impossible to tell anything about the sender.

Rogero paused halfway through the hatch as he answered. "Because if Midway's ground forces wanted you dead, Midway's mobile forces could have dropped rocks on you when they went past this planet."

"What does Midway want? What will they do to us?"

"Midway wants to destroy the alien base and keep the Syndicate from establishing a new base of its own. That's all. You must have heard that Midway takes prisoners. But we don't hold them. You want to go home, that's fine with us. You want to stay and work with us, that's fine. You want to go somewhere else, that's fine, too."

A long pause, while the time to drop approached and Rogero waited with growing impatience.

"We need proof," the voice finally said.

"Fine," Rogero said. "I told you that we're not going to attack you. We're landing a few kilometers from you, and will not fire on you. No prelanding bombardment, no suppression or covering fire from the shuttles. No weapons will be fired at you unless someone fires at us, and then we will target only the shooter. How's that?"

"How can *you* guarantee that?" the voice demanded suspiciously.

"Because I have a say in what happens," Rogero replied immediately, knowing that any hesitation in answering would look bad. "We have to start down now. Our transports need to have time to get clear of possible attacks by the enigmas. Expect the aliens to open fire on both your ground forces and ours as soon as they realize we are not attacking you."

The link cut off. With an exasperated curse muttered under his breath, Rogero entered the shuttle already crowded with other soldiers and locked one armored fist onto a strap hanging from the overhead. He scanned the status of his unit one last time before giving the launch order. Every one of his soldiers had their systems scrubbed clean of enigma worms, but all were also running outer shells that portrayed infected systems but were isolated from the main systems. Hopefully, that ruse would lead the enigmas to believe that the soldiers' armor was all still infected.

The time marker rolled down to zero. Time to go. His confirmation order went out to Leytenant Mack, all of the shuttle pilots, and every officer and soldier in his brigade. "Begin assault. No one is to fire on the Syndicate ground forces unless they fire on us, and then all return fire is to be aimed at any shooters and no one else. Be prepared to engage the entire Syndicate ground force if necessary, but only when you receive orders to do so. Do not forget that there are a lot of citizens down there among the ground forces, and the snakes with them will probably use those citizens as human shields if they can."

The shuttle lurched as it detached from the troop transport, swung about, then dropped toward the planet below. On his display, Rogero could see dozens of shuttles that had come off both transports mimicking the movement of his own.

An assault drop against a known opponent was bad enough, usually with assorted forms of flak filling the atmosphere and aiming to rip open or tear apart the descending shuttles. But this time as the shuttles fell toward the planet there was only an eerie quiet. The newly landed Syndicate ground forces hadn't been able to assemble any of their aerospace defenses yet, and the enigmas remained silent. Rogero had no doubt that they were watching, though. Watching, and waiting, for the two human forces to engage in the fratricidal warfare that they had seen humans perform many, many times.

But sometimes even humans could figure out how stupid that was.

And sometimes humans didn't do what everyone expected them to do.

Rogero's display showed five minutes left until the shuttles reached the surface. He triggered the comm circuit that covered the shuttles and the transports. "Assume hostile fire will commence the moment the shuttles lift. Initiate full countermeasures on lift. Transports, follow evasive orbiting maneuvers until you clear the planet. All units will drop false system shells at my command."

The shuttles fell in a perfect pattern, unshaken by any defensive fire, but still braking hard at the last to minimize their time at slow speed near the surface. Rogero braced himself against the momentum, letting his armor support his body as the shuttle he was on decelerated fast enough to make him feel like his feet were going to punch right through the lower deck.

The ramp at the rear of the shuttle slammed down at the same moment the shuttle touched dirt. "Go!" Rogero roared, and as he charged out, all around thirty-five more shuttles were also disgorging soldiers.

He went to one knee, scanning his display. Soldiers were scattering away from the shuttles, some dropping to cover their comrades, and as Rogero watched every shuttle finished unloading and leapt skyward at the same moment.

Not a shot had come from the Syndicate ground forces positions, though that might be because Rogero had placed his own drop at extreme range for the Syndicate hand weapons.

"All units, drop false system shells," he ordered, simultaneously activating a command that should ensure every individual soldier did exactly that.

He figured it would take the enigmas perhaps ten seconds to realize what had happened, as their precise information about what Rogero's soldiers and shuttles were doing suddenly vanished.

At five seconds, he had reached the edge of a very large crater where the enigma bombardment had once pulverized the human presence on this world, and slid into cover among the upthrust, broken rocks, checking his soldiers to see that they were all following instructions to do the same. At the edge of his display he could see part of the Syndicate positions, scattered red symbols marking individual soldiers deployed to defend against his own landing.

At eight seconds, his display lit up with a host of threat symbols and warnings. Fortunately, unlike the Syndicate soldiers who had been massacred here before, Rogero's soldiers did not have enigma worms hiding the incoming fire and providing homing information for it.

Rogero felt the ground shudder as enigma weapons plunged blindly into rock and dirt and exploded all around the area where his soldiers clung to whatever cover they had found. Above, enigma antiaerospace weapons were darting upward into a sky suddenly filled with flares, chaff, and smoke thrown out by the fleeing shuttles to confuse enemy seekers.

Five kilometers away, more enigma fire was ravaging the Syndicate positions. Rogero watched red symbols winking out, marking Syndicate soldiers killed, but saw that at least two-thirds of them were still alive. Some of the Syndicate workers had trusted him.

He wondered if the citizens were under cover, or exposed to the enigma barrage.

The first attack dwindled rapidly and then stopped. Rogero waited, controlling his breathing, his eyes locked on his display, where the sensors on every set of battle armor were linked into a net giving him as much information as possible.

If the enigmas were smart, and everything he knew about them argued that they were smart, then their next move was obvious.

"Everyone hold position," Rogero ordered. "All personnel set active countermeasures on auto."

The second wave of fire erupted from unseen launchers and swept across the area. The enigma weapons moved very fast, and this time they were using active seekers to spot the human soldiers. But the battle armor picked up those seeker signals and every soldier's armor began tossing out chaff rounds as well, forming a cloud that covered the unit.

Rogero saw some of his soldiers get hit and breathed a curse. A lot more of the Syndicate symbols were vanishing, but apparently someone on that side had also finally ordered active countermeasures to be employed because the losses slowed abruptly. Unfortunately, the countermeasures also blocked Rogero's view of not only the Syndicate positions but also the net linking his own soldiers.

The ground was shaking again, not in the spastic series of jolts that marked enigma weapons impacting nearby, but a prolonged and deep juddering that felt like the planet was tearing itself open.

Which, he realized, was exactly what was happening.

"—two kilometers . . . planet . . . again . . . two ki . . . north . . . drop z—"

The broken voice transmission from one of the transports, barely able to cut through the countermeasures, cut off completely. Rogero looked toward planetary north, not seeing anything in that direction, but his armor reported that the soil tremors were coming from there.

Whatever it was, it was big. He hoped the transports were already running for all they were worth.

Even through the dust and chaff Rogero saw to the north vast shapes suddenly hurling themselves skyward. Enigma warships. The aliens had launched another part of their ambush, opening some immense access just to the north of him, from which at least a dozen warships were heading into space as fast as they dared accelerate in atmosphere. *They must have hollowed out some huge hangars down there. How big is this base that I'm supposed to capture?*

Rogero hit the comm override which would boost his signal strength and use a special low-data-rate frequency which would punch through the chaff. "Everyone break north. All units except First Company advance toward expected very large access to the enemy base."

He glanced at the little information still showing on his display, remembering where his units had been before the picture went to pieces. "First Company, take up position screening our flank against any attack from the direction of the Syndicate forces." The Syndicate soldiers were probably still hunkered down against the chance of another incoming barrage, but if any snakes and supervisors had survived the enigma attacks they might order an assault. Or the Syndicate soldiers, confused, scared, and mostly leaderless, might panic and attack the only target they could see, which was Rogero's force.

Shutting off the special circuit, Rogero scrambled away from his position, knowing that the enigmas had probably spotted his transmission. He zigzagged toward the north, then as a warning appeared on his display Rogero flattened himself to the ground.

He and nearby rocks bounced as something big hit and exploded where Rogero had transmitted from. He felt both relieved and annoyed. Did the aliens think he was amateurish enough to have stayed in that spot? It was nice to be underestimated, especially when it kept you from being killed, but also insulting.

The enigmas had shifted their focus and were concentrating their fire on the area where the Syndicate soldiers and citizens were located. They were probably still getting some data from infected systems over there. Maybe they also thought they should focus on the larger group, though most of the Syndicate presence was civilians who posed no threat to the enigmas.

Nearing the edge of the chaff field, Rogero saw his display begin updating rapidly as his armor systems reestablished links. His forces were all moving, the majority north toward where the enigma hatch was located. Most of First Company, still under the drifting chaff, could not be seen, but intermittent detections of some showed them sliding sideways into the blocking positions that Rogero had ordered.

The Syndicate troops couldn't do the same, he knew. The Syndicate didn't want workers thinking for themselves, so Syndicate ground forces were required to carry out detailed plans. With many supervisors dead and countermeasures blocking net links, Syndicate-trained soldiers would be without any explicit instructions on what to do. If they moved, it would be a mob movement.

But, Rogero knew, when under fire and not knowing what to do, the average soldier would stay under cover. Which meant he shouldn't have to worry much about the Syndicate ground forces for a while.

"That is one BFH," an awed voice cut across the command circuit.

Annoyed again, this time by the undisciplined message on a critical circuit, Rogero was preparing to chastise the offender when someone else answered. "Yeah. Biggest hole I ever saw."

His display was updating again as information flowed in from the battle armor of the soldiers who had reached the near edge of the enigma hatch. Rogero stared in disbelief at the small section of arc that filled the upper part of his helmet's display. He pulled back the scale. He pulled it back again.

Twenty kilometers across. The enigma hole was twenty kilometers from side to side.

Rogero ran past soldiers who were lying or kneeling in covered positions, ran until he reached the edge of the hole and could peer across it and partway down.

It felt like looking into space from a hatch on a spacecraft.

"Send a probe down it," Rogero ordered one of his scouts, his message now able to go out through the unit net and therefore not broadcasting his position to the watching enigmas.

The scout pulled back an arm and hurled a probe out into the hole.

The probe, designed to be nearly invisible to defensive sensors, had barely begun to drop when an enigma weapon speared it and turned it into falling junk.

"Drop the next one instead of throwing it," Rogero said. Maybe the enigmas had spotted the motion . . .

A scout extended an arm holding a probe, only to have the probe shot out of her grasp and two other enigma shots slam into her lower arm.

As a medic dashed to the wounded scout, she wriggled back from the edge. "That didn't work, sir," she got out between teeth tightly clamped against the pain.

"This time I want every scout to launch a probe simultaneously," Rogero ordered.

The probes arched out over the hole. Rogero's systems registered dozens of shots coming out of the hole, and every probe went dead.

"Sir, we try to go over that edge, they'll take us apart," the scout commander reported. "It must be too easy for them to spot movement against the edge of the opening or above it."

"Try sending down gnats," Rogero said.

"It'll take a while for gnats to drop far," the scout commander cautioned.

"I know. But they're one of our stealthiest scout methods. Let's see what they can do." The gnats were the size of insects, with limited capability and range, but they were very hard to spot.

What they could do, Rogero quickly learned, was go silent when barely inside the hole as something knocked out every gnat.

It didn't take any particular sensitivity to the mood of the soldiers around him to know that none of them wanted to follow the probes or the gnats down that hole. They might follow him, Rogero thought, if he led the way. But since he would clearly die within a second or two of doing so, they were unlikely to follow him far.

They had a way down into the enigma base, but it was a death trap.

And they had yet to see a single enigma, or even any of the launchers raining death on them.

Another wave of enigma fire swept over, this time concentrated around the rim of the vast hole. Chaff filled the air as battle armor once again tried to protect the men and women wearing it.

Rogero looked upward through the haze of countermeasures, wondering whether the battles in space were going any better for humanity than the one down here.

CHAPTER FIFTEEN

LEYTENANT Mack had only been with Midway's mobile forces since he and his ship had been captured at Ulindi not all that long ago. It had been a pleasant surprise to learn that it was possible to fight for reasons other than avoiding court-martial and execution by your own side. He had genuinely enjoyed his time working with people like Colonel Rogero.

"All good things come to an end," Mack observed as he looked at his display.

The troop transport HTTU 332, along with Midway's other troop transport, was accelerating for all they were worth away from the planet where Rogero's soldiers had been dropped. Mack had taken Rogero's advice and directed both transports to chase down the vector of Midway's warships, reasoning that even though they had no chance of catching up with the friendly forces, it was at least movement in the only direction that offered any hope of survival. A few light minutes ahead of them were the Syndicate troop transports which had fled earlier, and much closer were the Syndicate freighters, which were lumbering desperately after the transports they had once accompanied but falling farther behind with every meter covered.

The maneuvers might have worked to keep the transports and the freighters safe. Might have, except for the thirty-three enigma warships that had spat out of a massive hole that had appeared on the surface of the planet. Those warships, once clearing atmosphere, had lined up on direct intercepts with Mack's transports, and beyond them the Syndicate freighters and transports. And, being considerably more nimble than the big transports, the enigmas were making up the distance fast.

"Should the crew abandon ship?" his senior specialist asked.

Mack sighed and spread his open hands in the age-old gesture of frustration. "You saw when they destroyed the Syndicate flotilla what they do to escape pods. We might as well die in what comfort this old ship offers." HTTU 332 had only been manufactured a year earlier, but since the life span of troop transports during the war was usually measured in months, that made 332 an old lady by the standards everyone used.

The senior specialist rubbed two fingers of one hand on her new insignia that marked her as a Midway forces specialist rather than a Syndicate worker. "I didn't really look forward to deciding who got to go in the escape pods," she admitted.

"The Syndicate told us to just line the people up and have them count off from a random start point," Mack reminded her. "Evens go, odds stay." The Syndicate, having calculated that on average a transport ship lost half the crew before being abandoned, only provided enough escape pods for the half of the crew that was assumed to still be alive. "I was an even, once."

"Me, too. I still remember the ones who were left behind. Didn't want to see that again." She checked her own display. "We've got less than an hour before they catch us. Those freighters up ahead have less than that. We're going to be passing them soon."

An alert sounded, causing the specialist to shift her attention. "The pirate's forces have changed their vector. Instead of going after our flotilla, they're now on a direct intercept with us as well."

Mack shook his head at his display, watching the arcs of the paths of ships through space converging on his own ship's projected movement. After so many near misses and so many escapes, this situation offered no hope at all. He wondered why he felt numb instead of frightened. "They'll get here about the same time the enigmas do. We should start a pool on which side kills us."

"What's the payoff?" the specialist asked.

"Bonus time off, at a future date to be determined," Mack said.

That got a tense smile from the specialist. The Syndicate liked to offer awards exactly like that, awards that often never actually got awarded. "I'll let the crew know."

He glanced her way, feeling the need to say something. "I've always treated the crew as decently as I could."

"Yes, sir, you have, and the crew appreciates that." She managed another rigid smile. "You never would have died at the hands of your own workers."

"That's something, I guess." No one knew how many Syndicate supervisors had been killed by their own workers, but the fact that the Syndicate officially denied it ever happened was a clear indicator of how often it did take place. A minor, fixable problem would have resulted in huge crackdowns that caused at least as much trouble as the problem they were designed to fix. But a big problem that couldn't be fixed by a crackdown had to be wished away, declared not to exist, even if the hatches to supervisors' staterooms were armored and alarmed and the supervisors always carried hand weapons.

Mack made a show of relaxing back into his seat, trying to fool himself as well as any members of the crew who could see him as he gazed at the display where two strong forces were racing to see which would be first to get close enough to destroy his ship. He hoped whoever managed it would then be destroyed by the other side.

"FIFTY-ONE of them," Marphissa said, her voice bleak. "With the thirty-three that popped out of that planet we now face more enigma warships than we did before that Syndicate flotilla sacrificed itself."

"We have the battleship," Kontos said.

"Damn Imallye. Instead of helping us, she's helping the enigmas. Does she actually think they'll be grateful and avoid destroying her afterward?"

"She must know better," Kontos said. He gave Marphissa a questioning glance. "We think Imallye's behavior is crazy. Would the enigmas? Given what they have seen of humans?"

"They probably consider it to be typical human behavior," Marphissa said. She frowned at him. "Are you thinking that maybe Imallye is playing a deeper game than it looks? President Iceni suggested the same to me. No one knows, though, and the Imallye I talked with at Moorea seemed to be absolutely serious. I have no doubt that she would have destroyed *Manticore* if she had caught us."

"Several more hours and we'll find out for sure," Kontos observed. "If she wipes out our transports on the way to catch us, that will make it clear that she means every word she said. Or she might bypass them and keep us guessing."

"If she messes with us any more I swear that I will make it hurt when I kill her," Marphissa grumbled, then refocused on the enigmas up ahead. The enigmas were coming to meet her flotilla straight on, probably intending to wipe out this force just as they had the Syndicate flotilla. It was possible that they would dodge at the last moment, though, intending to lure the two remaining human flotillas into combat with each other so they could finish off whoever survived that fight. Marphissa had no intention of permitting that. She would force a clash with the enigmas long before Imallye could come into contact, dealing with one implacable enemy at a time.

BRADAMONT'S plans to deal with the small Syndicate force at Midway that was bigger than her own received a rude interruption when another alert sounded.

"We have just detected the arrival of another Syndicate formation, this one at the hypernet gate," *Manticore*'s senior watch specialist reported. "One heavy cruiser, two light cruisers, and five Hunter-Killers."

"They've now got us outnumbered two to one," Diaz said. He didn't sound despairing about that. Instead, he seemed irritated at the enemy's moves.

"I'll have to change Kapitan Stein's orders," Bradamont said. She had to think before touching the proper comm controls. The Alliance always positioned that particular control *here* and the Syndicate always put it *there*. That was aggravating enough with physical controls, but especially maddening with virtual controls that the Syndicate Worlds had programmed in such a way that they couldn't be customized.

"Kapitan Stein," Bradamont sent, "cancel your previous orders to join up with us. You are to instead close on and shadow the Syndicate flotilla that arrived at the hypernet gate. If you have the opportunity to hit part of that flotilla without risking your entire force, do so, but avoid a straight-up engagement that might wipe out both that flotilla and your own formation. As long as you are close enough to hit them, that Syndicate force will have to spend its time worrying about what you'll do rather than pursuing its own mission."

She paused before ending the call, then decided what to say. "To the honor of our ancestors and for the people of Midway, Bradamont, out."

That new ending phrase, combining that of the Alliance and of these men and women from Midway, got her approving looks from the crew members on the bridge and a surprised smile from Kapitan Diaz. "You're becoming one of us, Captain!" he said. Then the smile faded, and Diaz nodded toward his display. "What will we do?"

"Keep them busy, Kapitan," Bradamont said. "Repeated firing passes. They'll keep trying to arrange those passes to hit us hard with all of their advantage in numbers, and we'll keep dodging their attacks and trying to hit portions of their formation with everything that we've got. We need to wear them down and keep them busy."

"I understand and—" Diaz broke off the old Syndic reply to an order and gave her a glance. "Yes, Captain."

She nodded firmly back at him. Bradamont knew Diaz well enough by this time to know that he realized how hard their task would be. Kapitan Stein could afford to make a few mistakes because the Syndicate flotilla from the hypernet gate roughly equaled her own force. But the Syndicate flotilla that she and Diaz were dealing with had enough superiority in numbers that a single mistake might result in a disastrous encounter.

And there would be far too many opportunities for such a mistake over the next few days as Midway's forces tried to wear down the Syndicate attackers.

COLONEL Rogero watched from a distance as carefully placed explosive charges toppled large rocks into the massive hole that was the exit hatch for enigma warships from their buried base. The rocks, all located near the edge of the hole, tipped over and were gone, plummeting into the dark soup below and vanishing from Rogero's sensors.

He and numerous scouts had extended whip-antenna-like surveillance probes from the shoulders of their uniforms so they could watch the rocks fall. The probes, limited in their capabilities by small dimensions meant to prevent them from being spotted, should have been able to get a decent look down the hole. But something not far inside that hole was blocking every bandwidth the probes could normally see.

"No reaction," reported the commander of the combat engineer detachment that had toppled the rocks.

"I noticed," Rogero replied. The enigmas had shown an extremely impressive ability to spot and almost instantly

destroy anything from Rogero's force that could either attack
down the hole or provide any information about what might
be beyond that murky shroud of concealment. Using the
rocks had been an attempt to see if a volley of useless decoys
could divert the attention and the fire of the enigmas enough
to get something else down the hole, but the aliens had
simply ignored the rocks.

He hoped the rocks would at least break something when
they hit the bottom, however far down that was.

His soldiers had been pinned down for several hours now,
their numbers being slowly whittled down by the unremit-
ting barrages of the enigmas, which alternated unpredictably
between periods of minor harassing fire and shorter but far
more intense torrents of incoming weapons. The medics,
moving despite the risks, were keeping as many alive and
capable as possible, but they couldn't do miracles.

Rogero ran down the status of his soldiers, studying the
data that scrolled past on his helmet display. Everyone was
running low on active countermeasures, and other critical
elements like power and water were being steadily depleted.
The enigmas weren't showing any signs of suffering from
limited supplies, though, especially when it came to expendable munitions. Either they had immense stockpiles in place
underground, or they had already set up the means to manu-
facture replacement weapons at a rate that could sustain
these continuing barrages.

"Colonel?" the commander of the engineer unit called.
"I've been thinking."

"Are you angling for a promotion or a court-martial?"
Rogero asked. This was the sort of situation that called for
dark humor.

"Not me, sir," she denied. "Neither one. The aliens must
have a way to close this hatch, but they haven't done it."

"Which means?"

"Which means they want to leave it open, and its being
open is why we're here around it, sir."

He got it. "It's bait. They left open a huge door, ringed

with defenses. And like moths drawn to a flame we've been sitting here."

"Yes, sir. You know I'm no coward, sir, but I think they want us to charge down that hole. I don't think we should."

"I was coming to the same conclusion." Rogero studied his display again. Scouts moving cautiously about the area had failed to spot any other openings into the base. There must be other hatches, there must be vents of some kind, but none had been found. Whatever the enigmas had placed beneath the soil was blocking the scout sensors as effectively as it had the sensors on the troop transport. He couldn't order the engineers to just dig down at random spots. That would generate enough activity that the enigmas would quickly detect it and destroy the diggers.

His soldiers had finally been able to find and destroy a few of the launchers being used to rain death down on them, but only a few. The enigmas had proven as good at hiding launchers as everything else.

They're better than us at this, Rogero realized. *Or so different that we don't know how to handle it. I can't even get into their base to attack it.*

He glanced upward again. The battle armor sensors had spotted the destruction of some large ships close enough to the planet that they must have been among those that had landed people here. Were all of the transports already gone? Would there be any pickup if Rogero called for evacuation now?

Space battles took time. He knew that. If the Kommodor beat their many enemies in space, she would come get Rogero and his troops afterward. And staying here in the meanwhile was simply wasting the lives of his soldiers.

Rogero traced out some troop orders on his display, then called all of his unit commanders. "Listen up. We're going to fall back by sections toward the positions that were occupied by the Syndicate ground forces. We don't know how many are left or if they are still hostile, but we need to get access to whatever supplies they managed to land. The scouts will continue to screen this hole in case any enigma ground forces issue from it to hit us as we reposition. Everyone else will regress toward the Syndicate ground forces site, firing on Syndicate soldiers only if first fired upon. Accept surrender if it is offered. Any questions? Move!"

Large numbers of soldiers began crawling and scuttling back toward the Syndicate site, while others held position and covered their movement.

The enigmas spotted something and launched another heavy barrage.

Rogero huddled between two substantial rocks, gazing grimly outward. It would take a while to get his soldiers moved between barrages, and then he would have to worry about surviving snakes or terrified Syndicate workers continuing the human war while the aliens lashed at both sides.

At least no flying monkeys had shown up yet.

LEYTENANT Mack had watched as the enigma pursuit got closer and closer to his ship at a steadily increasing rate as the alien ships outaccelerated what the troop transports could manage. He had watched, because that was all he could do. His transport lacked all but a few, minor weapons, lacked armor, and had fairly weak shields for a ship of its size.

But he was still better off than the four Syndicate freighters. Mack's two transports had surged past the freighters twenty minutes ago. The freighters, in a vain attempt to see if the enigmas would chase the transports instead of them, had angled off to the side and down. Mack had tried to think of ways to help the freighter crews, but their maneuver had taken them too far from the track of his transports. About twelve minutes after Mack's transports had passed them, the enigma formation had swung over and overtaken the freighters one by one, annihilating each in turn. The crews of two of the freighters had tried to flee in the one escape pod available on each freighter, but the enigmas had blown both pods apart with brutal efficiency.

The enigmas, having lost only a little time, eased back onto direct intercepts with Mack's ships.

In less than ten minutes, Mack's transports would meet the same fate as the freighters. The Syndicate troop transports would survive perhaps half an hour longer before the enigmas reached them as well.

Even if there had been any chance of evading the alien attack, the pirate flotilla charging toward the transports would have been impossible to escape.

Despite his attempts to avoid thinking about it, Mack found himself wondering if he would get a quick death, or if the pain would last awhile before the end came. He would learn the answer soon enough.

With both the enigmas and Imallye's formation converging on the two Midway troop transports, the aliens and the pirate's ships were roughly even with each other, Imallye's forces slightly higher and farther away from the star than were the enigmas who had launched from the planet. Imallye's ships had accelerated up to point three light speed, so they had come from behind the enigmas to a position slightly ahead. The enigmas were also accelerating, but since their launch from the planet had only made it up to point two light speed.

So when Imallye's ships suddenly altered their vectors a bit to starboard and slightly down, they rapidly closed to within range of their weapons, the relative speed between the pirate's ships and the alien warships slightly less than point one light speed.

Leytenant Mack stared in disbelief as the battle cruisers and heavy cruisers in Imallye's force unleashed missiles on the leading enigma warships, following quickly with hell lances and grapeshot as the range dwindled. The enigmas were firing back, but Imallye's pass was too swift and her track too far ahead of the alien formation for most of the enigma ships to engage her warships. A half dozen of the enigma craft at the front of their formation exploded or took damage serious enough to knock them out of the fight, while Imallye's ships took only a few hits.

In the wake of the attack the enigmas kept accelerating,

continuing their pursuit of the transports, en route to a linkup with the rest of the enigma armada.

But instead of swinging out wide, Imallye shifted her ships through a tight vector change to port, using her still-superior velocity and the small differences in the course of the two formations to veer across the front of the enigma formation again.

This time five enigma ships were knocked out.

With a third of their number lost, the enigmas finally broke off, bending downward in a vast curve that was still tighter than any human warship could manage.

"A message from *Vengeance*," the senior specialist gasped to Mack.

Feeling dazed, he accepted it, seeing the image of Granaile Imallye before him. Black skin suit, large knife, large hand weapon, glittering insignia, and a small smile on her lips. "I bought you some time, Iceni's minion. Keep going and hope she can protect you from the other group of enigmas. *This* group won't get past my ships."

Mack had to swallow before he could speak. "Th-thank you, honored . . . honored . . ."

Imallye made a cutting motion with one hand. "I'm busy. Contact those Syndicate transports ahead of you and tell them I'd be happy to accept them into my forces after this fight is over. Or they can die, if that's their preference. Out."

Her image vanished.

Mack managed to breathe in deeply, then gestured to his senior specialist with one hand that shook as he tried to point with it. "Get me a link to those Syndicate transports."

The specialist nodded, biting her lip. "You're going to do what she said?"

"Am I going to do what Imallye said? Hell, yes, I am going to do what Imallye said! Anyone who disapproves is welcome to trade places with me for the last hour!"

DESPITE the damage that *Manticore*'s formation had endured so far, Bradamont felt herself smiling. Kapitan Stein on *Gryphon* had caught the flotilla she was fighting in a perfect firing run, angling in from one side as the Syndicate formation tried to loop upward, that had knocked out one of the light cruisers and two of the Hunter-Killers. Stein had lost one of her HuKs, damaged and out of the fight but hopefully salvageable. But over two hours ago she had hurt the Syndicate flotilla facing *Gryphon*'s force badly enough that it had turned and run back for the hypernet gate. "Kapitan Stein, excellent work. Continue pursuit until the Syndicate flotilla you are fighting enters the hypernet gate, then come on and join us so we can get rid of this Syndicate flotilla as well."

It would take nearly half a day yet, but at some point Midway's combined flotilla would nearly equal the remaining Syndicate flotilla, and from what she had already seen of the Syndicate commander, she knew she could hold him off indefinitely with that force. Or at least until the rest of Midway's warships returned.

"Watch him," she warned Diaz. "The commander of the flotilla we're facing will have also seen the other flotilla fleeing and know that *Gryphon* will be coming to join with us. He'll be trying harder to knock us out fast and may take some unexpected risks. Don't give him any openings."

GWEN Iceni rubbed her chin as she saw that another reply had come in from Imallye. Sighing, she accepted the call.

Imallye wasn't on the bridge of her battle cruiser, but in what was obviously her stateroom, decorated with some small but ostentatious examples of the loot she must have acquired from conquered worlds. Imallye wore a smile this time. Not a friendly smile. More like the smile of a co-conspirator who didn't trust her cohorts. "I'll always hate you, Iceni, but I hate the Syndicate more. The Syndicate used you to get my father. They thought they could use me to help get you and other disloyal elements. I don't know what the enigmas think, but I can see what they did, and my sources within the Syndicate told me that Black Jack suspects the enigmas think they can use humans to get other humans."

She leaned closer, intent, her eyes searching as if they could see Iceni. "I sent agents to study you. I wanted to know who you were using, so I could use those people against you. But my agents said they couldn't find anyone. They kept reporting that you were acting so clean that the snakes were getting very suspicious of you. My agents wondered why any Syndicate CEO would fail to use people. They didn't realize that you might actually be feeling guilty."

Imallye leaned back again, smiling slightly once more. "Maybe you are. Do you know why I named this ship *Vengeance*? To always remind myself that only mindless machines let their actions be dictated by anger and attempts at revenge. The snakes didn't realize that, of course, though they didn't trust me, either. It took me a long time to find every snake that the Syndicate had planted among my crews and locate every piece of malware they had sown in my ships' systems. Your Kommodor helped with that when she employed that piece of snake malware against me since it provided me with an up-to-date example of the latest snake tricks. But I had to wait a little longer, until those governing the star systems I had allegedly conquered were ready to set in motion actual overthrows of Syndicate authority.

"I didn't want to reveal my intentions while the snakes held so many hostages on that planet, but your ground forces commander must have somehow figured out how to make the enigmas kill every snake on the ground for him. Once I had confirmed that, well . . ." She waved around casually. "A lot of snakes died a short time ago on my ships here. Some sort of epidemic, do you think? And all of their malware was rendered useless before it could cause catastrophic failures. I am free to act as I will. We have two common enemies. I will *always* hate you for what you caused to happen to my father, but I have admired from afar your repeated frustrating of the Syndicate's plans. And you have some powerful friends. One very powerful friend named Black Jack among them. I would like him to be my friend, too. Once we have swept the enigmas from this star system, we will talk about what to do with Iwa. My ships will not fire upon yours unless they are fired upon first, or if an attack seems imminent. I trust you will continue to operate with discretion. Now, if you will forgive me, I have some more enemies to dispose of."

Her lips quirked as if Imallye was fighting down another smile. "For the people, Imallye, out."

Iceni stared at the place where Imallye's image had been, then laughed. "You devious bitch! You completely fooled me. And you fooled the Syndicate into giving you the warships and star systems you now control. Brilliant. I do not want someone as dangerous as you as an enemy." She tapped a comm control. "Kommodor Marphissa, I am pleased to inform you that Imallye's flotilla will not attack us. She says she will deal with the enigma warships that launched from the planet."

Marphissa shook her head in denial. "Madam President, we can't afford to believe—" She looked to one side. "She's changed the vector on her ships. They're not heading to intercept our transports."

Iceni pulled up her own display, and watched as Imallye's warships in a couple of whipsaw passes took out a third of the enigma force chasing the transports. "I'd say that is pretty powerful proof that Imallye meant what she said."

"She could still stab us in the back," Marphissa argued.

"I agree. We will not give her the opportunity to do so. Focus your full attention on destroying the first enigma force, which is probably about to realize that their ambush has blown up in their faces, and I will maintain a watch on Imallye to see if she maneuvers at any point to be able to hit us by surprise."

THIRTY minutes to contact with enigma armada one," the senior watch specialist announced.

Marphissa eyed the oncoming enemy, who had long ago steadied out on vectors aiming straight for where the center of her formation would be when the two forces made contact. She had already pivoted her warships so the sterns, and the main propulsion units, were facing the enemy. It would be necessary to brake soon to ensure the meeting with the enigmas was slow enough to allow some hits on the enemy.

The enigmas would brake their velocity as well, she knew. The aliens wanted to destroy her flotilla as thoroughly as they had the Syndicate flotilla.

And she wouldn't make the mistake of assuming they would go straight through her formation and risk going head-to-head with the battleship. No, the enigmas would maneuver, and it wasn't hard to guess what their target would be.

What would the enigmas expect her to do?

After so many encounters with different foes, Marphissa was surprised at the answer that came to her. Yet it felt right.

"All units in Midway flotilla, immediate execute, reduce velocity to point one light speed." Having given that order, Marphissa swiftly tagged two people on her comm panel, then gestured Kontos to join the discussion.

"You don't need my approval," President Iceni began.

"I am not asking for approval," Marphissa explained. "I want your opinion. And those of Kapitans Mercia and Kontos as well. I was trying to anticipate what the enigmas would expect me to do, what final maneuver they would think I would conduct just before contact, and I realized they would not expect me to maneuver at all. They will expect me to hold course, straight through them."

She waited while the others reacted to her statement, then as they thought about it.

"Just as the CEO of the Syndicate flotilla did?" Kontos asked. "But we just saw his flotilla being destroyed."

Iceni was nodding, though. "How many flotillas were destroyed in a similar way during the war with the Alliance? We kept doing it. Both sides kept doing it. It was all we knew. And sometimes it worked."

"They know we have changed," Mercia said.

"Do they?" Marphissa asked. "We have not fought the

enigmas before. The Syndicate has, and the Syndicate continues to usually employ the same tactics it always has."

Iceni nodded again, her eyes thoughtful. "The enigmas know that Black Jack's fleet fights differently, but they also know that we are not Black Jack. What they know of warships like ours is that they fight like that CEO led them to fight."

"And that we do not let failure cause us to change our tactics," Marphissa said. "The enigmas will expect us to do the same as always. They have not fought us before. They have not seen us fight that we know of. We will surprise them if we maneuver on the final approach."

"Maneuver how?" Mercia asked.

"The enigmas will target *Pele* and our heavy cruisers. They can take out all three of those ships in their first pass if they can concentrate their fire on them. Agreed?" Everyone nodded. "So I will jog the formation upward, changing who the mass of enigma ships encounter."

"*Midway*," Kapitan Mercia said.

"Yes," Marphissa said. "Not a battle cruiser with limited armament and armor and shields, but a battleship."

Iceni looked down and off to the side, thinking. "Even a battleship will take some damage from an assault like that."

"Agreed," said Mercia. "But it is what battleships do. It's what *Midway* is made for."

"Is there a risk we'll lose *Midway*?" Iceni asked.

"Based on our analysis of what we've seen of the firepower of the enigma warships, there is only a small chance," Marphissa said. "Mostly due to the possibility of a suicide ramming such as the enigmas attempted against some of Black Jack's ships."

"They attempted the suicide ramming when that seemed their only remaining option," Kontos pointed out. "And if they are not expecting *Midway* to be where they encounter her, they will not have a ship in position to ram in any case."

"Hopefully," Marphissa agreed. "We could hurt them badly during the first engagement. We *must* hurt them badly then, because they will know to avoid the battleship after that, and a battleship cannot bring the battle to warships as agile as the enigma craft against their will."

There was a moment's silence as everyone waited for Iceni to render her opinion. Finally, Iceni nodded. "I think your reasoning is sound, Kommodor. I look forward to seeing it employed."

"Thank you, Madam President. Do you wish to transfer—?"

"No. I will remain aboard this ship."

Mercia nodded to Marphissa. "Let's show them what a real battleship can do."

"Stand by for maneuvering orders," Marphissa said, then ended the call.

"I wouldn't have thought of that," Kontos confessed. "The battleships are so slow, I think I stopped thinking about them as anything but defensive assets."

She shook her head at him. "The trick is getting the enemy to bash his head against your strongest point, right? These enigmas think they know us, but what they know is the Syndicate."

The enigmas had begun braking as well. Both forces were sweeping together for a first clash that might well decide who would triumph.

"YOU'RE in command?" Rogero asked as he knelt in the ruins of a portable command shelter littered with the remains of those who had been in the shelter when the initial enigma attack hit. Most of his soldiers had fallen back to this area, only some scouts remaining to watch the enigma hole for signs of new trouble.

The Syndicate soldier facing him nodded, the gesture wobbling with weariness. "Senior Worker Hams. All of our supervisors are dead, either in the first attack or soon afterward. Are you who I talked to before you landed? You sound like him."

Rogero nodded. "Yes. What about snakes?"

Hams managed a snort of laughter. "All dead. Some were

just wounded in the first strike, but they, uh, didn't survive their wounds. We made sure of that. What the hell are we fighting?"

"They're called enigmas. We know very little about them. But we've now learned they are very tough in ground combat situations."

"Yeah." Hams lowered his head, then raised it again with some difficulty. "We're about one-third strength, I think. Lost a lot of people."

"How are the citizens?" Rogero asked.

"Most of them are all right. They were separated from the ground forces and wearing nothing but survival suits, so the enemy weapons haven't targeted them."

A warning sounded on Rogero's armor. He and Worker Hams lay flat as another major barrage by the enigmas swept over the area.

"How long can they keep this up?" Hams asked despairingly as the assault waned again. "We've got nobody to shoot at. Just distance weapons tearing us up."

"Can your people pull back?" Rogero asked. "We're still sitting over what may be part of their base."

"We are? Damned CEOs! Why did they drop—"

"Answer," Rogero snapped, knowing the Syndicate-standard command would shock Hams out of his fatigue-induced rage.

"I understand and will comply." Hams gestured to his right. "If your unit helps, we can move. Cover us, help us get the wounded moved. We can do it. But the citizens . . . the aliens haven't targeted them yet. If they start moving, though . . ."

That was a problem. Rogero wished he could rub his forehead through his helmet visor, but the atmosphere of this wreck of a planet was even more toxic than usual thanks to all of the enigma weapons that had detonated in this area. "How many of your supplies are left? My people need active countermeasure reloads and replacement power packs."

Hams lowered his head again, shaking it slowly from side to side. "Nothing. All blown to pieces. The shuttles just dropped it all over the place, and the enemy weapons have been tearing it up ever since they opened fire. Sir, we're gone. It's over. Right? Nobody's coming for us."

"Wrong," Rogero said, as calmly and forcefully as he could. "My side has a flotilla up there, including a battle-ship."

"A battleship?" The hope in the question was easy to hear. "But we're just workers—"

"Listen. One of our heavy cruisers risked itself to pull three workers off this planet who had survived the attack that destroyed the Syndicate base here. You understand? They weren't our people. They weren't supervisors. They were just workers who needed help. And our mobile forces came for them. They'll come for us, too, and they'll pull you off with us." Rogero made that sound as if it were a certainty. And it would be, if the Midway flotilla survived the fights with the enigmas and the pirate.

Hams stayed silent, looking at Rogero. "Sir, that's . . . hard to believe."

"Two of them came back with my unit. They volunteered to come back. You can talk to them. But first, I need you to tell everyone in your unit that all humans down here are on the same side."

"Sir, you could have wiped us out if you wanted. I surrender the unit."

"I don't want you to surrender, I need you to keep fighting alongside my soldiers! Can you do that?"

Hams nodded. "I understand and will comply." He sounded a lot steadier now. "Let me get the word out."

"Go." Rogero settled back against a broken section of portable wall, breathing deeply and trying to believe that they still had a chance.

CHAPTER SIXTEEN

MARPHISSA held her flotilla's vectors as the enigmas arced slightly down and starward and her own force curved to meet them, rising slightly and angling a little bit to port. Having slowed to point one light speed, the warships had pivoted again so that their bows faced toward the enemy once more. It was a textbook approach to an engagement, technically perfect and totally lacking in imagination.

"All units," Marphissa broadcast. "Turn up zero one point five degree at time three seven." It was a very minor adjustment, but given the speeds being traveled and the distances covered, it would produce a significant change in the projected encounter. "Engage targets as they enter weapon envelopes."

When two formations were closing at a combined rate of sixty thousand kilometers per second, the enemy went from a very distant speck to *right there* in what felt like a moment of time. But even that was a bit of illusion created by the human mind. The ships were moving so fast relative to each other that they were never actually seen when close. They were far ahead, then far behind.

But in that instant, Marphissa felt a thrill of elation as

she realized she had guessed right. The enigmas had assumed her formation would not shift its vector.

The enigmas had run head-on into the firepower of a human battleship, while the battle cruiser *Pele* and the heavy cruisers *Basilisk* and *Kraken* skimmed the top of the enigma formation, only targeted by the enigma warships there and able to concentrate their fire on that same fraction of the alien armada.

Marphissa blinked, her eyes fixed on her display as the sensors on her ships evaluated a combat engagement whose duration was measured in much less than a second. Humans had not pulled any triggers in that engagement since their reflexes were far too slow. Only automated fire control systems could choose targets and fire in the time allowed. But with so little time to hit the enemy, the awesome firepower of the *Midway* had been in its element.

Thirty-three enigma warships had entered the engagement. Twelve of those in the center of the enigma formation had been blown to pieces by *Midway*'s broadside. A half-dozen others were staggering from damage inflicted by the battleship.

On top of the enigma formation, five more enigma warships had been knocked out by the combined fire of *Pele*, *Basilisk*, and *Kraken*.

Even the battleship's shields hadn't been sufficient to shrug off the enigma return fire, though, and in some places her armor had also been penetrated. Marphissa waited tensely as damage reports scrolled down, seeing that nothing critical had been hit on *Midway*. *Pele* had taken several hits, one knocking out a hell lance battery and another spearing through the shuttle hangar, but was still in fine combat shape, while the other ships in the Midway flotilla had suffered only minor damage as the enigmas tried to take out the human capital ships.

Sixteen enigma warships, six of them bearing significant damage, curved back around toward the human formation.

Marphissa seemed to hear Bradamont lecturing her. *"When the enigmas get hurt, when victory by conventional means suddenly slips from their grasp, that's when you have to worry about ramming tactics. You can't outmaneuver them. But you can hit them hard enough to knock them off a collision course."*

"All units in Midway flotilla," Marphissa ordered, "pivot zero eight zero degrees. Maintain current velocity."

"What are we doing?" Kontos asked, not frightened at all but intrigued.

Marphissa answered him with another transmission to everyone. "Assume the enemy intends to attempt to ram our largest warships. Set fire control systems to prioritize enemy ships on courses with smallest intercept distances."

Kontos nodded. "I see. That's why we're holding this vector. The enigmas will accelerate and catch us, but at a much smaller relative velocity, so we will have ample opportunity to destroy them on their approach. Did Captain Bradamont tell you of this enigma tactic?"

"Yes."

"That woman is an angel of death," Kontos said in admiring tones that made the label sound strangely seductive.

Marphissa gave him a startled glance, wondering if President Iceni now had a rival for Kapitan Kontos's chaste, martial admiration.

The flotilla was pivoting, every ship continuing along the same course at the same velocity, but facing nearly backward toward the enigmas who were coming out of their turn and lining up for another charge at the human formation.

About thirty light minutes behind the enigmas was the other enigma formation, tangling with Imallye's flotilla. The pirate queen had not let up, using the agility of her battle cruisers to hammer the enigmas on pass after pass until only a dozen now remained of the armada that had launched from the planet. Marphissa hesitated, then angrily touched another comm command. "Imallye, this is Kommodor Marphissa. Be advised that according to experience with the enigmas, when facing defeat they are likely to engage in suicide tactics including ramming of the largest human warships within reach. For the people, Marphissa, out."

"Let's hope the warning reaches her in time," Kontos said.

Marphissa turned a scowl on the young Kapitan. "She tried to kill me. She tried to destroy *Manticore*. And I have to warn her anyway. But I don't have to like it."

The enigmas came in at full acceleration, which was significantly better than any human ship could manage. But with Marphissa's flotilla moving away from them at point one light speed the alien ships were still exposed to human defensive fire for an unusually long run in.

Two of the remaining enigma ships blew up, a third broke in half, the two halves self-destructing as they tumbled away to prevent anyone from learning anything from the wreckage.

One of the smaller enigma ships suddenly veered toward the light cruiser *Falcon*, which had only moments to react. Fortunately, *Falcon*'s commanding officer did the only thing that could have saved the ship, putting the main propulsion on full and abruptly beginning to brake the light cruiser's velocity. The sudden change in vector threw off the enigma warship's approach so that it slid past a bare hundred meters from *Falcon*'s stern. Before the enigma could turn again, it was blown apart by fire from *Falcon*, the light cruiser *Eagle*, and the Hunter-Killers *Scout* and *Defender*.

Midway and *Pele* unleashed a stream of missiles that tore into the advancing enigmas and destroyed four more. *Kraken* and *Basilisk* each accounted for another.

And that was enough. The eight surviving enigma warships broke off, changing vectors rapidly so that the human defensive fire failed to hit. The remaining aliens kept accelerating for all they were worth, heading away from the star.

"They're going for that new jump point of theirs," Kontos said. "Shall I pursue?"

"No," Marphissa said. "Even *Pele* couldn't catch them if all they want to do is run." She looked to where Imallye had been fighting the other enigma group. As of thirty minutes ago, one of Imallye's heavy cruisers was limping away from the fight, but five surviving enigma warships had been tearing away in the same direction as the six fleeing from Marphissa's flotilla. "Let's hope we don't have to fight Imallye now that we've dealt with the common enemy."

"ANOTHER flotilla arrived at the jump point from Ulindi!" the senior watch specialist cried. "Three hours and twenty minutes ago. A heavy cruiser and two light cruisers!"

Bradamont had just begun muttering a curse when the specialist spoke again, this time sounding puzzled.

"I can't identify the unit recognition codes they are transmitting. It's not Syndicate."

Diaz swept his hand through his own display, peering intently at the data. "They're calling themselves Ulindi? It must be a trick. Ulindi doesn't have any warships."

"Incoming message from the new flotilla," the comm specialist reported. "It's addressed to the commander of Midway's flotilla, as well as President Iceni and General Drakon."

"At the moment, I'm the commander of Midway's flotilla," Bradamont said. "Let me have a look."

The man whose image appeared looked oddly familiar to her. Along with a satisfied smile, he was wearing a CEO suit that had been modified enough from its Syndicate origins to look distinct.

"I know him," Diaz said. "From when he was with the Reserve Flotilla, and when he commanded the Syndicate flotilla that Black Jack drove away from this star. That's CEO Jason Boyens."

"He was taken prisoner by Admiral Geary after the fight at Varandal and was most recently a prisoner of President Iceni," Bradamont said. "She told me she had released him not long ago and sent him to Ulindi. Why is he back and with those warships?"

"Another betrayal," Diaz said bitterly.

But Boyens's first words were unexpected. "Greetings from the newly independent star system of Ulindi to the people of Midway Star System," he said with a broad grin.

"And to President Iceni and General Drakon as well. I wanted them to know that their . . . what's the word? Oh, yes, their *trust* in me was well deserved."

Boyens indicated the heavy cruiser whose bridge he was on. "These three warships were part of the forces the Syndicate had been massing for a coordinated attack on you. With help and encouragement from covert agents I had sent out, the crews of this heavy cruiser and the two light cruisers mutinied against the Syndicate while in jump to Ulindi Star System, which they were to transit before jumping to Midway to hit you along with a couple of other flotillas. They didn't like that plan, because Syndicate ships sent to attack Midway have a tendency never to come home again, but were happy to tell us all about it when they arrived at Ulindi and requested asylum. We were in turn happy to grant them a place to stay in exchange for their becoming the first of Ulindi's own mobile defense forces!"

"I don't believe it," Diaz said, looking stunned.

"I'm not sure I do," Bradamont said. "But President Iceni said that Boyens might do some real service at Ulindi."

Boyens's grin had turned smug. "Since we knew you might be in need of a little help against the other attacks, I brought Ulindi's new fleet to assist. Just let me know what you need. Ulindi, and I, owe you a few favors. For the people! Boyens, out."

"I'll be damned," Diaz said. "What are we going to do?"

Bradamont indicated her display, where the Syndicate flotilla they had been fighting was already twisting about as quickly as possible. "Since they've figured out that one of their expected reinforcements has turned out to be reinforcements for us, I'd say we're going to chase these guys out of this star system. Once *Gryphon* joins up we'll more than match Boyens's flotilla, so we'll escort them toward the main world so he can talk to General Drakon in something like real time. Unless the general tells me otherwise. We've won, and one of our allies has picked up some decent firepower. Our ancestors are watching over us, Kapitan."

"You may make me a believer yet," Diaz said, grinning.

COLONEL Rogero checked his armor's power levels, then scrolled rapidly through his whole force to see how everyone else was doing. Not well. And the Syndicate ground forces and citizens were even worse off.

Another enigma bombardment swept past like a deadly hailstorm, but by now the human soldiers had learned the best means of hiding from the enigma seekers and few were targeted.

That wouldn't matter if everyone ran out of power, though. Without power for heat, oxygen regeneration, and water recycling, no one would last long on the surface of this planet.

"Colonel, that big hole is closing," a scout left in that area reported.

He didn't like the sound of that. "All scouts, get away from that hole and rejoin us. Move carefully. I want you back here in one piece."

What were the aliens up to now? Why had they finally sealed that access to their base?

A powerful signal cut through enigma interference that had increasingly been hindering the human comm net. "Colonel Rogero, this is Kommodor Marphissa. I understood there was a big hole I could drop some big rocks down, but it seems to have vanished. What is your situation?"

"Awful," Rogero said, feeling weak with relief as well as fatigue. "We're not capable of breaching their defenses. We've barely been able to hang on. The whole force needs to be pulled off planet, but the enigmas have a seemingly endless supply of munitions that they'll use against any shuttles that try to land now."

"The area to your southeast looks clear. Keep moving that way. When you're far enough from the enigma positions, I'm going to start dropping small rocks to keep the enigmas pinned down while we carry out the lift."

It wasn't easy, and they lost a few more people on the way, but Rogero got his unit, the Syndicate soldiers, and the citizens far enough to planetary southeast to be safe when the warships in orbit began dropping "small" rocks on the surface over the enigma base. Small meant metal projectiles falling at immense velocity to release their energy on impact, producing massive explosions that not only destroyed anything nearby such as enigma weapons launchers and sensors, but also threw up a lot of dust to help screen the human evacuation.

Rogero sent the citizens up first, dazed men, women, and children who weren't hysterical only because they were too tired to panic. He then started sending up groups of his soldiers along with the Syndicate soldiers who willingly gave up their weapons. Despite encouragement from President Iceni and Kommodor Marphissa, and perhaps a few orders that Rogero insisted he had not heard due to enigma jamming, he stubbornly refused to leave until the last shuttle came down to pick him and a dozen other remaining soldiers up.

Exhausted despite the up meds his battle armor was pumping into his bloodstream, Rogero realized with a start of surprise that two of those soldiers were Capek and Dinapoli, two of the three who had been rescued by *Manticore*. "You two are making a habit of being rescued from this planet," he said.

"I hope this is the last time," Capek said.

Dinapoli, weaving on her feet from tiredness, managed a nod. "We saved some citizens."

"Yes." Rogero let everyone else begin boarding the shuttle, feeling the reassuring vibration in the ground that marked the ongoing orbital bombardment of the surface above the enigma base. "But let's allow the mobile forces to finish this fight."

He went up the ramp last. The shuttle began rising while its ramp was still coming up, then as the ramp sealed the shuttle pivoted to face straight up and rocketed for space.

"THE last of our people is off the planet," Leytenant Mack reported to Marphissa. "The final shuttle lift has cleared atmosphere."

"Good." She ended the call and glared at her display. "Let's stop playing around. *Midway*, see what your big ones can do."

Battleships could carry some big rocks. *Midway* unloaded the biggest chunk of streamlined metal she had, and fired it downward from an altitude of twenty thousand kilometers above the ravaged surface of the planet. Picking up energy with every kilometer it fell, the rock impacted with the force of a multimegaton nuclear weapon, creating a massive crater directly above where the enigma base lay and shattering the planet's surface for a wide region around the site.

"My sensors can't tell if the shot penetrated the enigma base," Leytenant Mack reported. "But there doesn't seem to have been nearly enough subsidence of the surface. The enigmas must have dug out some huge spaces under that planet, and if we collapsed them we should see the surface drop a lot more than it has."

"Well . . . damn," Marphissa said. "We'll have to let the pirate have the last word on this."

Imallye had taken her flotilla out to where a natural asteroid about thirty kilometers across was swinging through the wide, elliptical orbit about the star Iwa which it had followed for countless years. Though occasionally crossing the orbit of the planet, and currently heading inward only thirty light seconds from the planet, it would never have come close enough to be caught in the planet's gravity and be pulled down to its doom.

But even though a thirty-kilometer-wide asteroid had a tremendous amount of mass and momentum, the amount of diversion necessary to change its path enough to meet that of the planet was within the capabilities of several human warships. With tow cables wrapped about the asteroid, they tugged it about, altering the age-old path, and setting it on a course for the planet.

It would take a little while to get there. But when it did, the impact would devastate half the planet and break everything on the other half.

"Maybe that will get their attention," Marphissa growled. "Just leave us alone! And we'll leave you alone!"

"The base, the armadas, this must have cost the enigmas a lot," Kontos suggested. "Even if they want to strike again, it will take them a while."

"It had better take them a long while." Marphissa leaned back, trying to relax after the long strain of the preparations for the fight and the actual engagements. But she couldn't relax, because President Iceni had ordered Marphissa to take her flotilla to rendezvous with Imallye's flotilla.

To negotiate.

"I have done this before," Marphissa had protested to Iceni. "At Moorea, I took my ship close to Imallye to negotiate. It didn't end well."

"This time we outgun her," Iceni had said.

"Not by much!"

"Make it happen, Kommodor."

THE virtual conference was centered on Iceni and Imallye, apparently facing each other across a table at which only Iceni was actually seated. To either side of Iceni were Kommodor Marphissa and Colonel Rogero. Imallye was alone. She still wore the black skin suit, the weapons, and the glittering insignia, but Imallye had added a long jacket that made the tight bodysuit less revealing. She lounged back in her seat, one elbow resting on the table, her chin lying on the palm of that arm's hand.

Iceni studied Imallye for a long moment, then nodded to her. "Granaile Imallye. Or Grace O'Malley, as you called yourself when I knew you."

"When you knew my father," Imallye replied. "We've both changed our names, haven't we, Madam President?"

"I was always Gwen Iceni, but now I have a different title." Iceni clasped her hands before her. "I have a pretty good idea of what happened, but I would appreciate your confirming it."

"I already told you," Imallye said. "The Syndicate was worried about suppressing your rebellion, and about more star systems around here following you out of the Syndicate. I suggested a false-flag operation, where I would pretend to be a pirate warlord who had rapidly taken over a few star systems and acquired some powerful Syndicate mobile forces. That would fool rebellious elements in those star systems into thinking they already had a new master and fool you into thinking I wasn't working hand in hand with the Syndicate. Having failed to take you down, and having put in place what it considered to be adequate safeguards against my betraying them, the Syndicate agreed to the idea."

Iceni could not resist shaking her head. "The same basic concept as the Syndicate tried at Ulindi, only bigger. Faced with one defeat, the Syndicate tried the same tactic but on a larger scale, hoping that the result would be different. But the Syndicate's safeguards against you were not adequate because you were not the CEO at Ulindi. You always intended to betray the Syndicate."

"Of course I did." Imallye waved toward the portion of space where the bulk of what remained of the Syndicate Worlds was located. "That's what they taught us, isn't it? Rules are for suckers. The strong do what they will, and the weak endure what they must. Do you know how old that quote is? Never mind. The point is, I owe you, because you created the opportunity I could exploit. Once I had those star systems under my nominal control, my agents could start setting things up for me to actually wrest control from the Syndicate. Same for the mobile forces that I had 'captured.' A lot of snakes died in a fairly short period of time. I don't know where the Syndicate has been getting so many fanatics, but they must be running short."

"You owe me." Iceni made it a statement and a question.

Imallye fixed a dark gaze on her. "Yes. Not as much as you owe me, though."

Colonel Rogero cleared his throat to break the resulting

silence. "Granaile Imallye, are any of your people among those we brought off the planet?"

"Why do you ask?"

"I'd like to transfer them to you."

"You would?" Imallye grimaced. "None are mine. The Syndicate brought that ground forces unit, and the mobile forces, and the families of those people, from another region. No ties around here. How bad was it?"

"On the surface?" Rogero inhaled, exhaled, then shook his head. "Pretty bad. At the current time, I think we, humanity that is, are outclassed by enigma ground defenses. We did recover some expended enigma weaponry that should help us identify their targeting mechanisms and other information. But we'll need to work out new tactics and get some new systems fielded before we can successfully take them on the ground."

"Interesting." Imallye looked at Iceni again. "I didn't know how this part would work out. I knew the Syndicate was planning to reoccupy Iwa, to lure you in, and I was supposed to hit you in the back while you were dealing with that. I came through Iwa so I could react to whatever happened, not to destroy you, even though you made such a major production of leaking your intention to also come to Iwa so I'd show up thirsting for your blood."

"You were very convincing," Iceni said.

"I'm always very convincing. Sincere? That's another matter."

"You say you did not intend attacking me, but there is the other matter of what happened when my ship *Manticore* visited Moorea Star System," Iceni said.

"Oh, that?" Imallye looked mildly regretful. "I had to maintain the illusion. The Syndicate expected me to offer no quarter to any of your followers. If I had let *Manticore* go the snakes would have suspected that I might be faking, and I was not prepared to make my move yet. I really was happy when your ship instead escaped, and in such a clever way." She smiled.

Iceni raised an eyebrow at her. "But if Kommodor Marphissa had not come up with a way to escape, you would have destroyed *Manticore*?"

"Of course I would have. You can't make a stew without gutting a few fish." Imallye grinned at Marphissa, and she smiled back, both of them looking like tigers baring their teeth at an opponent.

"What a lovely metaphor," Iceni observed, glad that the two other women weren't actually within physical reach of each other.

Marphissa spoke warily. "Mahadhevan commanding the HuK *Mahadhevan* was a fake? Not a real worker who had helped kill the officers and snakes on that ship?"

"Isn't he a brilliant actor?" Imallye said. "The Syndicate ordered him to pretend to be a worker who had led a mutiny on that unit and killed all the snakes aboard, and as things worked out, he really did turn out to be the leader of a mutiny who killed all of the snakes aboard. After you had met him, of course. Wheels within wheels, Kommodor. Never believe the first level of whatever you see."

"What are we to believe of what we see now?" Iceni asked. "What are your plans?"

Imallye gestured slightly with one hand. "The Syndicate is going to be a little upset. I need to defend against counterattacks by them. I also need to consolidate control of the three star systems that I actually do have charge of now and begin making some changes from the Syndicate way of doing things. I can't afford that much corruption and inefficiency, and I'd like to know that my star systems aren't likely to revolt against me the first time they see a good opportunity the way they would have against the Syndicate. What are we going to do with Iwa?"

"Neutral ground?"

"We need to keep an eye on it," Imallye insisted.

"I suppose we do," Iceni said, glad that she had manipulated Imallye into suggesting it. "We could alternate providing picket ships to watch the star system. I'm not enthusiastic about the idea of setting up any sort of orbiting or planetary base here."

Imallye shook her head. "A base would just be a target. What about the Syndicate ground forces and citizens you picked up?"

Iceni gestured to Rogero to answer.

He met Imallye's gaze. "We can't leave them at Iwa. Everything they brought to establish a new base on that planet was destroyed, and the planet itself isn't in too good a shape."

"It's going to be in a lot worse shape when that megarock hits it," Imallye said.

"Yes. As in the past when we have captured Syndicate personnel or found ourselves with Syndicate citizens, we are going to give them a choice. Join our forces or emigrate to one of the star systems associated with Midway if they agree to full security screening, or return to the Syndicate if they want to risk that."

"I don't get a shot at them?"

"That depends on how you mean *get a shot at them*," Rogero said.

Imallye bared her teeth in another grin. "I know about you, Colonel. What kind of man could get an Alliance fleet battle cruiser captain to give up her command for him? The sort of man who could survive that mess on the surface and rescue a lot of citizens as well, I think. I'll be blunt with you. I'm willing to offer them the same deal. The right to move to a star system under my control, or join my ground forces, if they agree to a full screening to ensure they aren't Syndicate agents."

"I have no problem with that," Iceni said.

"No quotas?" Imallye asked.

"No. If they all want to go to you, that's acceptable."

"Hmmm." Imallye canted her head slightly to one side as she studied Iceni. "I'll also be screening them to see if any are *your* agents."

"Of course. Are you willing to negotiate a boundary agreement?"

"Of course," Imallye mimicked Iceni. "How about a supporting forces agreement?"

Iceni raised her eyebrows in surprise. "You're willing to talk about mutual defense?"

"That's what we just did here, isn't it?" Imallye looked at Marphissa again, then at Rogero. "Besides, having seen your forces in action, I'd much rather be fighting alongside them than against them."

"I'm sure we can work that out." Iceni inhaled deeply, nerving herself for what she must say. "I want you to know that my expressions of regret were not a tactic driven by necessity. I dearly wish I had not accused your father and caused his death. I can never make that up."

"No. You can't." Imallye smiled slightly this time, the expression not conveying humor. "And I want you to know that my expressions of hatred for you were not a tactic driven by necessity. I really do hate you, and always will."

"Fair enough," Iceni said. "I'll keep an extra eye out for assassins."

Imallye smiled again and leaned a little closer. "No. Trying to kill you would lead to war, and war would lead to more fathers and more mothers dying and leaving their children to grieve and plot revenge. I won't have that on my conscience. There may be other assassins on your trail, but you are safe from me. I want you to live with your guilt."

"Fair enough," Iceni repeated, keeping her voice steady with some effort. "Your father would be proud of you."

Imallye sat back again, the smile gone. "I hope so. At the very least, I have made the Syndicate pay very dearly for what they did to him."

"You have," Iceni said. "They badly underestimated you. I never did."

"Lucky for you." Imallye nodded to Iceni, then to Marphissa and Rogero. "I'm going to send half my flotilla back to Moorea immediately, but leave the other half here until I see the rock hit. I'd advise you to do the same. The Syndicate did not apprise me of their other plans, but I have reason to believe they were intending to strike at Midway

Star System while you were gone. They can't have much available to do that, but the cruisers and HuKs you left behind might find themselves with a difficult fight."

"Thank you," Iceni said. "I will also send half of my flotilla home immediately. The ones that remain will help guard the transports until we've sorted out who wants to go where. Will you need any help with the Syndicate troop transports that you convinced to join you?"

"No. They seem to be eager to avoid giving me any reason to destroy them," Imallye said. "I will be leaving with the warships returning to Moorea, so I bid you farewell."

Her image vanished, leaving Iceni with those of Rogero and Marphissa.

Rogero shook his head. "I'm glad we're not fighting her."

"Not yet, anyway," Marphissa said darkly. "Madam President—"

Iceni held up a restraining hand. "I know. Don't trust her. Keep our guard up. Imallye will either be a very good neighbor to have or a very dangerous threat next door. She might be both. But she knows I have commanders like you working for Midway, and I believe Imallye was absolutely sincere about not wanting to tangle with either of you. Anyone smart enough to have scammed the Syndicate the way she did, to have made that whole pirate queen act look real enough to fool everyone, is going to be smart enough to know that making an enemy of Midway would be a very big mistake."

Marphissa nodded, mollified. "Will you really do what Imallye suggested?"

"Yes. We'll see very quickly if Imallye is actually heading back to Moorea with half her force. I'll leave you here in command of half of our flotilla, and take *Midway* along with the other half back home in case Captain Bradamont does need any help."

GENERAL Artur Drakon left his command center after watching the warships that made up Ulindi Star System's new fleet jump back to their new home. He still didn't trust

Jason Boyens, but had to admit that so far he had done just the sort of things that Gwen Iceni had hoped for. Boyens would probably end up effectively ruling Ulindi within a few years, but that wasn't necessarily a bad thing since someone so focused on self-interest and so high on the Syndicate's execute-on-sight list should work to make Ulindi strong and stable.

He found Bran Malin waiting in his office and automatically wondered where Morgan was. The two had been linked in their jobs for so long, it was still hard to realize that time was gone. "Is something up?" he asked Malin as Drakon sat down.

Malin nodded, standing respectfully, keeping any emotion from showing. Same old Malin. "General, I wanted to report a lack of activity."

From anyone else, Drakon would have suspected a joke. But not Colonel Malin. "On whose part?"

"Colonel Morgan and Mehmet Togo."

Drakon digested the news before speaking again. "Do you have any reason to think that either one is dead?"

"No, sir." Malin frowned slightly. "A lack of activity on both of their parts would imply both had died, and that seems very unlikely. I believe that both have gone to ground."

"Meaning that whatever they are planning is ready to go and they're just waiting for the right time?" It never occurred to Drakon to ask if either had given up. That didn't fit Morgan or Togo.

"I believe so, sir."

Drakon leaned back, pressing his palm against his forehead and closing his eyes to think. "Are there any clues to their plans?"

"Both have tested defenses, General. Togo here, and Morgan at President Iceni's offices."

"You're certain now that it was Morgan who tried to get to her, and not Togo?"

"Yes, sir." Malin hesitated. "She never made any secret of the fact that she thought you should be sole ruler of this star system. And now that you and the president have an openly acknowledged relationship, there is the possibility of a child. An heir."

"Another heir, you mean," Drakon said. "Morgan wouldn't want any offspring from me with anyone else. She thinks our daughter will conquer half the galaxy."

Malin seemed to grow a little colder. "There are reasons to believe that Morgan is . . . less able to separate reality from her dreams. She may have been injured at Ulindi in ways that affected her stability, and while physically recovered might still be mentally feeling the impact."

"And what about Togo?"

"I cannot be certain, but going through what is known and what was observed, I think Togo has his own dreams, General. President Iceni was not simply a boss to him."

Drakon grimaced at that. "I suspected . . . but Gwen . . . I mean, the president, told me that Togo never behaved inappropriately toward her. He never tried to go outside the bounds of their professional relationship."

"Not all forms of obsession manifest as physical desire," Malin said.

That tread perilously close to ground that Drakon did not want to get into with Malin. He had once thought Malin's relationship with Morgan was simply mutual loathing. But that didn't explain why Malin had stayed working next to her for so long and risked himself to save her life more than once.

He changed the subject. "How confident are you that we will be able to spot them if either of them makes their move?"

"Not confident at all," Malin said.

"Is there anything else we can do?"

"No, sir. Only wait, and keep our guard up."

Drakon sat at his desk, doing nothing, for a while after Malin left. He wondered how things had gone at Iwa. Hopefully, they would receive some word from there soon. Hopefully, Gwen was all right.

He wondered what Morgan was thinking. Her contact number had been remotely wiped soon after he had left her that message.

He wondered where his baby daughter was, and what she looked like.

After a long time, Drakon got to work, trying to forget everything else.

But even that effort was frustrated, because before the day was over the light arrived showing that an Alliance courier ship had popped out of the hypernet gate. Immediately after arriving, the ship had broadcast a coded message with an urgent priority heading.

CHAPTER SEVENTEEN

THE message wasn't addressed to him, and the code was one used only by the Alliance, but Drakon had no intention of letting an Alliance ship communicate directly with someone in this star system without his knowing what was being said.

He called *Manticore*.

"I assume that you are in receipt of the message from the Alliance courier ship, Captain Bradamont. I also assume that you have the necessary codes to read it. While we have respected your right to maintain security about Alliance matters, I nonetheless need to know if the message contains anything that bears on Midway Star System in any way. You may consider this a formal request for anything in that message that I or President Iceni should know. For the people, Drakon, out."

Fortunately, *Manticore* had remained fairly close after escorting Boyens's little flotilla to the planet. It only took fifteen minutes for the reply to come in.

"General Drakon," Captain Bradamont said. She had her most professional attitude on, was wearing an immaculate uniform, and looked very calm and very determined. Bradamont was not on *Manticore*'s bridge, but in the privacy of her stateroom. "I am in receipt of both the message from the Alliance courier ship and your message asking for its contents. I should first inform you that the message is classified, but I am using my discretion as the senior local Alliance officer to override that classification and discuss the matter with you."

Bradamont paused, then spoke slowly. "The message contains orders for me. It informs me that Admiral Geary's orders assigning me as liaison officer to Midway Star System have been canceled. I am directed to return to Alliance space aboard the courier ship for further assignment."

"Damn," Drakon muttered. Part of him felt relieved that his upset was focused on how this would impact Donal Rogero and not on the negative effects it would have on Midway's own defense. But it very definitely would hurt to lose Bradamont.

She was still speaking, but was having trouble keeping her voice steady. "My intent . . . General, my intent is to . . . to request that you grant me approval to remain at Midway in service to you and President Iceni. If you are willing to do so, I . . . I . . ." Bradamont paused, then got the words out. "I will inform the courier ship that I am resigning my commission as an officer in the Alliance Fleet and will not return with it. I hope you will regard my request with favor, and grant me a position here. Please inform me of . . . your decision. I will await your reply before answering the courier ship, which is demanding an immediate response. To the honor of our ancestors, Bradamont, out."

Drakon stared at the image of Bradamont for several seconds. He knew her well enough to know how hard that decision must have been. And how much it would mean to Rogero. But he could not let that drive his own decision, not given the stakes involved and how much they would impact everyone in this star system. He touched the reply command. "Captain Bradamont, I want you to know that I appreciate how difficult this is for you, and how much I personally appreciate your request. However, given my responsibilities, before making a decision I must receive some answers to

critical questions. First, will this action create ill will with
Black Jack? We can ill afford to have that happen. Second,
are you allowed by the Alliance to resign rather than obey
that order? Will this action place you in violation of Alliance
law? And, third, are you motivated in this matter purely by
your relationship with Colonel Rogero, or are there other
factors involved? Is your wish to serve Midway Star System
conditional on Colonel Rogero?

"I require your answers before I can make an interim
decision. I say interim because in a matter of this importance
President Iceni would have to approve any final deal. For
the people, Drakon, out."

This time the fifteen minutes spent waiting for Bradamont's reply seemed to take a very long time to pass.

Once again, she spoke with careful precision, trying to
keep emotion from her words. "General, the orders I have
received were not issued by Admiral Geary but by the admiral in charge of the fleet staff. Technically, that admiral
has authority to issue such orders. From what I know of
Admiral Geary, and from what he told me privately the last
time I saw him, he would not approve of those orders. I believe that he would support my decision. I intend sending a
private message to him back with the courier ship, explaining my reasons. As long as he knows this decision is mine,
made freely, he will not hold it against you or anyone at
Midway.

"If this were still a time of war, I would be prohibited by
Alliance fleet regulations from resigning my commission.
However, the Alliance is no longer legally at war. I took the
time to research the regulations covering my current situation, and I am permitted to take this action. I . . ." She
hesitated, her steely façade once again wavering a bit, "I am
nonetheless likely to be branded a renegade and possibly a
traitor to the Alliance by . . . certain parties. Legally, though,
I have every right to make this decision as a citizen of the
Alliance.

"You ask for my motivation. I would hope, based on those
services I have been able to provide Midway Star System,

that I would have earned the right to base my actions solely on my desire to remain with Colonel Rogero. But that is not my only reason. I have sacrificed that relationship to duty before this, and I would do so again if I believed it was necessary. Instead, I believe that duty now directs me to do all I can to continue to support you, and President Iceni, and all of those who fight to defend this star system and the new government you have built here.

"I want to stay and continue to help you, General, you and all of the citizens of this star system. I recognize that my status will have to be redefined, but I hope that can be accomplished in ways that allow me to follow my duty as I see it. To the honor of our ancestors, Bradamont, out."

Drakon smiled as he thought about her reply. He should have expected that Bradamont would have all of her official ducks in a regulation row. "Captain Bradamont, on my authority as commanding officer of Midway's ground forces and acting president in the absence of President Iceni, I hereby agree to your request, subject only to the approval of President Iceni upon her return, the exact terms of your remaining at Midway Star System to be determined later by mutual consent. Midway already owes you a great debt. I, personally, am extremely gratified that you wish to remain with us. Acknowledge receipt of this message and provide your acceptance of the terms I stated. For the people, Drakon, out."

This time, Bradamont couldn't hide her emotion. "Thank you, General. I accept the terms stated. I will inform the courier ship of my decision and my . . . resignation, and also provide it with the message for Admiral Geary. I will provide it as well with an update on the situation here which I have been keeping current in the event I would have an opportunity to send it. I cannot allow you to review that update before transmission because it is an official Alliance document, perhaps my last official act, but I assure you that nothing in it reflects badly on you or the president. I . . . thank you, sir. To the honor of our ancestors and our people, Bradamont, out."

It wasn't until the next day that he heard from her again. Bradamont looked a bit angry this time. "General Drakon, the courier ship's commander has responded to my messages. He insists that I must return to communicate my decision in person, and that I must comply with the orders I received. In light of the diplomatic aspects of this situation, I am informing you of this matter and request your guidance. Bradamont, out."

She *was* upset. Drakon considered the diplomatic issues, and the likelihood that Bradamont was as upset by the tone of whatever message the courier ship commander had sent as by the contents of that message.

A courier ship. An *Alliance* courier ship. And its commander was trying to play high-and-mighty with Captain Bradamont, who, all other issues aside, had always behaved with immaculate professionalism and was now effectively one of Drakon's subordinates.

He felt a little upset, too.

Drakon touched the message command. "Captain Bradamont, I will be sending a reply directly to the courier ship, copied to you. Drakon, out."

He checked the star system display, confirming that *Gryphon* and her escorts were orbiting within a few light minutes of the courier ship.

"To the Alliance courier vessel which has entered Midway Star System and so far not conducted routine identification and clearance procedures with Midway Star System authorities, this is General Drakon. I understand that you have a problem regarding an officer aboard one of our heavy cruisers. I have been assured by that officer that her response to you is within her legal and professional rights as a citizen of the Alliance, and I assure you that she has always represented the Alliance in a manner that has impressed everyone with whom she has come in contact."

That wasn't good enough. What would matter to Alliance people? Oh, yeah, that thing. "Her honor is unsurpassed and unblemished. It has deeply impressed all who have met her.

Given the services that she has rendered to the Free and Independent Midway Star System, under her orders from Alliance Admiral Black Jack Geary, I have accepted her offer to remain here and continue the tasks that she was given by Alliance Admiral Black Jack Geary. Since Alliance Admiral Black Jack Geary personally negotiated with me the terms of Captain Bradamont's assignment here, I will not have them redrawn by anyone but him, subject to the wishes of Captain Bradamont. I repeat that Captain Bradamont is aboard one of our warships, and that we will protect her from any threat or attempted coercion. You need not worry about her personal safety."

What else? There had to be something else. What had Bradamont spoken of the most?

"I must add that Captain Bradamont has always championed the principles which she says the Alliance stands for, and has done much to make this star system a freer and more just place. If you have any further questions, direct them to *me*, as senior authority in this star system as acknowledged by Alliance Admiral Black Jack Geary. If you intend remaining in this star system, then you must request clearance. Heavy cruiser *Gryphon* will assist you in that process if you have any questions. For the people, Drakon, out."

A little heavy-handed maybe, but no one listening to it could doubt that Bradamont had represented the Alliance well, and that Alliance Admiral Black Jack Geary wanted her here.

About nine hours later, Drakon was informed by his watch team that the Alliance courier ship had entered the hypernet gate, departing from Midway Star System without Captain Bradamont. He knew that it did have aboard not only his response, but also Bradamont's message to Black Jack and her report to the Alliance about this star system. None of those things worried him.

The return of half of Midway's flotilla to Iwa a few days later caused an initial rush of worry both because of so many ships not present and the battle damage visible on those that had returned. But coming in the wake of the light heralding their arrival were messages announcing the outcome of the Iwa campaign.

Drakon made a public announcement of the victory and of President Iceni's return, declared a half-day holiday for all workers, then sat in his office, smiling.

"Aren't you going to go out and celebrate, too?" Colonel Gozen asked.

"I'm celebrating," Drakon said. "Why are you still here?"

"My boss hasn't dismissed me," Gozen said. "Otherwise I'd be out getting seriously drunk already."

He gave her a look. "Be careful. The last time I got seriously drunk I did something seriously stupid."

"I think everybody who ever got seriously drunk can say the same thing." Gozen ran a searching gaze around the office. "I'm doubling security around the headquarters tonight. Anyone who wanted to get in might try to take advantage of the celebrating."

"Good idea. Thanks."

She left, and Drakon sat some more, then began assembling an update message for Gwen Iceni. That was his form of celebrating her return.

GIVEN the time for light to cover the distance to Iceni aboard *Midway* and back, her eventual reply came late that evening. "Thank you for the congratulations, though I had far less to do with the outcome than others did. I'll respect Captain Bradamont's wishes and not inform Colonel Rogero before we reach you. I have to say, Artur, that your responses were surprisingly diplomatic. Not as diplomatic as they could have been, but from you they were models of careful phrasing.

"We'll be in orbit the day after tomorrow. In light of her change of status, I've directed Captain Bradamont to turn over command of her flotilla's ships to Kapitan Mercia and to take a shuttle down so she can meet us when our shuttle arrives. I am concerned by your news regarding our two loose cannons and hope that between us, you and I can figure out a way to deal with them. See you soon, Artur."

He spent most of the intervening time reviewing and overseeing security for the return. Ideally, he would have brought Iceni's shuttle down in the middle of a vast deserted area with the several kilometers closest to the landing site swept clear of every piece of cover and a vast array of weaponry pointed outward.

But Gwen wanted the people to see her. He knew why and how important it was, so Drakon tried to work out a way to have her among the citizens yet safe from attack.

The day of Iceni's return was windy, wet, and gray at the shuttle landing site. That didn't discourage the people who wanted to cheer her arrival and packed every open spot around the cordoned-off landing site. Drakon had put together an "honor guard" which was actually composed of his deadliest and most dependable special forces soldiers, commanded by Colonel Gozen, and arranged them so that they could cover every possible approach to those leaving the shuttle. Colonel Malin had seeded the crowd with countless microsensors designed to spot weapons before they could be employed and was monitoring the actions of Iceni's own security teams.

It was not the most romantic of circumstances, but when the shuttle settled and dropped its ramp Drakon felt his heart leap. Iceni walked out first, her arms widespread as she waved to the onlookers, who howled with enthusiasm. She came straight to Drakon, wrapped her arms about him, and kissed him, which also generated a roar of approval from the crowd. Drakon barely noticed Colonel Rogero leaving the shuttle and rushing to embrace Bradamont, though displaying open surprise at the fact that she was wearing a civilian pantsuit rather than a uniform.

They were all escorted into the same armored limo, an action that also surprised Rogero, Drakon and Iceni sitting in the plush seats on one side while Rogero and Bradamont took the other. Drakon relaxed a bit once the armored doors sealed and the vehicle began moving.

Iceni gave Bradamont a stern look. "So, Captain Bradamont—"

Bradamont interrupted. "As I am sure General Drakon has explained, Madam President, I am no longer entitled to that rank."

"What?" Rogero stared at her.

"Wait," Iceni told him, then looked at Bradamont again. "I am the president of this star system and you are entitled to anything I think you are entitled to!" Iceni crossed her arms, studying Bradamont. "I have already formally accepted the deal agreed to by General Drakon. I understand that the details still need to be worked out. I'll offer you the rank of Kommodor in Midway's forces. You'll be coequal with Kommodor Marphissa, both reporting to me. You'll get all of the status, perks, and pay that come with that rank, with seniority based upon your total time in service, including with the Alliance. I will respect whatever agreements you made with the Alliance and not demand that you divulge any secrets or other protected information except at your own discretion. And you will be permitted to wear your Alliance awards and ribbons. As you no doubt expect, there is one catch to the deal."

"One catch?" Bradamont, who had been listening with growing amazement, looked warily at Iceni. "What is the catch, Madam President?"

"That you must continue to speak to me as frankly as you have in the past, offering your best assessments and advice, and not hesitating to point out any problems you perceive. Can you agree to those terms?"

"I . . ." Bradamont swallowed, regained her poise, and shot a glance at Rogero before replying. "You are extremely generous, Madam President. I accept your offer and am honored that you consider me worthy of it."

Iceni snorted derisively. "Do you know how badly I've wanted to have a second Kommodor I could count on? I assure you that I am getting by far the best of this deal. Perhaps Colonel Rogero can teach you to bargain better. You can make the formal commitment as a Kommodor in

Midway's forces tomorrow and keep calling yourself captain until then if you like."

"May I make one request?" Bradamont asked. "The uniforms that Midway uses, they are still obviously Syndicate in origin, and if I am to wear one I was hoping they might be further modified—"

Iceni waved away her words. "I've been meaning to get the uniforms changed, but something always comes up to distract me. Make that one of your first priorities as a Kommodor."

"What?" Rogero repeated. He had been listening with a look of growing incredulity and incomprehension. "What is going on?"

"Explain things to him," Iceni told Bradamont. "And while you're making the commitment to Midway you might kill two birds with one stone and make another more personal commitment, if your colonel isn't too hesitant."

She sat back next to Drakon, who knew he was smiling, while Bradamont talked quickly in a low voice to Rogero, who seemed unable to decide on which emotion to fix on his face. "What about you and me, Artur?" Iceni asked. "Still ready for that?"

"Yes," he said. "Colonel Gozen filled out the forms, so they'd be ready for us."

"How very romantic of you. Why do you sound worried?"

Drakon decided not to mince words. "Because after we submit the forms, there's a legally mandated twenty-four-hour cooling-off period, and you and I can't afford to ignore that when we're trying to make laws mean something. No matter how we protect the forms from disclosure, someone with sufficient hacking skills can find them and make their own preparations."

"Morgan and Togo?" Iceni gazed into the distance. "Neither of them would pass that up, would they?"

"It's predictable that they'd try for us then, but I'm willing to bet that both will think we'll be complacent about the amount of security around the ceremony, and they'll believe that they can each overcome that security."

"They wouldn't use any major weapons," Iceni mused. "Morgan wants me dead, Togo wants you dead, and neither wants to inflict collateral damage on the other of us. At least we don't have to worry about mass destruction weapons."

"I was afraid you'd want to put it off, given the threat," Drakon confessed.

"No. Let's get this done, let's get everything resolved, if we can. Because we can't live with this forever."

"General?" Rogero asked with uncharacteristic hesitancy. "I wish to request permission to—"

Drakon cut him off. "Oh, hell, Donal, you know you have permission. Go ahead and file the forms."

"After you discuss terms," Iceni said. "The general and I have staffs to review our terms. You two should make sure you are individually covered."

"We only held back," Rogero explained, "because we assumed she would be returning to the Alliance and . . . we don't need to discuss terms. Anything she wants," he added, gazing at Bradamont with a broad grin.

Iceni shook her head. "Neither of you can bargain. I suppose it's better that you partner each other rather than both of you wandering around waiting to be taken advantage of by someone else."

TWENTY-FOUR hours later, Drakon was wearing his dress uniform, which was liberally salted with weapons and defensive measures that were invisible to outside appearance. He was all too aware that for every defense there was a countermeasure, and any weapon was useless unless you got a chance to employ it.

Surrounded by bodyguards, he walked into the presidential complex. The bodyguards took up positions guarding doors and hallways as he walked, their numbers gradually dwindling until Drakon reached the last door alone.

Colonel Bran Malin waited there. Just Malin. That felt wrong, after so many years in which Malin and Morgan had been Drakon's right and left hands. But he had never broken faith with her. She was not here today because of Morgan's own choices.

Drakon could not help worrying about what choices Morgan might make today.

Malin saluted, looking as happy as Drakon had ever seen him. It wasn't much in the way of joy, but for Malin it was a lot. "This is an important moment," he said.

"I like to think so," Drakon said.

Malin blinked as if trying to understand the joke. "Oh. Yes. For you and for President Iceni. But also in terms of creating a stable governing structure—"

"Thank you, Bran. That's not why we're doing it. Anything to report?"

He shook his head. "No sign of either of them, sir."

"Bran, if there is anyone in this universe who might understand what Morgan is up to, it would be you." Drakon saw Malin stiffen a bit more, plainly unhappy at having his relationship to Morgan mentioned. "How much do I have to worry about her? Because I would much rather focus on worrying about Togo."

Malin did not answer for a long moment. "Morgan would never do anything that she did not think was in your best interests," he finally said. "As you are fully aware, General, her judgment on what is in your best interests can be seriously flawed. She will not attack you. But she may attack anyone who she thinks is a hindrance to you."

"Did she ever seriously attempt to kill you, Bran?"

Another long pause. "Not in cold blood. There were a few times, of which you are aware, when Morgan's temper nearly led to that."

Drakon weighed his next words carefully. "I want you to know something. I've been thinking about you and Morgan, and every action you've participated in. There were a lot of opportunities that Morgan could have used to bring about your death, Bran. Times when she could have paused for a second or two before acting, times when she could have gone left instead of right, times when she could have chosen other targets. But she never did."

"She didn't want the blame, General," Malin said. "She didn't want to alienate you, not until her plans were far enough along."

"I suppose that's possible." Drakon, knowing that if either Togo or Morgan had planned something, it would take place very soon, felt a reluctance to set things into motion by moving ahead. "There's something else. We've blamed a lot of the problems in the Syndicate on the Syndicate mind-set. The idea that all that matters is profit and efficiency, that self-interest is the ultimate good. But Togo and Morgan are acting out of a different mind-set, personal loyalty to either me or President Iceni, and that's producing the same results."

Malin shook his head. "No, sir. Both Morgan and Togo would declare that they are motivated by personal loyalty, but both are, in my opinion, merely using either you or President Iceni as tools for their own ambitions."

"And what about you, Colonel?"

"I hope I am motivated by higher goals, General, but I do not pretend to lack flaws, and personal delusion may be among them," Malin said, perfectly serious.

"I've met far worse people, Bran. I'm grateful to have worked with you. Before we go in, I want you to understand that if an attack goes down and you have to choose between protecting President Iceni or me, you choose her. Is that clear?"

Malin nodded. "I feel obligated to advise you, sir, that President Iceni has already ordered me to give your protection priority over her."

For some reason, that struck Drakon as funny. "I guess you'll just have to use your best judgment if it comes to that. All right. I've stalled long enough. Let's go." They entered the room, Malin in the lead as he scanned for threats, Drakon trying to do the same but losing his concentration when he saw Gwen Iceni in a practical but exceedingly flattering outfit. Her clothing was probably laced with as many defenses and weapons as Drakon's, but there was no way of telling that from where he stood.

Bradamont, Rogero, and Colonel Gozen entered as well to serve as official witnesses, but all of them had more eyes for their surroundings than for the couple. Drakon wondered just how many weapons were now in this room.

"The sooner, the better," Gwen said, with a look at him that told Drakon how much the tension was unnerving her as well. He walked up beside her and they stood before the scanner to register their commitment. It felt very odd to be making such a personal decision on a standard-looking form with touch-sensitive check boxes for things like "duration of commitment" and "number of previous commitments."

He was reaching toward the scanner when an explosion elsewhere in the building caused the room to shudder.

"Diversion!" Malin, Rogero, and Gozen all yelled at once, weapons appearing in their hands.

Drakon's defensive array sounded an alert.

"EMP burst outside the room," Malin reported. "The upgraded shields stopped it."

"Reports of penetration attempts at the east perimeter," Rogero said. "I can't confirm whether the reports are accurate."

Everything that had happened, every threat trying to draw their attention, was outside this room. Which meant—

"Someone is already inside," Iceni cried, having reached the same conclusion as Drakon.

Out of the corner of his eye Drakon saw part of the inside wall begin to move.

Drakon could never afterward sort out the sequence of everything that happened next. In his mind, it all seemed to take place at once. Only by reviewing security scans later was he able to break things down into a sequence.

Togo, in a chameleon suit that he had modified to fool sensors designed to spot it, swung one arm up to aim at Drakon.

Drakon's reflexes shoved a ready weapon into his hand, but the hand was still pointed toward the table.

Iceni lurched forward to block Togo's line of fire, another

weapon in her hand but also a wide arm swing away from being able to target Togo.

Malin already had a weapon out and almost on target, but he was so close to Iceni that Togo only had to shift his aim very slightly to put two shots into Malin before Malin could fire.

Another shot tore over Malin's shoulder as he fell, aimed at Togo but too high to hit him. Morgan had appeared out of nowhere, only to find that her line of fire was blocked by Malin. Later they discovered that she had burrowed through from a maintenance shaft, bypassing all alarms and defeating all barriers, breaking into the room just as the firing began. Instead of simply firing through Malin as Drakon would have expected of her, Morgan wasted one shot over his shoulder, then took a precious moment of time to sidestep more slowly than her usual deadly speed to get a clear shot at Togo.

Togo didn't pause for even that moment. He was firing quickly and with terrible accuracy. Malin staggered as two more rounds impacted on his head and chest, but he still got off one shot of his own before he fell.

Malin's shot smashed into Togo's shoulder, but Togo kept firing remorselessly with his other hand, swinging his barrel to cover Morgan. That moment spent clearing her line of fire cost Morgan dearly as several shots tore into her, but she still managed to fire three times, knocking Togo back with the impacts.

Before Morgan could hit the floor, Iceni and Rogero had pistols aimed at her, while Gozen and Drakon had lined up on Togo. Neither Iceni nor Rogero fired at Morgan as her limp form fell, but Drakon and Gozen shot rapidly, riddling Togo despite defensive elements in his suit that deflected a number of shots.

Pinned to the wall by the impacts, Togo dropped to his knees, even in death his expression betraying no clues to how he felt before he slammed face-first to the floor.

Her weapon sweeping the room in case of other threats, Gozen cautiously approached Togo.

Rogero knelt by Malin, checking for any signs of life.

Bradamont, her own weapon finally out, had moved to put her body between Iceni and where Morgan lay.

"Are you all right, Gwen?" Drakon asked Iceni, not taking his eyes or his weapon from Togo's fallen body.

"I'm fine," she said calmly. "Help is on the way."

Gozen had almost reached Togo when his body twitched. She emptied the rest of her clip into him to ensure the almost unstoppable Togo wouldn't be getting up again.

Several quick strides took Drakon to where Morgan lay. As Drakon moved he heard Rogero's strained voice. "Colonel Malin is dead, sir."

Drakon knelt next to Morgan, his gaze racing over the terrible wounds on her and coming to rest on her eyes, where the light of awareness somehow still gleamed. Those eyes rested on Drakon. ". . . got him?" Morgan managed to barely whisper.

"Togo is dead," Drakon said, slowly and clearly, wanting to be sure she understood.

"For . . . you." One of Morgan's hands was still locked on her pistol, but the other relaxed from a fist, allowing a bloodied data coin to roll out onto the floor and drop to lie flat. "Ours . . . raise . . . her . . . Gen . . . ral."

"I will," Drakon promised. If Morgan had been carrying that data coin, she must have believed that she would not survive this mission. "Medics are on the way."

Morgan's eyes rolled to one side as if trying to see into the room. "Ma . . . lin?"

"Bran Malin is dead."

"Damn." The word was barely audible. "I . . . al . . . ways . . . knew . . ."

Drakon saw the light go from her eyes and bowed his head, remembering the young officer who had joined his staff and served him so well for so long. He wished he remembered some of the beliefs that the Syndicate had worked to stomp out, that he remembered enough to say the right words to plead for Morgan's spirit. The reality of Malin's death hit home at the same moment, and he sent a wordless plea to whatever might be out there to welcome them both.

What had her last words meant? If it had been the old days, Drakon had no doubt they would have ended with a contemptuous dismissal. *I always knew he'd fail,* or something like that.

But even in the immediate aftermath of the exchange of fire, Drakon knew that Morgan could have gotten off the first shot, could possibly have killed Togo in that instant. But she had instead chosen to avoid hitting Malin.

Had she been about to say that she had always known that Malin was her son? When faced with the ultimate choice, had she sacrificed herself for him?

He would never know.

Drakon picked up the data coin carefully and stood, looking over at Iceni. "Are you sure you're all right, Gwen?"

"Not a scratch." She put away her own weapon as guards and on-call medics finally stormed into the room.

One medic checked Malin and immediately confirmed Rogero's assessment.

"He's gone. Zero recovery chance."

Another medic checked Togo and unsurprisingly announced that he was also beyond help.

A third reached Morgan and quickly scanned her. The medic gave Drakon an anxious look. "She has died, with multiple critical injuries, but there's a chance we could revive her and keep her going, sir. Not high, but it's there."

Drakon looked down on Morgan's still face. Was it just his imagination that saw there a serenity she had never revealed in her stormy life? "No. Don't try a revival."

Perhaps Morgan had not finally found her own peace. But as long as there was any chance that she had, he would not haul her back.

"Sir," the medic said as he got up, "I should mention that she's also got a badly healed injury to one leg that must have slowed her down, but that happened probably a few months ago. A rebuild unit could have fixed her up, but it would have required a few weeks of immobility to repair that much damage."

"Colonel Morgan clearly didn't think she could spare that amount of time immobilized," Drakon said. He could easily imagine her shrugging when asked about it. *"I had things I needed to do, General."*

Iceni came to stand beside him as the medics left, looking down at Morgan. "She saved your life."

"Our lives."

"No. Togo was trying to kill you, not me. Just as we thought. Right to the end he thought he was being loyal to me. But, from her position in this room, Morgan might have been planning to take me out. See? Look at the lines of sight. That meant she was slightly out of position to target Togo, but saving you was more important to her than killing me."

Drakon wanted to argue the point, but knew Iceni might well be right. "Two assassins who canceled each other out, and poor Bran Malin who took the shots that would have killed me." His gaze met Iceni's eyes. "He would have done the same for you."

"I know, and he did do it for me as well as for you. Malin took many risks for us. Without him as an intermediary to establish covert contact between us, we never would have worked together and would have both died at the hands of the snakes instead of successfully rebelling." She pointed to the bloodied data coin. "What's that?"

He looked at it. "Unless I miss my guess, this contains directions for finding my daughter and getting to her safely. Morgan . . . asked me to raise her."

Iceni paused, then nodded. "I couldn't ask you to abandon your daughter."

Drakon shook his head in reply. "I couldn't ask you to accept the daughter of myself and Morgan as our own."

"Excuse me, but I couldn't ask you first. She is your daughter, too." Iceni tilted her head to indicate where Malin's body lay. "And he was her son. Obviously, her blood has some good qualities." She shifted her gaze from the body of Morgan to that of Togo, then to Malin. "What exactly were they loyal to, Artur? Their own dreams. To what they thought we were, you and I. To what, in their eyes, we could become. The past lies dead around us. You and I need to continue to create the future that we want to see."

"We couldn't have achieved a chance at that future without their help," Drakon said. "They made it possible. And then it passed them by."

Gwen Iceni reached out and took his hand. "I won't let another innocent suffer, Artur Drakon. There's been too much of that. Find your daughter, and we will raise her as ours. Someday, she will be the sword and the shield that protects what you and I have built."

Read on for an exciting excerpt from
the first book in the Genesis Fleet series

VANGUARD

by Jack Campbell

Available May 2017 from Ace!

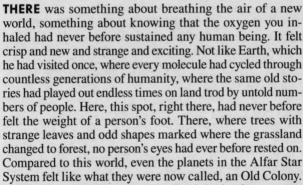

THERE was something about breathing the air of a new world, something about knowing that the oxygen you inhaled had never before sustained any human being. It felt crisp and new and strange and exciting. Not like Earth, which he had visited once, where every molecule had cycled through countless generations of humanity, where the same old stories had played out endless times on land trod by untold numbers of people. Here, this spot, right there, had never before felt the weight of a person's foot. There, where trees with strange leaves and odd shapes marked where the grassland changed to forest, no person's eyes had ever before rested on. Compared to this world, even the planets in the Alfar Star System felt like what they were now called, an Old Colony.

The sun overhead wasn't quite the right size for someone familiar with the sun that warmed the planets orbiting Alfar and looked a little too orange, but it was at the right distance from this world, so that the heat it gave off allowed a person to walk about in shirtsleeves at this latitude and this time of the planet's year. The air had that fresh relish to it and could be breathed by humans. The green of the plants felt a little too blue, but that was all right.

A flock of small, birdlike creatures rose into the air with a thunder of wings and high-pitched, warbling cries. Like every habitable world that humanity had discovered so far, this one held an array of native life but nothing that could be considered sentient. If other intelligent species existed in the galaxy, they were still somewhere out there, beyond the current boundaries of human exploration.

Robert Geary knelt and touched the grass, grinning. Behind him, he could hear the rumble of machinery coming off the landing shuttles that had brought the devices down from orbit. Soon enough, those machines would begin constructing the first buildings of a city. Not an old city, with memories of generations of people and buildings, but also something new, not burdened with history but still awaiting history's first imprint.

A new world. A new beginning.

Unlike Alfar, the Old Colony he had come from. In human terms, a new place that had become Old in a few generations. Where "how we do things here" had fossilized rapidly into a society where no one was supposed to rock the boat because the rules set forth by the first colonists were the best and only imaginable ways to do things.

And if you could imagine other ways? If you wanted to try something different? Or, worse, change the way things were? Who do you think you are?

I think I am Robert Geary; therefore I am not going to put up with this when I can go somewhere new with other people who want to be able to breathe. Somewhere we can make our own rules.

"Rob Geary?"

The call from his comm unit jarred Rob from his reverie. He frowned at the worried tone of it. Why would the president of the colony's governing council be calling him? "Here. Is something wrong?"

"A ship arrived at the jump point from Scatha five hours ago. They sent a message as soon as they showed up, which we have now received."

"And?"

"They say this star system is under their 'protection,' and we owe them what they call residency and defense fees."

"That's ridiculous," Rob said. "I thought we were granted full ownership here by the Interstellar Rights Authority."

"We were, and we intend on telling them that. But what if they don't listen?"

"Why are you asking me? I'm not on the governing council."

"Because that new arrival is a warship. And the warship is heading toward this world."

He gazed upward, where the blue of the daylight sky drowned out sight of the countless stars. Somewhere up there was . . . what? A warship belonging to some other recent colony? A private corporation wanting to sell security services in a new part of space? A pirate, absurd as that seemed? "What does the council expect me to do about it?"

"We need advice, Rob. Advice from someone who knows something about this kind of thing. And in this colony, that's you."

Rob Geary touched the place on his collar where he had once worn the insignia of a junior officer in the small fleet of Alfar Star System. He had thought he had put that part of his life aside forever.

But maybe not. Whether whoever controlled that other ship called themselves pirates or privateers or security professionals or part of whatever fleet Scatha had, they were playing a very ancient game. It looked like humanity had brought some old, bad habits along with it to new stars and new worlds. And as someone who had chafed at not being able to make changes, to make a difference, Rob wasn't in a very good position to refuse to help when asked.

FORTUNATELY, a shuttle had been about to lift back up into orbit to the ship, saving Rob time that could be valuable.

"What have we got?" Rob asked as he entered the command deck. The elderly passenger and bulk-cargo carrier *Wingate*, called the *Wingnut* by everyone, had been built to haul people and materials in a single star system, then had a new jump drive added on and instantly became an elderly interstellar transport. Aside from the up-to-the-minute jump control panel, the rest of the command deck was taken up by displays and controls that had been in service for decades—and showed it.

The main display flickered erratically until the *Wingnut*'s captain, a woman apparently as old as the ship, slammed her fist against a control unit in a spot already dented by many similar blows. As the display steadied, Rob squinted at the information about the ship that was demanding protection money. "It's a Buccaneer Class cutter?"

"Yep," the captain said. "Not good for much in the Old Colonies but still handy where there's not much else to threaten them."

"You don't seem to be very worried," Rob told her, not bothering to hide his irritation at her attitude.

"You already paid me," the captain said, "and those guys from Scatha won't give me a hard time because I already paid them a license fee to operate in this region."

"License fee? You mean extortion?"

The captain spread her hands. "Call it what you want. Do you have a better idea? You going to fight that Bucket with your fists?"

Frustrated, Rob took another look at the display, then stormed off in search of the colony's governing council.

Half the council were already gathered, crammed into *Wingnut*'s grandly named recreational room, which was just a compartment with several aging displays built in. The men and women of the rest of the council, still on the surface of the planet, could be seen on one of the displays. As Rob entered the compartment, a storm of argument dwindled as everyone looked at him. Council President Chisholm, looking unhappy, nodded at Rob. "Thank you for getting back up here quickly. What's your assessment?"

He didn't waste time asking why the leaders of the colony were calling on a lowly former lieutenant for his opinion. The Old Colonies tended to have really small military forces, which was why ex–junior officer Rob Geary was the most senior veteran among the initial group of roughly four thousand colonists settling this world.

"They have an old Buccaneer Class cutter," Rob told the council. "It arrived at the jump point from Scatha, about five light hours from this planet we're orbiting and colonizing. The information we have is still almost five hours light-delayed, but they were headed on an intercept for us at that time, and there's no reason to think they'd change vector. Their velocity is point zero five light speed, and they can't afford to push it any faster even if they had newer technology for their propulsion system. That means they'll get here in a little more than three and a half days."

"What can you tell us about the Buccaneer? How dangerous is it?"

Rob made an indecisive gesture with one hand. "Back home? Not very dangerous at all. The Buckets are nearly a century old, not very fast or maneuverable, and fairly small. They were built for law-enforcement duties like stopping smuggling and for search and rescue. All of the Old Colonies have retired and sold their Buckets, which is how a new colony like Scatha could get its hands on one for what was probably a cheap price. But in this star system, as the only ship equipped to fight, it's as dangerous as it needs to be. The sensors on the *Wingnut* are too badly maintained to tell us any details about the Bucket that showed up here, but it's probably got the standard weapons. That would be a single grapeshot launcher and a single pulse particle beam projector. Those are both close-in weapons. They'll have to be right on top of us to hit us, and their particle beam is probably early second-generation equipment, which means its hitting power is limited."

"But what can it do with those weapons?" Chisholm pressed.

Rob paused to think. "They could destroy our shuttles, preventing us from landing any more people or equipment, and stranding anyone up here in orbit. They could also decide to target this ship directly despite the owner's having paid them off earlier. Destroying the *Wingnut* would take a lot of work, but hitting critical areas like access hatches, air locks, and shuttle docking sites could cripple us."

"I kept saying we should invest in a warship of our own!" Council Member Kim complained.

"We didn't come out here to fight wars!" Chisholm snapped at Kim. "We went out to find the freedom and the room to follow our dreams! It's easy to say now what we should have done, but when all of us here decided where to put the money for this colony, we found that we couldn't afford even one warship like this Buccaneer cutter."

"We can't afford to lose any of our shuttles or pay this extortionate demand, either!" Kim tapped his comm pad furiously. "If we pay this, we'll barely be able to proceed with building the colony."

"According to the message from the warship, Scatha Star System says we need to be protected," another council member said. "Shouldn't we learn more before making a decision to reject their, um, offer?"

"They are not making an offer," Chisholm said. "Scatha is making a demand. That is not the action of someone seeking to help us."

"Do we know anything about Scatha?"

"All we know," Chisholm said, "is that the name they chose for their star system, Scatha, appears to be derived from that of an ancient warrior goddess. That and the fact that their first interaction with us is a demand that we pay them a very large sum."

"Appeal to Old Earth!" Council Member Odom urged. "When they hear—"

"They won't hear for months," Chisholm said. "And then what will they do? Old Earth has made it clear that while they love having their children spreading colonies among the stars, that love does not extend to actually helping them when they run into trouble."

"Old Earth got badly beaten up during the last Solar War," Kim grumbled. "They're still trying to rebuild. We can't expect them to help us. Which is why I wanted to buy our own protection!"

"Can't the police force do anything?" Council Member Odom asked plaintively.

"Twenty men and women with nonlethal weaponry?" Kim asked, his voice dripping with sarcasm.

"We have some weapons," Odom insisted.

"Hand weapons for hunting." Chisholm looked to Rob again. "What can we do?"

"I don't know," Rob said. "There are two other veterans among the current batch of colonists, and they're both former enlisted specialists from Alfar's fleet. They might know something about the Bucket that could help."

"You were an officer," Kim pointed out. "Surely you know more than any enlisted."

"Being an officer meant I knew enough about the systems on my ship to know how to best employ them," Rob said. "Most officers are generalists. The real equipment experts are the enlisted. I'll ask them. But regardless of what they tell me we *can* do, I need to know what we're willing to do."

Chisholm looked around, most of the other council members avoiding her gaze. "I know how criminals work," she told them all. "They'll take as much as they can, returning to hit us up repeatedly, while still leaving us enough to survive and generate more loot for them. We can't afford to give in to that. I need options beyond refusal and hoping they don't carry through on their threats," she finished, gazing at Rob once more.

"I'll see if we've got any," Rob told her.

Lyn "Ninja" Meltzer was still aboard the *Wingnut*, naturally enough. Also, naturally enough, she wasn't where the colony's individual locator software said she was on the ship even though that software was supposedly hack-proof. Rob punched her ID into his pad, hoping she would accept his call. "Ninja, where are you? We're dealing with a reality-bites situation."

Her reply came in moments later, showing her head

against the top of her bunk. He had only met Ninja a few times, but she smiled in welcome at seeing him. "Hey, Lieutenant! Reality for real?"

"Yeah. Break time is over. Do you know anything about the old Buccaneer cutters?"

"I might."

"What about Torres? Do you think he's familiar with them?"

Meltzer grinned. "Corbin Torres served six years on a Bucket."

"How do you know that?" Rob asked.

"He's the only other fleet vet with this mob. Who else am I going to swap stories with?" Meltzer eyed Geary. "I heard there's another ship in system. We're dealing with a Bucket?"

"Yes. Let's you and me and Torres get together and brainstorm this."

"Corbin isn't going to want to play."

Rob exhaled slowly. "Tell Corbin he either meets with me and you in the break room on the third deck in ten minutes, or the police will show up in fifteen minutes and drag him there."

"We're not being recalled, are we?" Meltzer asked. "Because I wouldn't like that, either."

"No one is being recalled. But the council, and all the other people with us, need you and me and Torres to figure out if there's anything we can do about that Bucket. If you and Torres want to go walkabout after we've hashed over the problem, I won't try to stop you."

Fourteen minutes later, as Rob was getting ready to call the council, Torres shuffled into the break room and sat down heavily in the seat next to Meltzer. In a colony group made up primarily of young people looking for a start in life and middle-aged people seeking a new start, Torres stood out for being older, his face bearing the lines of experience and the resentment of someone who thought life had not dealt out the rewards expected for a long life of work.

Acutely aware that his authority over Torres was limited,

Rob tried not to talk like the lieutenant he had been. "You two know the problem, right? And you both appear to know more than I do about Buckets. What can we offer the council as alternatives to surrendering and paying the protection money being demanded?"

Ninja made a face. "If they haven't upgraded their systems, they're probably still running on HEJU."

Corbin shook his head, speaking grudgingly. "Unless they gutted the systems, they're still using HEJU. Those things were designed around the operating system. That's why everybody sold their Buckets instead of upgrading them."

"HEJU," Rob commented. "Is that the one where you have to input commands backward?"

"Yeah," Ninja said, smiling.

"No," Torres insisted. "HEJU is designed to make you think through the entire process and your end goal before starting, so you have to enter command sequences in the reverse order you want them executed."

"Same thing," Ninja said. "That means their firewalls must be extremely obsolete. No one has coded in HEJU for at least twenty years, so there couldn't have been any upgrades in ages."

"The crew codes HEJU," Torres corrected again. "They have to. The operating system needs patches and repairs. But they're probably not any good at it, just stuff they learned on the job, so the patches and repairs are probably just able to get by."

"Do you think there's any way we can deal with that Bucket?" Rob asked him.

Torres paused, eyeing Rob as if trying to judge the sincerity of his outward respect for the former sailor's knowledge. "If we had anything better, and just about anything would be better, that Bucket would be toast. Even an old Sword Class destroyer could take it without breaking a sweat. But this old tub," he said as he kicked the deck of the *Wingnut* with his heel, "is useless. They didn't bring any weapons?" he demanded.

Rob shook his head. "No. Just hand weapons."

"Then you got a boarding party. That's something."

"A boarding party?" Ninja laughed. "Like some old pirate vid? We swing across to the Bucket with knives in our teeth? How do we get them to open a hatch for us?"

"Can't you do that, Ninja?" Rob asked her.

She paused to think. "You mean hack their systems? I don't know. If we had some stuff on HEJU aboard—"

Rob held up his pad. "I just checked. We do. In the colony library."

"Cool. Yeah, I can hack them. Just tell me what you want me to do."

"Can you disable their weapons?"

"Permanently?" Ninja frowned in thought.

Torres shook his head. "HEJU is an obsolete and gnarly system, but it's easy to patch. That's its only good feature. No matter how you hacked the weapons, they could do a work-around if they had time."

Ninja raised one eyebrow at Rob. "I could try to jinx the power core. Cause an overload. They wouldn't have time to patch that."

"An overload?" That would certainly solve the problem of the Bucket. But . . . "How many people do they have aboard? The database says standard crew size is twenty-four."

"You can run it long-term with six, as long as nothing big breaks," Torres said. "It'd be hard to handle a battle with that few, though. Or pack in as many as forty. What's the matter, Ninja? Don't want to have that many lives on your conscience? Don't worry. They're all just apes like us. Nobody important."

"Shut up, Corb," Ninja told him.

"I don't think we should blow it up," Rob said, trying to think beyond an immediate solution. One of the things that had frustrated him back on Alfar was the attitude that short-term solutions were fine because in the long-term, someone else would have to deal with the problem. "That would work for an immediate solution. But it would leave us without any defense against the next predator who showed up. If we could capture it—"

Torres glowered at Rob. "Don't even think about drafting me to help operate it!"

"I wasn't," Rob said, letting his voice grow cold and sharp. "I'd think you'd be interested in the idea of setting yourself up as a private contractor to help maintain the thing for the colony. Ninja, can you hack the systems on the Bucket to drop their shields and open a hatch? Without the Bucket's crew knowing right away, so they wouldn't try to override your hack?"

"Yeah," she said. "That should be doable. You're seriously thinking about a boarding operation? Does anybody with us know how to do that? And, just for the record, I don't."

Rob didn't bother asking Torres. "I went through a couple of drills. That's it. But it sounds like those are our two options. Either try to remotely override the controls on the Bucket's power core so it blows up or try to capture it."

"Or pay the money," Torres said.

"Yeah. Three options. Thank you," he said to both Ninja and Torres. "I'll let the council know and see what they say." He paused, once again having to focus on the fact that he could not give either Ninja or Corbin Torres orders. "Please stay where I can get in contact with you again quickly if the council has more questions."

The council was still in session when Rob returned to brief them. They didn't bother hiding their lack of enthusiasm for either of the options. "There has to be something else we can do," Council Member Odom insisted.

"You asked me to look at military options," Rob said, trying to keep his voice level. "That's what I did, along with Lyn Meltzer and Corbin Torres."

"Why can't your IT person shut down everything else on the cutter except the power core?" Council President Chisholm asked. "Then they wouldn't be a threat."

Rob used his hands to illustrate the movement of ships

as he spoke. "We could try that. Two things might happen. One is that the Bucket crew figures out how to get their systems working again, patches the damage done by Ninja, and comes back at us. Torres says they should be able to patch anything Ninja does if given enough time. The other thing that might happen is that the Bucket crew can't fix it, and their ship doesn't brake velocity before they reach us, instead being stuck on the same vector as they race past this planet and the star and onward out into the dark between stars, where they would slowly starve to death."

Council Member Kim smiled derisively. "Not a humane alternative, then?"

"The closest we have to a sure thing," Rob said, "is to task Ninja with trying to get the Bucket to blow up."

"But can she do that?" Chisholm asked. "I've met my share of programmers who say they can do what I need and end up delivering something far short of that."

"Ninja got asked to leave Alfar's fleet because she was too good at breaking and entering," Rob said. "I reviewed her case when she was getting pushed out. That's how we met back at Alfar. She got her nickname both because her code is so hard to spot that it can get into anywhere and because she never left footprints firm enough for anyone to nail her afterward. The service could never get enough evidence to charge her with anything, so finally they just pushed her out. If anyone can do it, Ninja can. But she hasn't promised she can do it. She needs to brush up on the programming language used on a Bucket, then probe their systems from long range to see what can be done."

"Then how can we know that she can support that other alternative, capturing the ship?" Odom complained.

"Supporting a boarding operation should be simpler," Rob said. "Power cores have a lot more safety interlocks built in. You've asked me for advice, so I think we should try to capture that Bucket and use it to defend this star system until we can get something better. I'm putting my money where my mouth is on this because I know I would have to lead any boarding effort. I'm the only one with our colony who knows anything about how to do it."

A long moment passed while the members of the council exchanged wordless glances. One finally spoke up. "There's a fourth option. Leave. If Scatha plans to prey on whoever occupies this star system—"

A furious eruption of voices drowned out the speaker.

"This star system is *ours*," Council President Chisholm said after she managed to silence the uproar. "We will not cut and run, leaving it to anyone who threatens us. So, Rob, you and this Ninja and Corbin Torres would be part of this boarding effort—"

"No," Rob said, shaking his head. "Ninja will be doing her thing aboard the *Wingnut*. Torres has no interest in participating and no training in that area. He's also not a young man, and a boarding operation can be extremely stressful physically. I was hoping the police force could assist."

"We'd have to ask for volunteers," another council member advised. "The contracts for the police force do not include this kind of thing. We have no authority to demand that they take part."

"We could ask for volunteers from everyone," Kim argued. "How many do you need?"

"Twenty," Rob said. "I'd only have three days to train them."

"Why are we even discussing this?" Odom said. "We don't have the means to take over that ship."

"Then I have to recommend that we try to blow it up," Rob said.

"We can't just decide to blow up another ship!" one of the members down on the planet protested.

"Self-defense," another chimed in.

Chisholm halted the babble of cross talk that followed. "We'll research this and consult with our legal team. We have almost three and a half days to make this decision and ensure that it is legally justifiable."

"Excuse me," Council Member Leigh Camagan said.

Short in stature but with intense eyes, her two words commanded everyone's attention. "What happens if we can't blow it up? Physically cannot. Citizen Geary said that is a possibility. If all we do is prepare for causing that ship's power core to overload, and we find out it cannot be done, we will have no alternative but to pay the extortion."

Silence fell until Council President Chisholm spoke again. "What do you suggest, Leigh?"

"Prepare for all possibilities, not just the one we prefer. Have Mr. Geary recruit some volunteers and train them. If we don't need them, we haven't lost anything. But at least we might have another option if the power core overload does not work."

Kim nodded. "I think Council Member Camagan is right."

The vote went in favor of pursuing both plans.

"Mr. Geary needs some authority if he's going to do his part," Leigh Camagan pointed out.

Another vote was taken, and Rob Geary, formerly a lieutenant in the small space force of the Old Colony Alfar Star System, found himself temporarily a lieutenant once more.

"Really?" Ninja asked once he had found her again. "A temporary lieutenant in what?"

"The otherwise nonexistent defense forces of this star system," Rob said.

"So you're, like, the most senior officer, and the most junior officer, and you've got no enlisted? Who's going to do all the work?"

"Are you interested?"

"No way."

"I do have a budget, so there's money in it for you," Rob pointed out. "And a challenge to your skills."

"The money is enough," Ninja assured him, "if it's enough money."

It was.

He was pleasantly surprised when ten of the twenty-officer police force volunteered for the possible boarding operation. Those ten contacted friends who they thought might be interested, and in short order, Rob had the twenty volunteers he needed.

"I also need battle armor and military-grade weapons," he commented to his new second-in-command.

Val Tanaka was a police veteran of the tough district around the largest spaceport on the surface of Alfar's primary world. She was at least ten years older than Rob, one of the middle-aged types looking for a change. Rob had met her once on Alfar while bailing some of his sailors out of jail after their night on the town had gotten seriously out of hand. "What you've got are survival suits and nonlethal shockers," Val commented. "Why exactly don't we have any lethal weaponry?"

"Because we wouldn't need lethal weaponry," Rob explained. "Or so they told me. Because we'd all get along, and everyone else would leave us alone because it's such a big universe."

"Did they ask anybody who actually lives in this universe whether that made sense?"

Rob shrugged. "It came down to money. They had other things that were regarded as higher priorities."

"Sure," Val said. "I bet they found enough money for insurance, though, didn't they?"

"You're right. Investing in some military forces would have been another form of insurance. But what would they buy? A full-on space combatant like that Bucket? Aerospace craft for defending a planet? Ground forces? Get them all, and that's really expensive for a new colony that has a lot of other things they need to spend money on." Rob gestured toward the outside of the *Wingnut*, where infinite space held uncounted stars. "But the main reason is because they're still thinking in Old Colony, pre–jump drive terms. Space is too big, so aggression between star systems is too hard, and even minimal defenses will prevent anyone's being tempted. And if anybody does try anything serious, Old Earth will jump in and put things right. The jump drive changed all that, but the jump drive is too recent, less than a couple of decades old, so a lot of decision makers are still caught in the past. Trips that required years between neighboring stars now only take a week or two. The same thing that made it affordable for us to plant this colony makes it profitable for somebody on Scatha to shake us down using an old warship."

"And because we can go so much farther, Old Earth is a long, long ways off. So what's our plan?" Val asked.

"We act pretty much helpless."

"We *are* pretty much helpless."

Rob grinned. "Then that ought to make our act believable, right?"

THE LOST STARS
by JACK CAMPBELL

In the far reaches of the galaxy, the Syndicate Worlds
lords its totalitarian regime over the colonized planets.
But President Gwen Iceni and General Artur Drakon,
leaders of a rebellion seeking to establish a government
for the people, refuse to fall in line...

Find more books by Jack Campbell
by visiting prh.com/nextread

"If there is at this present time a better writer of pure
popcorn explosive-BOOM military space opera working in
the field, I haven't found them." –Tor.com

"A fast-paced thrill ride that leaps nimbly from
harrowing to heartbreaking to heroic." –*Publishers Weekly*

jack-campbell.com